LEVELED UP LOVE

A Gamelit Romantic Comedy

TAO WONG
A.G. MARSHALL

Contents

Leveled Up Love

Copyright © 2020 Tao Wong and A.G. Marshall. All rights reserved.

Cover Copyright © 2021 Elle Maxwell

A Starlit Publishing Book

Published by Starlit Publishing

69 Teslin Rd

Whitehorse, YT

Y1A 3M5

Canada

starlitpublishing.com

Ebook ISBN: 9781989994320

Paperback ISBN: 9781989994306

Hardcover ISBN: 9781989994313

❀ Created with Vellum

Chapter One

ZACK SILENCED the incessant ringing of the doorbell with a quick eye-tracked command on his OptiGlasses. Blessed silence arrived as the smart-house system muted the noisy interruption, allowing Zack to return to Star Fury. He could not afford the distraction when he was in the midst of an intense dogfight. Virtual stars flashed past as he kicked in the afterburners and his integrated, state-of-the-art leather gaming chair tilted him in place, adding to the immersion of the game.

Speakers whined, providing the surround-sound effect of his straining engines and the audible ping of lasers striking energy shields. Zack turned up the volume with another swipe of his Opti-Glasses as repeated thumps and muffled shouts originating from the heavy front door provided the insistent intrusion of unwanted reality. His new speakers drowned out the thumps with ease. The upgraded system was the best on the market right now. He'd even had to get techs in to install them weeks ago. Nothing but the best for Star Fury.

The muffled shouts rivaled the speakers though, and Zack missed a key input. His ship spiraled into darkness and flames as his shields failed and lasers tore his ship apart. Swearing, the generously padded young man pulled himself out of his chair and stalked to the door. He adjusted his stained shirt and sweatpants, which had stuck to his pasty skin as he walked, and smacked his lips. Days-old flat pop had left an overly sweet, furry sensation lingering in his mouth.

"What?" Zack snarled as he yanked open the door, bypassing the automatic commands just to vent his fury.

On the other side of the door stood Zack's ex-guardian and present trustee, Philip MacComack. Zack hadn't needed a guardian since he turned eighteen over six years ago, but that didn't stop Phil from interfering. Phil's forehead was shiny from sweat, and he was panting. His skin was too dark to turn bright red the way Zack's did when he overexerted himself, but Phil was still flushed from the effort he had put into assaulting Zack's door. The graying older gentleman's tie was askew, his coat unbuttoned and his foot half-raised as he readied another kick at the door. Phil placed his shiny leather foot down before Zack could shut the door, pushed the younger man aside, and stalked in. Moving Zack was absurdly easy, considering Phil was at least three decades older and smaller than Zack, but athletics had never been Zack's strength.

"Damn it, Zack, why did you stop returning my calls?" Phil demanded.

"I was busy."

"And running your trust isn't a full-time job? I had to fly in from New York for this. And you know how much I hate the heat of Oklahoma City."

Phil stormed past Zack and slapped his briefcase down on a nearby table. The briefcase landed with a squelch that turned Phil's expression from anger to disgust. He wrinkled his nose as he finally noticed the mess he had walked into.

A wall of smudged windows showed a stunning view of Oklahoma City: sleek silver buildings, crowded multi-level highways, and a meandering river with an expanse of parks and shops dotted along the bank. But the panoramic scenery was overshadowed by the layers of grime and clutter in the open plan black and white marble condo. To the right of the entrance hall, the luxurious gray and white kitchen with a granite-top island was cluttered with empty pizza boxes, discarded plates, and abandoned coffee mugs. Directly in front, past the dining room table that Phil now regretted using, sat the pride of Zack's existence—his state-of-the-art, multi-monitor gaming rig.

The only decoration in the apartment hung beside the monitors: a promotional poster for the Star Fury tournament, featuring super-model host Zoe Cross wearing a skimpy version of the Armada dress uniform. Zoe's thick black hair hung loose around her shoulders, and her exposed skin glowed golden on the glossy poster. The redesigned uniform showed a lot of skin. Zack had yet to put up the other posters he had of her, collected from the very start of her modeling contracts with Star Fury years ago. Of course, she'd branched into acting and hosting video game shows since her debut over a decade ago. Ever since then, she'd captured the hearts and loins of gamers everywhere.

Zack and his teammates were Corsairs—basically space pirates who played by their own rules—but he could appreciate a woman in uniform. Besides, Star Fury hadn't released a promotional poster for the Corsairs since the last model retired. Rather than be upset about the clear favoritism being shown to Armada scum, Zack had decided to appreciate what was available.

Not a hardship when it was Zoe.

The poster and gaming console were the only clean items in the room. His gaming chair was surrounded by discarded clothing, pizza boxes, and empty pop bottles. A pathway through the mess led to the bathroom to the left and his bedroom beyond that.

"What is this?" Phil asked. "And what happened to the cleaning service?"

"Pizza. I told them to take a break till the tournament is over." Zack turned to look back at his massive computer setup, eyes hungry as his ship's escape pod floated in space, waiting for him to return and respawn. "The tournament which I'm currently training for. The first round is this afternoon, and—"

"Your damn games again," Phil said as he wiped the bottom of his briefcase with a discarded napkin.

"You know, they're not just damn games…" When Phil opened his mouth to argue, Zack sighed and shook his head. "Forget it. I don't have time to argue about this right now. Why are you here?"

"The year-end audit and next year's proposed budget. We've put off submitting the documents as much as we can, but if we don't get it signed in the next week, we'll be fined."

"Okay, so do it."

"Oh, for the love of Moses!" Phil took a deep breath to regain his composure. "We do this every year, Zacharius… you're the named beneficiary. Accordingly, we need *you* to sign off on the audited statements. Where are you going!?!"

"Got to respawn," Zack said as he walked back to his seat and began the process of getting his pod to respawn at the nearest station. "I thought we changed that bylaw."

Phil drew a deep, long-suffering breath as he popped open his briefcase and retrieved a tablet and stylus. "You wanted to. I refused."

"Oh, right. Why did we do that again?"

"Do you care? Are you even going to pay attention to the explanation?"

Zack shrugged, not taking his eyes off the screen. Phil huffed, and in the reflection from his monitors, Zack caught the old man's eyes narrowing. He almost felt a little guilty. Almost—until Phil thrust the electronic tablet at him.

"Sign."

"Why can't we do this remotely?" Zack muttered. He grabbed the tablet and tossed it onto a nearby couch. A precariously perched, half-filled coffee mug nearly tipped over.

Phil caught the mug and looked around vainly for a safe place to discard it. He settled for a relatively clear place on the floor. "We. Tried." Phil drew a deep breath as he struggled to stay calm. "Someone sent us to spam."

"Oh, right."

Zack vaguely remembered that. The trust had sent some bothersome email in the midst of a fleet battle for Veobos IV, and Zack had nearly been ganked because of it. Somehow, they'd used an override to ping his OptiGlasses, forcing him to deal with it to stop the notifications. That was when they got added to the spam folder.

They just didn't know when to quit.

"So you'll go away once I sign this?"

"Review what you sign first!" Phil said.

"It's fine, it's fine." Zack turned on autopilot as his ship launched from the station, then he took the stylus. He held it toward the tablet Phil offered, then pulled back his hand. "What about the foundation?"

"Zack, that's the least of—"

"Did the board cut the budget? Is that why you're telling me to review this?"

"Zack—"

Zack pulled the tablet from Phil's grip and scrolled through until he found the paragraph outlining the budget for his charitable foundation. Sure enough, his bilge-sucking board had proposed a fifteen percent cut to the funding. Zack gritted his teeth.

"Double it."

"Zack, is that—"

"Double the foundation budget, or I don't sign."

Phil sighed. "The proposed budget is more than enough to support the current hospitals and doctors. The board—"

"Then find another hospital to support and put another doctor on the committee."

"You know I appreciate your dedication to the charity your parents started. They would appreciate it as well, but you should also take an interest in the business they founded. They wouldn't want you left destitute."

Zack laughed. "Destitute? I'm about as far from destitute as you can get."

He gestured to the luxurious apartment. Phil looked around, once again grimacing as he took in the mess. His face said that Zack was a lot closer to destitute than he realized.

Zack's ship blared a warning, and he turned his attention to the screen. Blast. An Armada patrol was moving in fast. They must have been hanging out just outside the station's sensor range to catch respawns.

"Look, make the change so I can sign."

"Zack—"

"It will annoy the board and help sick kids. I call that a win."

"You really should review—"

"Just make it work."

Zack turned off autopilot and executed a quick succession of offensive maneuvers, putting his newest laser cannon through its paces while Phil edited the document on his tablet. Zack no longer had time to pay attention to Phil. Three against one was no laughing matter, even if the ships were a class below his.

Anyway, Zack wanted to get a little more practice with the weapon before he decided on his final setup for the tournament round that afternoon. Using something so new in competition was risky, but it also would keep his opponents on their toes.

Phil punctuated his tapping on the tablet with long-suffering sighs that Zack ignored. He had ten years of practice learning to ignore Phil. The trustee was always complaining about something or other, but in the end, he managed to give Zack what he wanted with minimum effort on Zack's part. It was why Zack kept him around in spite of Phil's occasional meddling.

Zack had destroyed the entire patrol by the time Phil shoved the tablet at him again. That laser canon had been worth every coin. He took his eyes off the screen long enough to glance at Phil's face and confirm that the trustee had done as Zack had asked. Phil look grim and resolved. That was about right.

"One more thing. Somebody on my gaming forum just lost his job. Send him something to help ends meet, all right?" Zack used his eyes to make a few swipes on his OptiGlasses and send the user's contact information to Phil.

The trustee sighed but didn't protest. "Anonymous as usual?"

Zack shrugged. "Say he won a raffle or something."

"You know, it isn't easy to—"

"Hey, it's what I pay you for."

"About that. You really should review the rest of this document before signing."

"Nah, I'm good." Zack pulled the tablet and stylus from Phil's hands and began to sign the marked sections.

His speakers blared again as Armada drones spawned and blasted him with laser fire. Zack swore and dropped the tablet to maneuver away. His ship had taken minimal damage, but he couldn't let something like that slide. Getting caught by patrol drones was a noob move. Their programming was so basic that any decent player paying attention could defeat them without any effort. Getting hit at all was insulting.

Zack set the autopilot to begin a counter maneuver and resumed his signing with renewed energy. Why was the document so long? He was sure there weren't normally this many boxes to sign. His speakers chimed, letting Zack know that the drones had caused more damage.

Zack's signature turned into a squiggled line as he blazed through the rest of the forms until he reached the end. The tablet sent a prompt to his OptiGlasses requesting biometric confirmation, and Zack looked straight ahead while the app scanned his retinas to make sure it was really him. It was a security measure Phil had insisted on implementing last year after Zack had tried to avoid the hassle of paperwork by hiring a body double to go to the office and sign for him.

That had been fun while it lasted.

The biometric scanning app chimed to confirm his identity and prompted him for one more signature on the tablet. Zack signed the final box with a flourish and tossed the tablet onto a nearby pile of dirty laundry.

Paperwork dealt with, Zack dropped a bomb big enough to obliterate the drones and hyperjumped away from the quadrant before the weapon detonated. That would take care of the drones, but he needed to find the outpost that had sent them and get revenge for the damage they had caused. Should he get his revenge alone or wait for his team to come online and back him up? Either he was slipping or the Armada had finally figured out a way to make their drones more effective. In either case, he needed to figure it out before the qualifying round of the tournament in a few hours. Some backup and input from his teammates might be—

"What the hell?"

One after the other, his screens turned off. The incessant hum of the CPU fan died. It looked as if the power had been cut, but none of the other electronics in the room had been affected. What had happened? Zack tossed his game controller onto the couch and knelt—with some effort—to stare at the external power supply beneath the table. It flickered at him, the green lights glowing as cheerfully as always.

So the power was still on. What was the problem then? This setup was new and state of the art. It shouldn't die like that. Zack pressed the power button on his computer a few times, but nothing happened. He wheezed with the effort of bending over as he checked everything a second time, hoping he had missed something obvious.

"I'll be taking that…" Phil extracted the tablet from the laundry and walked over to his briefcase. He slipped the tablet inside with a satisfied smile.

The smile slipped when Phil picked up the leather case and noticed the slice of pizza stuck to it. Face twisting in disgust, he peeled off the dried pizza and cleaned the leather with a handkerchief. Then he stood and watched Zack poke and prod at computer wires under his desk.

A second later, Zack jerked upward, banging his head on the table and clutching the injury. As he rubbed the sore spot, pink hearts flooded his vision on the OptiGlasses. Before Zack could react, text scrolled across the lenses.

DaEvo installing…

…

DaEvo installed.

DaEvo initiating connections with smart household.

Authorization confirmed.

Assessing DaEvo user…

…

Initiating user protocols.

The text faded away, and Zack blinked. "What the hell is DaEvo?"

"Dating Evolution. Alpha version 1.1. It's what you agreed to alpha test for us," Philip said, his smile growing truly wolfish. "I told you to review what you signed. Now, I've got to get going."

"What? No. I didn't agree to anything…" Zack scrolled through the menu of his OptiGlasses to delete whatever weird app Phil had installed, but all of his icons were covered with pink heart-shaped locks and wouldn't open. "Phil, what is happening?"

But Phil was already halfway out the door. The older man had a bounce to his steps that he had not had before, while Zack leaned against the wall and tried to regain his equilibrium.

"Phil! Why is my computer dead? What did you do?"

"Zack Moore User Protocols Initiated. Electronic use limited until minimum attributes and quest reached."

The computerized voice came through the bone conduction headphones built into Zack's OptiGlasses, so only he heard them. It was velvety soft, a voice that caressed and calmed. Not that Zack was feeling particularly calm at the moment.

"What is happening?" Zack whirled toward Phil.

The older man held the door open just a bit and peeked through. "Right, have fun. Let us know how it works out!"

"How what works out? What does it mean that my electronics use is limited?"

Zack dove for the door, but Phil was too fast. The trustee slammed it shut, and the automatic locks for the smart house system clicked into place. Zack pulled on the door, but it wouldn't budge.

He cursed out his trustee as he pressed the code into the keypad. The numbers flashed as he entered the door code, but the bolts remained firmly in place.

"Phil! Phil, what are you doing? Why won't this open? Phil!"

DaEvo initiating… Please wait… Thank you for helping to make DaEvo a success…

Zack ignored the scrolling text and used his eye path to select the menu on his OptiGlasses. The video calling apps were blocked out with pink hearts and wouldn't open, but the basic calling app was still available. He opened it and groaned. All his contacts were blocked except for Phil. He dialed the number and tried to force the door open while the phone rang.

"Hello. Phil speaking—"

"Phil, I'm locked in—"

"Thanks for calling, but I'm not available right now. Leave a message, and I'll get back to you when I can."

Zack gritted his teeth and kicked the door. "What the hell, Phil? You work for me! Did you forget that? My trust pays your salary! Pick up this phone right now, or you're fired!"

An email notification flashed on the OptiGlasses screen. From Phil. Zack opened it with a quick flick of his eyes.

It was a section of the documents he had signed, a few lines highlighted.

I, Zack Moore, do hereby agree not to hold Philip MacComack liable for any consequences of the Alpha Test of the Dating Evolution App and hereby relinquish control over my electronic key to the App.

The line below the highlighted text contained Zack's signature and his biometric print.

Zack swore and kicked the door again. Pain shot up his leg, and another line of text scrolled across his glasses. In addition to agreeing to alpha test Dating Evolution, Zack had signed documents to extend Phil's contract and give him a raise.

A substantial raise.

"You've got to be kidding me."

It wasn't as if Zack couldn't afford to pay Phil's raise. Or that the man didn't deserve it. Phil had stood between Zack and his odious board for years and made sure Zack had a comfortable life. Unfortunately, Zack and Phil sometimes disagreed about what that comfortable life should look like. So Zack liked yanking Phil's chain, making the trustee's life as miserable as Phil made his, with his endless prattling about responsibility and making Zack sign things.

It looked as though Phil had finally had enough.

Zack tried the door one more time, then turned his attention to his gaming setup. Being locked in was annoying, but it wasn't as if he really needed to go outside. Food could be delivered through the mail slot if necessary. He probably had enough leftover pizza scattered around the apartment to last through a few tournament rounds.

But none of that would do him any good if he couldn't access Star Fury, and the first round of the tournament was a few hours away.

Zack checked all his messaging apps again, just in case, but they were still blocked out. He could call or email Phil, but the app had hijacked every other form of communication with the outside world.

Zack narrowed his eyes and glared at the cheerful pink heart icon that now filled the corner of his OptiGlasses. He gritted his teeth and opened the app. Time to see exactly what he was dealing with.

Cheesy music and a stream of pink hearts accompanied the opening of the app. The words "Dating Evolution" scrolled across his vision in an ornate font.

Then the fancy graphics gave way to basic text, and the hearts and music disappeared. Apparently, the alpha version was still pretty rough. Maybe that was for the best. Zack would rather snap his OptiGlasses in half than see everything through pink heart filters.

User protocols initiated. Sending first quest. Please accept and complete!

Minimum Hygiene Levels not Met
Please take a shower and change into a clean pair of clothes.
Reward: Access to external environment

As the words scrolled past his glasses, Zack groaned. "What did you do to me, Phil?"

Chapter Two

WATER, water everywhere, and most of it on the bathroom floor. Getting the faucet fixed was on Zack's long list of things to do, but there was always something more important on that list – like the next Star Fury raid, a new book or Marvel movie, or the latest forum discussion on ship builds. Pretty much anything was more appealing than dealing with reality, and the virtual world had plenty to keep him busy. Since Star Fury released new weapon, armor, engine, and shield modules every month, the metagame constantly evolved. Sometimes drastically.

Zack shook his head, wincing at his hazy silhouette in the bathroom mirror as he dried off. He had never been particularly athletic, but at least in college he had been forced to walk to and from classes. Even if he did skip a good quarter of his classes – barely passing the attendance requirements for many – he had still left the doom room, burned some calories, and gotten some sun. Now that he was out of his teenage years, the calories he consumed on a daily basis had nowhere to go but to round out his soft stomach, and his skin was pasty from constantly being indoors. He put a hand on his stomach, jiggled it a bit, and winced.

"Not a pretty sight."

Nothing.

Ever since Zack had taken off his OptiGlasses, those annoying notifications had disappeared. No matter what he did, DaEvo had refused to let him out of the house or turn on his computer, tablet, smartphone, or e-reader. So Zack had finally relented and taken a shower, which was how he found himself jiggling his paunch.

"Well, let's see if this worked."

Zack put on his OptiGlasses and waited. And waited.

"Damn it! I knew it was a scam."

How a program was scamming him by making him shower, Zack wasn't sure. Rather than follow that particular line of thought, Zack stalked out of his bathroom to the front door, turned the handle, and yanked on it. This time, he did receive a notification.

Warning! Minimum Public Decency Requirements Not Met

Please dress yourself appropriately according to local public decency laws.
Enacting blackout protocols.

"Blackout…"

As Zack wondered what the words meant, the windows darkened, making the mid-day sun disappear behind the now-darkened windows. In response to the lowered lighting threshold, his smart lights turned on, bathing him in a pleasant yellow glow.

"A little buggy, aren't you?" Zack snarled, not expecting a reply.

The app chimed cheerfully through his glasses.

Your alpha test bug report has been logged.

Thank you for your help in making DaEvo a success!

When the app offered no further explanation, Zack stomped back to his room in search of clothes. He snatched up the first T-shirt he saw, only to pause with his hands above his head as another notification floated across the lenses.

***Warning! Current chosen wear does not meet
minimum hygiene standards.***
*Please select an article of clothing that has been freshly laundered or has
an olfactory factor < 0.8*

"It's fine. It doesn't smell that bad!" Zack huffed and continued
pulling on his shirt.

Another message appeared.

***Continuing your current actions will result in the
failure of your current quest (Meet Minimum
Hygiene Standards).***
Quest Failure Penalty: Restricted access to external environment.

For a second, Zack's stubbornness at being told what to do
warred with the reality of the situation. In the end, he pulled off the
shirt, almost knocking off the glasses in his haste. Tossing the
clothing to the corner, Zack spent the next twenty minutes searching
for something that met DaEvo's standards. All the while cursing his
need to get the best gadgets—including the luxury, limited edition
OptiGlass suite that included an olfactory sensor. What the hell did
he need an olfactory sensor on his AR glasses for!?!

Zack cursed out past-Zack as he searched. This was ridiculous.
He needed to get through this and pretend to learn whatever lesson
Phil was trying to teach him so he could get back to Star Fury. The
first tournament round was fast approaching, and he was supposed
to be warming up with his team.

Finally, he found some long-forgotten clothes under his bed that
didn't offend DaEvo's olfactory standards and put them on. When
nothing happened, he moved to study himself in the full-length
mirror that had come with his condo to see what the app could
possibly object to now.

He wore a geeky gamer T-shirt that said "My brain has too
many tabs open" that he'd picked up at some vintage store and a
pair of entirely too tight jeans that he had bought while in college.
The ill-fitting clothes made him look even more out of shape than

he actually was, pushing his stomach up into a sort of mushroom shape. At least, Zack mused as he stroked his chin, he still had his boyish good looks. Even if he did need a shave and a haircut. He may not look great, but it was the most presentable he had looked since he began training for the tournament.

DaEvo seemed to agree. The app flashed a new notification on his OptiGlasses.

Success! Minimum Hygiene Requirements Met!
Reward provided. User now has access to external environment via front door.

Starting dataset for user has been fully loaded.
Would you like to see your starting attributes?
(Y/N)

A small blinking cursor followed his gaze. Having played a few rather poorly programmed games for his Augmented Reality glasses, Zack knew exactly what to do. He turned his gaze to the yes button, letting his eyes rest on it until the cursor depressed. In return, a new screen formed on the glasses.

Zack Moore Current Attributes (Social Level 8)
Physique: 31
Style: 19
Reputation: -18
Occupation: 0

"Stats?" Zack muttered, a side of his mouth turning up in spite of everything.

He liked stats. He loved stats. They were one of the few things in life that made sense and one of the reasons Zack loved Star Fury. It was a game filled with numbers, from fire rate to turret momentum, relative velocities and turning angles. Unlike the real world, numbers never lied. They never broke your heart by dying in a car crash in the middle of the night.

"Those numbers seem low. Is this out of a hundred? A thousand? Arithmetic, geometric, or logarithmic progressions?" DaEvo chimed.

Attributes are calculated based on current shown variables and arithmetically allocated on a scale of one hundred.

"Oh good, someone did program a basic help file." Zack paused, then repeated, "Help? Index? Settings?" Getting no answer, Zack huffed and tried the last, dreaded word for any real gamer. "Tutorial?"

Tutorial files are still under development and will be added as soon as they are completed. DaEvo thanks you for your patience!

Unsure if he should feel relieved or disappointed, Zack shrugged. "Right. Based off a scale of one hundred, we'll assume fifty is the average. Whose average, we won't ask, because I'm certainly not a level eight compared to the average American."

Talking to himself was a habit he had grown into over the last few years. It helped him think and filled his apartment with noise.

"Either way, fifty is probably the 'passing mark' in this stupid software. That means I'm failing in all aspects, especially Reputation." The app gave no answer, so Zack spoke again to prompt it. "Display Reputation calculation."

Due to proprietary algorithms, calculations on all attributes are not provided.

"That's because you're a half-finished pile of drone waste!"

Your alpha test bug report has been logged.
Thank you for your help in making DaEvo a success!

"Fine. Whatever. I can get out the door now. But how do I gain access to my computer?"

DaEvo Life and Dating Protocols Initiated.
Quests initiated…
Abort
Zack Moore protocols in use.
Searching…

Quest Found!
Hold a conversation with a woman face-to-face!
Restrictions: In-person. Non-VR generated. Unpaid interaction.
Difficulty: Variable
Reward: Access to electronics and internet

Accept Quest?

Zack stared at the words. Talk to a woman?

"What kind of a quest is that? Why does that matter?"

In response to his question, a flood of pink hearts and script text covered his OptiGlass screen. The cheesy music blasted through his headset as an enthusiastic voice read the text out loud.

"Dating Evolution is the next generation of relationship gaming with a real-world twist! Did you ever wish your online skills translated into the real world? Now they can! Follow our quests to level up your love life and earn real life rewards!"

The music cut off abruptly, as if the composer hadn't had time to write an ending, and the pink hearts disappeared. Zack blinked. A dating sim. Phil had trapped him in an augmented reality dating sim.

Zack swore and stomped around the room, kicking discarded clothing and garbage as he vented his fury. Of all the games he could be caught in, why did it have to be a dating sim? What real gamer would ever play a dating sim? Certainly not Zack. Those were for teenage girls and hopeless romantics.

Damn. This was bad.

"So if I talk to a woman for a minute, you'll give me access to my computers again?"

Instead of responding, DaEvo flashed the quest prompt again.

Quest Found!

Hold a conversation with a woman face-to-face!
Restrictions: In-person. Non-VR generated. Unpaid interaction.
Difficulty: Variable
Reward: Access to electronics and internet

Accept Quest?

Zack glanced at the clock in the corner of his OptiGlass display. He was scheduled to meet his team for warmups in twenty minutes and had no way to contact them since DaEvo had restricted his electronics use. No way to ask for help out of the situation or explain why he was late.

And if he didn't fix this fast, he would miss the first round of the tournament completely.

Phil had left him no choice. He had to fulfill the quest to get his electronics back. Zack gritted his teeth and swore to fire the trustee as soon as he was able to communicate with the outside world again.

"Accept Quest."

DaEvo chimed, and a heart icon labeled "Active Quests" appeared in the corner of Zack's screen.

Twenty minutes until warmups, and he needed to complete a one-minute conversation to earn the privilege of using his electronics.

In theory, he had time for twenty conversations, but first he had to find a woman.

That was a pain, but not too difficult all things considered. Find a woman. Talk to her. Then he would have his electronic access back and this nightmare would end. Phil would have had his little joke and could go back to managing the trust from afar and letting Zack do whatever he wanted.

Right now, he wanted to play Star Fury and find a good lawyer to see about firing Phil. But Star Fury had priority.

Resolved, Zack pulled on a pair of sneakers and walked to the door. He typed in the code, then hesitated before resolutely pushing down on the handle. It turned. Letting out a surreptitious breath of relief, Zack walked out of his apartment for the first time in months. The smart locks clicked the bolt back into place as the door closed behind him.

Maybe he shouldn't have gotten everything wired up. But it had seemed like a good idea at the time…

Chapter Three

Quest!
Hold a conversation with a woman face-to-face!
Restrictions: In-person. Non-VR generated. Unpaid interaction.
Difficulty: Variable
Reward: Access to electronics and internet

ZACK STUDIED the notification as he rode down the elevator. After a few moments' thought, he had decided to find a woman at the building's fitness center. That should be easy enough. Find someone. Talk about the weather or something. Get back to his life.

He pushed the door open and scanned the fitness room. Men and women of all ages were scattered around the gym, using the various types of fitness equipment. Most of them wore sleek workout outfits along with customized armbands to measure their performance and offer suggestions for improvements.

For a moment, nothing happened. Then DaEvo flashed a few pink hearts across his OptiGlasses, and numbers appeared above the women's heads. Data populated first for those he could see fully or glimpse via the mirrors around the room, then for those hidden

TAO WONG & A.G. MARSHALL

from view who had open social connections via their wearable tech. Zack grinned. More stats. Maybe this app would be useful after all.

Please choose difficulty:
Easy / Medium / Hard

Zack considered this. The app didn't go into details on what rewards he would earn for each level, but he assumed he would get something better for completing more difficult quests. He selected Hard from the menu and watched the quest parameters expand.

Quest!
Hold a significant conversation with a woman face-to-face!
Restrictions: In-person. Non-VR generated. Unpaid interaction.
Difficulty: Hard
Requirements: Select a female with an overall level of 75 or higher
Bonus Points: Use a sexy growl
Bonus Points: Make her laugh
Bonus Points: Make physical contact

Zack winced, recalling his own Level of eight. But he *knew* the app was buggy. There was no way he was a noob. So obviously, Level Seventy-Five would be wrong too. Anyway, he just needed to have a minute of conversation with one of these women. He looked around the room for the best option. His OptiGlasses highlighted all the level Seventy-Five and above women by superimposing a pink heart above their heads. Augmented Reality at its finest. Unfortunately, everyone was focused on their workouts and didn't look to be in a chatty mood.

Maybe he should have started off with easy mode to get an understanding of the baseline difficulty levels. Jumping into a game without understanding the basics was such a noob move. But he wasn't willing to admit defeat now, and he didn't have time to waste figuring out how to change the difficulty level.

"Hey," Zack whispered, trying to figure out how to produce a sexy growl so he could get the bonus points.

His OptiGlass screen remained blank, but Zack couldn't shake the feeling that the app was laughing at him. A pink heart flashed on his screen.

Quest tip: Try "Hey, babe."

"Hey, babe."

A man built like a bodybuilder walked past and gave Zack a questioning look.

Zack grimaced and tapped his OptiGlasses. "Sorry. Talking to my girlfriend."

The bodybuilder rolled his eyes and kept walking. Zack looked at the clock. Ten minutes had passed already. He needed to pick a woman and make this happen.

Zack looked around to make sure no one was within earshot and tried again, looking in a mirror this time to test out facial expressions. His crumpled, overweight reflection stared back at him. "Hey, babe."

He couldn't remember ever saying that to a woman, but then again, he had never been particularly successful in relationships. Maybe this app would actually prove useful. A sort of tutorial for life. Did it have save points? Save points would be great.

It had been a while since Zack had dated. He'd had several girlfriends in college, even if none of the relationships had lasted more than a few months. They were always looking for couple time and never agreed that gaming together counted.

The growl wasn't quite right. Zack searched his memory for some sort of reference point and settled on those old Batman movies. Who didn't like Batman? He smoothed his tangled mop of brown hair to the side and once again faced the mirror.

"Hey, babe. I'm Batman." His growl was more of a rasp and tickled the back of his throat. He coughed to clear it.

Would you like to complete a tutorial level to prepare for this quest?

Zack glared at the screen and dismissed the prompt. Now it

offered help? No, he didn't want to complete a damn tutorial level. He had eight minutes to find a woman, speak to her with his best sexy growl, and spend the rest of the day competing with his team and pretending this had never happened.

He scanned the gym and settled on the highest level woman there. Might as well get as many points as possible, whatever that meant in this context. He selected the heart above her head by staring at it for a few seconds, and DaEvo popped up a notification with the woman's stats.

Kayla Taylor (Social Level 86)
Physique: 89
Style: 82
Reputation: 89
Occupation: 85

A flood of social media posts followed the stats. Mostly pictures from Kayla's career as a model. Advertisement spreads, red carpet events, and selfies with an endless stream of celebrities, including a few with Zoe Cross. All of them showed "KayTay," as her fans called her, in gorgeous gowns on the runway or swimsuits on exotic beaches. She was always perfectly styled, with just the right amount of makeup to highlight her blue eyes and strawberry-blond hair.

She looked significantly less polished now, with a dusting of freckles not visible in her modeling portfolio and her hair pulled back into a messy bun. But she was still hot, her tight workout gear showing off her body just as much as the formal gowns did.

Zack pushed aside his nerves and forced himself to smile as he walked over to Kayla's elliptical. Maybe DaEvo wouldn't be so bad. Kayla was no Zoe, but she was still a hot model. And thanks to the game, he was going to talk to her.

"Hey, babe."

The sexy growl was more of a wheeze, and Kayla didn't seem to hear him over the whir of the machine and whatever she was listening to with her earbuds. She stared straight ahead, running on her elliptical with an intensity that Zack found a little intimidating.

24

Apparently, that body required some maintenance to stay swimsuit-ready.

"Kayla?" Zack tried again.

Kayla looked down at him, frowned a little, and redoubled her efforts on the elliptical as if she were actually moving and could run away from him.

If she did decide to run, Zack would have no chance of catching her. DaEvo now displayed a sixty-second timer in the corner of his OptiGlasses, but it hadn't started yet.

"Hey! Kayla!"

"Can't. Stop. Now."

She said the words on an exhale, breathing deeply between them. Sweat poured down her face as she ran even faster. DaEvo chimed and started the timer. Success! Apparently, he just had to get her to respond. Now he could stand there for a minute and let the timer run down.

But when Kayla said nothing else for ten seconds, the timer flashed red and reset.

Crap.

"Hey."

Zack whirled around and found himself face to face with the bodybuilder from earlier. He swallowed. "Yeah?"

"You're interrupting our workouts."

The muscled man gestured to the gym, and Zack realized that everyone but Kayla had stopped what they were doing to stare at him.

Reputation -0.1

"What the hell?"

Had DaEvo really docked his reputation just because some muscled jocks were annoyed?

DaEvo calculates user Reputation using an in-person, real-time algorithm as well as other proprietary calculations for baseline information.

"What did you say to me?" The bodybuilder leaned closer, looming over Zack.

Behind them, Kayla Taylor was still sprinting on the elliptical, seemingly oblivious to it all.

"Oh, I wasn't talking to you," Zack said. "I, uh—"

"Maybe you should leave," the bodybuilder said. "You don't look like you belong here anyway."

He laughed, looking at Zack from head to toe and apparently finding his flab amusing. Zack felt his cheeks burning red. Who cared about muscles? It wasn't as if they helped you win game tournaments or get a job. Not that he had a job himself, but most manual jobs these days were done by machines. What was the point of putting so much effort into physical activity?

"Look, I'm not causing any trouble. I just need to talk to—"

"And I think you're done here. She doesn't want to talk to you."

Zack and the bodybuilder looked back at Kayla, who was still ignoring their conversation.

"Is there a problem over here?" Another muscled gym user came over. This one was even bigger than the first, which Zack would not have thought possible.

DaEvo flashed again.

Reputation -0.1

"Fine. Whatever," Zack said, raising his hands in surrender as he backed away and made a hurried exit from the gym, checking the clock as he did so.

Damn. He was two minutes late for the rendezvous with his team and no closer to getting back his electronics privileges. If this kept up, he would miss warmups entirely. And that was unacceptable.

Zack gritted his teeth as he steeled his resolve. Find a woman. Have a conversation. He had to do this for Star Fury and his team.

Maybe he should have made an effort to get to know his neighbors when he moved in. He didn't know a single person in the building, male or female. He had toured the facilities when purchasing the condo, then promptly forgotten about them. Knowing his neighbors wasn't exactly a priority—not like the new triple redundancy fiber optic cable they had laid during the condo's development. It was one of the fastest networks in the nation, perfect for gaming.

But not even lightning fast internet would save him now. He needed a woman.

Zack took the elevator to the ground floor. Maybe he could catch someone in the lobby.

No luck. The lobby was empty. He would have to take this outside if he wanted to get his gaming system back.

That was just unfair. Firing Phil moved up Zack's list of priorities as he took a deep breath and walked out of the apartment building for the first time in weeks. Heat wafted up from the sidewalk and washed over him in waves. Apparently, his decision to stay inside had been a good one. Walking into the Oklahoma summer was like walking into an oven. But weather had been low on his priorities when he moved from New York. He had been far more interested in fiber optic lines, the innovative green tech in the apartment building, and the new Star Fury main servers located downtown.

The building stretched above him, tall, sleek, and blinding in the afternoon sun. Solar energy panels covered every bit of the surface that wasn't a window, and small wind turbines sat on the roof. Supposedly there was even a rooftop garden up there. Wind gusted past, nearly knocking Zack over, and he gritted his teeth. No wonder they had decided to put a green building here. The sun and wind were strong enough to power a tier-two server center, so providing light to the apartment should be a piece of cake.

Zack ducked into a small patch of shade under a nearby tree and dismissed the idle thought. Renewable energy was the least of his concerns right now. He opened the calling app. It showed three missed calls from his teammates, as well as a number of texts, but DaEvo had blocked his ability to do anything other than see that the calls had come in. He couldn't even read the messages.

Zack dialed Phil again. The call went to voicemail. "Look, you've had your laugh. I'm outside in literal hell trying to find a woman while my team probably thinks I'm dead or ditching them. The tournament starts today! You're ruining my life, man!"

As Zack hung up, a text message from Phil opened.

A little sunshine never hurt anyone.

A little sunshine? That was the understatement of the century. The afternoon sun was blinding and giving him a headache. Zack opened the settings for his OptiGlasses and tinted the lenses to reduce the glare. Normally that would happen automatically, but apparently, that feature required an internet connection or had been blocked by DaEvo as non-essential.

Zack took a deep breath and stomped away from the building. He was officially late for warmups. If he hurried, maybe he could still make it in time to discuss the Armada drones he had encountered before they began the tournament. He just had to play along until he satisfied DaEvo or until the freaking heat killed him. He was already sweating and undoing all the good from his shower.

He scrolled through DaEvo's menu as he paced the sidewalk, which was annoyingly empty of people and offering no options for a conversation. The app cared about his hygiene and public decency. Maybe there were other ways to get points that didn't require interacting with another human. Some quick poking around showed that there were other rewards available, but they were all locked out at this time.

He had one quest available. Talk to a woman.

Damn dating sim.

Zack swore and walked, staying in the shade whenever possible to minimize exposure to the heat. There was a park nearby. Maybe he would have better luck there. When he finally reached the park, he winced. Whoever thought a park should be made up of flat ground, sparse trees, an unmanned basketball court, and a jogging track really needed to be forced to stand outside in the Oklahoma sun as punishment. At least the lack of trees let the breeze through, though the hot air did little to cool his sweating body.

On the other hand, sure enough, a woman was jogging along the track. She looked a little older than him but based on what he had seen in the gym, she should still be fairly high level. Zack waited for DaEvo to populate her stats, but instead received a different notification.

Social network scan unable to complete. Please provide a complete facial view to activate facial recognition.

She must have her social network privacy features turned to maximum. Damn luddites and privacy enthusiasts. Zack watched her jog and tried to get his overheated brain to form a plan. Providing a complete facial view was easier said than done. The only way to get a good view of her face was to get on the track and jog in the opposite direction. Jogging was the last thing he wanted to do, but she was the only woman around. Zack had no choice.

"Stupid buggy app."

Your alpha test bug report has been logged.
Thank you for your help in making DaEvo a success!

Zack swore softly and stepped onto the track. He jogged, his feet pounding against the pavement. The wind grew stronger and rushed through his still-damp hair. Ten steps in, the light sweat he'd worked up became a flood. Zack felt sweat beads popping out of his face as he panted for breath.

Detected increased heart rate and low oxygen level.
Fitness quests not yet available.
Scanning status.
Attempted exercise…
Please reduce physical exertion levels to achieve optimal results.
Complete current quest before attempting others.

Current Quest!
Hold a conversation with a woman face-to-face!
Restrictions: In-person. Non-VR generated. Unpaid interaction.
Difficulty: Variable
Reward: Access to electronics and internet

Zack swiped away the notifications as fast as they came. He could barely read them anyway since sweat was pouring into his eyes.

Maybe he should walk instead. Walking would give the app a better view of the woman's face. That was why he was slowing down. He just needed the program to work if he was going to complete this quest and get back to his team.

Zack walked at a brisk pace so he could pass the woman on the track sooner and get this whole nonsense quest over with. He was hyper-aware of every second that passed. How long would his team wait for him before they decided he had bailed?

The track seemed a lot longer once you were actually on it. Heat radiated off the concrete and burned his feet. He might as well exercise in an oven.

Halfway around the track, Zack stopped and leaned against a lamppost to catch his breath. He looked at the woman, who had rounded the corner and was jogging toward him. How did she keep moving so quickly? A light sheen of sweat covered her tanned skin, but she didn't seem to be putting out much effort. Her long black hair was pulled into a ponytail that swished behind her as she ran, and her dark eyes showed no signs of exhaustion or even heavy exertion.

She noticed Zack and nodded a greeting as she passed him. DaEvo chimed.

Facial view acquired. Beginning facial recognition and importing stats.
Target does not meet current difficulty requirements (Hard, over
level 75)
Would you like to downgrade difficulty to medium?

Zack selected yes, and a stream of data filled his vision as DaEvo calculated the woman's level. In short order, Zack had a glimpse of her life as she had shown it to the world. Admittedly, that wasn't much. Her social media profiles showed her job as a pediatrician, links to her blog, and a blog in which she posted about her latest meal recipe for a chicken salad. DaEvo seemed to be pulling more information, maybe bypassing her privacy settings, but most of it flashed by too quickly for Zack to read. A moment later, the data consolidated.

Cassie Jones (Social Level 65)
Physique: 81
Style: 59
Reputation: 34
Occupation: 87

Zack glanced through the stats. She wasn't anywhere near Kayla's level, but maybe it would work better to start off easier. He just had to talk to her. Bonus points for the sexy growl, laughter, and physical contact.

By the time Zack had read the stats, Cassie was nearly around the track again. Honestly, how did she move so quickly? He pushed away from the lamppost and continued walking along the track.

Target acquired. Moving in for the kill. This was easy, just a milk run like the first missions in Star Fury, where you had to do a delivery quest to prove you had what it took to be a Corsair.

Talk to Cassie for one minute and get his life back. Simple.

Zack cleared his throat and wondered if he should have brushed his teeth. Just in case this went well and he moved in for the physical contact bonus. Maybe he should have picked up after himself in his apartment too.

He shook his head. He couldn't let this stupid app distract him. He just needed to complete the quest and get back to his real mission: playing Star Fury. Every second he spent out here was a second away from preparing for the tournament. The first round would be easy. A simple outpost destruction timed event to weed out noobs before the real fun began. But if he didn't compete, the team would be down one ship with the corresponding lower damage per second.

How was Cassie still jogging? She was coming in fast. He would only get one shot at this.

Zack leaned against another lamppost. Partly for support and partly because he had once read that leaning against things made you look like a bad boy. It definitely had nothing to do with the fact that walking halfway around the track had left him winded and shaking.

Definitely not.

"Hey, babe."

It came out as more of a gasp than a growl. Cassie looked at him, as if unsure that he was speaking to her. Zack nodded to show that he was.

"Um, hi?"

The heart-shaped timer flashed and counted down. Zack watched the seconds tick by. Only sixty of them. He just needed to keep Cassie talking for sixty seconds.

"Do you need help?" Cassie said. "I'm a doctor. I can check your vitals if you think you're having a heart attack."

As if a pediatrician could do anything for a heart attack. Zack smiled. Cassie was already making excuses to move closer. He definitely should have brushed his teeth.

"No, I'm fine," Zack wheezed. "How you doing?"

He punctuated this with a nod and single eyebrow raise. Classic move. It had worked like a charm in college.

Cassie's eyebrows knit together in confusion. "I'm sorry, do I know you?"

"I'm Zack." Zack extended a very sweaty hand.

Cassie eyed it but didn't take it. So much for physical contact. "If you don't need help, I need to go. I'll be late for work."

She turned to jog away. No! She couldn't leave yet! They had only been talking for thirty seconds, and he hadn't earned bonus points for the sexy growl, laugh, or physical contact.

"Do you want to hear a joke?"

It was far from his best line, but Cassie turned back around. "What?"

"A joke! I heard a good one the other day."

Only twenty seconds left. He could do this.

Cassie rolled her eyes but gestured for him to continue. Zack opened his mouth to tell the joke, but his mind had gone completely blank. A joke. What was a good joke?

"Um, knock, knock?"

"I don't have time for this."

She turned to jog away. Zack gritted his teeth. Fifteen seconds remaining. He was so close!

"Cassie, wait!"

She turned around, her posture defensive. "How do you know my name?"

Zack's mind raced for an explanation. "It showed up through my social app. You know how these wearables like to share information." He tapped his OptiGlasses.

Cassie's eyes narrowed. "I'm not wearing any tech."

"And we went to school together! You really don't remember?"

Zack expected this to make her relax, but her scowl only deepened. "What was the name of the school?"

"Oh. It was—you know what, I must be thinking of someone else."

"Because I seriously doubt you went to the Chickasaw Nation School for Girls."

"Um, nope. Definitely thinking of someone else."

Zack hoped that would be the end of it, but Cassie stayed put.

"So how do you know my name? Are you stalking me?"

"What? No. Definitely not. I—um, I saw you last time I was at the hospital. I—"

"Leave me alone, you creep. If I see you again, I'm calling the cops."

Cassie sprinted away. She really did have some kind of superhuman strength, sprinting after all that jogging. Zack was still huffing from his brisk walk. DaEvo definitely should have given her stronger physique stats.

DaEvo's cheerful theme music sounded through the conduction headphones, and a notification flashed across his screen.

Quest Complete! You spoke with a woman for 1:15!
Rewards: Electronics and internet privileges!
Bonus: None

Score! Zack pumped a fist in the air and opened his settings menu. Most of the pink hearts blocking out the apps had disappeared. Hopefully that meant the ban on his gaming system had been lifted as well. The app said it had restored his electronics privileges. Surely that included Star Fury.

It was over. He had won.

Reputation update: -0.5

What? How had he lost reputation points even though he completed the quest? His conversation with Cassie hadn't gone that badly!

Whatever. He didn't care about this stupid app and its stupid stats. His team was waiting. If he hurried, he would make it back just in time for the start of the qualifier round. He sent a quick text saying he was on his way and sprinted toward his building as fast as he could, ignoring the app's warnings that he should slow down and rest. Sweat poured down his body, and the increased pace left him wheezing. DaEvo played somber music and flashed another stat.

Physique update: -0.1

Chapter Four

DaEvo flashed constant warnings to slow down and rest as Zack jogged home. Apparently, the app had access to the fitness tracking devices built into his wearable tech. Zack ignored the notifications until he was back in his building and riding the elevator up to his condo.

He ignored the stream of messages incoming from his teammates and leaned against the elevator wall, leaving streaks of sweat on the mirrors as he struggled to catch his breath and shivered in the air-conditioning. The clothes that had been fairly clean when he put them on were now drenched with sweat and sticking to his skin. He looked at himself in the mirror and winced. His face was tomato red, and the pools of sweat on the T-shirt outlined his gut. It wasn't pretty. Maybe those bodybuilders had a point about exercise. Not a big point, but as Zack stared at his reflection, he almost wished he had taken advantage of the gym when he first moved in.

Style Update: -0.1

Yeah, yeah. Zack pulled off his OptiGlasses and crammed them into his jeans pocket. DaEvo couldn't judge him if it couldn't see him.

Once he reached his apartment, he punched in the code and pushed open the door. He gagged as the overwhelming smell of dirty clothes and rotting food washed over him. It hadn't smelled that bad in here this morning.

He pulled off the sweat-drenched shirt, grabbed an energy drink from the fridge, and sank into his gaming chair. The leather stuck to his wet skin, but he didn't care. He didn't plan to move from that spot for the rest of the day anyway.

Zack picked up the controller for his gaming system and pressed the power button. He breathed a sigh of relief as the screens flickered to life. Then he unbuttoned his jeans so he could slouch comfortably.

This was more like it.

The Star Fury theme music blared through his surround sound speakers, and Zack took a long swig of his energy drink. He had missed the strategy session with the team, but thankfully he would be in time for the tournament. He even had a little bit of extra time.

This was a big tournament, and Zack planned to finish on top. Teams of four from all over the world would compete in several rounds over the next few months, and the teams that made the finals would travel to an in-person televised event at the Star Fury Convention in Las Vegas to show off their skills. The winning team would receive global recognition and join the pro circuit. This was Zack's chance to prove once and for all that he was the best. The ultimate quest.

The fact that Zoe Cross was hosting the event and interviewing winners didn't hurt anything.

Zack glanced at the poster of Zoe in the Armada uniform and grinned. No, that didn't hurt at all.

He wouldn't let Phil and a stupid dating sim take that away from him.

Zack launched out of the station, growled as he realized he was in the wrong star system, and hit the hyperspace thrusters. Good thing he'd way-pointed their training map.

"You're here!"

"Where have you been?"

"What the hell is going on, Zack?"

His teammates' chatter boomed through the apartment as they talked over each other in a clammer of accusations and relief. Judging from the background noise, they were under heavy fire.

Zack checked the timing and groaned internally. "Long story, but I'm on my way!"

"Yeah, yeah, just hurry up, would ya? We were supposed to be testing out the new formation, and it doesn't work without you."

Fazilnoor Kapoor, known to most as Faz, sounded truly peeved. His irritation made his Wisconsin accent stronger, which Zack found hilarious in spite of everything that had happened so far. When he first met Faz in college, he had found his classmate's nasal accent combined with the Sikh's traditional wear a little jarring. Now he didn't think twice about the combination of traditional turban and cheesehead slang.

Faz kept ranting, but Zack turned his attention to piloting his spacecraft. His team was on the other side of an asteroid belt, so he needed to get through there quickly to reach them. Maybe he could break his record while he was at it.

He pushed his thrusters into overdrive and zipped around the asteroids. The ship maneuvered easily through the field, twisting and turning with the touch of a key and the yank of the joystick.

Zack sank further into his chair. His sweaty back sticking to the leather was the only reminder of the unpleasant morning.

A notification on the screen confirmed he had beaten his previous record for navigating the asteroid belt. Nice. It looked as though things were finally going his way. The actual base location and fight was in a well-known asteroid belt, and the team had run the entire thing multiple times. It was the closest approximation they had to what they expected the first round would be like.

As he neared the battle, bright flashes of light indicating unrealistic laser fire, streaks of moving light that were homing missiles and tiny dots for drones came into view. The speakers rumbled and buzzed, adding to the atmosphere, while in the corner, chat from the

TAO WONG & A.G. MARSHALL

viewing Star Fury community flashed past. Just because they couldn't take part didn't mean they couldn't watch.

The team was in the middle of the fight, trying to blast through the defenses, but the outpost had a layered defense system. Mines on the outside, drones farther in, then automated NPC Armada ships on the inside.

Zack opened up his thrusters to maximum and sped toward the battle. His team was in the thick of it. They had formed up in close formation, driving straight through—which would work beautifully once he was there to complete the formation. Without him, they didn't have the DPS to cut through the respawning drones.

"Better late than never," Jenny Romero said as Zack entered hailing distance. The only female in the group was used to giving as good as she got.

Zack called it the "short woman ego issue"—when she wasn't around. He had no desire to get his head taken off.

Jenny was in the back as usual, playing the long game by having her drones drop auto-targeting laser mines in enemy space, ensuring the backup drones that were populating behind them couldn't reach the team. The mine and drone strategy was a bit old-fashioned, considered spammy by some and dishonorable by the most stalwart Armada members, but Jenny refused to upgrade and said Corsairs didn't care about honorable strategies as long as they worked. The bulky, multi-spherical drone deployer she maneuvered took hits from the Armada and shrugged them off, the thick hull plating more than adequate for the current rate of fire.

Greg Miller, their heavy-hitting missile and artillery boat, ran a much sleeker vessel than Jenny. He relied more on speed and force shields, allowing the sleek, bullet-nosed craft to provide cover for Jenny and watch Faz's back. Greg was what others might consider a typical gamer: overweight, working a dead-end job in a grocery store, with an irascible personality.

Fazilnoor Kapoor—Faz—was in front with his ship acting as scout and interceptor, the smallest ship of the group. Probably the smartest member of the team—discounting Zack himself, of course

—Faz was taking a year-long break, playing Star Fury in an attempt to sow his wild oats before his parents made him go to medical school.

Where Greg was fast for a medium-weight ship, Faz was just fast. And rather than use multiple weapon systems, he'd thrown nearly everything into concentrating his weapon system on his forward laser turret.

All around the team, the Armada ships swirled and spun, hammering at the close-held formation. Faz and Greg focused on picking off the drones in front of them, not yet daring to break out into a dogfight. The deeper they got, the more Jenny's mines played their part, the automatic targeting on the mine lasers expanding their zone of control.

Zack cut his thrusters as he entered the back of the zone, cruising in on built-in velocity, and fired a blast from his new laser cannon to clear a path through a new set of populating drones. His ship was the linchpin of the operation, nearly as fast and maneuverable as Faz's but more heavily armed. Also, less armored and a hell of a lot more expensive to replace when it was inevitably blown up from time to time. Unlike real-world money, Star Fury credits had to be earned. Good thing Zack spent so much time running missions.

Zack barked orders to the team, his voice cutting off complaints as he controlled the team's maneuvers. Since he'd just joined, he had a full bank of energy and he let loose, damaging Armada ships and tearing through force shields with impunity before he slid into position.

"You're loose, Faz."

Now that Zack was there, Faz peeled off to harry the ships the team had damaged but not taken down. "For cripe's sake, it's about time!"

"Chill. We got this. Marauder on your right, Faz. Greg, that Zed-3 is trying to get onto your six. Jenny, switch over to the… mine spread formation seven." Rattling off orders, Zack maneuvered his ship, blasting away at enemy ships.

Long minutes drew on as they took down ship after ship and

even the automated drone deployers on the base. With the entire area around them littered with half-disabled ships, they were finally getting back on track.

"Finish them!" Jenny said. "I'm swamped over here."

Zack blasted all the disabled ships within range with the laser cannon, then flushed his entire rack of missiles again. His monitors went white from the force of the explosions, the rumble from the ship making him grin. Everyone knew it was unrealistic, but it sure was fun. Jenny squeaked in alarm, and Faz swore.

"Dude! A little warning next time? You almost hit me."

"You said to finish them," Zack said defensively. "Let's pull back and regroup. The tournament starts soon."

"And we still haven't tested our new formations," Jenny said. "You were supposed to be here an hour ago."

"Yeah, what happened?" Greg asked.

Greg covered Jenny as she recalled her drones and backed away from the battle. Faz flew circles around them, both showing off and scouting for anyone who might try to hinder their retreat.

"Long story," Zack said. "I'll tell you after the tournament round."

They settled in a safe distance away from the battle, having given up on finishing off the base. A countdown to the tournament appeared in the corner of Zack's gaming monitor, and he guided his ship into its place in their formation. They would be automatically teleported to the tournament once the countdown reached zero, and they needed to be prepared. Luckily, all their expendable munitions would be refilled automatically, so that wasn't a concern.

"Any last-minute words of wisdom, Captain?" Jenny said with more than a hint of sarcasm.

Zack sat up straighter, remembering his encounter that morning before Phil had interrupted him. "Yeah, I ran into some weird, automated Armada drones earlier. They were stronger than they should have been and landed a few hits on me. It might be something from the latest update, so watch out for those."

"That would have been nice to know about in time to actually do something about it," Jenny said.

"Focus," Greg said. "It's time!"

The battle in front of them faded to black as they were teleported to the tournament dungeon. They respawned in a different quadrant of space, empty except for the four of them and a nearby star with jets of plasma shooting from its surface. Before Zack could comment, a wave of enemy ships flew out from behind the star and raced toward them.

"Take out the destroyers first," Zack said. "Watch your sensors for plasma bursts. Alpha formation, go!"

His teammates seamlessly fell into place as they blazed toward the ships. This was a timed mission, so there was no point waiting for the enemy to come to them. They needed to be aggressive and efficient.

Zack called out orders, and his teammates obeyed in a flawless display of teamwork that they had honed through years of playing together. Jenny stayed back and deployed her drones. They weren't quite as effective against AI players as they were against humans, but even computers couldn't avoid her traps forever. Soon a large pile of disabled ships floated around the battlefield.

"Pull around," Zack said. "I'll take them out."

Greg and Jenny pulled back to harass the large ships at the outer edge of the fleet. Faz darted forward, picking off smaller ships at the inside one by one. Zack armed his new cannon and destroyed the mass of disabled ships with a single blast.

"Nice cannon," Greg said with grudging admiration.

"Worth every credit."

When the explosions died away enough for Zack to see the screen again, his teammates had regrouped on the other side of the enemy fleet. He squinted with concentration, studying the pattern of the enemy's laser fire. If he timed this just right, he could slip through the center of the fleet without taking damage and assume his place in the formation rather than wasting time by flying around. Taking out every ship in his path would just be a bonus.

He took a deep breath and rested his thumb against the trigger that would engage his thruster. This move would require precision.

Wait.

Wait.

Now!

Zack pressed the trigger.

His screen went black.

"What the hell?" Zack let out a frustrated scream and followed it with a string of profanity.

Pressing the power button on his gaming controller had no effect. He tried to leap to his feet, but his back stuck to the leather and held him in place. He leaned forward, peeling out of the chair, and stood. His pants fell down around his ankles, and the lock on his door clicked shut.

Warning! Minimum Public Decency Requirements Not Met

Please dress yourself appropriately according to local public decency laws.

Enacting blackout protocols.

The words echoed through his surround sound system, and DaEvo's cheerful theme music accompanied them. The windows darkened, and the overhead lights brightened. Zack tried to sprint for the door, tripped on the jeans around his ankles, and fell face-first into a pile of dirty laundry.

The good news was that it broke his fall. The bad news was that it smelled awful.

Zack rolled over, pulled the OptiGlasses out of the pocket, and shoved them onto his face. The public decency warning flashed across the screen. Zack cursed the dating sim as he flicked his eyes to the calling app and dialed Phil. The phone rang once then went to voicemail.

Zack ended the call without leaving a message, untangled himself from his clothes, and stood. DaEvo flashed notifications across his screen.

Minimum Hygiene Levels not Met
Please take a shower and change into a clean pair of clothes.
Reward: Access to door

"I already did that!"

Your alpha test bug report has been logged.
Thank you for your help in making DaEvo a success!

A ringing in his conduction headphones interrupted Zack before he could do anything further. He answered. "Phil?"

"Dude, where are you?" Faz said.

"I got kicked out."

"Connection issues?" Greg asked.

Apparently, Faz had made a group call. The sound of laser fire and whine of engines sounded in the background.

"We're in the middle of the qualifying round!" Jenny's said. "Get your butt back here!"

"How long 'til you're back? Faz asked. "We can cover you until you reboot but make it quick."

DaEvo flashed a notification across the screen.

Zack glared at it. "Just a second."

"What do you mean, just a second?" Jenny shrieked. "We don't have a second. Greg, to your right!"

Greg released a series of muffled grunts punctuated by Faz's swearing while Zack flipped through DaEvo's menu of rewards, upgrades, and achievements that he had unlocked.

Rewards, Upgrades, and Achievements
Access to Front Door—locked. Please meet minimum hygiene and public decency standards
Electronics Privileges—unlocked
Essential Internet Privileges—unlocked
Non-Essential Internet Privileges—locked, time expired

"What do you mean my time expired?"
DaEvo flashed another screen.

Non-Essential Internet Privileges earned : 30 minutes
Non-Essential Internet Privileges spent : 30 minutes
Non-Essential Internet Privileges remaining: 0 minutes

Please complete more quests to unlock more rewards, upgrades, and achievements.

"Star Fury is essential!" Zack yelled.

Your alpha test bug report has been logged.
Thank you for your help in making DaEvo a success!

Faz stopped swearing. "Essential? What are you talking about? When are you coming back?"

Zack swallowed and stared longingly at the sleek surfaces of his screens. They remained dark mirrors, reflecting his sweaty, half-dressed image.

"I don't think I am."

"You're ditching us?" Greg said. "In the middle of the tournament? You're just leaving?"

"Of all the bilge-sucking, hornswaggling muckspouts—" Jenny continued a tirade of the pirate-based insults favored by the Corsairs.

Zack turned down the volume of the call with a quick swipe of his eyes as he tried to gather his wits enough to explain. "Phil pulled a fast one this morning, and I'm locked out of my account. My console won't even turn on."

"So go to a café and reset your password," Jenny said, abandoning the stream of insults in favor of solving the problem. "If you hurry, you can respawn and join us. The tournament officials lied. This isn't a three-tier base. This looks more to be seven. Faz, on your left."

Zack waited for the laser fire to die down before he answered. "Yeah, I don't think it'll be that easy. I'm also locked in my apartment."

"You're what?" Faz's voice rose, half in incredulity, half in surprise. And maybe another quarter in pure mirth.

"Forget him and focus," Jenny said. "This is a timed round, and we're down a player. Zack, do what you need to do and get back here if you can."

"I'm trying," Zack said. "Phil hooked me up to some kind of app that's restricting all my stuff. Apparently, I have to earn screen time to access my account."

"Earn screen time? You're legally an adult. He can't do that to you," Greg said.

"Just call tech support and report that your account was hacked and you need back in," Jenny said.

"And do it real quick," Faz said.

The sound of laser fire in the background intensified, and Zack winced as Jenny and Greg yelled for Faz to focus.

"Just get back online," Faz said. "Whatever it takes, get back here."

Faz hung up, and the room went silent. Zack stared at his screen for a moment, then shook himself out of his shock and looked up the number for Star Fury support. He'd never had to deal with them before. The game had always been perfect.

He dialed the number and paced as the OptiGlasses rang. The qualifying round should last at least thirty minutes if it was seven tiers. Hopefully longer, so he would be able to fix this and get back in time to help his team. DaEvo flashed the public decency warning again, and Zack considered stripping completely nude in protest. It seemed like the only act of defiance he had left.

Detected increased heart rate to a dangerous level.
Scanning status.
Accelerated stress…
Please assume a reclined position and breathe deeply to ease stress levels.

"You're the one stressing me out!" Zack shouted, but of course DaEvo had nothing useful to say to that.

The app just kept flashing the warning. Zack gritted his teeth. He would recline when this was fixed and he was safely back in his ship. What did a stupid app know about his health?

"Welcome to the Star Fury support line. Please enable retina scan with your OptiGlasses to confirm your account identity."

The computerized voice was the same one as his AI co-pilot in the game. Zack sighed and stared straight ahead as his OptiGlasses scanned his eyes.

"Thank you. Please log in to your Star Fury account to allow diagnostic scanning."

"I'm locked out of my account."

"Please complete password reset protocol to regain access to your account."

Zack sighed. He really hated dealing with tech support. "I can't access password reset."

"Have you tried turning your device off and back on again?"

Zack ground his teeth. "Yes."

"Hesitation detected. Are you sure you tried turning your device off and back on again?"

Stupid uppity AI with its stupid condescending suggestions.

"Of course I did!"

"Have you checked to make sure your device is plugged in?"

"I checked everything, okay? It won't work no matter what I do. Please transfer me to a real person!"

He could practically hear the automated voice sigh.

"Malfunction reported. Please hold for a human representative."

The Star Fury theme played. And played. Zack paced around the piles of dirty clothes. His stomach growled, reminding him that he hadn't eaten anything yet. He pulled a piece of pizza from one of the boxes on the floor and gnawed on it while he walked. It was a little stale. Probably time to order a fresh one.

He looked at the door. Was there anything in the apartment solid enough to break it down? At this point, he would rather do that than fulfill any of DaEvo's stupid hygiene quests to unlock it.

"Star Fury support, Gary speaking. How may I help you?"

Gary sounded almost as robotic as the AI. Zack took a deep breath. Just stay calm and explain the situation. That was all he needed to do.

"Yeah, I'm having trouble accessing my account. This is urgent. I was competing in the tournament when I got kicked off."

"No need to worry, sir. Just start the program on your game console, and—"

"I can't."

"One moment please."

Gary hummed to himself as he searched for whatever he was looking for. The out-of-tune music did nothing to ease Zack's frustration.

Detected increased heart rate to a dangerous level and low oxygen level.
Scanning status.
Accelerated stress...
Please assume a reclined position and breathe deeply to ease stress levels.

Zack paced faster just to spite the app. But the combination of adrenaline, exercise, and energy drink was catching up with him.

"Okay, here we go. Can you give me your login handle?"

"Omniscious23x."

"Right. Can you spell that for me?"

Zack spelled it.

"Thank you. Now please confirm your home address."

Zack did.

Gary hummed again. "My records say you live in New York."

"I moved."

"And you didn't update your address?"

"Apparently not." Zack gave his old New York address to confirm what Gary's information was telling him and agreed to update his account information. He tapped his fingers against his leg, punching in combinations for combat maneuvers that he should be performing with his team right now.

"One moment, sir. I'll need a second verification method as well." Gary hummed again while he checked something.

Zack bounced on his toes in frustration. "Look, you confirmed my retinal scan. Isn't that enough?"

"One moment, sir. We thank you for your patience."

Zack rolled his eyes at the sound of pages flipping. Apparently, his request required Gary to look through his employee handbook.

"Yes, the retinal scan is enough. I can confirm your account identity and reset your password through your game system, but it doesn't seem to be online right now. We'll just go through a few steps to make sure your system is functioning properly. First, please make sure your unit is plugged in."

"What?" Zack had started to tune Gary out but snapped back into focus.

"The unit won't function without power. We need to make sure—"

"Of course it's plugged in! I'm not an idiot. Can you transfer me to someone who actually knows what they're talking about? I'm in a hurry!"

There was a beat of silence interrupted by rustling paper, then Gary continued. "First, please make sure your unit is plugged in."

"Are you reading from a script?" Zack clenched his fists, trying to keep his temper in check.

Another pause.

Zack snapped. "Look, you bilge-sucker, it's plugged in. Just skip ahead to the part where you check my account."

"First, please make sure—"

"Fine!"

Zack stalked over to the game system. He glared at the plug and blinked. The smart sensors were orange, indicating that they weren't transmitting power.

Damn it. They had been green that morning.

Zack unplugged the smart surge protector and plugged the gaming console directly into the wall outlet. Not recommended, of course, but it was the only way to bypass the surge protector that was apparently now under DaEvo's control. He could always buy a new console if it fried.

"Ah, there we are," Gary said. "I'm receiving transmissions from your system now. Give me a moment to upload them."

He sounded smug. Self-satisfied idiot. Anybody could read from a script.

Zack gritted his teeth and waited. His TV turned on, transforming the screen from glossy black to glowing blue. It was an improvement. The game console turned on as well but didn't transmit anything to the screen.

Zack described what he was seeing to Gary, who continued humming.

"I'm telling you, I just need to reset my password."

"Aha!" Gary sounded even smugger than before.

Zack swallowed. "Yeah? What did you find?"

"Your account has not been compromised. You've activated intervention mode."

"What? No, I didn't."

A smirk crept into Gary's voice. "The paperwork was submitted this morning, and you signed it."

Phil. Damn it, he hadn't wasted any time.

"So what exactly is intervention mode?" Zack asked.

"Intervention mode limits your access to video games based on the parameters you agreed to ahead of time. We introduced the feature after people complained that Star Fury was interfering with their life."

"Star Fury is my life. How do I remove the restrictions?"

"It depends on the contract you signed. Most people restrict hours so they can't play during work or specify that they must complete tasks like exercise before they log in."

"I don't have a job, and I don't exercise. I want my account back."

"Sounds like you made the right choice accepting the intervention."

"I didn't agree to this! I'm in the middle of a tournament!"

"A lot of addicts regret signing the contract, especially at first, but we have a legal responsibility to uphold the terms of your agreement."

"I'm. Not. Addicted."

"Of course not, sir. You signed over control of your account to Philip MacComack. You'll have to talk to him about lifting the ban."

"He tricked me! I didn't mean to sign it. The tournament is happening now, and my team is stranded without me."

Gary chuckled. "I'm sorry. There's nothing I can do. Have a good day, Mr. Moore."

The call ended. Zack growled in frustration.

Detected increased heart rate to a dangerous level and low oxygen level. Scanning status.
Accelerated stress…
Please assume a reclined position and breathe deeply to ease stress levels.

"I'll show you stress!"

Zack pulled off the OptiGlasses and threw them across the room. They landed in a pile of dirty underwear.

Great. Just great. He would have to put those glasses back on his face at some point.

Zack finally took DaEvo's advice and sank into a chair. His sweaty skin stuck to the leather as he reclined. Around him, yellow sunlight bulbs illuminated the room, the skyline of the city hidden behind the darkened windows. He closed his eyes as reality settled in around him.

He was going to miss the first round of the tournament. He was trapped in his apartment without access to the internet, leaving his team a player short and at a huge disadvantage. Even if they did make it through the round without him, they would be behind in the leaderboards and have to fight to make it back to the top.

All because he was trapped in a damn dating sim.

Zack took a deep breath, trying to clear his head and form some kind of plan.

DaEvo chimed, its soft, velvety tones coming across his expensive surround sound speakers.

Reminder! Minimum Public Decency Requirements Not Met

Please dress yourself appropriately according to local public decency laws to lift blackout protocols.

Chapter Five

Zack stared at the pools of water on his bathroom floor. If showering was going to become a regular thing, he really should move the faucet repair up on his list of priorities. Or at least invest in a shower curtain. He ran a towel over his hair to stop it from dripping and began the search for clothes that would meet DaEvo's minimum hygiene levels.

He pulled a T-shirt from the top of the nearest pile of clothes and held it up to his nose. Not the worst, but not exactly fresh. He doused it with a lemon-scented cleaning spray left behind by the last housekeeper and put it on.

The pants were more difficult. Why did none of them fit? It was weird that all of them had shrunk when they hadn't been washed recently. Finally, Zack found a pair of stretchy sweats shoved under a chair. He gave them the same deodorizing treatment and pulled them on. Then he put on his OptiGlasses and looked in the mirror.

Success! Minimum Hygiene Requirements Met!
Reward provided. User now has access to front door.

He could tell the software was in the alpha version. They didn't even code the quest information to be similar. Or was it running a test? Checking which set of notifications elicited a better reaction? In fact, Zack would not put it past DaEvo to do that.

Success! Minimum Public Decency Requirements Met!
Blackout protocols removed

The front door unlocked, and the windows brightened. Before Zack could feel too satisfied about that, another notification flashed across his screen.

Style update: -0.1

"Oh come on! I look fine!"

Your alpha test bug report has been logged.
Thank you for your help in making DaEvo a success!

Damn it. He really hated this app.

Zack cast a longing glance at his gaming setup. The screen was on now that it was plugged into the wall, but Star Fury still refused to start. His teammates hadn't made contact yet. Either they weren't speaking to him, or they were still fighting in the tournament round.

Neither scenario was good. It had been almost an hour. All the competent teams would be finished already. If Zack's team was still fighting, they might not make it to the next round.

Zack sighed. It looked as though it was time to leave the house again. Phil may have disabled Zack's gaming system and account, but he couldn't disable access to the game everywhere. Maybe Zack could get around the restrictions if he logged in from a gaming café instead of his personal devices. Even if he was locked out of his main account, he did have an alt. Not that it would help the tournament, but he was grasping at straws. The secondary account would at least give him a way to check the leaderboards and communicate with his team.

A notification flashed across his OptiGlasses as soon as his hand touched the doorknob.

Quest!
Hold a two-minute conversation with a woman face-to-face!
Restrictions: In-person. Non-VR generated. Unpaid interaction.
Difficulty: Variable
Reward: Online access time for non-essential electronics

Easy level (Rank 0-50): 3 minutes of game time
Medium level (Rank 51-74): 6 minutes of game time
Hard level (Rank 75-100): 9 minutes of game time

"Nine minutes? Why is it so low? Why'd it drop!?!"

Zack scrolled through the rest of the quest parameters. Even if he was able to complete the quest with a high-level target, nine minutes wasn't enough game time to do anything meaningful. It would barely be enough time to check the leaderboards and see which teams had advanced to the next round.

DaEvo chimed a belated response to his question.

Quest rewards are determined by calculating a combination of your level and your date's level. Level up your personal stats to gain more points and unlock more valuable quests.

This was followed by a stream of his stats. Zack glanced through it and groaned.

Zack Moore Current Attributes (Social Level 7)
Physique: 30.9
Style: 18.8
Reputation: -20.5
Occupation: 0

The Style and Reputation points he had lost were putting a serious strain on his rewards and available quests. He'd even dropped an entire Social Level. Not to mention the conversation with Cassie had almost given him a heart attack, and that had been a medium level. So he could kill himself to earn six minutes of Star Fury access, or he could game the system.

"How do I level up my stats?"

DaEvo flashed a wave of pink hearts across his OptiGlasses.

Quest!
It's hard to attract the ladies when you look like a slob. Lucky for you, Style is one of the easiest stats to level up! Complete this makeover tutorial to level up your style.
Restrictions: None
Difficulty: Low
Reward: Increased style points

Zack ground his teeth and stalked to the elevator. Hell would freeze before he let some stupid dating sim give him a makeover. He looked fine. His OptiGlasses tinted automatically as he stepped into the bright Oklahoma sun. Thank goodness they were back online. With a few eye swipes, Zack called a car with his ride app and directed the driver to take him to Gord's Gaming Center. He could buy a car, but it never made sense. Not as a New Yorker with cabs on every street and ride shares everywhere. And certainly not for the environment. Now, technically it was close enough to walk, but he was still winded from chasing Cassie. Besides, it was hot as hell and he didn't want to sweat and trigger DaEvo's Hygiene Requirements again.

Two showers in a day was already one too many. No need to add a third.

Zack took a deep breath as he stepped into the gaming café, appreciating the scent of coffee, pizza, and electronics. He hadn't visited Gord's since he'd gotten his own place fully set up, but the gaming center had a good reputation, with two levels of space for the average user, a half-dozen private rooms for super-users, the latest gaming technology, and even an in-house café with instant noodles, pizza, and coffee on hand.

Small, discreet tabs let the servers come to you directly at each station, and you could also make orders from the café for food to be delivered. The entire place was lit with low-intensity lights to reduce glare, and it had marble flooring and black metal railings that gave the place a modern, sleek vibe. The minimalist style was interrupted only by the numerous gaming posters hung around the gaming café, many of them featuring Gord's logo. It was busy today, and the room was filled with the sounds of soft conversations and pressing buttons. If his condo wasn't so nice, Zack would have made Gord's his home too.

"Hi, how can I help you?"

Zack nodded to acknowledge the server at the counter and stared at the menu, the café menu and the hourly rates showing on either side above her. Even more personalized advertisements floated in his OptiGlasses as the café's system pulled his order history and offered him special deals.

Zack dismissed the deals, although a few of them were tempting. He was on a mission. No distractions. "Yeah, I'll take a latte, two slices of pepperoni pizza, and three hours of access in one of your private rooms."

"Sure thing. Just give me a minute."

Zack surveyed the main lobby as the cashier pressed buttons on her display screen. The room was full of gamers. Most of them were playing Star Fury, though there were a scattering of the usual casual browsers, job seekers, and first-player shooter gamers. The upcoming Star Fury tournament had given the game a boost in popularity, and it dominated the attention of real gamers.

A large monitor in the corner flashed the preliminary results of the tournament as they came in. As Zack had suspected, lots of teams had completed the dungeon already. Sixty-five of them, to be precise. There were only one hundred slots up for grabs.

"Come on, guys. You can do it."

Zack studied the screen of the nearest Star Fury player. He was at a massive scrimmage at a two-star battlefield but was fighting on the Armada side. Zack couldn't see much of the player. Just a ball cap featuring the Armada's military logo. No matter. Zack was much more interested in what was happening on the screen. From the looks of things, the Armada vastly outnumbered the raiding Corsairs and were close to wiping them out. Judging by the intensity of the battle, it looked like the players were getting bored just watching.

Zack gritted his teeth. He should be there. He squinted at the screen, hoping to catch a glimpse of his teammates and confirm that they had also completed the round and joined this battle. Maybe they just hadn't been added to the leaderboard yet. Not as if there weren't a million battlefields, but he was getting desperate.

DaEvo flashed a notification, but Zack flicked it away with a swipe of his eyes. Hopefully logging in at Gord's would fool the system and he would never have to hear from DaEvo again. If his team managed to qualify without him, he could join them in future battles. They would work up the ranks and—

"Paying by OptiGlass?"

Zack nodded, and the price flashed across his screen. He approved the purchase and gave Gord's permission to run a tab and make further charges without his approving them. No need for distractions.

"As you can see, we're pretty full today. Well, every day with the tournament coming up. Normally you'd have to reserve a private room ahead of time, but one will be open in about five minutes thanks to a cancellation. If you don't mind waiting here, I'll get your food ready while they clean the station for you."

"Hmm? Yeah, sure. Whatever," Zack muttered, his attention still focused on the Armada player's screen. Worse things worse, he'd log into his alt account and join the battle. It wasn't as tricked out as his main, but it would at least give him a chance to help the Corsairs and vent his frustration at the situation. Maybe the tournament organizers would let his team make a substitution to the alt account if he explained that the other had been put into intervention mode. There was no need for them to know that the same person would be playing.

"You're interested in the Star Fury tournament?" the cashier asked.

"Yeah."

More interested than she could know. Zack studied the other gamers with narrowed eyes. Were any of them serious competition? If he wasn't able to log in with his alt, a fellow Star Fury player might have some ideas about how to get past the restrictions of intervention mode. But Zack would rather start over with a completely new account and make milk runs than let his competition know that his life had been taken over by a dating sim. Especially Armada scum like the player in the baseball cap who had just blown up three Corsairs in battle. Zack really hoped those explosions weren't all that was left of his teammates.

"What kind of milk do you want in your latte?"

"You got any Veobos Raptor Cow left?"

"What?" She sounded so alarmed that Zack looked over. The cashier's brown eyes were wide with confusion.

"You know, like in Star Fury? It was a joke."

"Sorry. Never played it," her voice was relaxed now, as the misfired joke flopped around in the past.

"You've never played Star Fury?" Zack looked at the cashier, actually seeing her for the first time. What kind of person worked at Gord's but had never played Star Fury?

She was shorter than him, although the auburn hair that stuck out in unsuccessfully restrained curls added a little height, mandated hat failing to achieve the desired effect. Her brown eyes sparkled with mischief that her smirk accentuated. The khaki pants and black polo shirt that all Gord's Gaming Center employees wore weren't doing her any favors, but Zack suspected she would look pretty good in something that fit her better. The name tag pinned to her chest informed Zack that the non-gamer's name was Ashley.

Ashley laughed and held her hands up in mock surrender. "You got me. I'm not a gamer. I only play one on TV. I'll give you two percent milk if that's ok?"

Zack blinked, still not sure what to make of her. Ashley shrugged and turned around to make the latte. The back of her uniform was much more flattering than the front.

Zack shook his head to regain his focus and get back to the

matter at hand. "You work in Gord's Gaming Center, and you've never played Star Fury? How did you even get this job?"

"Believe it or not, they were more interested in my past job experience as a waitress than my gaming preferences."

"Really?"

"Yeah. Really." A scowl replaced Ashley's smirk, and her eyes glinted with a steely expression. She gripped the latte so tightly that Zack half-expected her to crush the mug and send hot liquid all over the counter.

He swallowed. "Right. I suppose that makes sense."

She handed him the latte, and her fingers brushed against his as he took the cup. DaEvo flashed a notification, and Zack pushed it aside. Ashley checked a notification on her computer and cast a sideways glance at Zack.

"Your room is clean. Upstairs and first door on the right. I'll get the pizza over to you as soon as it's ready."

"Great."

Zack wrapped his hands around the warm mug and hurried upstairs. He paused at the top of the stairs to check a monitor displaying the leaderboard. Eighty-five slots had been filled, and his team still wasn't on the list. He sprinted to his private room, spilling a little of the coffee on his shirt as he did so. If they were still fighting, maybe he could join them after all. He set the cup on a side table and ran his hand over the controller. Please, this had to work.

The console started up. Star Fury activated, and Zack held his breath. So far so good. Now the app would complete a retinal scan to log him into his account and—

Account Access Denied. Please contact Star Fury support.

"Damn it!"

Zack slammed the controller down and glared at the screen as if he could bully it into submission. When that yielded no results, he drew a deep breath. Time to try the alternate account. A minute later, he swore again. Of course, he'd linked both accounts to the same credit card and they'd flagged them both. Zack sighed, closing his eyes, then opened them again. There had to be a way around this.

Movement on his OptiGlasses caught his eye. DaEvo was flashing a pink heart in the corner. Zack sighed and flicked open the icon. A flood of pink hearts filled his vision, and cheerful music blared through his headphones.

> ***Quest Complete! You spoke with a woman for 4:35! You have earned non-essential electronics and internet privileges!***
> *Reward, easy difficulty—+3*
> *Bonus Achieved – Make her laugh. +10 Minutes Use Time*
> *Bonus Achieved—Make physical contact +20 Minutes Use Time*
> *Reputation increased: +0.1*

"Wait, what?"

Zack flipped through DaEvo's menu. He had completed a quest, but how? With whom?

He hadn't even realized he'd said the last sentence out loud. But a social media feed filled his screen, followed by a stream of stats.

> ***Ashley Barnes (Social Level 49)***
> *Physique: 71*
> *Style: 41*
> *Reputation: 61*
> *Occupation: 26*

Zack looked over the pictures on the feed. He had been right. Ashley looked much better in street clothes than her work uniform. Her profile picture showed her smiling with a young girl who had to be related to her somehow. They had the same auburn hair and mischievous expression.

Zack thought back to his interaction with Ashley. Yeah, she had laughed. He hadn't been trying to make her laugh, but apparently, DaEvo didn't know that. But what about the physical contact? He had received some serious bonus points for that.

Right, their hands had touched when he took his coffee.

But hadn't DaEvo said that paid interactions didn't count? If all Zack had to do to earn game time was chat with cashiers, this might be easier than he thought. Zack's lips pulled apart in a vulpine grin as he plotted how to exploit the system. Dating game or not, Zack was still a gamer and a damn good one.

And now he had thirty-three minutes of game time to make the Armada scum pay.

He sipped the coffee and stared straight ahead while the Opti-Glasses completed a retinal scan and logged him into his account. The Star Fury theme music filled the room, and the familiar computerized voice welcomed him back to his ship.

Zack hadn't quite forgiven that voice for aiding Gary at customer support, but he pushed the frustration aside and engaged his boosters. He had spawned back where he had been teleported. All alone. Not in the tournament. He sank back in the chair as a final wave of reality washed over him. He really had missed it.

"What the hell, Zack?"

Jenny's voice cut over the sound of laser fire, and Zack sat up straighter. "You're here? How did it go? What happened?"

"What happened?" Greg said. "We're the ones who should be asking that question. Where did you go?"

"Long story."

"We have time," Faz said.

"Did we qualify?" Zack asked, putting off the inevitable explanation for as long as possible. A quick check verified their location and Zack plugged the information into the hyperspace computer.

"We?" Jenny said. "What's this talk about we? You disappeared. We covered for you and barely made it out alive."

The Star Fury theme music blasted through the speakers, and a notification appeared in the corner of the gaming monitor. The final results.

Zack tensed as he pressed the button to open the notification. He scrolled to the bottom of the list and whooped in triumph when he saw his team listed as the 98th qualifier. His teammates temporarily forgot their anger and joined him in celebrating.

When the excited screams gave way to awkward silence, Zack said, "You guys are amazing!"

"We were lucky," Jenny said. "Seriously, Zack, what happened? We can't have team members disappearing in the middle of competitions."

"You said something about Phil?" Faz prompted.

Zack sighed. "Phil tricked me and linked my account to an app running intervention mode. I have limited game time. I didn't realize quite how limited, and it ran out."

"Cripes," Faz said.

"And not to avoid the issue, but I only have—" Zack looked at the pink timer in the corner of his OptiGlasses. DaEvo was counting down the time he spent playing the game, and five minutes had passed already. "I only have twenty-eight minutes of game time left right now. So maybe we could test out our new formations in that battle and talk about this later?"

His teammates' swearing echoed through the room, but thankfully, they weren't far away. The moment his ship appeared, they fell into place for their attack formation. Zack led the course toward the Armada base, the team flying through the swirl of lasers, missiles, and artillery fire.

"That's not nearly enough time," Faz said. "We have a lot of gear to test out."

"You think I'm happy about this?"

"What exactly is intervention mode?" Jenny asked. "You said he installed an app. What do you have to do to earn game time?"

Zack looked hopefully at the DaEvo icon, but no timer started at the sound of Jenny's voice. Apparently, DaEvo meant it when it said in-person interactions only. So why did it count Ashley when it said no paid interactions? "Hey, when you have a conversation with a cashier, would you say you're paying to talk to her?"

"What does that have to do with anything?" Greg asked.

"Just trying to settle a bet."

"About how long you can talk to a girl you're not paying to be there?"

"Is now really the time to settle a bet about girls?" Jenny asked. "Greg, on your left."

"Got it," Greg said.

Zack swerved as an Armada cruiser tried to ram into him. "You're right, Jenny. Forget the girl. Let's try gamma formation on that cluster of Armada scum up ahead."

The team switched formations, and Faz led the attack by dodging between the ships. He distracted them with acrobatics while Jenny planted mines and Zack got into position to blast them with the laser cannon.

While Zack waited for Greg to lure the enemy ships close enough to each other to destroy in a single blast, his mind went back to Ashley. If DaEvo didn't count the interaction with Ashley as paid, the logistics didn't matter. Zack had paid for coffee, not Ashley's time. That seemed like a technicality, but maybe the app was too buggy to know the difference. Either way, he would exploit that knowledge however he could.

"Get clear on my mark," Zack said. "This laser has a bit of kick."

"It's the new Mark VIII, right?" Greg said. "Reviews of that are mixed online."

"That thing almost blew me up along with the target earlier," Jenny said. "I say no laser cannon."

"The laser cannon is awesome!" Faz said.

"I agree," Zack said. "We could win the whole tournament with it."

"Or we could all die in the crossfire. If you bother to show up at all."

Zack sighed. It looked like Jenny was not going to let that go.

"Go!" he said, forcing himself to push away his frustrations to deal with later.

His teammates scattered, and Zack blasted the cluster of ships with the laser cannon. The gaming chair shook with the force of the explosion, and the sound of shrapnel hitting his shields filled the room.

"Nice," Greg said. "We might be able to break through their front line over on the west side."

"Good idea," Zack said. "Let's try jellyfish formation. Greg, you lead this one."

"I remember."

Greg led the charge while Jenny flew behind him, fanning out a swarm of drones like jellyfish tentacles. Zack and Faz hid in the swarm, ready to dart out and—

Someone knocked, and the door to his room opened. Ashley waved and held up his pizza. "Sorry to interrupt, but the delivery bay for this room is out of order. I'll set this on the table, okay?"

DaEvo chimed.

Quest!
Hold a two-minute conversation with a woman face-to-face!
Restrictions: In-person. Non-VR generated. Unpaid interaction.
Difficulty: Variable
Reward: Online access time for unrestricted internet privileges

Easy level (Rank 0-50): 3 minutes of game time
Medium level (Rank 51-74): 6 minutes of game time
Hard level (Rank 75-100): 9 minutes of game time

The pink timer counted down, and Zack grinned. The conversation was a repeatable quest, and DaEvo really didn't count the workers at Gord's as paid interaction! If he could get Ashley talking, he might earn enough game time to test out the rest of the team's formations. Zack waved for Ashley to stay and set his autopilot to keep him hovering under the cover of Jenny's swarm.

"Hang tight, guys. I'll be right back."

"Not again!" Greg said.

Faz let out a stream of profanity.

Zack quickly muted the comms and turned back to Ashley. "Sorry about that."

"Did you want something else?"

The timer was still counting down. Ashley stood in the doorway, watching Zack with her arms crossed. She did not seem pleased that he was keeping her from work.

Think! What could he say? Jokes hadn't worked on Cassie, but weren't jokes the best way to get her laughing? This would be a fantastic time for DaEvo to offer help, but the app remained silent. The pink timer flashed red, warning Zack that the conversation was lagging enough to reset it. He said the first thing that came to mind.

"Do you want to see my ship?"

Ashley raised an eyebrow. "You want me to stand around watching you play your game?"

Zack's pulse raced at her words, a close echo to Phil's every time he came over. Of course she was just like every other non-gamer, thinking that video games were beneath her.

"I need to get back to work," Ashley said. "Please excuse me."

DaEvo chimed.

Bonus Quest

Your lady seems upset. Find out what's bothering her and make her feel better to earn bonus points.

Zack blinked. Why would DaEvo think Ashley was upset? Did the app have some kind of facial expression software built into it?

He took a closer look at her face. She did look a little tense. Ashley glared at him and turned to go.

"Wait!"

"What? I mean, do you need anything else?"

"Are you okay? You seem upset."

Not the smoothest move in the book, but Zack had never claimed to be smooth with the ladies. That was what DaEvo was for, and the app said Ashley was upset. At this point, he had no choice but to trust it. If nothing else, it would keep the conversation going.

Ashley stared at him for a few moments. Then her shoulders slumped. "Sorry. I'm just tired of customers making fun of me because I don't know anything about Star Fury. I get that it's popular, but I'm just here to serve pizza. Why does it matter what I do with my spare time? I have better things to do than research every video game our clients play." Ashley's voice rose and her chest heaved. She took deep breaths to calm herself.

Zack blinked. Unbelievable. DaEvo had been right. He struggled to think of a suitable response. "Sorry. That sucks."

Wow. He was really bad at this.

Ashley shrugged. "It's fine. You just caught me on a bad day. Please don't tell my boss I was rude to you, okay? It won't happen again."

She turned to go, and Zack checked his timer. No! He still had five seconds to go, and he hadn't completed any of the bonus quests. The battle raged behind him on his screen, reminding him what was at stake.

"I could teach you!"

Ashley turned around and looked at him, some of the humor returning to her eyes. "What?"

"I could teach you about Star Fury. You know, so they don't make fun of you."

She laughed, and DaEvo chimed congratulations. "Thanks, but I'm not really interested in space battles."

The conversation timer flashed to let him know he had reached two minutes, but now Zack's mind was racing with ideas. "You don't need to know much. Just enough to shut down the jerks who are bothering you."

"I'm listening."

Zack thought hard. He needed something easy for her to remember. Something that would shut down casual gamers and dedicated fans alike. "Tell them you're a Veridian."

"A Veridian? What does that mean? If it's something gross—" She stepped toward Zack, her eyes sparking. Either she was especially defensive, or the other gamers at Gord's really had been giving her a hard time.

"Nothing bad," Zack said quickly. "It's an order of assassins. The only time they reveal their identity is if someone is annoying them while they're undercover and they're considering bumping them off to make the mission easier."

"Veridian. Thanks." Ashley still looked suspicious, but she smiled at Zack.

"No problem."

Ashley looked at his monitor and laughed. "You'd better get back to your game. I think your team misses you."

Zack turned back to the screen. His teammates had figured out he had muted them and were spewing profanity via the text chat available in the game. The text that scrolled across the bottom of the screen was not exactly complimentary.

"Yeah, I'd better get back." Zack held up his hand for a fist bump. The physical contact bonus had been the best one. He really needed that.

Ashley raised an eyebrow and stared at his outstretched arm.

"For the Veridians," he said, trying to sound more confident than he felt.

She laughed and bumped her fist against his. "For the Veridians." As soon as Ashley left, DaEvo chimed.

Quest Complete! You spoke with a woman for 3:12.
You have earned non-essential electronics and
internet privileges!
Reward, easy difficulty—+3
Bonus Achieved – Make her laugh. +10 Minutes Use Time
Bonus Achieved – Make her laugh. +10 Minutes Use Time
Bonus Achieved – Make her laugh. +10 Minutes Use Time
Bonus Achieved—Make physical contact +20 Minutes Use Time
Bonus Achieved—cheer her up +25 Minutes Use Time
Reputation increased: +0.1

Sweet! He had done it. Zack turned the comms back on in order to hear his teammates screaming warnings at him. He blinked at the screen and realized that his ship was on a collision course with an Armada drone. He reclaimed the controls and swerved away just in time.

"Sorry, I was talking to someone."

"Seriously?" Greg said. "Zack, we're trying to go pro. If you're not going to take this seriously—"

"I am taking it seriously! I was earning more game time."

Zack looked at the countdown timer in the corner of his Opti-Glasses. The conversation with Ashley had cost him three minutes but gained him over an hour. Not a bad return on investment.

"I have almost two hours of game time now. Let's show these Armada scum what happens when they cross the Corsairs."

Zack let out a war cry and blasted into the battle.

Chapter Six

———————

A CORSAIR BATTLE frigate swooped by, burping a dozen missiles that slammed into the Armada base. Unrealistic explosions blared from the speakers, along with the curses of their enemy. Zack laughed and joined the rest of the Corsairs in using his afterburners to buzz the exploding base and capitalize on the Armada scum's surprise as the energy drain field the base had been putting out stopped working. The battle had finally turned, and it was only a matter of time now. The Armada may outnumber them, but nobody stood a chance against him and his team. And the other Corsairs, of course.

"Just cleanup now," Jenny said. "Hopefully, we pick up some good gear once this thing finally blows."

"And then we need to discuss the new weapons releases," Greg said. "We've got to have the latest if we want—"

DaEvo chimed and flashed a pink heart timer.

00:00:10 Game Time Remaining

Zack swore. How had two hours gone by already? "I'm out of time, guys. Got to run."

He hit the autopilot warp button, sending his ship on a course back to home base. If he logged out in the middle of enemy space, he would likely get blown up and have to replace all his gear.

"Later, Zack. Let's meet tonight to discuss—"

His game disconnected and cut back to the Star Fury logo screen. Zack leaned back in his chair, feeling the familiar rush of a successful raid. The base wasn't quite gone yet, but it would be in a few minutes. It was a shame he couldn't stick around to see the fireworks, but at least he had contributed to the victory.

Zack grinned and hurried down to the lobby. Maybe he could watch. It wasn't the same as being there and firing the final shot, but it was better than nothing.

He walked to the counter and ordered another coffee. Ashley's shift must be over because a male cashier named Stan had taken her place. DaEvo did not offer points for the interaction, so Zack took his coffee and found an inconspicuous seat where he could watch the Armada player's screen.

The gamer looked grim as he furiously pushed buttons on his controller, trying to stop the inevitable Corsair victory. Half of the base was already gone, and Zack saw how Jenny's mines were being deposited by her drones to further expand the damage. Zack couldn't help but grin, because the initial break in the shield's defenses had come from his main laser.

The laser was definitely worth all the other weapons he'd ditched for it, though it made his energy levels fluctuate like crazy. He needed more practice with it. Timing on the firing of the main cannon needed to be a major focus.

Faz and Greg were leading a group of fellow Corsairs in the charge to finish the mission. Jenny had pulled back to lay minefields on the outer layer, joining a group of other drone users in preventing defeated Armada ships from escaping.

Zack's OptiGlasses chimed. Not DaEvo this time, thank goodness. It was the group messaging app that he used to communicate with his team when they weren't playing.

. . .

Jenny: *So how does this app work exactly? We need a plan so you don't keep running out of game time right when we need you.*

Zack sighed, trying to decide exactly how much to tell his team.

Zack: *It's called intervention mode. I have to do things in real life to earn game time.*
    Greg: *Dude, that sucks!*
    Jenny: *No way to get around it?*
    Zack: *Not according to Star Fury support, but I'll keep looking.*
    Faz: *So what kind of things do you have to do to earn game time?*
    Zack: *Hey, focus on the mission. You've got some Armada scum sneaking up behind you.*

Zack watched on the Armada player's screen as Faz turned around to intercept his sneak attack. The player swore and retreated when he lost the element of surprise, and Faz turned back to bombing the base and interrogating Zack.

Faz: *Don't avoid the question. Is it super embarrassing?*

Zack gritted his teeth. If he admitted he was trapped in a dating sim, he'd never hear the end of it. Better to keep that part secret for now.

Zack: *Basic stuff. Take a shower. Clean my apartment.*

That was less embarrassing, but not by much. He could practically hear their laughter in the silence that followed. Or maybe they were focused on the mission. The Corsairs dealt a final blow with a coordinated strike on the base, and the Armada player's screen erupted with explosions. He swore loudly and engaged hyperdrive to escape the battle. Unfortunately, he warped straight into one of Jenny's mines. His screen turned white as his ship exploded. The player threw down his controller and jumped out of his seat, spewing profanity.

The Gord's worker ran over. "Steve, we've talked about this. You want to rage, you rent a private room."

Zack scoffed into his coffee. Steve was typical Armada scum, dressed head to toe in Armada regalia and decorated with medals earned from missions as if he had something to prove. Corsairs preferred to fly under the radar, building a reputation until everyone knew who they were without them having to say a thing.

Faz: *Mission accomplished. Now go take a shower or put on deodorant or whatever else you need to do to be ready to train tomorrow.*

Greg: *Don't forget to use soap.*

Zack: *Ha, ha.*

If only it was that easy. Zack called a ride and sent a message to Phil during the drive back to his condo.

Zack: *You win. What do I need to do to uninstall this app?*

To his surprise, Phil answered almost immediately.

Phil: *Beat the game.*

Beat the game. How exactly did you beat a dating sim?

Zack searched online wikis during the elevator ride up to his condo. Apparently, most dating sims ended when you found love. More specifically, when you started dating someone exclusively or got married.

Crap.

Zack punched in the door code and slumped into his apartment. He gagged at the smell. How was it getting worse every time he left? Maybe he shouldn't have canceled that cleaning service after all.

No matter. He had bigger problems now.

"How do I win?"

He wasn't exactly expecting an answer, but DaEvo chimed cheerfully and popped a notification onto his OptiGlasses.

Dating Evolution is the next generation of relationship gaming with a real-world twist! Did you ever wish your online skills translated into the real world? Now they can! Follow our quests to level up your love life and earn real life rewards!

"Yeah, but what does that mean exactly? How do I prove that I've won and don't need DaEvo anymore?"

Dating Evolution understands that you won't need us forever. When you find love and a committed relationship, your quest is complete. However, given your current stats, you will need to complete quests and level up before you're ready for your final mission.

Okay, he had his answer. The dating sim wanted him to date. Annoying, but not exactly a surprise. In fact, he was pretty certain that Phil had bugged Zack about his increasing reticence and lack of social contact since he left New York.

He just needed to get a girlfriend to end this nightmare and get back to gaming.

Except getting a girl required him to be able to talk to one. Which, thus far, had been less than successful and given pretty pathetic gaming rewards for the work involved. That meant he needed to level up. Each time his social level fell, he'd get even worse rewards, so he'd have to grind and improve his stats. Zack flipped through the app's menu until he found his character sheet.

Zack Moore Current Attributes (Social Level 8)
Physique: 30.9
Style: 18.9
Reputation: -20.3
Occupation: 0

On the one hand, DaEvo had ridiculously underscored him. On the other, that would make leveling up that much easier. Maybe the app's bugginess could work to his advantage.

Zack searched for the Quest Menu and found it hidden under his attributes. He clicked on the top option, Physique, and scrolled through the available quests.

Physique Quests
Have a healthy meal (Repeatable)
Walk 2km (Repeatable)
Run 2km (Locked)
Lose 5lbs (Repeatable with limits)
Take a weightlifting class
~~Lift weights~~ (Locked)
(more...)

Nope. Physique was out. That sounded like way too much work. Repeatable quests were often easily exploitable, but he wanted to get more points, fast.

Next on the attribute list, Style.

That should be easier. He had money, and Style was all about money, right?

Style Quests
Shop for new clothes
Wash laundry and remove worn and torn clothing
Get a haircut from the 21st century
Manicure
Pedicure
Skin treatment
Manscaping
~~Take a deportment class and pass~~ (locked)
~~Learn to dance (Choose dance type)~~ (locked)
(more…)

Zack looked at the time display in the corner of his OptiGlasses. Just past seven. Maybe he could squeeze in some grinding before the shops closed. If he got good enough rewards for the quests, he might even be able to squeeze in more Star Fury training tonight. Plus, the higher level would mean more points and time earned the next time he talked to a woman.

He focused on the top style quest, Shop for new clothes, until it selected. DaEvo chimed the cheerful quest music that Zack was beginning to hate.

Quest!
Impress the ladies and level up by improving your style from (Current-style: Unemployed Hobo). Please journey to one of the highlighted stores to begin your makeover quest.

Zack ground his teeth at the word makeover. And then again at the Unemployed Hobo label. He registered a bug report, although that hadn't accomplished anything so far, and went back to glaring at the word makeover. If any of his friends ever found out he had completed a makeover quest for a dating sim…

He would just have to be careful that no one ever found out. Luckily, all his friends were either online or lived in New York. If they didn't see him in person, they would never know he had changed his look.

A map of Oklahoma City marked with highlighted stores filled the OptiGlass screen, and Zack turned his attention to it. If he was going to complete a makeover quest, he was going to do it right and get as many points as possible.

Please select Quest difficulty:
Easy
Medium
Hard

Zack selected Hard. If he was going to play this game, he was going to play it right and win. DaEvo cut down the number of highlighted stores to only those with the highest value points. They were spread across the metro, but the greatest concentration was to the north in an area marked Gaillardia. Zack called a ride to take him there.

As they drove, he zoomed in on specific stores, searching for his first target. As soon as Zack started zooming in, a belated pop-up arrived.

Developer Note:
Style Calculations are currently being amalgamated from crowd-sourced opinion polls, social media images, influential bloggers, and fashion magazines.
We have been able to achieve 85% fidelity to style points but are having issues with both ends of the spectrum. Hobo-chic, high fashion, and other areas may cause algorithm malfunctions.

Zack glared at the notification. Then a wide grin spread across his face. Bugs. What gamer didn't like to exploit bugs? And if there was a bug here, he was going to min-max as much as possible.

He zoomed in on the stores. Most were centered around the Gaillardia Mall, which was apparently very new and very chic. Not his usual shopping preference, but it would be perfect for this.

Zack started with Infinity & Beyond, his usual go-to when he needed new clothes. Granted, he usually bought things online when they were on sale, but it was a start.

Infinity & Beyond
Style Increase: +13—+14.5

...

Comments: Clothing purchased here is perfectly adequate for watching Rocky Horror *remakes and attending your local comic convention. Paired with clean, fitting wear, this would be adequate for everyday tasks.*

Okay, maybe that wasn't the best option. He could hit those points by doing laundry and finding jeans that fit. This was a makeover quest, and adequate was not enough. The whole point was to come away looking different and to level up.

Zack changed the menu settings so the highest-level stores were displayed first. He selected the option at the top of the list. Maximum points.

WesterNeon
Fashion forward apparel for the modern cowman. Designer David Davidson is the hottest new thing on the runway, with work featured in Vogue, Elle, *and more. Lauded as the second coming of....*

There was more info, but Zack skipped ahead to the stats. He raised an eyebrow as DaEvo displayed the numbers for WesterNeon.

Style Increase: +51.2—+77.5

That was incredible. If he got the highest level, he'd be in the top 90s! If the app was anything like a game, breaking into the top percentile might even get him a Title or an exclusive badge.

The price range displayed was equally high, but that wasn't a problem.

Zack grinned. Maybe this would be easier than he thought. Go to the mall and buy some things. Get points for wearing them. Then he could go back to the gaming center, have a few conversations with Ashley, and get enough time to run training sessions with his team. The level up would also open up more quests and maybe increase his chances of succeeding in conversations with higher level women. The possibilities made his head spin.

While Zack was lost in his thoughts, they reached the mall and slid to a stop at the front entrance. Zack tipped his driver with a swipe of his OptiGlasses and eyed the entrance of the Gaillardia shopping center. It was as luxe as the internet had promised, built from light stone with elegant arches, and it looked more like a private mansion than a retail location. Zack couldn't remember the last time he had been in a physical store. Online shopping was so much easier.

But as fast as drone shipping was, Zack needed clothes and points *now*. Would DaEvo give him points for buying things online? It was worth checking into later. If spending money could earn him points and game time, Zack was all for it. That was certainly easier than talking to women.

A few well-dressed shoppers eyed him suspiciously, and Zack hurried inside before they could comment and further damage his Reputation stats. He walked through the sleek glass doors and stared at the array of brightly colored storefronts and advertisements. A blast of cold air provided a welcome relief from the muggy evening. Zack was sweaty again from the humidity, but thankfully DaEvo hadn't noticed. The last thing he needed was for the app to complain and force him to shower again.

Pink hearts similar to the ones that had appeared above the women in the gym appeared over the storefronts. Zack took note of the stats as he walked through the mall, just in case any of the stores were better than WesterNeon. A formal wear store offering custom tuxedos was ranked highly, but their window advertised that they could finish a custom tuxedo in four days—as if that were a good thing.

Zack needed clothes now.

He reached his destination, a glossy white storefront with "WesterNeon" printed over it in different colors, and hurried inside. Neon lights and electronic music assaulted his senses. His OptiGlasses tinted automatically to dim the bright lights a little. Zack stood in the entrance, wondering if he had wandered into a rave by mistake. Everything was oversaturated. The walls were decorated with a neon grid of cow silhouettes that flashed and changed colors in time with the music.

Speaking of music, what the hell was he listening to? Some kind of fusion of old school country and modern electronic dance. Twangy guitars mixed with synthesizers, accented by the occasional auto-tuned "yeehaw." It was one of the strangest things Zack had ever heard.

They apparently took the "neon" part of WesterNeon very seriously.

"Howdy. How may I help you?"

Zack jumped as a store clerk materialized. He hadn't seen the man approach. Probably because his brightly colored hair and outfit acted like a sort of camouflage in this technicolor jungle.

If colors were camouflage, the muted palette of Zack's outfit was like a beacon in this place. The clerk, who was dressed in an outfit that looked like an old-time saloon barkeeper in an Andy Warhol painting, was staring at Zack as if he were something found squished on the bottom of a starship after a crash landing.

"Yeah, I—" Zack swallowed, rethinking his decision to complete the makeover quest.

Maybe he should go for fitness instead? He dismissed that thought, but maybe there was another, better quest? Those negative Reputation points were hurting his stats the most but fixing that might require him to be more social. Talking to a single person was bad enough. Convincing society as a whole that he was worth their notice would be even worse. Still, maybe he should—

No. Style was the easiest option. It was just that min-maxing in the game was one thing, but in real life, where he'd actually have to wear this....

DaEvo popped up with a cheerful chime, assigning point values to the various items of clothing displayed throughout the store.

Zack's jaw dropped as he stared at the closest display—a rack of hats.

Skyline (Green Neon) Stetson +3.8-7.3*
Lavar (Gray) Premier Cowboy Hat +2.7—7.1*

"Yeah, okay. I can do this. I want some clothes," said Zack.

Sometimes, you just had to trust the system. If this was fashion, who was he to argue?

"May I inquire about the occasion, sir? This establishment is dedicated to serving the modern cowman's every need, but of course such service comes at a premium. I want to make sure we're the proper fit for you. I'm afraid we do require proof of funds before patrons try on any items of clothing."

Zack fought the urge to roll his eyes. The snooty cowboy butler clown clearly had no idea who he was dealing with. Zack flicked his eyes to the credit app in his OptiGlasses and sent a credit approval rating to the store's system—the equivalent of flashing a black card. Unbelievable as it was, some people still felt the need to carry those things around. Damn luddites.

The clerk's eyes widened as he accessed the information on his —was he wearing an OptiGlass monocle? Zack had been too distracted by the clerk's clothes to notice it. Where in the hell had the man gotten an OptiGlass monocle?

And was it worth more points than regular OptiGlasses? Because Zack was willing to switch for the sake of his stats.

But DaEvo didn't offer any stats for the OptiMonocle. Probably because it wasn't actually for sale in the store.

"Ah, very good, sir. Are you familiar with the WesterNeon collection?"

Zack shook his head and scanned the room for high-level items. Everything in there had pretty good stats, but of course some items were better than others. He tried to find the logic behind the numbers, but everything seemed to run on a scaling basis without an explanation for the range.

"WesterNeon is the brainchild of designer David Davidson. He was inspired by Oklahoma sunsets and the desire to provide fashion forward apparel for the modern cowman."

The clerk droned on. Something about the designer's process and everything being handmade. Too bad the worker wasn't a woman. That would be earning Zack some serious conversation points without any effort at all. But in spite of the bright colors, this seemed to be a menswear store run by men.

Shame.

Zack ignored the history lesson on David Davidson's career and walked around the store, gathering the highest-level items. He manually tinted his OptiGlasses a little darker. Staring at all the neon was giving him a headache.

As were all the options. The pink hearts with stats floating above the racks, assigning points to each item of clothing, were getting overwhelming. Zack opened DaEvo and adjusted the settings so that only the highest-level items were displayed. The sea of hearts diminished, and Zack quickly sorted through the remaining options.

The neon green jeans in the center display would raise his Style score by eighteen points. A pink-and-yellow striped jacket with orange leather fringe on a display mannequin was worth twenty.

Score.

"I'll take this as well." Zack pulled the jacket off the mannequin. The fringe swished as he did so.

The clerk had been so engrossed in his speech that he hadn't noticed Zack shopping. He blinked at the pile of clothing in Zack's arms. "Ah, an excellent choice. That jacket was recently featured on the cover of *Fashion* magazine. Might I suggest these trousers to complete your look? We could recreate the entire editorial if you prefer." He pointed at bright orange jeans hanging next to the jacket.

Zack checked the stats. Only worth sixteen points. Not as good as the green. "Nah, I'll take these."

He nodded at the green jeans in his arms, and the clerk raised an eyebrow.

"I see. Well, you certainly have an adventurous sense of style. Perhaps one of our button-up shirts to complete the ensemble?"

He eyed Zack for a moment, squinting into his OptiMonocle, then led him to a rack of shirts. Some were covered with the same repeating cow print that was on the walls, and some were decorated with the repeating motif of the WesterNeon logo like the outside of the store.

Zack flipped through the shirts until he found one with bright pink cows on it that was worth twelve points. He tried to check the size, but the labels had mysterious cow designs where the sizes should have been.

"We at WesterNeon don't believe in sorting cowmen into arbitrary sizes," the clerk said. "Each item is handmade with unique proportions. Allow me to select one for you." Once again, he studied Zack for a moment through the OptiMonocle, then pulled a different pink shirt from the rack. "This should do. Would you like to try your items on now?"

Zack nodded and followed the man to a florescent orange dressing room that was bright enough to make Zack's OptiGlasses darken another shade. He slipped on the lime green pants, salmon pink shirt, and fringed jacket. Apparently, the saloon clown clerk knew his stuff because they all fit perfectly. Much better than any of Zack's current clothes actually.

He looked in the mirror, and DaEvo chimed enthusiastically and flashed a new style score.

Style Points
Shirt: 12
Pants: 18
Jacket: 20
Accessories: 0
Combo: -10
Total: 40

"What the hell?" Zack swore. "What are combo points?"
DaEvo answered with a help screen.

Style is scored in the following way.
Shirt: 0-22.5 points
Pants: 0-22.5 points
Jacket: 0-22.5 points
Accessories: 0-22.5 points
In addition to base points, the combination of specific items may add or subtract up to 10 points from your score.
Style points may be adjusted for local taste and climate as well.

Great. Just great.

Zack stared at himself in the mirror. He could understand DaEvo's point. It wasn't exactly a cohesive ensemble. Then again, nothing in this place actually looked good. He took a deep breath, absently noted the slight floral and desert hints in the air, and reminded himself that looking good didn't matter. He was gaming the system. Min-maxing.

Which meant he needed to understand how the system actually worked.

"Show me how you calculate fashion scores again."

Developer Note:
Style Calculations are currently being amalgamated from crowd-sourced opinion polls, social media images, influential bloggers, and fashion magazines.
We have been able to achieve 85% fidelity to style points but are having issues with both ends of the spectrum. Hobo-chic, high fashion, and other areas are causing the algorithm to fritz.

Fashion magazines. The technicolor butler had mentioned something about that, hadn't he?

Zack stuck his head out of the dressing room, where the clerk stood patiently waiting. "What did you say about a fashion magazine cover?"

The man grinned, somehow managing to make it look pleased and yet, not condescending. "Ah, you want to try the editorial look. An excellent choice. One moment."

He turned away and, in a short minute, had a basket of clothing ready. He shoved the basket into Zack's hands while giving orders. "Keep the jacket. Replace everything else with what's in here."

Zack rolled his eyes but complied. He started out with trading the green jeans with the orange ones. As he straightened, DaEvo chimed.

Combo bonus: +1

Zack grinned. That was more like it. He quickly replaced the pink cow print shirt with a maroon button-down with WesterNeon embroidered above the pocket. The combination was still eye-searing, but less so than it had been before. DaEvo agreed.

Style Points
Shirt: 10
Pants: 16
Jacket: 20
Accessories: 0
Combo: 5
Total: 51

Sweet!

Zack eyed the empty Accessories slot. Normally he would never wear accessories. At home, he barely wore clothes. But if he was going to do this, he needed to do it right.

DaEvo chimed as if agreeing with him.

Great style! Don't forget to maximize your points with accessories.

Zack eyed his reflection critically. Orange fringe wasn't his usual style, but that didn't matter if he could earn bonus points and get back to playing Star Fury faster. If this outfit gamed DaEvo's system, his problems were over. Yes, the colors were a little bright, but apparently that was what was in fashion. In truth, Zack had no idea, but that was what the magazines were for, wasn't it? Their entire job was to stay "on trend."

And now they would help Zack stay on trend as well.

He stepped out of the dressing room and nodded to the clerk. "I'll take everything I'm wearing. Do you have accessories?"

"Of course."

Zack glanced around to make sure no one was watching him shop for jewelry. Then he followed the clerk to the display.

In the editorial photo, the model wore a yellow cowboy hat. Zack tried it on and received eight accessory points and an additional combo point. DaEvo popped hearts over a selection of plastic cuff bracelets and brightly patterned socks. Zack selected the highest stat items and slipped them on, choosing more than he typically would in the quest to get as many points as possible. That only added one point and took away two combo points.

He sighed and removed all of the bracelets. Apparently, there was an art to accessories. What was he missing? There had to be a way to max out accessories without losing combo points.

He looked down at his well-worn sneakers.

DaEvo chimed and pointed an arrow across the store. Zack followed it to a rack of polka-dotted cowboy boots. His eyes widened, and his blood pumped a little. Maybe he could see the point in shopping in-person once in a while.

It took him a bit of swapping around before he found a pair that didn't clash with his outfit and gave him the highest points possible. Weirdly, it was a pair of white boots with purple spots. The clerk hovered, ready to offer suggestions when asked, but Zack had hit a stride and didn't want to ask for help. It felt too much like relying on a tutorial.

He looked at himself in the mirror, and DaEvo flashed his new stats.

Style Points
Shirt: 20.3
Pants: 20
Jacket: 21
Accessories: 19
Combo: 9
Total: 73

That was more like it! But why hadn't his level upgraded?

Maybe he needed to actually purchase the clothes first. Zack looked around for a cash register or payment station to log his Opti-Glasses, but all he saw was a sea of neon clothes.

The clerk cleared his throat softly. "Our store app will take your payment whenever you're ready. We use an extra layer of security since we are a premium product. Are you ready to make your purchase?"

"Yeah, sure." Zack shrugged a little. Thankfully, they didn't have pesky things like labels to take off, which made wearing all this out a simple matter.

The WesterNeon logo appeared on his OptiGlasses, temporarily blinding Zack in a flood of color. He swiped the pay button as fast as he could to make it go away. His credit card app popped up a warning.

Potentially fraudulent activity detected. Did you make this purchase?
WesterNeon Apparel, Inc. $56,723.19

Zack swallowed. Man, those stats did not come cheap.

Whatever. It was worth it. He didn't actually spend his allowance on anything anyway. Takeout pizza—even good takeout pizza—wasn't enough to put a dent in his finances.

He approved the transaction with a flick of his eyes. DaEvo chimed triumphantly and provided Zack with his new style points and social level. It even put a nice pink circle around everything. Which, when you considered who they were marketing to, might be an issue. He doubted all this pink was meant for the guys, but whatever. That wasn't a Zack issue.

Style Points: 89.3
Social Level: 25.0

Reward: You have gained the title: Stylish!
Access to VIP line for UpWings! Royal Texas, Big Shift, Trinity, (more...)

Zack didn't recognize most of those names, but the Royal Texas was a couple of blocks from his condo. It was a nightclub, always packed, so those others were likely more of the same. Not much use to him, but a reward was a reward.

"Most stylish, sir. I have taken the liberty of packaging your old clothing. Unless you would prefer I burn them?" The clerk held out a lime green bag decorated with the cow print and wrinkled his nose as if it smelled bad.

Actually, it did smell bad. The sneakers had a distinct odor that was more apparent now that they weren't on his feet.

But those were his favorite sweats. Zack took the bag and nodded to the clerk. "Thanks."

Then he hurried out of the store. The mall looked dark, and for a moment Zack wondered how long he had been in WesterNeon. Had the mall closed while he was shopping?

Then his OptiGlasses lightened their tint, and Zack sighed in relief. He called a ride and used Gord's app to reserve a room for tomorrow. Only one left. Ashley hadn't been kidding about them being packed. Hopefully she was working tomorrow. Talking to her in his new leveled up clothes would be way easier than searching for another woman to talk to.

His new style level hadn't given him any game time, which was disappointing. Zack swiped to the quest menu and checked the conversation quest.

Quest Upgrade!
Hold a significant conversation with a woman.
Reward: unrestricted internet privileges and non-essential electronic privileges
Easy: 15 minutes
Medium: 30 minutes
Hard: 45 minutes

That was more like it. Talking with Ashley had been pretty easy, and now he would get even more points for it. Hopefully the bonuses would also be worth more now that he was Stylish. And if he kept leveling up, he could have conversations with higher level women, get even more points, and have unlimited time to play Star Fury.

Things were finally looking up.

Chapter Seven

DaEvo chimed a quest prompt as soon as Zack entered his apartment. He ignored it and the smell that permeated the place and went to his room to change out of the WesterNeon outfit. The style points were great, but the outfit wasn't exactly comfortable.

Zack collapsed into bed in his sweats and T-shirt, feeling exhausted. DaEvo chimed.

Quest!
A good night's sleep will leave you rested and ready to find love. Get—

Zack pulled the glasses off his face and slammed them on his nightstand. Maybe this was all a bad dream. Maybe he would wake up with everything reset. That would be great. Then he could skip the quests needed to get game time to complete training and go over new gear with his team tomorrow. If the style upgrade wasn't enough—

Zack shuddered and buried his head in his pillow. The style

upgrade would do the trick. It had to. He refused to let anything get in the way of his success in the Star Fury tournament. No matter what others might say, he loved gaming. He wanted, needed, to win and prove himself.

————

Zack woke up to sunlight and a vague sense of dread. He stared at his OptiGlasses, the near field charging station on his nightstand having done their job he was sure. They sat, waiting, looking far too innocent. He reached for them, then pulled back his hand. Would DaEvo still restrict everything if he didn't put them on? The app was buggy. Surely there was a way to trick it.

Zack flicked the small power switch on his glasses. DaEvo had access to his whole life, but it ran through the OptiGlasses. Maybe it would stop functioning if they were turned off.

He ran to the living room and tried to turn on his gaming console. Nothing happened.

Crap.

Zack sighed and made his way back to his bedroom. He wasn't dreaming. This was his life now. He turned the OptiGlasses back on and slowly slid them onto his face. DaEvo chimed cheerfully and greeted him with a flood of pink hearts.

Quest Complete!
Get a good night's sleep.
Physique + 0.1

Points for sleeping. Nice. If he didn't have the tournament, Zack would forget about dating and nap his way to success. But the fifty-six missed messages in the team's group chat reminded him what was at stake. Zack scrolled through them to see if he had missed anything important. Most of the messages were about the qualifying round Zack had missed. He skipped past those to the more recent ones.

Faz: *Has anyone heard from Zack yet?*

Jenny: *No, but he usually sleeps in.*

Greg: *Hey, Zack, get out of bed and do your chores so you can train with us today.*

Zack chewed on a stale slice of cold pizza while he answered. DaEvo chimed to protest his choice of breakfast, and he swiped away the notification.

Zack: *Ha, ha, very funny. I'll see you guys at the usual time and place.*

The Gord's Gaming Center's app had sent him a notification to remind him that he had reserved a room. Zack checked the time. He had an hour to get there.

Much as he hated to admit it, he should probably take a shower.

Crap. The app was getting in his head.

Zack delayed putting the OptiGlasses back on until he was dried off and fully dressed in the WesterNeon outfit. He placed the bright yellow cowboy hat on his head and looked at his reflection with skepticism. Was this really fashionable? He had never seen anyone wear anything like this.

As if answering his question, DaEvo chimed.

New Quest Unlocked! Styling!
You've got the look, now get the ladies! Catch her attention and get a compliment on your outfit.
Requirements: Receive a positive compliment on your new outfit from a woman.
Reward: 30 minutes of online access.
Bonus Rewards: Additional online access. Hidden.

Zack stood a little straighter and accepted the quest with a swipe of his eyes. He was wearing the same outfit that had graced the cover of *Fashion* magazine. He was bound to get a few compliments. This quest would be a breeze.

He called a ride and left his apartment. DaEvo chimed.

Quest!
Breakfast is the most important meal of the day. Eat a healthy breakfast to level up your physique.

Apparently, the app was so buggy, it had forgotten he had already eaten. Was that another bug that could be exploited? During the elevator ride, Zack looked through the suggested breakfasts and quickly rejected the quest. No way was he eating a kale smoothie for breakfast. It wasn't even something you ate. A drink didn't count as a meal.

He spent the ride to Gord's browsing through the new unlocked quests and noting potentially good ones. He had more style quest options now, including online shopping. Zack grinned. He could min/max without leaving his house. He was opening a shopping app when he was interrupted.

"You getting out, buddy?"

Zack blinked. He had been so caught up in his planning that he hadn't realized they had reached Gord's. He quickly tipped the driver and crawled out of the car. The heat hit him like a ton of bricks, and he wondered if this was really what cowboys wore. The thick fringed jacket made him feel as if he was wrapped in a blanket while being blasted with an enormous blow-dryer. The wind added to the blow-dryer effect, rustling the fringe and gusting it into his face.

Oh well. It was fashion. That was what mattered right now.

Zack swaggered into Gord's Gaming Center with the confidence that only leveling up could give him, choosing to ignore the layer of sweat that had formed on his forehead. He already needed another shower, but that would have to wait.

Zack scanned the room and grinned when he saw Ashley was once again working as the cashier. He sauntered over to the register. The purple-polka-dotted cowboy boots pinched his feet, but hopefully the slight unevenness of his gait added swagger. Unfortunately, Ashley was too busy scraping something sticky off the counter to notice him.

Zack stood for a moment, then cleared his throat when Ashley didn't look up. He considered trying the "Hey, babe" line, but that hadn't gone well with Cassie. Maybe it was better to let the clothes do the talking.

Ashley looked up and blinked in surprise. She squinted and held a hand in front of her eyes as she took in the brightly colored outfit. She wasn't wearing OptiGlasses, so she didn't have any automatic tinting to help her.

Zack puffed out his chest as Ashley regained her composure. He had definitely created an impression. The compliments and bonus points would come rolling in any minute.

"Zack? Is that you?"

Zack nodded and tipped his new hat for good measure. This was going well. Ashley looked completely overwhelmed by his new style. DaEvo started the conversation timer and offered a prompt.

Quest Hint!

You've caught her attention! Try an eyebrow raise and smoldering smile to seal the deal!

That was accompanied by an animated emoji demonstrating the expression. Zack watched it for a moment, then did his best to copy it. DaEvo flashed a thumbs-up.

Ashley laughed.

It started as a giggle. She pressed her hands over her mouth, trying to muffle the sound. Then tears welled, and she gave up on staying quiet. She waved her hands in an apology as her laughter rang through the gaming center. A few gamers looked up, annoyed to have their concentration interrupted. They chuckled at Zack before turning back to their gaming consoles.

This wasn't right. Zack tried the smile and eyebrow raise combo again. Ashley laughed even harder, until she had to lean against the counter for support. She seemed to be having trouble breathing.

What was so funny? He hadn't even said anything.

DaEvo chimed in, adding bonus points for Ashley's laughter, but Zack had the nagging feeling that those points weren't quite the victory they appeared to be.

Ashley pressed her lips together and wiped tears from her eyes as she continued to silently giggle. When she finally stopped laughing, her face was red and her eyes sparkled.

"Sorry. Did you want to order something?" Ashley said.

"Yeah, I—" Zack started.

DaEvo chimed in, letting Zack know that he had completed a conversation quest and was now earning bonus points. But he still hadn't received the compliment he had come for. Somehow, this mission had gone completely wrong.

"I'll take a pizza to go."

As soon as he said it, Ashley's computer chimed. She looked from it to Zack with a strange expression. "To go? But you reserved a room for the hour. Are you feeling all right?"

Ashley seemed concerned, which annoyed Zack for some reason he couldn't quite place. "Yeah, I just changed my mind. Need to take care of some things at home."

Ashley swallowed. "I can't give you a refund for it. Company policy."

A gamer across the room stood and looked over his seat. "Is somebody canceling a room? I'll take it."

It was the Armada scum from the raid yesterday. Steve? Stan?

Something like that. He looked at Zack as if he was a piece of garbage washed up in the intergalactic tides.

"I thought you couldn't afford private rooms right now," another gamer said. "Did you find another job already?"

"Nah, I won a raffle. Don't even remember entering. Girlfriend doesn't know, so she's still covering all the bills. Which means I can take that room and rage all I want."

Zack stared. Surely it was a coincidence. Surely his act of generosity hadn't gone to help this Armada scum?

"The room is already reserved," Ashley said in a stiff voice that managed to be both pleasant and condescending.

Apparently, she wasn't a fan of the Armada scum either.

"Yeah, but the cowboy doesn't want it anymore. You can give it to someone else." He sauntered over.

Ashley frowned and looked at Zack. "I guess you could let Steve use it if you want to. I can give you a refund if someone else takes the reservation."

DaEvo chimed and a new notification floated up Zack's glasses.

Quest!
Your lady is upset. Fix her problem and earn bonus points!
Reward: +30 Minutes game time

Zack looked back at Ashley. She had the same tension around her eyes that she'd had yesterday when he told her about the Veridians. Was this part of the same problem? Had Steve been one of the guys making fun of Ashley for not playing Star Fury? That was just low.

Never mind that Zack had done exactly the same thing to Ashley yesterday. He was on a quest to cheer her up now, and that made Steve the enemy.

Zack looked around the room, searching for a solution. He definitely wasn't staying. Not when half the gamers had stopped whatever they were doing to stare at him. The attention was making him sweat more than the humidity had. Apparently, WesterNeon was too high end for Gord's.

Stupid app.

He searched the room for someone to pass his reserved time to. Someone other than Steve. No way was he letting that jerk get what he wanted, and if Zack canceled his reservation, he had no doubt Steve would complain until he got it.

Zack scanned the other people in the room. If he was going to cheer up Ashley, he needed to choose someone who had never teased her. But it was hard to tell that at a glance, especially when most of the people in the room not wrapped up in gaming were snickering at him.

Bilge-sucking muckspouts.

Zack's gaze settled on the far corner of the room, where a young girl sat reading a gaming magazine about the upcoming Star Fury tournament. Zack guessed she was about twelve, but he was no good guessing kids' ages. She had the same auburn hair as Ashley, although it was subdued by a headband with the Corsair logo: a space helmet and crossbones. Was she the same girl who had been in Ashley's social media photos? Zack didn't have time to check the pictures to confirm his theory. The gamers' looks and snickers were beginning to turn into all-out laughter.

"Give it to her," Zack said, pointing.

"Oh come on," Steve said. "I can pay."

Ashley gave Zack a look of surprise. "Really?"

"Yeah, why not? She looks like she'd make good use of it." He dropped his voice, and added for Ashley's sake, "Better than Armada scum, right?"

"Look, man, I'll pay you for it," Steve said. "I'll make it worth your while."

Zack crossed his fingers and thumped them against his chest. Among Corsairs, it was a friendly gesture, but the Armada considered it extremely rude.

Steve's face flushed. "Corsair drone waste."

"Armada scum."

Steve returned Zack's gesture with one of his own, then turned back to his gaming console. He seemed to be restocking his new ship and rebuilding inventory after his encounter with Jenny's mines.

Ashley's smile widened, and she waved across the room. "Hey, Amber! Come here!"

Amber set down the magazine and hurried over. "I didn't do anything wrong! I've been sitting there not making a sound, just like you said!"

Ashley reached across the counter and ruffled the girl's hair fondly. "Yeah, you've been good. This is Zack. He reserved a room but can't use it now, so he offered to let you use it so you can play."

Amber looked at Zack. She seemed less fazed by his outfit than Ashley had been. DaEvo didn't populate stats for her. That made sense. She was way too young to be on the app's radar, and it hadn't pulled stats for the store clerk or any other men either. Apparently, it only cared about potential matches. Zack wasn't sure where DaEvo got its data, but it seemed to know his age and that he preferred women. Maybe from his social media and dating profiles. He had probably given it access to accounts other than Star Fury when he signed Phil's documents. Or maybe that was just the default setting.

Amber's eyes lit up and she was almost bouncing on her feet. "Really? You'd let me use your room?"

Zack shrugged. Or at least, he tried to. The button-up shirt was sticking to his sweaty skin, and the heavy fringe of the leather jacket made it difficult to move. "Yeah, why not? Have fun, kid."

Amber made a sort of excited squeal, and Zack winced at the sound. "You're the best! And your outfit is super cool!"

She darted off to the gaming room. Zack waited for DaEvo to give him points for Amber's compliment, but nothing happened. Apparently, it didn't count unless it came from a potential match.

Ashley handed him the pizza box, and Zack paid quickly. He was in too much of a hurry to remember to brush his hand against hers as he took the box. Crap. Physical contact was worth serious bonus points, and he could have used that right now.

"Thanks," Ashley said. "She'll be talking about that for weeks. Plus, it kept Steve from getting what he wanted."

"Huh? Yeah, sure thing. No big deal."

Zack carried the pizza out. He sent a quick message to his team to let them know he would be late, then he flicked through his stats on the ride back to his condo.

Style Quest Failed!

Conversation Quest Succeeded
Rewards: +15 minutes online time
Bonus: make her laugh +30 minutes
Bonus: make her laugh +30 minutes
Bonus: make her laugh +30 minutes
Bonus: cheer her up +30 minutes

Not as much time as he had hoped for, but it should be enough to get through the latest gear releases and put together and test a strategy for the next round. Zack checked the group chat on his OptiGlasses as he walked through the lobby, gathering rendezvous coordinates from the team and letting them know he'd be online in a few minutes. They could do some planning offline after his time ran out but switching out loads and testing fire wasn't something that could be accomplished via chat. They would need to work efficiently to get through it all.

Zack grinned as he fell into the familiar rhythm of working out Star Fury plans in his head. He was finally back in the zone. Pizza and sweatpants were calling his name as he headed for the elevator.

"Nice outfit."

Zack looked up to see who had spoken, turning as he did so. The words had sounded sincere, and the voice familiar somehow.

A woman stood in the exit, tall and imperious in the bright sunlight. Silhouetted in the doorway, the sunlight obscured her face. Before Zack could think of a response, she was gone in a rustle of tanned legs and stiletto heels. The lobby doors closed, and DaEvo popped up stats from the fleeing form.

Zoe Cross (Social Level 91)
Physique: 94
Style: 84
Reputation: 95
Occupation: 91

Wait, what?

Zack sprinted out the door, crushing his pizza in the process, but the woman was already gone. Possibly in the limo pulling out of sight down the street. He stood in the sun a few moments, sweating and searching the sidewalks as if she might suddenly appear again.

"Probably a bug," he muttered finally.

Your alpha test bug report has been logged.
Thank you for your help in making DaEvo a success!

Zack walked to the elevator in a trance. Somehow, he ended up back in his condo. He threw the crushed pizza onto his cluttered couch, not hungry anymore.

Zoe Cross. Had that actually been Zoe Cross?

Why would she be in his building? Or in Oklahoma City at all?

She had complimented his outfit. Why hadn't he said something clever? Or at least said thank you?

DaEvo chimed at him again, and Zack opened up the menu to distract himself from his circular thoughts.

A flood of stats filled his screen.

Style Quest Complete!
You got a compliment! It looks like your style upgrade paid off!
Rewards: +30 Minutes Gaming time
Bonus Rewards: +60 minutes (received compliment from woman >50 points over social level)

Zack sank into his gaming chair. Well. It definitely was Zoe Cross.

Chapter Eight

FAZ: *Hey, you coming?*

Jenny: *Sorry I'm running late, guys. Got held up at work. A lady threw a fit about her salmon not being free range.*

Greg: *What does that even mean?*

Jenny: *Nothing. It's literally not a thing. But I still had to talk her down until the next shift manager clocked in.*

Faz: *I was talking to Zack. Are you going to make it, or do you have to finish your math homework first?*

Zack: *Be right there.*

First, he needed to shed the WesterNeon apparel. No way was he training in all that.

Zack pulled off the fringed jacket and scowled when DaEvo removed points from his stats. He kept the "Stylish" title, but his stats continued to lower as he pulled off the polka dot boots, jeans, and button-up shirt.

Whatever.

Zack took a quick shower, tossed a dirty towel over the pool of water that the broken faucet had made on the floor, and pulled on the cleanest of his old clothes. DaEvo chimed a warning.

Warning! Current chosen wear does not meet minimum hygiene standards.
Please select an article of clothing that has been freshly laundered or has an olfactory factor < 0.8

"Yeah, yeah."

Zack ignored his lowered stats, retrieved an energy drink and his neglected pizza, and settled into his gaming chair. His gaming system sprang to life, and the Star Fury theme music blasted through his surround sound speakers.

Finally. All was right with the world again.

All except the pink timer in the corner of his OptiGlass screen, reminding him that he would be cut off after a few hours.

"Hey, you actually made it!" Faz said when Zack arrived at the rendezvous point. "You do all your chores and earn some screen time?"

Zack let out a theatrical groan and glanced around his surroundings to gain his bearings after the jump through hyperspace. In spite of her troubles with salmon, Jenny had beat him to the rendezvous point.

Zack sighed. He hated being the last to arrive. "Very funny. I have just over three and a half hours. What's our objective?"

"Oh, wow. Three and a half whole hours? What did you do to get that? Vacuum the carpet and put fresh sheets on your bed?"

"Sure." No way was Zack going to tell the team about Wester-Neon and the makeover quest. Although… "Guys! I think I saw Zoe Cross today!"

"What? No way," Faz said.

"What do you mean you think you saw her?" Greg said. "Do you mean you saw someone who looks like her? Don't you know what she looks like?"

Zack cast a quick glance at the poster on his wall. Yeah, he knew what Zoe looked like. Or at least, he knew what she looked like on

TV. She would probably look different in person. Kayla had looked different at the gym than she had in her social media pictures.

"It was probably just a tall brunette in tight clothes," Jenny said. "Unless you have a secret career at a modeling agency that we don't know about."

"The sun was in my eyes," Zack said. "But it sounded like her."

"You talked to her?" Faz sounded more impressed.

"What did you say?" Greg asked.

"Um—" Zack swallowed. There was no way they would believe that Zoe Cross had complimented his normal clothes, and there was no way he was explaining WesterNeon to them. "Um, the weather. We talked about the weather."

"You met Zoe Cross, and you talked about the weather?" Greg sounded skeptical.

Zack's sensors pinged, and he checked them to make sure the team wasn't under attack. But it was just Jenny deploying a few scouts to lure targets their way. They were skipping base battles today in favor of wide-open space where they could test out new weapons and strategies on patrol drones.

"It's hot as hell here, man," Zack said. "Everybody talks about the weather."

"Zoe's hot as hell, and there's no way you met her."

"It could have been her."

"No way. Don't you live in Oklahoma City? Why would she be in Oklahoma City?"

Zack said, "She drove away in a limo."

"Sure."

Zack sighed. He had told his team he lived in an apartment, knowing they would picture something different than the luxury condo he actually called home. Now that was coming back to bite him. "It's a nice apartment."

"No way is Zoe Cross hanging out in an apartment in Oklahoma City."

"Hey!" Jenny said. "If we want to talk instead of train, we should help Zack figure out how to get out of intervention mode. I looked it up last night, and it's no joke."

"Or maybe we should just fly in and help him with his chores," Faz said.

"Ha, ha. Very funny," Zack said.

"But really, how messy is your apartment?" Faz asked. "It seems pretty extreme for Phil to put you in intervention mode just because your place is a mess."

"Guys, focus," Greg said. "We're on a time limit, and we have a lot of weapons to test out."

"Yeah," Zack said, glad to take the focus off his problems. "Let's train."

"Fine," Jenny said, "Let's make the most of the time Zack has, but we need to talk about this later."

Zack pushed DaEvo and Zoe from his mind and turned his attention back to Star Fury. Jenny was right. He needed to make the most of his time.

They settled into formation and went over the latest game releases, debating their merits. In the tournament, they would be fighting teams from all over the world, Corsair and Armada alike. Eventually at least. In the first round of the tournament, they were all fighting those in the same bracket—which meant people drawn from the same servers in the same time zone.

To win, they'd need a balanced strategy to deal with the wide array of fighting styles and environments that the tournament would pitch them in. Everything from timed dungeons to escort quests were on the table, though the final battles would be team-based dogfights.

The tournament itself consisted of multiple rounds. It started with online elimination rounds in each server bracket, with the winners of each bracket being allowed to move onto the final, in-person battles at the convention where they'd face further eliminations. The final battle at the convention would then be televised and streamed worldwide.

Early qualification rounds required teams to run a series of missions—basically, dungeons—and come out with the highest score. The types of missions varied from the basic warp, hunt-and-kill missions to timed race courses through asteroid fields or even—

most dreaded of all—escort missions. Teams were scored on their effectiveness at completing the mission objectives and total time taken, so teamwork was crucial. There were even solo dogfighting battles planned between members of opposing teams, with the battles considered bonus points that were added or subtracted from a team's score.

Once players were seeded, they would be pitted against one another in direct PvP rounds and randomly seeded team melees in Vegas, duking it out at the conference itself. They'd earn points for each opponent they defeated, and the highest qualifying teams from each server bracket would fight it out in the televised Vegas finals.

It was a grueling gauntlet of events that required gamers to show off their skills in multiple situations, but Zack's strategy was to take it one step at a time. And the first step was to make sure their gear setups were optimized for each of the missions. The problem was, over-optimization would bite them in the ass, because even regular Star Fury missions were known to throw curveballs. A basic "destroy the prison outpost mission" could easily become "safeguard the fleeing prisoner ships." Points were cumulative, and it would be a lot harder to gain ground later when all the noobs were eliminated.

Zack blasted an incoming patrol drone with his new laser cannon.

Jenny made a frustrated noise. "Every time you use that thing, it sends off an EM pulse."

"So?" Zack said.

"It sets off my mines."

As if to prove her point, a series of explosions lit up the screen. Zack's monitor beeped, letting him know that his shields had engaged to protect him from the impact.

"Fair point. Any ideas?" Zack asked.

"Save the cannon for emergencies?" she said.

"And give up a weapon that can take out ten ships at once? There has to be a solution. Can you set your mines farther out?"

"Not if you want them to hit anything. Drones won't run away to protect themselves like real players will."

"Incoming," Greg said.

Another wave of patrol drones appeared on Zack's radar.

"Fine, let's test something else," Zack said. "Faz, you want to try out that upgraded photon blaster and see if we have the same EMP problem with it?"

Faz let out an evil chuckle and took his place in the ship formation.

Zack quickly settled into a rhythm. Target the enemies Faz found, swoop in and clean up whatever ships weren't destroyed by Greg's initial attack, then get back into formation while dodging Jenny's mines. Occasionally, he'd set them off by firing too close to the mines, but Jenny was already playing with shielding options on her side.

They defeated that wave and regrouped to debrief until the next one came.

"Those drones had a weird shielding," Faz said. "It took more hits than it should have to defeat them."

"Or maybe the photon blaster just isn't as effective? I'll have to look at the logs later to see what's happening," Zack said. "The laser cannon is definitely faster, and we need to be fast in the timed rounds."

"It isn't faster," Jenny said. "It's just stronger. If you don't time your recharges, it's actually slower."

"What about the new sniper turret version?" Greg said. "Accuracy over power? Faz is fast enough to pull it off."

"Darn right I am," Faz said.

"And he doesn't need to destroy the drones," Jenny said. "Just disable them. It just needs enough penetration to get through their shieldings and take out their engines. Then maybe Zack could use the upgraded photon blaster to finish the job. Lower power drain, so we have more room for error."

Zack tried to be objective and put aside his love for his new favorite weapon in favor of overall strategy. "It's worth a shot. We'll test that out on the next round. I want to run a few more tests, get the log data for these fights, then we can test the new build. Jenny, can you bring us another round of drones to fight?"

"Already on it."

The next wave arrived a few moments later, and Zack settled into the familiar rhythm yet again. While data from one fight should be correct, Star Fury took a bunch of details into consideration when it came to actual damage. Everything from angle of fire to distance, so that damage done always had a variation. The more data Zack had, the more he could isolate the variables and work out if it was the new shielding or the weapons that were the problem. That Jenny and Greg hadn't upgraded their weapons helped, so he had all that data on-hand for comparison.

It still meant hours of crunching numbers, but Zack loved that kind of thing. He had spreadsheets after spreadsheets of game data.

Once they finished this round, they docked, swapped out weaponry, and went out and did it again. Faz proved to be lightning fast with the sniper turret. So fast, in fact, that Zack had trouble keeping up with the cleanup. He gave up on the photon blaster and cycled through other secondary weapons, hoping to find a middle ground in what they already had. Worst case scenario, they'd run the test again with even more variations of weaponry.

As he called out instructions and directed the team, Zack's thoughts strayed ahead to the rest of the tournament. He would need to find time to train for the solo rounds, as well as practicing with the team. Thanks to DaEvo, he would probably need to complete a lot of those practice sessions at Gord's so he could level grind with the dating sim to earn time. He needed to shine in the solo PvP battles to make up for the points he had cost his team by missing the first round.

Lucky for everyone involved, PvP was one of the things Zack did best. He was confident he would be able to earn the points needed to get the team to Vegas. Competition in the final round would be stiff, but they had as good a chance as anybody, and the rewards made it worth the effort. The winning team would receive a half-a-million-dollar contract to join the pro league.

Zack didn't care about the money. He wanted to win to show the world how good he was. In fact, he planned to give his portion of the winnings to his teammates, although he hadn't told them yet. That money would set them up for success, which would be as much a win as anything else they got out of the tournament.

Zack shook his head, dismissing thoughts of the pro leagues as they finished off the last of the drones. He checked the time it had taken them to defeat their enemies and shook his head.

"The sniper turret is good," he said, "but the photon blaster isn't as fast as the cannon. I don't even need to run the math to make that call. Maybe an artillery cannon, but I doubt it. Particle accelerators are still a little slow, but they've got a good rate of fire. In these timed rounds, we need to be fast."

"We're fast enough," Jenny said.

"The sniper turret is legit," Faz said. "Is there anything else in the new releases that would help you keep up with me?"

Zack narrowed his eyes at the smugness in Faz's voice. "Keep up with you? What's that supposed to mean?"

"I like the looks of the new anti-matter blaster," Greg said.

"No anti-matter," Jenny, Faz, and Zack said in unison.

They had learned that lesson the hard way.

"Fine, fine," Greg said with a laugh. "If you'd rather defeat enemies one at a time instead of all at once, we'll do it your way."

"I'd rather not tear a hole through time and space across three quadrants," Faz grumbled.

"Incoming," Jenny said.

"Right," Zack said. "Faz, keep the sniper turret. I'll keep looking for something that complements it. Jenny, how are things on your end?"

"Peachy."

"Greg?"

"I might test out that photon blaster if you're not using it. Unless you want to change your mind about the anti-matter."

"There are some different settings on the photon blaster, so make sure you cycle through them. No anti-matter."

The team returned to their formation and faced the wave of incoming drones.

It seemed as if they had only been training for a few moments when DaEvo chimed a warning. Updating the settings to give him a warning had been a simple enough matter once he got around to it.

Zack checked his OptiGlasses and sighed. "Guys, I've got five minutes left. Let's finish this latest wave, then I've got to go."

"I think we should do a group call afterward," Jenny said. "We can help you figure this out."

"No, it's fine. I've figured out how to game the system. I just need a few days to build up my levels, and I'll have all the time I need."

"I hope so. Don't forget to double-check your math homework," Faz teased, then added, "And make sure to do your real math homework too. And I mean the math for the weapon damage."

"I know. Everyone knows," Zack said dryly.

"Also, make sure to fold your underwear neatly in your drawer. I hear that gives you extra points," Greg added.

"Ha. Very funny."

"And say hi to Zoe for me," Faz said.

If only it were that easy. Zack had received massive bonus points for talking to Zoe since she was such a high social level. A few more conversations with her really would solve all his problems.

He shook his head. Those points had probably been from a bug. Even if it really had been Zoe, he couldn't rely on chance meetings with celebrities to solve his problems.

"You can say hi to her yourself during our interview at the tournament. Let's go!"

Zack engaged his boosters, and his ship blasted into the starry sky. He gave the enemy fleet all the firepower he had left. His ship flashed warnings, letting him know that he was overheating some crucial systems, but Zack ignored them. If he had more mission time left, that would matter, but he didn't. So he had to make these last few moments count.

The hits landed, and the opposing fleet exploded like an interstellar fireworks show. As DaEvo's countdown got close, he hit the autopilot. Then Zack's screen went dark. He groaned and leaned back in his gaming chair to stare at the ceiling.

DaEvo played a cheerful tune.

You're out of time! Would you like to complete a quest to earn more?

As if he had any choice. Zack opened the quest menu and looked over the fitness quests. They were repeatable. Maybe it was worth—

Nah.

He opened the makeover quest menu again. There was still the opportunity to spend some cash and do a little min/maxing. Leveling up his style had paid off pretty well so far.

Style Quests
· *Shop for new clothes (repeatable)*
· *Wash laundry and remove worn and torn clothing*
· *Get a haircut from the 21st century*
· *Manicure*
· *Pedicure*
· *Skin treatment*
· *Manscaping*
· ~~*Take a deportment class and pass*~~ *(locked—see details)*
· ~~*Learn to dance (Choose dance type)*~~ *(locked)*
· *(more...)*

The haircut might be worth looking into. That was easy enough. Manicures and pedicures would be easy as well, although he would have to make sure no one ever found out about them. Dance and deportment sounded like more work than the fitness quests. Maybe manscaping? What did that even mean?

Zack selected one of the websites DaEvo recommended for manscaping and skimmed through a description of their services. He closed the site just as quickly.

Hell. No.

Why would they...? He opened the website again, looked at it again, and shook his head.

No. Definitely not.

That left doing his laundry and buying more clothes.

Maybe laundry wasn't such a bad idea anyway. Since DaEvo kept reminding him about olfactory stats, Zack had become aware that his dirty clothes were giving his apartment a certain odor. Improving the olfactory stats wouldn't be the worst thing in the world.

But first, time to get the easy points.

Zack clicked on the Style Makeover category and chose the online shopping option he had unlocked. Sure enough, DaEvo had included a list of recommended online retailers. A rather long list. Zack sorted it so he only saw the high point options, but there were still a lot of stores.

Where to start? Going with the highest point option had backfired with WesterNeon. He needed to make sure that didn't happen.

"How does it calculate style stats?" Zack said, running his hands through his hair in frustration.

DaEvo chimed.

Style stats are calculated in five categories: physical style (e.g. haircuts, beards, etc.), tops, bottoms, peripherals, and accessories. Peripherals include larger extra items such as shoes and jackets, while accessories are smaller items such as watches or hats. Every item contains an inherent point value, but it may gain bonus points when combined with other items. Fashion is art!

Fashion was a pain. And apparently, Zack needed a whole new wardrobe.

He sorted the list by clothing categories and selected fitness. Not that he planned to actually complete any of the fitness quests if he could help it, but there had been lots of high-level women at the gym. Maybe they would be more likely to talk to him if he looked the part. Workout clothes might be a way to take his level grinding to a whole new level without having to leave his building.

Zack selected the highest-level fitness store and skimmed through their store description. If it had been featured on the cover of a fashion magazine, he was taking his business elsewhere.

Fit Life: High performance athletic gear for fashion-conscious athletes. This brand is consistently well-reviewed by extreme athletes and weekend warriors for comfort, durability, and style.

Sure. That seemed promising. Zack sorted the clothes according to their point values and picked the top one on the list.

Workout Shirt (Black) Cooling Fabric
Shirt: +14 Style Points
Pro athletes and fitness enthusiasts alike love this high performance—

Yeah, yeah. He would care more about that if he was actually planning to work out. Zack selected the shirt, matching shorts, and a pair of limited edition sneakers. He added a few designer sweat bands and limited edition socks to fill out the accessory portion of his outfit and clicked the buy button.

Potentially fraudulent activity detected. Did you make this purchase?
Fit Life Clothing. $1,204.72

Good grief, style stats did not come cheap. Zack approved the purchase, and DaEvo chimed with approval. It didn't add any stats for the new items yet. That would probably have to wait until they arrived tomorrow morning and he tried them on.

Lacking anything better to do, Zack scrolled through a few more online stores and bought more clothes. These weren't quite as high level as the WesterNeon outfit, but he couldn't wear the same thing every day. Having a few more options in his fashion arsenal would be good.

And maybe he could wear these without Ashley laughing in his face.

Zack still didn't understand her reaction. The fashion magazines said WesterNeon was fashionable. Zoe, or whoever he had talked to in the lobby, had liked the outfit. So why hadn't Ashley?

Zack looked around his apartment. Usually he would stay up all night playing Star Fury. What was he supposed to do with his evening without the game? It wasn't that late.

Wherever he looked, his eyes settled on piles of laundry. He opened DaEvo's menu and went to the style quests.

Wash laundry and remove worn and torn clothing

Sometimes cleanliness alone is enough to upgrade your look! Clean up your act by cleaning your clothes! Bonus points to remove anything that is too worn to meet style standards.
Style attributes increases (variable—dependent on washed articles)
Reputation increase +0.2

Zack picked up an armful of clothes and gagged at the smell. DaEvo flashed an olfactory warning, and Zack dropped the pile. This wasn't worth it. At least, it wasn't worth doing himself.

He opened his condo's app and scrolled through the menu until he found the cleaning service. Cleanliness could be bought just as easily as new clothes. It seemed pointless since the apartment would get dirty again, but DaEvo hadn't given him a choice. It was time to reengage the cleaning staff.

Chapter Nine

ZACK AWOKE to the sound of his OptiGlasses ringing. He squirmed a little on his Egyptian cotton sheets, one of the few luxuries he'd brought into the apartment—other than his gaming console. Good sheets and a good bed made such a difference. The ringing came again, and Zack groaned. At least it wasn't the overly cheerful DaEvo tune, thank goodness. Just a normal ringtone from his video calling app. He fumbled with the glasses, stabbing himself in the eye before he managed to put them on.

Phil's face filled Zack's field of vision. The trustee did not look happy.

"What the hell is this?" he asked, waving a tablet too quickly for Zack to see what was on the screen.

"Morning," Zack muttered, rubbing his eyes and once again wishing this was a bad dream. He missed the days when Phil had left him alone to play video games, only occasionally interrupting to ask Zack to sign something over email. You never knew what you had until it was gone.

"How did you manage to spend seventy thousand dollars on clothes?" Phil demanded. "Clothes! In one day! Your bank called me, convinced you had been hacked or kidnapped by a deranged fashionista."

Zack shrugged. He had stopped paying attention to prices and credit card notifications after the first few online purchases last night. It had been much easier to scan the store for the curated ensemble with the highest stats and combo points, order it, and move on to the next target. Zack had become rather proficient at that after a while. It took a lot less brainpower than working out the exact right combination of weapons, shields, and speed on Star Fury for his ships.

"Just playing the game."

"Dating Evolution was supposed to make you take a break from video games and talk to women, not turn you into a shopaholic!

"Sometimes things don't work out the way we want. Frustrating, isn't it?"

Phil sputtered, and Zack yawned. Partly because he was still sleepy, and partly because he knew it would drive Phil crazy if he looked as if he didn't care.

His trustee swore softly and took a deep breath to calm himself. "You can't buy your way through life. That's not how this works."

"It's worked out fine so far, but tell you what. Cancel the alpha test, and I swear I won't buy any new clothes for the rest of the year. Actually, make that the rest of the decade."

Phil ground his teeth as his desire to curb Zack's spending warred with the desire to teach him a lesson. Zack held his breath and waited. If Phil agreed, Zack would have his life back. He could train for the PvP portion of the tournament without completing any of DaEvo's ridiculous tasks. He could spend all day testing new weapon combinations with his team. He could—

"No," Phil said finally. "It's only been a couple of days. The developers assured me that Dating Evolution would help you realize your potential and connect with people. It just needs time."

Zack laughed. "The developers are morons. This is the worst app I've ever seen, and I've seen a lot. Come on, Phil. Let me off the hook. I'll give you another raise if you do."

Phil's eyes narrowed, and he shook his head. "You have to learn. I'm sorry, but you have to learn."

The trustee hung up, leaving Zack alone with a flood of pink hearts as DaEvo booted up for the morning.

Health Quest Complete!

You got a full night's sleep! Keep making healthy choices to level up your life.
+0.01 Physique

Damn it. Phil had been close to cracking, but Zack had played it the wrong way. If only Phil was greedy and money motivated like every other member of Zack's board, the offer of another raise would have worked. His parents had promoted Phil because of his integrity, and Zack kept him around for the same reason.

That integrity was now coming back to bite him.

DaEvo offered Zack a quest to eat a healthy breakfast, and Zack swiped it away without reading it. He still had pizza in the fridge and a shred of self-respect in his soul. The app may dictate what he wore, but he wouldn't let it dictate anything else.

The condo app chimed to let Zack know that his packages had arrived via drone and been left on his doorstep.

Perfect.

Zack opened the door and blinked at the mass of boxes in the hallway. They were stacked neatly in piles that reached up to his shoulders and lined the wall halfway to the next condo door. Maybe he had gotten carried away last night. Boredom and a desire to game the system may have fueled him to take his shopping a bit too far.

Whatever. Those clothes were key to his strategy to beat DaEvo. He needed to min/max his Style stats so his conversations gave him more game time. Less work, more play.

Zack sighed and moved the boxes into his condo. Most were light, so he pushed the stacks rather than picking up individual boxes. When the stacks fell over, he kicked the boxes one by one into his already cluttered living room.

DaEvo chimed.

Workout Detected

Your increased heart rate indicates that you're working out. Accept an official quest to level up your physique.

Zack glanced quickly through the list offered.

Physique Quests

· *Have a healthy meal (Repeatable)*
· *Walk 2km (Repeatable)*
· *Run 2km (Locked)*
· *Lose 5lbs (Repeatable with limits)*
· *Take a weightlifting class*
· ~~*Lift weights*~~ *(Locked)*
· …

He rejected them just as quickly. Such dumb software. If it detected him exercising, shouldn't it at least give him points for it? Almost, Zack registered a bug, but decided to skip it. He wasn't going to help them fix their damn buggy software that he'd been conned into testing. Anyway, he had almost finished moving the boxes. There was no need to get carried away.

Zack kicked the last box into his apartment. It gave a satisfying thud, and he sank into his gaming chair to examine his loot. If his apartment had looked cluttered before, it now looked as though it belonged to a hoarder. Luckily, most of the boxes were decorated with the brand logos, which would help him sort through them later. The sleek packaging was a strange contrast to the piles of dirty laundry scattered around the room.

Zack retrieved his pizza from the fridge and ate it while he opened a few boxes. DaEvo rated the clothes as he pulled them out, overlaying each item with a pink heart filled with stats. Zack set aside a striped polo shirt, dark wash jeans, and tennis shoes that DaEvo had given high combo points to the night before. He needed to be smart about this if he wanted to win the game. Ashley had laughed at his high fashion ensemble, but Zoe had complimented it.

If it really had been Zoe. Zack didn't trust DaEvo enough to say for sure. But even if it wasn't Zoe, it was probably still someone fashionable with a very high social level.

He'd made the classic mistake of using the same kind of weapon on every kind of opponent. Mass accelerators were great for blowing holes in outposts, but not fast enough to handle high-speed drones that ducked out of the way. You needed guided missiles, a high-speed railgun, or lasers for them.

If DaEvo was programmed to work like a game, Zack needed to assume his Style stats worked the same way. Use high stat, high fashion items on high fashion women. And lower value items on low level women like Ashley.

Zack started to pull on the striped shirt, and DaEvo flashed a warning.

Minimum Hygiene Levels not Met
Please take a shower before changing into a clean pair of clothes.

Good grief, he wasn't that sweaty. But there was no point arguing with the app.

Zack took a quick shower to wash away the sweat he had built up while moving the boxes. He tossed a dirty T-shirt over the pool of water created by the leaking faucet and put on his new outfit. DaEvo chimed when he looked in the mirror.

Style: 58.5

Congratulations! You've taken your style from Unemployed Hobo to Boy Next Door! Consistency in dress matters! Keep going to earn even more rewards.

This was accompanied by a list of other style quests.

Style Quests
· *Shop for new clothes*
· *Wash laundry and remove worn and torn clothing*
· *Get a haircut from the 21st century*
· *Manicure*
· *Pedicure*
· *Skin treatment*
· *Manscaping*
· ~~*Take a deportment class and pass*~~ *(locked)*
· ~~*Learn to dance (Choose dance type)*~~ *(locked)*
· *(more...)*

Zack studied the list. His first instinct was to swipe it away and forget it existed, but if he wanted to maximize his Style stats, he would have to face these eventually. "What do I get for a haircut?"

DaEvo chimed.

Proper physical grooming is important to maximize points available from your clothing purchases.
Even if you have physical shortcomings, there's no reason to look like a slob.
Style Combo Maximum Upgraded
Physique +4

"Why didn't you mention that yesterday?"

DaEvo remained silent.

Stupid, buggy app. Zack suddenly felt suspicious. Even his high fashion WesterNeon outfit had only reached eighty-nine or so points. That seemed low, considering how cutting edge those clothes were. And some of the best outfits he had bought online were only worth forty-five points. On top of that, this was the second time he'd seen style and physique cross-pollinate. There was definitely something going on.

"What else affects my style points?"

DaEvo chimed.

Even great clothes won't look their best on you if you're out of shape.
Physique stats affect Style stats. A pig wearing makeup is still a pig.

"Pig? Who are you calling a pig, you blasted…" Zack paused as the usual bug report flashed up.

He drew a deep breath. It seemed that the alpha test still had the developers' placeholder descriptions. Either that or DaEvo really thought the sarcastic-insulting tone was the way to get more customers.

Maybe it did work for some people. But this was ridiculous. After all that shopping, he could only min/max up to a certain point before he was forced to work on Physique. So much for exploiting the system.

Still, he had leveled up significantly in one day. His level grind with Ashley should give him way more points now. Hopefully enough that he could train for individual combat without needing to do any more quests for the day.

Or maybe he should hang out in the condo lobby for a while to see if Zoe walked by again.

Tempting, but Zack decided against it. There was no guarantee she would pass by. Or that it had even been her in the first place. And that was like making a World Boss run without bothering to grind the space slugs in the starting area. Better to start small and level up first.

Even without working out, he was leveling up his physique by sleeping. And he still had Style quests he could complete before that stat was maxed out.

Zack sighed and scheduled an appointment with the barber located on the first floor of the condo. As much as it pained him to admit that the app was right, a haircut probably wasn't the worst idea in the world.

Chapter Ten

ZACK WALKED into Gord's with significantly less swagger than he had possessed the previous day. His stats were lower than they had been in the WesterNeon outfit, but the barber and several other patrons had assured him he looked good. His throat tightened when he saw Ashley. The gaming café was less busy now that the first round of the tournament was over, but Zack still had no desire to repeat the public humiliation he had experienced yesterday. If she laughed in his face again, he would walk out of Gord's and never come back.

Which would be a shame. This was by far the nicest gaming café in town, and it would be so convenient to complete his DaEvo quests here then go straight to the private gaming room he had reserved for the rest of the month. Not to mention it would be a pain to find another place to do his level grinding.

Ashley grinned when she noticed Zack standing awkwardly in the doorway. With a ribbon bookmark, she marked her place in the book she was reading and waved him over. "Hey, I'm sorry about yesterday."

DaEvo started the conversation timer, and Zack coughed to buy himself time. The last thing he wanted to do was talk about yesterday.

Ashley's forehead wrinkled in concern. "Seriously, I didn't mean to laugh."

"That was a lot of unintentional laughter."

She smirked, looking as if she might burst into "unintentional laughter" all over again. "You just looked—anyway, I'm sorry. Why were you dressed like that?"

Apparently, Ashley did not subscribe to *Fashion* magazine.

Zack shrugged. "Just a project for a friend."

"Oh. Well, you look nice today."

DaEvo chimed and gave Zack a compliment bonus.

Style Quest Complete!
You got a compliment! It looks like your style upgrade paid off!
Rewards: +30 Minutes Gaming time

Zack read through the notification with satisfaction, then realized Ashley was still waiting for him to respond. "Oh. Thanks."

Ashley looked at the counter, and Zack looked at the ceiling. DaEvo flashed a warning that the conversation was lagging. If one of them didn't say something soon, he would lose the conversation time he had gathered without gaining any points.

Zack opened his mouth to order a pizza, but Ashley spoke first. "Thank you for yesterday. That is—Amber was so excited about the room. She's been talking about it nonstop."

"What? Oh, yeah. It was nothing."

Really, it had been nothing. Just a way to annoy the man and get points for cheering up Ashley. Apparently, the cheering up had worked well. Ashley looked happier than she had in their previous two encounters as she smiled at Zack.

"Right. Anyway, thanks." Ashley gave Zack a look, her eyes searching his face for something.

Zack hoped she wasn't thinking about how hideous his new haircut was. Maybe DaEvo and the barber had lied to him and he looked as ridiculous now as he had in the WesterNeon ensemble. He had fashion trust issues after the debacle yesterday.

DaEvo chimed.

Your conversation is going well! Get bonus points and level up your relationship by:
Complimenting her
Asking about her interests
Giving her a gift

Zack swallowed and studied Ashley for something to compliment. She was pretty, but the Gord's uniform wasn't particularly flattering. The baggy polo shirt completely obscured her waist and—

Ashley cleared her throat when she noticed him staring and Zack felt his face warming. Yes, he had been checking her out, but it wasn't what she thought. Not that he could explain that.

Ashley put her hands on her hips, and DaEvo repeated its conversation warning. Zack ran a hand through his hair, his eyes flicking around the desktop and alighting on the book on the counter.

"So you like reading?" Zack said quickly.

Ashley followed his gaze to her discarded book and made a face. "Usually. This one's a bit dry."

"Sociology," Zack read aloud. "Why are you reading a book about sociology?"

"For a class." Her tone suggested he had asked a very stupid question.

DaEvo chimed.

Bonus Objective Completed! You asked about her interests. For additional bonus points:
Compliment her
Give her a gift

Zack looked from the notification to the book to Ashley. He

wanted those bonus points. But how should he phrase his compliment so that DaEvo would recognize it as one? He noticed a tiny question mark over the bonus quest and pressed it with a flick of his eyes.

Suggestion*!*
To compliment her, be specific. Let her know that you admire something about her.

Zack thought for a moment to sort out his wording in a way that was likely to trigger DaEvo. "It's really cool that you're studying. You know, for a class. It's awesome that you're taking a class."

DaEvo did not give him points, and Zack cursed the app in his head.

Ashley looked mildly amused. "More than one. I'm working on my master's."

"Oh. Wow. I thought—you know—"

"You thought I was a slacker nobody who works at a gaming café but knows nothing about gaming?" Ashley arched a single eyebrow.

Zack swallowed, feeling his back grow damp under her scrutiny. Yeah, that was about right, but even he knew better than to admit that. DaEvo chimed again, once again encouraging him to compliment her and flustering him even further.

"It's cool. You're kind of a nerd too. That's cool. I mean, you're cool. Sociology is great." He was rambling, trying to find the right wording so DaEvo would recognize the compliment. For once, Zack wished that one of the morning gamers—all too few right now—would come and interrupt the conversation. Maybe demand she fix their mouse or something.

Finally the app chimed.

Bonus Objective Completed! You complimented her.
For additional bonus points:
Give her a gift

Zack stared at the notification. How in the world was he supposed to give her a gift on such short notice? Zack looked for a tutorial, but apparently, that hadn't been added yet. Maybe they should add a shopping app link too. That'd be a great way to make more money...

Zack kicked himself mentally, getting his brain back on track.

Before he could speak, Ashley's computer chimed. She flashed Zack an apologetic grin and checked it. "Sorry, Room Three is requesting more coffee. Give me a second."

She turned to make the coffee, and Zack checked DaEvo. He had earned bonus points for asking about her interests and complimenting her, and game time for the repeatable conversation quest. He suspected he would get some kind of combo bonus for giving her a gift and completing all three quests, but he had no idea how to pull that off. His OptiGlasses chimed.

Faz: *So, how's solo training going? Or are you still doing the dishes to earn screen time?*

Zack: *Shut up.*

Zack could practically hear his friend laughing through the text. He swiped the messaging app to close it and realized that Ashley had returned and asked him something. "Sorry, what?"

"Do you want anything before I deliver this?"

DaEvo flashed the bonus challenge again, and Zack swallowed a sigh. He didn't have time to run out and get a gift now. Hopefully he could do it later and still get the combo points.

"Can you bring a latte to my room when you have time? I need to start training."

"Raptor Cow milk as usual?"

Zack laughed. "Always."

Ashley winked and hurried away to deliver the coffee. Zack watched her go, then hurried up to his reserved room. Star Fury was calling his name.

DaEvo chimed and awarded him points for the conversation.

***Quest Complete! You spoke with a woman for 5:47.
You have earned non-essential electronics and
internet privileges!***
Reward, easy difficulty—+15 minutes
Bonus Time Awarded—+30 Minutes Use Time
Bonus Achieved – Ask about her interests. +30 Minutes Use Time
Bonus Achieved – Compliment her. +30 Minutes Use Time

Zack sighed as he slumped into his chair in his private room.
That wasn't a lot of time, but it was better than nothing. Just over
two hours when he included his Style quest. It didn't take him long
to boot up the game, and while he went through the routine, he
glanced at the quest information again. He had once again gotten a
good return on investment for the time spent in the conversation. If
he could keep the conversation going, the Bonus time seemed to
increment in two-minute slots. Which seemed a little broken if you
thought about it. If he had an hour-long conversation, Zack would
have more time than he ever needed.

There was probably a limiter in there. Maybe a logarithmic
decrease in time? In either case, having a higher social level meant
that he received even more time than before. Almost twice as much
—and that was without bonuses for laughing or touch. He'd been a
little too flustered, trying to achieve the other bonus goals, to hit
those this time.

Still, Zack smirked. His strategy was working. It would work
even better if he found some higher-level women to talk to, but right
now, the level grind with Ashley was going fine. Maybe in a couple
of hours, he'd go down and get some coffee. Maybe use the excuse
of stretching his legs.

His pod spawned at the usual Corsair outpost, and he went
through his pre-flight check to make sure everything was ready for
training. Once he was satisfied with his setup, he set his scanners to
search for a PvP opponent and opened up long-range comms to his
team.

"Hey, guys! How's it going?"

Laser fire and the high-pitched whining of tracker missiles answered him.

After a few moments, Faz answered. "Welcome back, Zack. Finally finish your chores?"

"You know, you may be overusing that joke," Zack said. "I think it's time to develop some new material."

"No way. This situation is comedy gold."

Zack waited for Greg or Jenny to chime in and tell Faz that their teammate disappearing in the middle of a tournament round was not funny, but the comms remained silent.

"Nobody else is on?" he asked.

"Jenny got called in to cover for a waitress with food poisoning, and Greg is working overtime to save up for the flight to Vegas," Faz said. "You know how it is."

"Yeah," Zack said noncommittally.

He did not, in fact, know how it was. After graduating college, Zack had declined Phil's offer of an internship in his own company and thrown himself into gaming. He understood on an intellectual level that people had jobs and needed to earn money, but the day to day reality of it was hard to grasp.

Although now that he was trapped in DaEvo, he was rapidly developing sympathy for his teammates and their work schedules.

"Won't have to worry about jobs once we go pro," Faz said cheerfully.

"You don't have to worry about it now," Zack said.

"I don't have to worry about it for another ten months," Faz corrected. "Then my gap year is officially over, and I will fulfill my destiny of becoming a doctor."

He said that without his usual cheerful enthusiasm, and Zack frowned. He didn't know many doctors who played video games. Would Faz have to give up Star Fury once he started medical school? Certainly, he would have to cut back.

"You don't think your parents will ease up about that when we make the pro circuit?" he asked. "That's a way bigger deal than going to medical school."

Faz laughed. Zack waited politely for his friend to stop, but he just kept going. Eventually, Zack had to clear his throat to get Faz back on track.

"We can dream anyway. You find anybody good to fight yet?" Faz asked.

Zack turned back to his ship's sensors, which were scanning his quadrant of space for opponents at his level. "Not yet. Might have to jump somewhere else."

While Star Fury was an international sensation, to deal with its massive number of users, players were relegated to servers based off time zones. Of course, they generally tried to mix enough people around so that there were people on at all times, but sometimes, it didn't work. That's where the low sec space was useful. Low sec space was all international, shared servers and meant that you could often find non-English speaking opponents.

If anyone local was logged in right now, fighting them would be faster than hyperjumping to international space. Transition time between his local servers and the international servers occasionally caused severe lag. Problem was, the odds of finding someone at Zack's level who was also live weren't great. He had never actually checked server rank boards before, preferring to take the time to travel to international battlefields and fight the best in the world. But he was trying to save time now. Although, sitting here running his scanners wasn't saving him much time either.

"Wait, I've got somebody." Zack checked his dashboard.

An Armada ship was patrolling nearby, level grinding by blowing up NPC Corsair ships and automated drones. Its stats looked comparable to his, and their ships were in the average tech level. Zack hailed it with a picture of the Corsair flag, the standard invitation to single combat between the factions. He added an emoji sticking out its tongue for good measure. That should get his attention.

Sure enough, the ship responded with the Armada insignia and a skull emoji and changed course to intercept him. Zack grinned wolfishly and settled back for the ride. His comms pinged to let him know another of his teammates had come online.

"Hey, guys," Jenny said. "How's it—"

A blast of laser fire and explosions swallowed the rest of her words.

"You all right over there?" Faz said.

Zack flipped through his available weapons and adjusted the energy levels for his favorites, wanting to get a quick first kill. If he managed to do it fast enough, it often angered his opponents and they'd come rushing back for a second helping.

"Fine," Jenny said. "Just trying to adjust the shield frequencies on all my drones while also flying my ship. Looks like we're not the only ones to notice the EMP-inducing laser cannon."

"Yeah, that last update was a doozy," Faz said. "But hey, that's why we practice, right?"

"Good pep talk," Jenny said sarcastically. "Now if you'll excuse me, I need to focus."

She muted her comms, and Faz chuckled. "She's going to be insufferable once she finally figures out that EMP problem. Don't tell her I said that."

Zack laughed. There were three theoretical ways he knew of to fix the issue. Increase the shield strength overall—but that drained energy faster. Wasn't an issue with full-sized ships, but Jenny's drones had smaller engines or, in some cases, just energy batteries. Second was to figure out the frequency that was being cut through and adjust the shield frequency to match. That required more fiddling with the backend and could leave the drones vulnerable to other, previously shielded, attacks. And lastly, you could combine the two options to blunt the edge of the EMP while widening the distance between your drone and mine layouts.

Zack's musings were interrupted as his screen flashed an incoming warning. The Armada ship had sent some missiles on a dead burn in a lame attempt to catch him off guard. Maybe he should have flown to international space after all. If that was the best this guy had, this match wouldn't be much good for training.

Zack destroyed the missiles with the photon blaster and started the warmup sequence for his laser cannon. Time to see how this thing did in single combat.

Zack's gaming chair shook, and the room's ambient lighting flashed red as his shields dropped to 95% efficiency. What? How had that guy hit him?

Zack swore softly as he checked all his readouts and tried to figure out where the hit had come from. It hadn't been a strong attack, but the Armada scum had drawn first blood. Unacceptable.

"I've got to go, Faz. Looks like this guy has a few tricks up his sleeves."

"Have fun. Don't forget to take a break and eat your vegetables to earn game time."

"Seriously, that's not funny anymore."

Faz just laughed.

Zack muted his comms and grinned as he swooped into evasive maneuvers. To keep his opponent on his toes, Zack dropped off a pair of missiles on a delayed burn intercept course.

Time to get down to business and destroy this Armada scum.

Chapter Eleven

ZACK SWORE as his laser cannon's beam went wide again. The Armada ship was fast. Too fast for the cannon's turret rotation speed and targeting software to get a reliable read on. He'd been attempting to compensate with better flying skills, but he had to admit, the Armada scum knew how to fly.

Damn it. It looked as though the cannon wouldn't be a good choice for PvP after all.

He tapped away on the keyboard, switching energy shunts and recharge levels to his secondaries. If he dedicated the vast majority of his energy recharge to the secondary lasers, he'd be able to increase damage levels. A quick tap released a new stream of seeker missiles to deal with another of the cloaked drones the Armada scum had been using.

Sneaky devil had hidden the initial cloaked drone with its bomb behind his missiles. Zack was both impressed and annoyed at how clever his opponent had been.

He was vaguely aware of a door opening and someone setting coffee next to him on the table, but he didn't look up. He was too busy dodging laser fire while trying to get his secondaries in the target zone.

Zack felt himself slipping deep into the zone. It had been a while since he did PvP with someone so evenly matched with him. His usual tricks weren't working, and the guy was using weapon combos Zack hadn't seen before. He had thoroughly reviewed the latest releases, but apparently, he hadn't been thorough enough. He needed to do more research on the recent releases. Maybe scan the forums to see if someone had created blueprints he hadn't seen from existing tech. Some of the attacks should have been out of current tech abilities, but he was still getting hit.

If he could reverse engineer what the man had, maybe they could add it to their arsenal. Or at least adjust their flying styles. Maybe squeeze in a percent or two more efficiency to their weapons and shields.

The fight continued, and Zack lost himself in the battle. His world was lasers and missiles, adjusting energy draw and recharge rates while piloting his ship. Sure, you could fly with a bog-standard setup, but that was for newbies. To eke out the most from your ship, you constantly had to adjust. It was what made Star Fury the best.

As Zack's coffee cooled, he flew and fought until DaEvo chimed. He swore as he looked at the timer counting down in the corner. He had five minutes to end the latest round of their duel. This was the... fifth? Sixth round? Zack wasn't even sure, what with the need to fly back and forth after a ship was destroyed.

That wasn't enough time to bring this match to a close. Since his main laser cannon hadn't been effective, Zack had been forced to shift things up. Now, he was using a massed series of lasers delivering low damage hits, but a lot of them all the time. Wearing down the Armada's shields.

Zack was winning, he could tell. There were issues with this configuration for PvP, but it worked, even if it took time. Time he no longer had.

Zack swerved to avoid an incoming missile and considered his options. He could forfeit the match and retreat back to the Corsair base, but that would cost him reputation points. He could fly in close and destroy the Armada scum with a hyperbomb, but the resulting explosion at close range would likely destroy Zack as well.

At the least, it would cause damage that would require costly repairs. Which wasn't a huge thing for him, but it was still a loss.

Or he could live up to his Corsair reputation and do something underhanded and unexpected. Zack grinned and armed the anti-matter blaster. He'd added it because of Greg's insistence, but the slow warmup time and high energy cost to keep it running meant he'd kept it off for the duel thus far. It was a little hard to aim, but the Armada ship had sustained engine damage earlier. If Zack could land a hit, he could end this and make it back to the Corsair base relatively intact.

Worth a shot.

Zack bit his lip as he brought his opponent in close. In one corner of his eyes, he watched the amount of time he had left counting down. In the other, the energy levels of the anti-matter cannon as it warmed up. To make sure his opponent didn't suspect anything, Zack was lobbing missiles at him every chance he got and overheating his engine. He couldn't keep that up for much longer, but it'd work.

A modified S-curve managed to maneuver the Armada ship into Zack's shooting hairs. He fired a blast of anti-matter ahead of the Armada ship, then pulled back as hard as he could, switching off everything but shields and accelerators.

The anti-matter, unseen and unnoticed, was flown into by the Armada ship. It stuck to an engine like a wad of chewed gum before it crawled up along the wing.

Extremely volatile chewed gum.

Zack watched as his screen went white. The game auto-tinted his monitors as he lost all sensors, all external views from the massive explosion the anti-matter had created. The release of energy was many times more powerful than the "nukes" their normal missiles used and damaged his ship even as he ran away.

Luckily, Zack had already started the hyperspace jump, so he was barely able to escape. Sadly, hyperspace would be unstable in the quadrant for the new few days, which would create an unstable wormhole location. Sometimes, Star Fury generated automatic dungeons; sometimes, ships just got torn apart when they traversed too close.

No one liked losing ships for no good reason, which was why anti-matter was considered dangerous and insane to use, even by Corsairs.

Still, he had won. His game screen flashed with the points and achievements from the match. Zack idly watched his ranks update, then groaned as DaEvo warned him again of the impending shut-down. A quick tap set up his autopilot, since there were no Armada patrols around.

It was a shame about the loot. If only he had more time—

As if reading his mind, DaEvo chimed and counted down his final thirty seconds of game time.

Zack groaned and leaned back in his chair, watching the stars fly by as he took a sip of his now-cold coffee. Maybe if he had paid attention and gotten up when he meant to get his coffee, rather than order another one, he could have added more time.

The timer reached zero and the Star Fury theme music played as the game returned to the title screen then flashed the notification that he would have to contact customer support to access his account. Zack glared at it a moment, then slowly stood and stretched. There was nothing more he could do here. Much as he hated to admit it, he needed to spend the rest of the day with DaEvo and earn game time for his next team training session.

Zack walked back to the lobby, where a Gord's employee was trying to reason with an irate customer.

"You can't rage in the common room, Steve. You know the drill."

"Corsair scum! Did you see what he did to me? Did you see—"

Zack searched for Ashley, but she wasn't there. He leaned against the counter to wait for her, and the employee talking to Steve waved at him in apology. DaEvo flashed stats for her.

Candace Cook (Social Level 49)
Physique: 63
Style: 52
Reputation: 53
Occupation: 26

Candace wore her dark dreadlocks pulled back into a high ponytail and bright yellow eyeshadow that complemented her brown skin. Zack wondered briefly if the bold makeup choice meant she would appreciate his WesterNeon outfit. He could run home, change, and be back in ten minutes.

"Anti-matter!" Steve said. "Out of nowhere. We're sparring, then he blasts me with anti-matter. I thought he was vaguely honorable, unlike more Corsair scum."

Zack smirked. Knowing that he had beaten the scum who had been giving Ashley a hard time was rather satisfying, even if it was rather amusingly coincidental. Or not. Really, to be at their level, most people had to devote years to the game. And most people didn't have the time.

Zack looked Steve over with interest. He didn't often get to see his opponents in person. Maybe that didn't matter. Other than the ridiculous amount of Armada regalia pinned to his jacket, Steve was pretty unremarkable. And given how annoying he was being right now, the anti-matter had been a good call.

Candace put her hands on her hips. "Look, you know the rules. Are you going to settle down, or do I have to kick you out?"

Steve glared at her then turned back to his station. Zack could almost swear Steve was sulking as he walked back.

Candace hurried over to the counter and smiled at Zack. "Sorry about that. What can I get for you?"

DaEvo chimed and started a conversation timer. Zack grinned. Might as well resume his level grinding and bank time for the next training session.

"I'll take a pizza to go."

"Sure thing." Candace turned to make the pizza without offering further comment.

DaEvo flashed the conversation warning but no helpful suggestions. What had it said last time? To compliment Ashley or ask about her interests? Would that work on Candace?

Worth a shot.

"Nice eye shadow," Zack said. It was the most noticeable thing about her.

Candace turned and gave him a strange look, then shrugged. "Thanks."

DaEvo chimed a compliment bonus, and Zack grinned. This was getting easier.

"That guy give you a lot of trouble?" he said, gesturing to Steve.

Candace laughed. "Just when he loses. I can't really blame him. Some idiot Corsair used anti-matter during a PvP match."

Zack struggled to keep his face neutral. "Yeah? I mean, that's not exactly typical, but it sounds like it worked."

"Oh, you must be Corsair," Candace said. "No sense of honor. No offense, of course."

"You Armada think you can add 'no offense' after any insult and say whatever you want."

Candace laughed, and DaEvo offered a bonus for it. "Come on though, anti-matter? That's the cheapest way to avoid a loss I've ever seen. I'd be ticked if someone did that to me. It's not even a great build—the cannon takes up too many slots and it recharges too slow for anything but aggro kills." Candace pulled the pizza from the oven, put it in a box, and set it on the counter.

Zack swiped his OptiGlasses to pay. "More like an expensive way. Have you seen the cost of anti-matter these days? Maybe he had a good reason."

"More like he realized he was about to lose." Candace laughed again, as if she had said something funny.

DaEvo chimed with another bonus that Zack was tempted to reject on principle. The anti-matter had been his best option in a difficult situation. Not some sort of joke.

But he needed the time and had no idea if it was possible to reject bonus points. Probably not, given how buggy DaEvo was. Candace was chatty but annoying. It would make sense to earn more conversation points before he went home, but he'd rather talk to Ashley.

"Hey, where's Ashley?"

"Gone."

"She quit?" Zack's voice rose in alarm. Had the other gamers annoyed Ashley so much that she found employment elsewhere? He had been sure the Veridian solution would fix the problem. Ashley had been his most successful contact so far in DaEvo. If she left Gord's—

"Family emergency," Candace said. "She'll be back tomorrow. Why do you care?"

Zack swallowed at the wary note in Candace's tone. "Oh, right. No reason." He flashed a smile and waved. Hopefully she didn't think he was a creep or a weirdo stalker.

He took the pizza and hurried out of Gord's. DaEvo flashed a notification for the successful conversation quest, and Zack scanned through it on the ride back to his condo. The conversation with Candace had given him some time, but not enough. If he was going to endure more inane conversations like that, he needed to grind his personal level up so they'd be worth more.

As soon as he returned home, Zack dug into the pizza. The pepperoni left his hands covered with grease. He made a quick visual sweep of the room, looking for paper towels, but it would be impossible to find anything under the layer of boxes from his online shopping. He shrugged and wiped his hands on his polo shirt instead. Finding a clean shirt now that he had bought new clothes would be easy enough, and the cleaning service would do laundry when they arrived.

Which would hopefully be soon. The stench of his apartment was killing his appetite. Zack stuffed the rest of the pizza in the fridge, and DaEvo flashed a notification.

Quest!
Level up your life by improving your physique. Eat a healthy lunch for
bonus points.
Kale salad
Oven Roasted Caesar Salad
Fruit bowl
Whole wheat BLT
Avocado toast with pepper on whole grain bread
(more...)

Zack swiped away the notification with a grimace. He wasn't that desperate for points, and he hoped he never would be. He was getting the hang of talking to women the way DaEvo wanted him to. He had successfully leveled up his style and still had quests there that could be completed to get him even more points. He was well on his way to gaming the system with minimum effort. No need to get crazy with Physique quests.

He pulled a slice of pizza out of the fridge, deciding he was hungry after all. Small acts of rebellion were still rebellion, and Zack was determined to give the app as little control over his life as possible.

His phone rang as soon as he took the first bite, lukewarm pizza turning cold as he saw the name.

Phil.

Zack quickly chewed the pizza. Maybe Phil had changed his mind and decided to let him off the hook after all. Zack swallowed and answered the call.

Phil's face filled the OptiGlass screen. He did not look happy.

Chapter Twelve

"Sup?" Zack said. He took a bite of his pizza and chewed it loudly to annoy the trustee.

Phil sighed. "I don't suppose you've completed any of the etiquette quests in that app. The developers assured me it would improve your manners."

Zack swallowed the pizza and shrugged. "You change your mind about letting me loose?"

"I have an update about the charity. Since that's the one aspect of your business that apparently interests you, I thought you'd like to hear it."

"What is there to hear? You doubled the budget like I asked, right?"

"Yes, which has created its own difficulties. As I have said before, you can't just throw money at problems to solve them."

Zack frowned. "The hospitals aren't happy with more funds?"

"Of course they are, but it's already creating infrastructure problems. On our end and theirs. We need someone to manage the extra funding and research. Someone who knows this field and how to evaluate the effectiveness of our efforts."

"So find someone." Zack took another bite of his pizza and

wondered absentmindedly just how far Phil's eyes could bug out of his head. He had annoyed the trustee plenty over the years, but DaEvo seemed to be pushing him to another level.

Maybe the app had that effect on everyone.

"You know, you're capable of doing that," Phil said. "If you really want to help the charity, you could put some effort into it."

"Nah, you're better at that sort of thing. You find someone yet?"

Phil sighed. "As a matter of fact, I have someone in mind. Doctor Jones is perfect for the job, but reluctant to take it. She wants to meet you first."

"She?"

Zack's mind spun. A doctor should be high level, right? Her Occupation and Reputation stats should be good anyway. If she had decent Physique and Style, he could get some serious conversation points in a face-to-face meeting. Working out all the details for the trust might take hours. He could compliment her ideas for bonus points. Maybe get some physical contact when they passed papers back and forth.

"Yes, *she*. Please don't tell me you don't think a woman can—"

"I'll meet her," Zack said. "Where and when? And preferably as soon as possible."

Phil blinked at him suspiciously. "This is an important meeting for the trust. We all agree that Doctor Jones is perfect for this position, but she wants to meet the person behind the money before she agrees. Apparently, she's a little suspicious of big organizations. I don't want to scare her off."

"You just said you wanted me to take an interest in the trust," Zack said. "This is me taking an interest, and I'll be a perfect gentleman. After all, I've got an app for that now."

He tapped his OptiGlasses, and Phil sighed. "I guess I don't have a choice. Fine. Lucky for you, she works in Oklahoma City. I'll set the meeting and let you know the time."

"It's a date," Zack said with a grin.

"It is not a date," Phil said. "It is a business meeting. And if you do anything inappropriate, I will enact the budget clause you signed."

"The what?"

Zack's OptiGlasses flashed a highlighted portion of the contract as Phil sent it over.

In instances when the beneficiary exceeds regular expenses or the budgeted expense limit by 25%, the beneficiary agrees to the expansion of expense oversight by the trustee. This oversight may include:

- *restrictions on spending*
- *increased guidelines on expenses charged to the trust*
- *a decrease in current budgeted allowance for the beneficiary*
- *...*

Zack swore.

"I did warn you to read through what you signed," Phil said smugly.

The trustee's good spirits seemed to have returned a little. Zack glared at him and hung up the call.

A text message came through a few moments later.

Phil: *Be respectful toward the doctor, and I won't need to use that.*

Zack rolled his eyes. Of course he would be respectful to the doctor. He would compliment her and ask about her interests and get bonus points for all of it. He should bring some gifts just in case. What did doctors like? A stethoscope?

Maybe he should look up some jokes to make her laugh. Laughter was worth serious bonus points, and it was repeatable.

Zack ate another slice of pizza while he scrolled through websites of medical jokes and rolled his eyes. They were terrible. He would be better off winging it.

A message from Faz interrupted him.

Faz: *We're running dungeons tonight to train. You in?*

Zack typed yes without thinking, then groaned as he remembered he was low on game time. The conversation with Candace hadn't given him nearly enough time to run dungeons, and he wasn't eager to speak with her again. Ashley had gone home early, so he couldn't have a conversation with her either. He would have to get points another way.

He surveyed the boxes filling his living room. Whatever he did, he would get the Style bonus while doing it. That was something.

He opened DaEvo and scrolled through the quests. He had just about maxed out Style unless he wanted to get a manicure and pedicure. Or... worse things. Zack swiped those away and looked at Physique. Boosting that would also raise his Style, but that would require eating healthy or exercising.

That left Reputation and Occupation.

Hmm. Occupation was sitting at zero. How much would a job improve his stats?

Occupation Quests

- *Browse job listings*
- *Fill out an application*
- *Complete an interview*
- *Complete your first day*
- *Complete your first week*
- *Suggested Careers based off current work history*
- *Grocery Cashier (+7)*
- *Night Janitor (+5)*
- *Busboy (+3)*
- *Roadside cleaner (+6)*
- *Warehouse packer (+4)*

- *Parking Lot Attendant (+6)*
- *---(locked)*

"What the hell?"

Why would he become a night janitor for +5 Occupation points? It definitely was not worth the amount of time he'd be giving up gaming. For that matter, those kinds of jobs were becoming rarer and rarer as drones and automated machinery took over the work. These days, half the job involved standing around pushing buttons and making sure the machines didn't get stuck.

Zack closed the Occupation quests and opened Reputation. DaEvo had obviously miscalculated this category. It was in the negatives right now, undoing all the work he had done to level up his Style.

Reputation Quests

- *Join a volunteer organization*
- *Join a charitable organization*
- *Join your local religious organization, the [...- error, unable to find nearest location for the 'Church of the Flying Spaghetti Monster']*
- *Spend time at the local retirement home*
- *Answer questions on local bulletin board (helpfully!)*
- *...*

Nope. Zack pulled off his OptiGlasses and glared at them. Those were even worse than the Occupation quests. If that was the sort of stupid thing the app used to calculate Reputation, it was no wonder he had such a low score. It didn't explain the negative score though. Just because he wasn't making the world a better place didn't mean he should be in the negatives.

"Show me Reputation score calculations."

DaEvo attribute calculations are proprietary information...

Zack dismissed the notification with a huff before he finished reading it. Yeah. He should have remembered that. So. How'd he get the information for the Style points? He cudgelled his brain a bit, trying different methods to get the system to give up some information. Nothing worked.

Eventually, Zack slumped back in his chair, muttering into the open air, "Why are my Reputation scores negative?"

Reputation scores are taken from negative and positive interactions with others in public and other social situations, as well as the overall reputation of an individual in greater society.

Developer Note:
We're using facial recognition tech for real-time reputation updates, but we're weighing heavily toward public reputation scores. We're getting decent statistical correlation among the test group here, with general reputation scores ranging from 40-60. Except Cindy from HR and her bake sales. She's a 70.

Still, there's concern that we might be weighing too heavily on public reputation levels, especially for past incidents. We might need to adjust the time decay of reputation scores. In the meantime, don't pee on your neighbor's lawn.

How was I to know she had a cam streaming everything in the middle of the night!—Tim

Zack blinked at the developer note. If those were accidentally slipping through, the app was even buggier than he thought. Still, it was another bug he could exploit. Apparently, bake sales would help his Reputation and public urination would not. He just needed to look through his public record and find whatever content DaEvo objected to.

A quick search through his social media feeds found a few

offenders. Angry posts from high school after his parents had died. Photos of partying from his college days. A few off-color jokes.

Zack deleted those and moved on to gaming forums. He may have occasionally had heated arguments with Armada scum and typed some things DaEvo would likely object to. He found the most obscene posts and deleted those as well, scowling as he did so. Stupid dating sim.

Then he moved to the internet at large, doing a search for both his name and his picture to take advantage of facial recognition. To his surprise, several news headlines popped up in the search.

Nature or Nurture: A Study on Second-Generation Business Owners

Moore Enterprises Continues to Thrive in Spite of Absent Owner

The Idle Rich: A Case for Higher Inheritance Taxes and Fixing Trust Fund Loopholes

The Idle Rich: How the Next Generation Spends Their Time

The articles were far from flattering, and they couldn't be deleted as easily as a forum post. He would have to put some effort in if he wanted to adjust his Reputation stats any further. Zack stared at a photo of him stumbling out of a New York bar during his college years. Was that how everyone saw him?

As Zack bit his lip, considering sending the magazine a rude email, DaEvo chimed and showed the fruits of his labor.

Success! Your Reputation has Improved
Reputation: +3.21
Your new Social Level is: 19.2
For improving your reputation, you have gained +30 non-essential electronic minutes

All that done, Zack eyed his gaming monitors. All that work and he'd barely gained any time from it. He still needed points if he was going to run dungeons tonight. How was he going to get them?

As if answering his question, DaEvo chimed.

Quest!
Level up your life by improving your physique. Eat a healthy lunch for bonus points.

- *Kale salad*
- *Oven Roasted Caesar Salad*
- *Fruit bowl*
- *Whole wheat BLT*
- *Avocado toast with pepper on whole grain bread*
- *...*

"I already ate lunch."

Your alpha test bug report has been logged.
Thank you for your help in making DaEvo a success!

But the quest remained. Apparently, DaEvo didn't care if he ate two lunches.

Zack sighed. The quest was repeatable and didn't involve getting a job, talking to reporters, or getting his nails done. How far would DaEvo let him exploit this particular bug? Only one way to find out.

He accepted the meal quest.

Quest Begun!
Eat a healthy lunch.

- *Kale salad*
- *Oven Roasted Caesar Salad*
- *Fruit bowl*
- *Whole wheat BLT*
- *Avocado toast with pepper on whole grain bread*
- ...

Zack grimaced as he read through the list. None of them sounded appealing. Especially since he had just finished half a pizza. Maybe it would be easier to go find another woman to speak to and earn time that way.

Except looking for random women hadn't gone well for him so far. He had been accused of stalking by Cassie and completely ignored by Kayla. Candace had insulted his PvP skills. So far, he had only managed to have successful conversations with Ashley, and he had no way to find her at the moment.

Granted, he had leveled up since his encounters with Cassie and Kayla. Maybe looking for a woman to talk to would go better this time. There would probably be women at whatever restaurant had healthy lunches. At the least there would be waitresses. He could double up on quest points by eating a second lunch and working in some conversations.

In the end, did he really have a choice?

"Fine. Where do I find these healthy lunches?"

DaEvo suggested a few options, and Zack blinked. The nearest one was in his building. Apparently, the condo gym also offered food. He could get points without leaving his building.

Score.

Zack waded through the boxes in his living room until he found the box marked with the Fit Life logo. He pulled it open and eyed the gym clothes suspiciously. They sat in the box, neatly folded and harmless. Just black shorts and a shirt. No big deal.

Zack rolled his eyes and put them on. They were surprisingly comfortable. Light, breathable fabric with just enough stretch. The online reviews hadn't lied about that. He added the limited edition socks, sneakers, and sweat bands, and looked at himself in the mirror so DaEvo could populate his stats.

Gym Stylish!
Style: 63.2

Zack stood straighter so his gut didn't stick out quite as much. He honestly didn't look bad. These clothes would be the perfect camouflage to infiltrate the gym without drawing negative attention like last time. He grinned at his reflection. There had been some high-level ladies at the gym. A lot of high-level ladies.

Maybe his Style upgrade would be enough to get them to talk to him. If he could have a few conversations with women whose scores were +50 over his, he would have no problem getting enough game time to run dungeons. He might not even need to eat the healthy lunch DaEvo kept pestering him about.

There was only one way to find out.

Chapter Thirteen

THE GYM WAS LESS CROWDED in the afternoon. Apparently, the serious fitness enthusiasts in Zack's building preferred to work out earlier in the day. He scanned the room, taking in the numerous cycling machines, the ellipticals and treadmills, and the weight racks in the back. He grinned when he saw Kayla. According to the pink hearts hovering around the room, she was still the highest-level woman in the gym. She was doing crunches on a machine, her forehead glistening with a light sheen of sweat.

Seeing her sweat reminded Zack about the lack of smell here. Unlike his high school gym, the condo had state-of-the-art facilities including air circulation, which meant it smelled pretty neutral except for a foresty smell. Maybe pine? Really, Zack had no clue. It was foresty.

Zack moved toward her, but DaEvo flashed a notification.

Quest!
Eat a healthy lunch.
Would you like to abandon your current quest for a conversation?
(Abandoning quest will delay gains in Physique attributes)
Yes/No

Zack glared at the notification, considering his options. If he gained Physique points first, he would earn more time from the conversation. And as much as he didn't want to do it, he would have to work on Physique eventually if he wanted to max out Style.

He would eat lunch as fast as he could and hope Kayla was still there when he finished. Zack used his gaze to let DaEvo know that he would continue the lunch quest, then he looked around in confusion.

"Where's the café?"

A pink arrow appeared in the corner of his glasses, pointing him through a doorway to another room.

Just how big was this place?

Zack walked through the door and found himself in a spacious room with large windows that showed a panoramic view of the surroundings. Sleek tables and chairs lined the space around the windows. A double door at the end of the room led to a counter with an open grill where people were ordering food cooked to order. Zack frowned at the long line. Kayla might be gone if he waited that long to get food.

He turned his attention to a self-serve counter in the middle of the room, covered with protein powders, supplements, and fresh fruits and vegetables. That was more like it. The other patrons were mixing their selections in blenders at the end of the counter. DaEvo popped up stats for the various items and the occasional combo bonus when someone blended something particularly high level. Zack grinned. The whole thing reminded him of a potion shop. Mix a few high-level ingredients to improve potency. Level up your Physique stats.

Why had no one ever told him it was that easy?

He grabbed a clean blender jar and lid from the counter, and a notification appeared on his OptiGlasses. The condo app asking for payment. Zack swiped to give consent and scanned the counter for the highest value items available.

"How do I know which ones to combine?"

DaEvo popped up a complicated nutrition chart suggesting that combo points were based on ratios of macro and micro nutrients being in perfection proportion to each other.

Zack stared at it, trying to make sense of it all, then noticed a new icon in the corner. Tutorial.

Now the app offered him that option? For a stupid smoothie?

Zack glared at the icon, hardly noticing that the other patrons were carefully moving around him as they chose their ingredients. Finally, he gritted his teeth and selected it.

Flashing arrows replaced the pink hearts. Zack selected the recommended ingredients without really looking at them. Kale, coconut water, protein powder. A few mysterious liquids that he assumed were vitamin supplements.

He finished it off with ice cubes and beets, put the lid on his blender, and crushed the ingredients into oblivion. The crunch and grind of his blender joined the symphony of those around him, setting Zack's teeth on edge. Even if they were high-quality blenders, they were still noisy.

When he was done, DaEvo chimed and offered stats for the sickly brown mixture Zack poured into a glass.

Grind-Up! ® Kale Vitamin Smoothie

A trademarked recipe from Grind-Up! and part of your balanced workout meal. Guaranteed to provide all your nutrition needs after a Grind-Up! light or medium workout. Would you like more nutritional information?

Reward for Consumption: +0.15

A few of the other patrons watched him out of the corner of their eyes. Probably wondering how he knew how to make such an effective drink. Or why he wasn't in better shape if this was the sort of thing he normally ate.

Zack grinned and selected an empty table with a view of the river. He was still annoyed that DaEvo was bossing him around, but maybe the Physique quests weren't so bad after all. This quest was repeatable. He could drink a bunch of these concoctions and level up without ever touching any exercise equipment. Zack settled back in his chair and took a drink.

He gagged. It tasted like dirt. Chocolate dirt with a faint hint of coconut and vomit thrown in for good measure.

DaEvo chimed.

Quest Begun!
Eat a healthy lunch.
Reward: +0.15 Physique

Zack swallowed, trying to erase the taste from his mouth, and stared at the glass. It looked bigger than it had a moment ago. Sickly strands of kale floated through the muddy mixture, reminding him of hair in a witch's brew. Maybe he should have abandoned this quest after all.

Zack heard snickering from the other side of the room. The bodybuilders who had run him away from Kayla were watching him from the corners of their eyes and hiding their laughter by taking drinks of their own smoothies.

They obviously expected him to fail. Just like the jocks who'd laughed at Zack in gym class. Why was it important to climb a damn rope? Unless you were a mountain climber, it was an utterly useless skill.

Well, he'd show them.

Zack took another drink and somehow managed to swallow it. Video games never mentioned how potions tasted, but come to think of it, some of them were made with some pretty nasty ingredients.

This was likely worse.

The bodybuilders nudged each other and laughed some more. DaEvo flashed a warning.

Reputation -0.1

Stupid fitness jerks. He would not let them damage his Reputation after he had taken the trouble to fix it! Zack took another drink and fought the urge to throw up. Think of the points. Think of Star Fury and running dungeons with his team. He had almost finished a quarter of the glass. Just a few more swallows.

He kept expecting to get used to the taste, but if anything, it got even more disgusting. The smoothie sat heavy in his stomach, competing for space with the pizza. Maybe eating two lunches hadn't been a great idea after all.

He took another drink. You got used to the dirt taste after a while. Kind of. It was the dirt mixed with fake chocolate that threw him off.

And the coconut aftertaste.

No, it was still disgusting.

Halfway there.

"It helps to put some fruit in," someone said.

Zack looked up in surprise as one of the bodybuilders sat in the empty chair at his table.

"Helps what?" Zack said, glaring and wishing the man would leave him alone in his misery. The last thing Zack wanted right now was company.

"The taste. I know it's tempting to cram every healthy thing in that you can, but if you don't actually like the taste, you'll never keep up the habit."

"I'll keep that in mind," Zack said with as much venom as he could muster, wishing the man would go away and leave him alone.

Instead, the bodybuilder grinned. "It's the same with the workouts. Find something you actually enjoy. This is a great facility. Not many buildings have gyms like this."

"Sure." Zack forced down another swallow and eyed the nearly empty glass. He was so close. He couldn't wait to get back to his condo and wash this down with a soda.

"You must be new," the bodybuilder said. "I haven't seen you around. You should come to boot camp Tuesday mornings. It's a great class."

"I don't think he's interested in boot camp," one of the other bodybuilders called.

"Hey, we all have to start somewhere. See you later, man. Hit me up next time you want a smoothie. We can swap recipes. I guarantee I can make you something better than that."

The man grinned and left the café with his buddies. In the corner of Zack's vision, he was surprised by a contact request. He hadn't even noticed the man use his tech to send it over. Must have been on one of his wearables. Zack glared after them. Stupid, smug, arrogant jocks thought they knew everything.

Zack looked at the clock on his OptiGlass screen. It had taken him almost thirty minutes to make and consume the smoothie. So much for getting through it quickly and getting back to speak to Kayla. He drained the rest of the glass, slammed it on the table, and fought the urge to vomit. Leveling up was so satisfying in video games. In real life, there was no symphonic music, no happy little dings. Just a lingering aftertaste.

Quest Complete!
+0.15 Physique

Zack stared at his OptiGlasses. Repeatable quest or not, that had been way too much trouble for that many points. He stood, fought back a wave of nausea, then walked into the workout room. This was stupid. What was the point of eating healthy if it made you feel worse?

The bodybuilders were nowhere in sight. Zack noticed a few other doors that probably led to classrooms or other weight rooms. How big was this place?

No matter. He just needed to find someone to talk to. Was Kayla still there? He filtered DaEvo's hearts to show only the highest-level ladies and grinned. She was still there, once again running frantically on the elliptical. Zack walked casually toward her machine, hoping to catch her eye and impress her with his stylish new outfit. Unfortunately, she didn't look up.

Zack casually claimed the elliptical next to Kayla's and ran. At least, he tried to run. The machine wobbled as he tried to use it, and Zack grabbed the handles for balance. He looked at Kayla. She glanced in his direction, nodded slightly to acknowledge Zack, then focused her gaze straight ahead.

"Hey, do you mind showing me how to use this thing?"

It was as good an opening as anything else he had come up with. Unfortunately, she either didn't hear him because of her headphones or she was completely ignoring him.

"You're really good at using it," Zack said, going for the compliment bonus. "I thought—"

"It helps if you type in your height so the machine can adjust for you," a female voice said behind him.

Zack looked down from his place clutching the handles and almost fell over again. Apparently, his stylish upgrade had paid off. The women were coming to him now!

Cheri Wells (Social Level 79)
Physique: 92
Style: 74
Reputation: 78
Occupation: 71

Zack scanned through the rest of Cheri's information. She was a personal trainer who also did bodybuilding competitions. He could have guessed that from looking at her. She was seriously toned. She could probably pick him up and throw him across the room without any effort.

Still, all those muscles gave her amazing Physique stats.

DaEvo flashed a warning that the conversation was lagging, and Zack realized he had been staring at Cheri's stats longer than he should have. "Right. Thanks."

"Let me show you around," Cheri said. "You'll get better results if you know how to use everything properly."

Sweet! She was into him! Zack grinned at Cheri and climbed off the elliptical. His stomach churned as he followed her around the gym. Zack pretended to be interested in the machines, adding just enough commentary for DaEvo to keep the conversation timer going. He hadn't managed to make her laugh yet, but Cheri had touched his arm a few times to correct his form as she showed him how to use the equipment.

"So that's all there is to it," Cheri said. "Of course, there's the free weight room in the back and all the classrooms, but I'd start out here first."

"Thanks."

The conversation seemed to be wrapping up. Zack glanced at the timer. It had been almost thirty minutes. A long conversation, all things considered, but he still had several hours to go until it was time to meet his team. He might as well keep her talking if he could. It was a shame the cleaning service hadn't cleaned his apartment yet. He could have invited her over and—

"We've got personal training available as well," Cheri said. "My schedule is open for the next hour if you want me to help you put together a fitness plan."

Wait, what? Zack looked at Cheri in confusion, then noticed the nametag pinned to her tank top.

Crap. She was a personal trainer here.

So much for him getting better at attracting women. Cheri had simply been doing her job and helping a fitness noob learn the ropes.

Whatever. At least he was getting points for it.

DaEvo chimed.

Quest!
Take a weightlifting class to unlock new Fitness and Physique quests

Zack glared at the notification. He didn't want to take a stupid weightlifting class. He didn't want to be here. But if he accepted it, he would get both conversation points and complete the quest. Game time and improved Physique.

He sighed. The smoothie had settled into his stomach like a rock, and he wanted nothing more than to go back to his bed and take a nap. But Cheri was waiting for him to decide, and DaEvo flashed a warning that the conversation was lagging.

"Yeah, sure," Zack heard himself say. "Let's do some weights."

He acknowledged the contract and liability waiver Cheri flicked over to him, slowing down long enough to scan through for any potential issues. After the incident with Phil, Zack wasn't about to just agree to a contract without reading. Luckily, this one was pretty simple. Just an acknowledgement of dangers from exercising—ha! he already knew exercising was dangerous—and a standard waiver. She had set him up for a ten-class trial period, which seemed high. But he could always skip it once he figured out how to get points another way.

Cheri grinned. "That's the spirit! I can program a routine directly into your OptiGlasses so the machines will adjust to fit your routine and you can do it without me tomorrow. You should see a notification in just a moment."

She retrieved a tablet from behind a nearby counter and typed something into it. A notification flashed onto Zack's OptiGlasses, and he swiped to download the gym's app so it could interface with the weight machines. Hopefully that wouldn't come back to bite him later. Attaching his door to a smart app had seemed innocent enough and look where that had led.

Still, nothing to be done about it now.

"Let's start with the seated press," Cheri said, leading Zack to the nearest weight machine. "We'll just need to figure out your starting weights to program the settings. Let's try five to start."

Zack looked around the gym at the other users. Even those who weren't in great shape were lifting quite a bit of weight. Certainly more than five pounds. His competitive side kicked in, and he spoke without thinking. "Five? I'm sure I can handle more than that."

"It's just a starting point. You'll build up over time."

Zack sighed and gripped the handles as Cheri instructed. It was probably better to go with the lower weight. He was trying to satisfy DaEvo, not actually get in shape. He pushed.

Nothing happened. The machine didn't move. Zack's stomach churned as he pushed harder.

Cheri frowned. "Let me just lower that a little."

Zack tried again. Cheri lowered the weight again. Finally, he managed to move the bar.

"One pound," Cheri said, tapping on her tablet. "Let's have you do two sets of ten reps since you're just getting into this."

With growing horror, Zack realized that Cheri meant for him to push the bar up again. What the hell? This was supposed to be a class, not an actual workout. She was just supposed to show him how to use the machines and program a routine, not actually have him complete it.

"I don't—"

"I can lower the weight to zero if it's still too heavy. The bar has weight, and even moving your arms without weight is a good start."

Cheri's offer seemed genuine, but Zack couldn't help suspecting some sarcasm in her tone. He glared at her and pushed the bar up again. And again.

This was the absolute worst. His arms were shaking, and his breath came in ragged gasps. He needed to get out of here. Now.

Tapping at the tablet, Cheri cast a critical eye over Zack's shaking limbs. "Maybe just one set on this one. Let's do some legs and call it a day. It's best to start off easy and add in extra sets gradually."

Zack's eyes grew wide with horror. Another machine? She honestly expected him to complete exercises on another machine?

"I should probably go," he said.

"You're sure? We haven't finished your routine yet."

DaEvo chimed.

Quit Current Quest?

Please note, there are no save points in this quest. You will be required to begin the quest from the start if you quit. Additional reputation losses may occur.

Yes/No

Damn. It. All.

Zack gritted his teeth and followed Cheri to the next machine. This one required him to squat and push himself back up.

Cheri looked over Zack's body with a professionally critical eye. "Let's start with no extra weight for this one. For squats, we'll want to make sure you get your form right before we do anything else."

She gave Zack a friendly smile. He fought the urge to reply that he didn't want to do it at all. But now that he had started this blasted quest, he needed to finish it. Then he could leave this hell-hole of a gym and never come back.

DaEvo chimed bonus points as Cheri lightly tapped Zack's shoulders to correct his form. He gritted his teeth as he squatted and lifted himself back up. This wasn't a big deal. No big deal at all. Just like getting out of a chair. He did that every day. Multiple times a day.

So why was he sweating so much?

Cheri made him do two sets on that machine. Zack's whole body trembled when she finally told him to stop.

"Nicely done," she said. "You'll want to add some cardio as well, but for now let's walk a few laps for a cooldown."

Zack nodded and followed her to the track. He caught a glimpse of himself in a mirror and winced. His hair was plastered to his head in a sweaty mess, and his face was bright red and splotchy. His legs trembled as he tried to match Cheri's pace during their time around the track.

"Great," Cheri said. "Now let's do some stretching."

She bent over, demonstrating the stretch. Zack tried to follow suit, and his stomach heaved. He made a frantic dash for the nearest trash can as the smoothie and pizza resurfaced.

DaEvo chimed.

Health Warning!

Purging is not a medically healthy form of weight control. Please see a licensed dietitian or follow DaEvo's tutorial on healthy eating habits for additional, medically appropriate weight control methods.

Points acquired for Physique Quest: Eat a Healthy Lunch! have been removed

Zack could only groan into the trash can and hope that his Reputation points didn't drop further.

Chapter Fourteen

ZACK WOBBLED BACK to his apartment on shaking legs. He collapsed into his gaming chair and looked over his base stats.

Physique: 35.2
Style: 58.5
Reputation: -16.99
Occupation: 0

He'd gotten nearly the same amount for the workout as having a proper night's sleep, which was rather ridiculous. About the only good thing was the conversation with Cheri. He'd gained enough time to run dungeons with his team tonight. He had been a little worried that her training him would invalidate her, but it seemed the app hadn't caught on. Yet.

Zack craned his neck and looked at his fridge. He was thirsty, but it was all the way across his apartment. That distance seemed immense at the moment. He leaned forward, trying to stand. His entire body protested, and he collapsed back into the chair.

Forget it. He didn't need a drink that badly.

He hadn't bothered to change out of the Fit Life clothes. DaEvo chimed with a hygiene warning that Zack swiped away. Most of the sweat had dried, and the Fit Life clothes wicked away moisture as promised. Much as he hated to admit it, the workout clothes were even more comfortable than his usual sweats and T-shirt. This was one DaEvo upgrade he might keep around once he got out of this ridiculous situation.

Zack spent the next few hours reading detailed blogs about the latest Star Fury update and looking for clues about the strange drones he had encountered a few days ago. Steve's use of drones to open their PvP match had suggested that something interesting was happening on the Armada side of space.

But the blogs, while detailed and informative, offered no clues about what Zack had seen. The latest update had included a few patches to fix bugs in older model drones, but nothing else that was helpful. It looked as though the developers had focused their energy on lasers and blasters this time around. That was a good way to ensure lots of fireworks at the tournament, especially since they'd made missiles the last round a touch too powerful. The increased range of the previous update had caused problems until everyone had switched to better point-defense.

The lasers and blasters, combined with hiring Zoe Cross as the face of the tournament, should help them boost ratings. Zack gave up on the drone question and turned his attention to inputting the new weapon data into his spreadsheet. He'd been putting that off and he really shouldn't have. He needed to work out a better balance for their ships, especially for the dungeons they had to run tonight. Even something as small as finding space for an additional shield booster could give him a major advantage if the numbers lined up correctly.

When he was satisfied that he had exhausted the existing resources, Zack forced himself out of his chair to grab dinner. His legs trembled as he navigated the canyon winding through the piles of laundry and unopened boxes. He cursed DaEvo, fitness, Cheri, smoothies, and the world in general as he hobbled around his kitchen, gathering supplies for the dungeon run.

DaEvo offered a quest to eat a healthy dinner, and Zack swiped it away as he retrieved the rest of the pizza from his fridge. He balanced as many energy drinks and sodas as he could on top of the box and made the perilous return journey to his gaming chair. He was sweating by the time he reached it, and his arms shook with the effort of hauling his spoils across the room. He tilted the box and dumped the cans onto a pile of clothes within reach of his gaming station, then sank into his chair.

He logged into Star Fury and ate the pizza as he checked his spreadsheet. His eyes darted from side to side as he programmed the shipyard with the various weapon configurations, verifying that his spreadsheet was correct at each point before saving the configurations. It'd make hot-swapping to a new configuration easier later on.

When he was done eating and shopping, Zack wiped his greasy hands on his FitLife shorts, grabbed an energy drink off the stack of laundry, and proceeded to make the series of hyperjumps to the dungeon.

His arms shook as he lifted the controller. Blasted fitness quests. What had he been thinking, doing a weightlifting class?

Zack directed his autopilot to take him to the rendezvous point and set the controller on his lap as he stretched his arms and tried to loosen them. He wasn't surprised when he was hailed by Greg the moment his friend came on.

"You go through the updates yet? I'm torn between two of the new blasters."

"Just finished. I'll send you my results."

Zack made sure to send over his recommendations to the team as a whole. Of course, they wouldn't take his suggestions at face value, but whatever they chose to go with, they'd send back and he'd put it into his sheet to ensure they had the right amount of DPS, defense, and webbing.

"Sweet," Greg said. "I'll try these out tonight and see how they do. How was your PvP?"

"Great. Took out an Armada maggot who was in the same gaming café as me. He almost got kicked out for whining after I beat him."

"I got crushed," Jenny said as she hyperjumped into their quadrant. "He had some kind of new laser that took out my drones as fast as I could spawn them."

"You need a tutorial in heavy artillery?" Greg said. "Or somebody to avenge you?"

Jenny scoffed. "I can avenge myself, thanks. I note you didn't do much better—your ranking's down."

"Bah! Just bad matchups."

"That's what losers always say," Faz said as his ship materialized.

A few moments later, Greg's appeared as he spawned in the local Corsair outpost.

It didn't take long for the group to gather now that they were all in-system. Zack turned off autopilot so he could guide his ship into formation. His arms trembled as he maneuvered, and he twitched, nearly crashing into Faz.

"Cripes, watch out!"

"Sorry!" Zack quickly corrected his course. He once again cursed Cheri, the gym, the weight machine, and DaEvo. He added Phil and the smoothie for good measure. He was better than this. He couldn't let them throw him off his game. "Ready?"

His teammates voiced their agreement, and Zack led the charge through the wormhole that would lead them to the dungeon. It started off easy enough—a few rogue patrols and AI ships that Jenny easily disabled with her drones. Zack fired up his laser cannon and blasted the disabled ships into oblivion. His thumb on the joystick slipped though, sweaty and tired, and he fired when he shouldn't have, clipping Faz.

"Watch it!"

"My bad!"

Faz corrected his course and engaged a rep, and Zack glared at his hands as if they had personally betrayed him. Which they had, in a way.

"Sorry. I'm a little shaky today."

"Well, pull it together," Faz said.

"Incoming!" Greg snapped.

Zack took a deep breath and wiped his hands on his shirt as

another wave of ships approached. He couldn't choke now. He couldn't let DaEvo win.

He let out a war cry and poured all his remaining energy into the battle. Time flew by in a rush of explosions and laser blasts. The final boss was an enormous space station. The team split up. Jenny and Greg kept the station defenses busy with drones and heavy-hitting artillery while Zack and Faz flew through the mobile defenses and landed critical hits on weak points.

Finally, the space station exploded in a glorious display of color. The sound roared through Zack's surround sound system, and he whooped in triumph. He tried to raise his hands in victory but gave it up when his muscles protested.

"Nice one!" Greg said.

Zack's OptiGlasses chimed. He expected it to be DaEvo, but instead the condo app popped up a notification.

A resident has filed a noise complaint. Please be mindful of other residents in the complex.

Zack rolled his eyes. He had been much louder than this before without a problem. Then again, the building constantly had a rotating group of residents as real estate flippers tried to make a buck and the developer rented out their furnished apartments. Maybe someone new had arrived. He waited for his teammates' chatter to die down before speaking.

"That was good, guys. Let's debrief. What formations worked best?"

Greg groaned. "Do we have to strategize now? Let us enjoy our victory for a bit."

"Sorry, no can do. I've got"—Zack cast a quick glance at his OptiGlasses—"forty-five minutes of game time left. We need to debrief and make a plan for tomorrow's session."

"Fine," Faz said. "Let's debrief so Zack can get to bed on time."

"Ha, ha. Let's try that formation we used on the third wave again. I think it might work better if Faz pulls more to the right."

The team quickly settled into training mode, running through the various formations and discussing gear until DaEvo chimed to let Zack know his time was almost up.

"Sorry, guys. Gotta go."

His teammates groaned.

"You're going to have enough time for the next tournament round, right?" Jenny said.

"Yeah, I've got it under control."

"You'd better," Greg said.

"Don't forget to brush your teeth," Faz said.

Zack logged off and tried to lean forward in his chair, but his muscles refused. He sighed. Repeatable quests weren't any good if he was physically incapable of repeating them. And he would rather run milk delivery missions than drink any more health smoothies or lift weights.

If he couldn't level up Physique, Reputation, or Occupation, he was back to Style. He scanned through the remaining Style quests. The haircut had been pretty painless, all things considered. He might as well complete more grooming quests and max out his Style points as much as he could.

Zack gritted his teeth and selected *manicure* from the offered quests. It would be fine. No one had to know.

He had a sudden vision of himself in a frilly pink nail salon and groaned. Forget that it would be filled with women he could talk to. It wasn't worth it. He would rather do another weightlifting session with Cheri than set foot in a nail salon.

Okay, that wasn't quite true. He would rather not do either ever again. But that wasn't an option.

Maybe it wouldn't be so bad. Zack selected the first nail salon from DaEvo's list and checked the pictures that accompanied the online reviews.

Crap, it was worse than he'd pictured. Pink with flowers everywhere.

He turned his gaze to the top to close the website and stopped. At-home appointments. Did that mean—

He quickly selected the option from the menu, and a wide grin spread over his face. The nail salon offered in-home appointments.

He could level up his Style without leaving his condo. Without leaving his gaming chair! That was more like it.

Zack booked the first available appointment without bothering to check the date or time and quickly scrolled through the rest of the grooming quests, scheduling as many in-home visits as he could.

Leveling up was easy again.

His condo app sent him a notification, and Zack frowned as he read it.

Thank you for choosing Sunshine Cleaning!
Your cleaning appointment is set for August 8 at 2:00pm.
At that time, weekly cleaning services will be resumed.

That was way too late! Before Zack could respond and demand that they move him up the list, DaEvo chimed.

Bonus Quest!
You are on a roll! Keep improving to maximize your gains.
Achieve an average social level of 25 for 3 days
Reward: +240 minutes Online Time

Zack did some quick calculations. The Style quests would get him close, but he would have to wear WesterNeon all the time. That would not work at all. If he wanted that bonus time, he would have to explore another category. He had already ruled out Occupation and Reputation as being too much work. Literally for the former. Physique was repeatable in theory, but not in practice.

Think. There had to be a way around this. Another way to game the system. Smarter, not harder. That was what he needed now.

Of the remaining categories, Physique seemed the easiest to scam. Pretending to work out seemed easier than pretending to get a job.

Zack's mind raced as he tried to find a way to cheat the system. DaEvo was brand new, so there weren't any fellow dating sim sufferers he could ask for help in beating it. But DaEvo wasn't the only thing keeping people from playing Star Fury. That incompetent moron at Star Fury support had mentioned exercise and work, not dating. If other gamers were locked out of their accounts because of intervention mode, other gamers would also be searching for hacks.

Zack opened his web browser with a flick of his eyes and went to his favorite Star Fury forum. As he suspected, there were no posts about DaEvo. That made sense. It was still in alpha, and even if other gamers had been tricked into similar situations, they were likely keeping quiet about it. Zack was certainly not willing to admit his situation in a public space full of gamers.

Hopefully he wouldn't need to.

Zack expanded his search to include any kind of intervention mode, and his screen lit up with responses. There were whole sections of the forum dedicated to cheating the intervention criteria. As Zack had suspected, his fellow gamers wouldn't give up Star Fury without a fight.

Man, a lot of people had been tricked into this. The forum was divided into categories by whatever vice the users were supposed to be overcoming. Jobs. School. Alcohol. Diets. Exercise.

Luckily, that last one seemed to be a popular sub-topic. Zack clicked through and scanned the posts for something useful.

Scurvyman55: *It's set to measure time I spend in the gym but doesn't actually track activity. Any way to fool the GPS into thinking I'm at the gym without actually going there?*

Anvil2time: *The time log has to be signed by a physical trainer. Is anyone here a licensed physical trainer willing to sign it for me?*

Harambelives1247: *It's connected to my heart rate tracker and measures movement and pulse. Any way to hack that?*

. . .

Zack selected the third one. That seemed to be what DaEvo was doing to him, since it asked if he was exercising every time his heart rate increased. All the smart gear had seemed like a good idea when he bought it, but now it just gave DaEvo unlimited access to his information.

Cactustrash8: *Heart Rate detectors are hard to fool, but not impossible. Watches are the easiest types to hack. I put mine on my dog like a collar and got points while she ran around the yard. All I had to do was throw a ball for her.*

B@conislife97: *Tried this with my dog, but he didn't move enough. My watch thought I was sick because the dog slept all day. :(*

Byronasaurusrex: *I'm having the same issue, but my dog runs around like crazy, so this worked for me! Thanks for the idea, Cactustrash8.*

Zack grinned. That was more like it. He skimmed the rest of the posts. Lots of users had cheated the system with their pets. Their wearable tech wasn't the same model as his, but the hack should still work.

There was just one problem. He didn't have a pet.

Well, he could fix that.

Chapter Fifteen

ZACK LAY FLAT on his back and opened his eyes, groaning as the morning beat him with its insufferable presence once again. Sunlight streamed through the windows, letting him know that he had slept in even later than usual. So why did he feel as if he had been run over by a steamroller?

He tried to sit up, and his muscles screamed in protest. He collapsed back onto the pillow and groaned.

What in the world had happened yesterday? He hadn't woken up this groggy and in pain since his party days in college.

Had he gone to a party? That didn't sound right. But something had obviously happened yesterday. Something big.

Music played through the surround sound system in his bedroom. Peppy, cheerful music that had no business being so pleased with itself so early in the morning. Zack tried to scratch an itch on his forehead, but his arm refused to move. Why wouldn't his arm move? Had he been drugged? Mugged and somehow crawled back home?

The music chimed again, and everything came flooding back.

DaEvo.

Physique quests.

Health smoothies.

Zack let loose a stream of profanity. It made him feel slightly better, but he wasn't sure it was worth the effort of speaking aloud. Everything hurt. He hadn't been this sore since... well, never. He had never felt this miserable in his life.

Stupid app.

DaEvo chimed again. Zack forced himself to roll over, retrieved his OptiGlasses from his bedside table, and put them on. A flood of hearts covered the screen, and he swore again as pink filled his vision.

Health Quest Complete!

You got a full night's sleep! Keep making healthy choices to level up your life.

+0.1 Physique

Fat chance. Healthy choices were the literal worst.

Zack rolled over again until he reached the edge of the bed. Somehow he managed to swing his legs around and pull himself up to a sitting position. His entire body trembled from the effort.

He flexed his fingers to make sure they still worked. They were all he really needed to play Star Fury. If worse came to worst, the app had accessibility features that would let him control his ship with his eyes via the OptiGlasses. It wasn't precise enough for him to perform as well as he did with his joystick and keyboard, but it was an option.

Zack swore again. He shouldn't be wondering if he would be able to use his hands the day before the next qualifying round of the tournament. He should be looking over the new weapon releases, adjusting his setup, and training with the new equipment until he knew how it performed inside and out.

His OptiGlasses chimed. Not DaEvo this time. Zack opened the condo app.

Your package has arrived and been delivered via drone.

This was followed by a picture of a box sitting outside his door, taken by the courier to show its delivery. A white box covered with purple paw prints. What had he—

Oh, right.

Zack grinned in spite of everything. DaEvo thought it was so smart, but he'd show it who was boss. He'd level up his Physique without lifting a finger.

But first he had to get out of bed.

With great effort, Zack pulled himself forward and extended his legs. They shook as he put weight on them. He stumbled forward and caught his balance on the wall. He was so tired, the smell in his condo didn't even bother him anymore. He hobbled through the condo, using furniture and stacks of clothing boxes for support until he reached the door and opened it with shaky hands. He frowned at the box. If he bent to pick it up, he might not make it back to an upright position.

He gently slid the box through the door with his foot. Something rustled inside as the box moved. Zack almost couldn't believe his plan had worked. Apparently, you really could order anything online these days.

Zack pushed aside boxes to clear a space and collapsed onto a bar stool by his counter. He slowly bent over to pick up the box, pulled tape off the flaps, and opened them.

Beady black eyes stared up at him. Zack blinked. The hamster didn't. It seemed to be sizing him up, deciding if it could take him in a fight.

The way Zack was feeling, it probably could.

He pulled the cage out of the box and carefully set it on the kitchen counter. The hamster was contained in a small enclosure attached to the larger cage by a tunnel.

Peppy music blared through his headphones, and an animated hamster appeared on Zack's OptiGlasses.

"Hi, I'm your new best friend! Pull the tab to let me wander free in my habitat!"

This was accompanied by an animation showing Zack where to pull on a tab and open the door from the small enclosure to the large one. He pulled, glaring at both the animated and real hamster as he did so. The animated hamster's voice was high-pitched and squeaky. Almost more annoying than DaEvo.

Almost.

"Thanks! Now I need a name!"

The animated hamster jumped up and did a flip around a blinking cursor on the OptiGlass screen. Zack stared at it, slowly realizing he was supposed to give the hamster a name.

"Veobos," he said, naming the first Star Fury planet that popped into his head.

"Yay! I love it!"

The animated hamster did another dance, and Zack gritted his teeth. Man, that was annoying.

"Now I'll show you how to take care of me!"

The animated hamster showed him how to fill the water bottle, put seeds in the dish, and pour fresh bedding in the bottom of the cage. Zack skipped through the presentation and did as it said as quickly as he could, then he hobbled over to the fridge and pulled out a slice of pizza. DaEvo chimed.

Physique Quest!
If you eat better, you'll feel better. Try a healthy—

Zack quickly swiped away the notification and stuffed half the pizza in his mouth. He wasn't falling for that again. He wasn't going anywhere near the gym with its poisonous potions and sadistic personal trainers.

He had another plan.

Zack eyed the hamster. It was running in its wheel, creating a soft whirring sound as its little feet pounded against the plastic. It looked like an active creature. Perfect. All he had to do was put his smartwatch on it, and he would get all the Physique points he needed.

Zack took off his watch and reached into the cage. The hamster dodged his hand and burrowed under the bedding.

"Hey! Get back here!" Zack grabbed a handful of bedding, hoping the hamster would come with it, and grinned when he pulled the rodent out of its cage. "Hold. Still."

The hamster kept wriggling. After some struggle, Zack slid the band around it and grinned as the fitness watch automatically adjusted to fit the hamster's girth. Finally, one of his technology upgrades was paying off.

The hamster bit Zack's finger as the band grew snug around its waist.

"Ouch!"

Zack dropped the hamster in surprise and gritted his teeth when he realized the creature had drawn blood. The hamster darted away and disappeared under a couch. Having staunched the bleeding with some quick pressure, Zack stared at his finger and wondered if hamsters got rabies.

DaEvo flashed a notification.

Workout Detected

Your elevated heart rate indicates you're working out. Would you like to start a workout quest?

Error! OptiGlasses Optical Fitness Monitoring has noted a significant (>10%) discrepancy between your eFitBand and OFM heart rate.

Zack lips pursed, then quickly flipped through the options. It didn't take him long to reset the options to choose his fitness band over the OFM when both were providing information. Of course, when the watch stopped working or provided no data, it'd just default back to the OFM.

Problem solved, Zack turned back to his quest. A quick confirmation and Zack received a new notification.

Workout Quest Started!
Keep it up to level up your Physique!

Zack grinned and leaned against the counter as he finished his pizza. He sniggered as he scrolled through the data he had collected from last night's dungeon runs.

Finally, something was going right.

Chapter Sixteen

Warning: Elevated heart rate detected. Please—

ZACK SWIPED AWAY the notification and returned to sorting through data. He had imported the combat logs from their dungeon run into his spreadsheet and was checking the numbers to see if any different weapon combinations could have shaved off some time.

Idly, Zack wondered if he could make a spreadsheet that ran the comparison of damage, shield sustainability, maneuverability, and engine recharge times for specific obstacles. It'd take some finagling, and he'd want to create sufficient input options to make it reusable for multiple dungeons, but he had one somewhat similar. Maybe if he...

DaEvo chimed.

Quest!
Don't forget to finish wooing Ashley Barnes by:
Complimenting her (Completed)
Asking about her interests (Completed)
Giving her a gift (In Progress)

"I'm not wooing her," Zack said.

But he stared at the notification anyway, considering it. He was bound to get bonus points for completing all three parts of the quest, and giving a gift was easy enough. He thought about Ashley. He didn't know a lot about her. She worked at Gord's but didn't game. She was smart. She had a little sister.

He considered purchasing a beginner's guide to Star Fury for her but dismissed the thought reluctantly. She would probably laugh in his face again, and DaEvo was unlikely to recognize the gift as a romantic gesture.

Then again, she did like to read. Maybe a book wasn't the worst idea. But if Ashley didn't want to read about Star Fury, what else would she want to read about?

"What on earth should I give her?"

Lucky for Zack, DaEvo chimed and offered a list.

Ladies love getting gifts. Consider one of the following:

- *Flowers*
- *Chocolate*
- *Jewelry*
- *Candles*

There was definitely something a little chauvinistic about that entire list. What about books? A good gaming console? Intimate lingerie?

Maybe he should just stick to the list.

Someone knocked on the door before Zack could look through the retailers DaEvo suggested. He started to stand up, but his legs refused to cooperate. Instead he unlocked the door through his app and called for the person to come in. That should be his first appointment of the day.

The manicurist stood in the doorway, his eyes wide at the sight of the cluttered apartment. Zack swallowed his disappointment that the manicurist was a man. He had assumed it would be a woman and he would be able to get conversation points as well. Perhaps he should have specified that when booking the appointment.

"You're Zack?" the man finally said.

"Yep. Let's get this over with."

"Um, yeah. Give me a minute to set up. You want to sit in that chair?"

"Yep."

The manicurist looked at the mess around the gaming chair and swallowed. "I'll need to clear a space, if that's okay?"

"Do what you need to do."

The man moved boxes and shoved aside piles of laundry to make space for a small folding table and rolling cart full of equipment. Veobos ran by, and the man yelped in surprise.

"My hamster," Zack said. He watched the manicurist a little warily, curiosity overtaking his initial apprehension. He'd never had a manicure before after all. "He likes to run free."

"Oh. Of course. I'm ready to start if you are."

His voice was a little strained. Zack wouldn't have thought that being a traveling beautician was particularly stressful, but maybe he was wrong.

The man sat on a stool and gestured for Zack to give him his left hand. As he filed down the nails, DaEvo chimed.

Quest Begun!
Get a manicure

Zack watched warily for a moment, but the man's actions didn't seem inherently evil. Zack turned his attention back to studying data from the dungeon run while the manicurist worked.

Warning: Elevated heart rate detec—

Zack swiped away the notification. He was comparing specs on laser cannons, trying to decide which one had the most power while putting off a low enough EMP that he could use it without setting off Jenny's drones. He thought he'd figured out the changes they'd made in the lasers to make the updates work the way they did. But of course, there was all the other issues—recharge rate, penetration, turret tracking speed, etc.

"Oh, I forgot, you ordered a pedicure as well. We should start soaking your feet."

Zack looked up and realized that the man had pulled out a small foot bath and was staring at Zack's feet. Honestly, he couldn't remember what he had ordered. He hoped DaEvo hadn't sneaked some manscaping into his order when he wasn't paying attention. It would be just like the app to do a thing like that. But the man just seemed interested in the pedicure for now.

Zack shrugged. "Yeah, sure thing."

He placed his feet in the tub and returned to checking stats while the man navigated the maze of boxes and trash to bring water for the small foot-soaking tub. When he turned it on, it bubbled and massaged Zack's feet. Honestly, this style quest wasn't so bad. Kind of relaxing, if he was honest.

Quest Begun
Get a pedicure

Zack opened up his message app to contact his team.

Zack: *Jenny, will this EMP level be too high for your drones? Anybody else see a potential problem with it?*

He attached a screenshot of the stats with his message and relaxed into his chair as he waited for his teammates to answer.

Jenny: *I'm at work, but I'll look through this on my break.*

Greg: *There's rumors someone is selling a new build for Armada seeker missiles that might be a problem.*

Zack: *A new build?*

Greg: *Yeah. He got it from an easter egg blueprint. Rumor is, it came out a while ago, but no one found it till now.*

Warning: Elevated heart—

Zack swiped away the notification and pressed his lips together to avoid laughing as the beautician worked on his feet. It tickled.

A red light flashed in the corner of Zack's OptiGlasses. He ignored it and went back to the chat.

Zack: *Crap. What makes you think it will be a problem?*

Greg: *Some kind of new cloaking device, but the Armada players aren't talking. I haven't been able to find the actual blueprint or missile stats yet.*

Jenny: *So if it exists, it's probably being saved for the tournament. Any idea how real the rumors are?*

Greg: *I'm asking around. If it's real, I should be able to confirm existence. No guarantee on stats though.*

Zack scrolled through forums as his teammates speculated. Whatever blueprints had been found, they either weren't a big deal or were being kept carefully under wraps. Either was possible. In addition to frequent new item releases, the Star Fury developers sometimes hid Easter eggs in dungeons or outposts. Special limited edition items or blueprints with instructions for modifying existing items.

If someone had found something like that, it could give them a major advantage in the tournament.

Was that how that Armada scum had landed a hit in the PvP round yesterday? Had he adapted the seeker missile build to his drone? If so, it'd explain why when he'd gone over his sensor logs later on, he still hadn't been able to find information on the drone.

Thankfully, downloading sensor logs and reviewing them, along with the blogs and his spreadsheet were all done on 'productivity' apps, rather than being considered non-essential electronics.

Zack: *We'll just have to keep our ears open. Jenny, any way you could use drones to boost our sensors and help fight the superior cloaking? It would be cheaper than upgrading each of our ships ourselves.*

Jenny: *I'll work on it. If we had specifications, it'd help.*

Zack: *Obviously. Just do your best. Both of you.*

Someone knocked on the door. Well, pounded really. Must be the facial treatment Zack had ordered. Hopefully this one was a woman so he could get some conversation points.

He opened his door with a swipe of his OptiGlasses. Two women wearing medical scrubs burst into the apartment, pulling a wheeled stretcher behind them. Zack and the manicurist stared at them with wide eyes, and Zack's heart pounded. Apparently, facial treatments were a little more involved than he had realized.

Still, he could get double conversation points. Not bad.

"Zack Moore?"

Zack nodded, and the women rushed over to him.

"Your OptiGlasses detected unusual heart rate activity and called us. How are you feeling?"

"What? I'm fine."

DaEvo started a conversation timer.

"Give us some space, please," the first woman said, brushing aside the manicurist.

DaEvo flashed.

Quests Interrupted: Style

Get a manicure

Get a pedicure

The woman took Zack's hand and checked his pulse.

"I said I'm fine! You know how buggy wearable tech is."

Your alpha test bug report has been logged.
Thank you for your help in making DaEvo a success!

Zack pulled his hand away and shoved it toward the manicurist. He needed those points.
DaEvo chimed.

Conversation Tip!
Yelling at your lady is not the way to win her over. If you're having an argument, try:

- *Listening to her*
- *Taking a deep breath*
- *Repeating positive affirmations until you calm down*

"Like hell I will."
"Heart rate is spiking again," the first paramedic said, showing a tablet to her colleague.
"What? How are you getting that information?"
Zack tried to stand so he could see the tablet. His legs gave out, and his feet slipped in the foot bath when he tried to catch his balance. He toppled forward and crashed into a pile of dirty laundry.
"Sir, are you all right?"
The paramedic hovered over him. Zack swatted her away and tried to stand. His arms shook, and he collapsed onto the floor.
"We'd better bring him in," the first paramedic said. "He's in bad shape."
"I'm fine! Get out of my condo!"
The second paramedic scrolled quickly through a document on a tablet. "He signed the medical consent form that comes with the smart tech. We can bring him in against his will if he's incoherent or in obvious distress."
"I didn't sign that!"

"Just relax, sir. We're going to take you to the hospital and get you checked out. Everything will be just fine."

"I said I'm fine!" Zack gathered all his strength and managed to stand. He tried to walk back to his chair, but his feet slipped, and he fell again. Apparently, there had been some kind of oil or soap in the foot bath. His lack of balance definitely had nothing to do with his shaking legs and sore muscles. Nothing at all.

"Get him on the stretcher," the first paramedic said. "He'll hurt himself if he keeps that up."

The second paramedic cleared a path through the room for the stretcher. As she moved a box, Veobos scampered out from beneath it and took refuge under the couch.

"Heart rate just spiked again."

"It's the hamster!" Zack protested as the paramedics strapped him onto the stretcher. He pulled a hand free and gestured wildly to the couch.

"You can go," the paramedic said to the alarmed manicurist. "He'll have to reschedule."

She caught Zack's arm in a firm grip. His arm trembled as he fought for his freedom.

Quest failed!
Get a manicure
Get a pedicure

"Don't leave! I need to finish the manicure! Let me go! It's the hamster!" Zack swore, one hand clipping the side of the paramedic's face as he struggled against the bands that held him on the stretcher.

"Should we sedate him?" the paramedic said, twisting away from the flailing hand and gripping it even tighter.

Zack tried to follow DaEvo's advice and took a deep breath. It didn't help, and the paramedic took advantage of Zack's relaxation to strap his arm tightly to the stretcher.

"This is ridiculous! The heart rate is from the hamster. I'm fine. I'll pay you whatever you want, just let me go!"

"Yeah, we'd better sedate him. He's delusional, and that heart rate is way too high."

Zack caught a glimpse of a needle out of the corner of his eye, then everything went fuzzy. DaEvo chimed.

Conversation Quest Failed
Reputation -0.25

Chapter Seventeen

ZACK OPENED his eyes and stared at the bright white lights above him, trying to figure out where he was.

Dead. That was the first thing that came to mind. He was dead and waiting to respawn.

No, that wasn't right. He wasn't playing a game. Even the most advanced VR games he'd played couldn't simulate something like his pounding headache and the itchy sheets. He glanced down and made a face at the putrid green sheets. He was in a bed somewhere. Somewhere not his room. For one thing, these were definitely not thousand thread count Egyptian cotton. If they were two thread counts, he'd be surprised. And worse, they were olive green.

Who chose olive-green sheets?

At least they matched the wall colors. Not that that was saying much.

A sharp ping sounded, and the white light above Zack's head transformed into a screen. A video of a smiling man in scrubs appeared on the screen.

"Hi, I'm Doctor Patel. Welcome to Compassion Hospital."

The hospital? What in the world had happened?

Memories flooded back. Women in scrubs. A needle. The manicurist packing up his cart and sprinting away at top speed.

"Just relax and lean back," the video of Doctor Patel said. "A nurse will be with you shortly."

Zack searched the room for a clock and swore when he found one on the bedside table. At least they'd gotten him a private room, but he had been unconscious for hours. Not how he had planned to spend his day. "I need to get out of here."

Doctor Patel smiled again. There was a pause while whatever program controlling the video processed Zack's words. Then the screen glitched, and another video of Doctor Patel appeared. "I'm sure you're eager to go home, but first we need to make sure your condition has stabilized. You were suffering from *dehydration*."

The recorded face switched briefly to a realistically animated version of Doctor Patel as it named the symptom. Zack rolled his eyes. He understood why hospitals wanted to use AIs and recordings to increase efficiency, but surely they could do a better job than this.

"How long will it take to check out?"

"I'm sure you're eager to go home, but first we need to make sure your condition has stabilized. You were suffering—"

"That's it. I'm out of here."

"I don't recommend that, *Zack*." The video glitched again as it switched to the animated version to say Zack's name.

Zack ignored Doctor Patel's continued warnings and sat up. His muscles still hurt, but whatever they had given him for dehydration had apparently helped the soreness. He looked at his bandaged arm and realized they had given him an IV at some point.

Ugh.

Zack searched the room until he found his clothes, and in the bathroom, he quickly changed out of the hospital gown. Back in the room, the recording of Doctor Patel was playing pre-recorded messages telling Zack to settle down and get back into bed until the nurse came.

He tossed the crumpled hospital gown onto the bed and gave a sarcastic salute to the digital doctor. He wished he could saunter out of the room, but his legs were still shaky from the workout.

As Zack limped down the hall, a nurse looked at him suspiciously.

"Leg day at the gym," he said, trying to sound casual. "Just visiting my grandma."

She rolled her eyes and hurried past him. Zack quickened his pace as soon as she turned the corner. How in the world did he get out of here?

He followed a trail of exit signs until he came to a wide double door that marked the end of whatever hospital wing he had been in. Zack pushed through it and sighed with relief. That much closer to freedom.

Pristine white hallways gave way to colorful murals of flowers. Zack blinked at the painted walls. Maybe he was dead after all. Maybe this was the trippy part of the afterlife.

He kept following the exit signs until he reached a circular reception desk painted to look like a giant red mushroom with white polka dots. Weird, but the receptionist looked normal enough in her pale pink scrubs. She was on the phone but waved to Zack to let him know she'd be with him when she finished.

Zack stared at the mushroom desk a moment longer, then noticed the sign above the receptionist's head.

Pediatric Wing

Oh, thank goodness. He wasn't dead. Just lost in some well-meaning idiot's attempt to cheer up sick kids. Zack understood the idea behind decorating the wing, but did any child really want to be greeted by a woman sitting behind a giant mushroom?

A plaque on the wall caught Zack's eye.

Redecorating initiative sponsored by the Moore Medical Trust.

. . .

Crap. He was the well-meaning idiot responsible, and he had just given them twice as much money for projects like this. Phil was right. The hospital needed oversight. Were all the hospitals the company sponsored like this? They could have at least used the money to get some solar panels and reduced the cost of running all these expensive machines.

"Sorry about that. Can I help you?"

The receptionist smiled at him, and Zack couldn't help thinking of the Cheshire Cat. Or was it the caterpillar that sat on the mushroom? Whatever. It was weird. DaEvo popped up stats and started the conversation timer, but Zack swiped them away. For once, he didn't care about the points. He just wanted to get out of there.

"Yeah, I'm a little lost. How do I get to the parking lot?"

"Down that hallway. Take the second door to the right and go down the elevator."

Zack nodded his thanks and limped in the direction the woman pointed. He was almost out. With any luck, he would make it to the elevator without meeting anyone else.

Luck was not on his side. Zack rounded the corner and collided with a woman. His legs nearly gave out, and he leaned on the wall for support as she bent over to retrieve the tablet she had dropped. When she stood, DaEvo populated stats for her.

Cassie Jones (Social Level 65)
Physique: 81
Style: 59
Reputation: 34
Occupation: 87

She looked familiar. Why did she—

Cassie's eyes widened with recognition at the same time Zack remembered where he had seen her.

Crap. This was bad.

"You?" she said. "What are you doing here?"

"Um, visiting someone?"

"What room? What's the patient's name?" Cassie brandished her tablet, ready to check his story.

She was dressed for work in navy scrubs and had her dark hair pulled back in a tight ponytail. It was no different than what the rest of the doctors and nurses wore, but somehow it looked intimidating on her. Zack edged away from the wall. He could see the elevator behind her. The way to freedom. He just needed to outrun her.

His legs shook, and he remembered the way Cassie had sprinted effortlessly around the track. Outrunning her was unlikely.

Think, Zack, think. There had to be a way out of this.

"I knew it," Cassie said. "You really are stalking me. Don't move. I'm calling security."

The elevator opened, distracting them for a moment. Zack stared longingly at the sliding doors. Freedom was so close. He just needed to get around Cassie.

The only person in the elevator stepped out, and Zack caught a glimpse of familiar auburn curls. "Ashley?"

"Zack? Hey! Good to see you!" Ashley smiled. She wore tight jeans and a flower print shirt that was way more flattering than her Gord's uniform.

DaEvo agreed. It started a conversation timer and flashed her stats.

Ashley Barnes (Social Level 52.5)

Physique: 71
Style: 52
Reputation: 61
Occupation: 26

Zack's gaze lingered on Ashley for a few moments. Those jeans were worth way more than five extra points in his opinion. They looked good. Really good.

Cassie looked from Zack to Ashley. Zack sauntered over to Ashley's side, hoping to give the impression that they were together. Maybe it would fool Cassie. Please let it fool Cassie.

The doctor's smart watch flashed red. She read the notification on it and swore. She looked at Zack and Ashley and opened her mouth to say something. The watch flashed again, and she shook her head and sprinted down the hallway.

"What was that about?" Ashley gave Zack a questioning look.

He shrugged. "No idea. I was just leaving, and she started asking me all these questions."

"I wouldn't take it personally. Doctor Jones is militant about protecting her patients' privacy."

"Right." For the first time, Zack noticed the small vase of flowers in Ashley's hands. She had a heavy-looking tote bag slung over her shoulder and was struggling to balance everything. "You're visiting someone?"

She nodded, and pain flashed across her face. "Amber just woke up from her surgery. My grandma was sitting with her, but she needs to go home and get some sleep."

"Oh."

Zack didn't know what else to say. It hadn't occurred to him that Ashley had a life outside of Gord's. Of course, the other cashier had said she'd had a family emergency. Could that have been her little sister's surgery?

"Who are you visiting?" Ashley asked, walking down the hall.

Zack cast a quick glance at the elevator then followed her. He had almost completed the conversation quest. He might as well get a few points while he could. It wasn't as if talking to Ashley was hard. "No one. I came in for a checkup and got lost on my way out."

Ashley laughed, and Zack swiped away DaEvo's bonus notification. "Yeah, this place is a maze. You can't mistake this wing for anywhere else though." She gestured to a neon yellow butterfly painted on the ceiling. "The face on that one always creeps me out."

Zack looked more closely at the face and shuddered. Yeah, they needed someone competent to oversee the medical trust. "You're right. That thing is going to give kids nightmares."

"That one's not much better." Ashley pointed at another butterfly, and her bag slipped off her shoulder as she moved.

Zack caught it without thinking, and pain shot through his arm as his tired muscles strained. Actions like that never hurt in video games. He glared at the bag as if personally offended. "That thing is heavy!"

Ashley laughed. "Textbooks. Here, I can take it."

She reached for the bag, but Zack shook his head and slung it over his shoulder. His muscles screamed in protest, but he ignored them.

Ashley gave him a look. "Seriously, I can carry my own bag."

"You're carrying the flowers."

"Yes, and obviously I can't carry both because flowers are so heavy."

She arched her eyebrow in a challenge. Zack tightened his grip on the bag, although he wasn't sure exactly why. Ashley stared at him for a moment, then shrugged.

"All right, suit yourself. We're here anyway." She gestured to a room door painted with a bright purple flower with the number 412 in the middle of a petal.

Zack stared at it, feeling awkward. "I should go."

"You can come in and say hi if you want. Amber would love to thank you in person for letting her use your room at Gord's."

She opened the door and motioned for Zack to enter. He peeked into the room. Amber lay on the hospital bed, covered in wires and surrounded by monitors. She was asleep, as was the elderly woman slumped in the chair next to her bed. The room had apparently not been included in the redecorating initiative. It was beige and bare. The tiny bouquet in Ashley's hands would do little to brighten it up.

Zack's throat went dry. He hadn't been in a hospital room since his parents—

The memory was hazy. Barely a memory at all. More of an emotion that he thought he had buried so deep it didn't exist anymore. But it was resurfacing now like a zombie determined to tear him to shreds and eat his vital organs.

"Hey, are you okay?" Ashley said. Her voice had dropped, her eyes narrowed as she regarded Zack.

"Yeah. Sorry, I've got to go. Looks like they're asleep anyway."

Zack shoved the bag into Ashley's hands and hurried away. He passed the butterflies on the ceiling and made it to the elevator without running into anyone who might question his presence there. As the elevator descended, Zack leaned against the wall and swiped away DaEvo's notifications for the successful conversation quest, as well as a few messages from his team. He couldn't deal with it right now. Not with any of it.

The doors opened, and Zack walked across the lobby to the revolving doors that marked the exit. Sunlight beckoned, promising him freedom from this dreary place. He would have sprinted if his legs weren't shaking so badly.

A flash of color caught his eye, and he looked to the side. A gift shop. The vision of the beige hospital room flashed through his mind, and he stopped walking to stare at the flower arrangements and brightly colored balloons bouncing in the window. He might question the wisdom of painting hallways with demonic butterflies, but real flowers would go a long way to brightening up a room.

Zack turned away from the exit and hurried into the shop.

"Can I help you?" An elderly man in a striped apron smiled at him.

Zack swallowed. "Yeah, can you deliver flowers to one of the rooms?"

The man laughed. "That's why we're here! What room?"

"412 in the children's wing."

The man tapped the number into his tablet. "Got it. What would you like to send?"

That was a good question. Zack looked around the room. Most of the flowers were pretty standard arrangements. They would add some color to the room, but he could do better than that. What would a kid like?

He selected a giant teddy bear holding a bright bouquet of daisies and added some balloons for good measure. He saw a single Star Fury balloon hiding in the corner. Zack grabbed it and tied it into the bouquet.

"Got it," the man said, grinning. "Just give me a minute to send the bill to your OptiGlasses. Our system can be temperamental." He tapped the tablet.

DaEvo popped up a notification while Zack waited.

Quest!

Don't forget to finish wooing _Ashley Barnes_ by:

- *Complimenting her (Completed)*
- *Asking about her interests (Completed)*
- *Giving her a gift (In Progress)*
- *Consider one of the following:*
- *Flowers*
- *Chocolate*
- *Jewelry*
- *Candles*

Zack glanced around the room. The gift shop didn't have any jewelry, but it did have flowers, chocolate, and candles. "Hang on, I want to send something else."

Sending all three seemed a bit excessive. Zack selected a bouquet of sunflowers and stared at it. How would DaEvo know that he was giving this to Ashley? He wrote a quick note on the card so DaEvo would give him points.

To Ashley, From Zack

"Very heartfelt message," the man said.

Whatever. Zack paid for the flowers with a swipe of his Opti-Glasses. Apparently, DaEvo trusted the shop to deliver the flowers, because it chimed as soon as his payment went through.

Quest Complete!

Congratulations! You have successfully wooed Ashley Barnes!
+30 minutes for Giving her a Gift
+180 minutes for completion of Relationship Bonus Goals!
Take things to the next level by asking her out!

New Relationship Quest!

Ask Ashley Barnes out!

Spend some one-on-one time with your special lady by asking her out on a date. Completing this quest will unlock Relationship Milestone bonuses and additional quests.

A successful date will unlock the Lovemeter and unlimited access to non-essential internet privileges.

Zack ignored the cheesiness of whatever the "Lovemeter" was and stared at the last sentence of the notification

Unlimited access.

One date would unlock unlimited access to Star Fury.

But first he had to make the date happen.

Ask her out. That was the point of this whole thing, wasn't it? To ask someone out and get a girlfriend? He just needed to play along with DaEvo until he had satisfied the ridiculous app and could get back to sweatpants and Star Fury. Simple.

So why was his throat dry?

Zack checked for a tutorial, but apparently, that hadn't been added yet.

Ask her out. It wouldn't be hard. He could catch her at Gord's tomorrow and do it then.

Except she might not be at work tomorrow. What if she took another personal day to be with Amber? Zack pulled the card out of the flower arrangement and scribbled his phone number on the bottom.

The old man grinned. "That's more like it. You want to add a few roses to that bouquet? No extra charge."

The man winked, and Zack felt his face flushing. This was ridiculous. Stupid DaEvo and stupid nosy hospital employees. Ashley probably wouldn't even call him.

He turned toward the hospital lobby to hide his red face from the grinning cashier. A nurse was pushing a young boy in a wheel-chair toward the elevator. Zack's stomach churned. The kid's face was pale, and he looked depressed. Hopeless. What was wrong with him?

In the end, what did it matter?

Was the boy going back to a cheerless beige room like Amber's? Did he have family to come visit him? From the look on his face, things were pretty bleak.

Zack turned back to the man. "I'll take a balloon and bouquet for every room in the children's wing."

The man gaped. "Every room? Son, there are four hundred—"

"You heard me." Zack opened his credit app and sent his credentials to the hospital's payment system. "Charge this when you've got the amount figured out."

He gave the credit app advance permission for the charges, OptiGlass's version of prepaying. The old man sputtered in surprise, and Zack quickly left the hospital.

It was hot as hell outside, but he would rather deal with that than the cold, stark lobby. He ducked under a tree and waited for the car he had called to arrive.

His OptiGlasses chimed. Phil.

Zack rolled his eyes and answered the video call. "Yo."

"Twenty thousand dollars on flowers?"

Zack leaned against the tree and made a mental note that Phil's eyes could bug farther out of his head than previously thought. Interesting. Maybe it was a genetic defect. He should probably go to the doctor and get that checked out.

"First the clothes, now this? How the hell do you spend twenty thousand dollars on flowers? If you're trying to impress a woman, maybe buy her a car next time! It will cost less and last longer!" Phil's ranting turned into an incoherent sputter.

Zack watched in amusement. He hadn't seen his guardian this unsettled since his college days.

"And the hospital? You were admitted to the hospital, and then you sneak out? They just sent me a notification that you're missing from your room. Do you even know what that looks like? It's like your eighteen again!"

Zack shrugged. "I'm fine. There was never anything really wrong with me, so I checked myself out. Just smooth it over with them, will you?"

"Checked yourself out? You can't just check yourself out of the hospital. They said your heartbeat was erratic and you were dehydrated. That you were behaving irrationally and couldn't even stand on your own."

"I'm standing now."

Zack's car arrived. He climbed in and confirmed his address with the driver before continuing the conversation.

"It was nothing, Phil. Just a life hack gone wrong. Side note, the children's hospital wing is hideous. You're right. We need someone overseeing that project."

"I want you to get a checkup. A full physical. And I want an explanation about the flower bill. I meant what I said about the budget clause."

Zack sighed. "I sent flowers and balloons to everyone in the children's wing. Some of the kids didn't have anything in their rooms, and it was depressing. Satisfied?"

For once, Phil was silent. His eyes returned to their normal place as he stared at Zack. "You— were in the children's rooms? You—"

The OptiGlasses chimed.

Incoming call. Ashley Barnes

Zack's heartbeat quickened, and he tried to keep the excitement from his voice as he said, "Sorry, man, getting another call. Talk to you later."

Phil sputtered as Zack hung up to take the other call.

"Hello?"

"Hi, Zack? It's Ashley."

Zack's stomach caught in his throat. The call was voice only. Apparently, Ashley had a regular phone rather than OptiGlasses or a newer model that supported video. That was good, because he was pretty sure his face had turned red again.

"Oh. Hey, Ashley."

DaEvo chimed.

Relationship Quest!

Ask her out!
*Spend some one-on-one time with your special lady by asking her out on
a date. Completing this quest will unlock Relationship Milestone
bonuses and additional quests.*
*A successful date will unlock the Lovemeter and unlimited access to non-
essential internet privileges.*

Zack swiped away the notification and wiped his hands on his
pants. For some reason, his palms were sweating.

"Hey, I just wanted to say thanks for the flowers. That was really
sweet of you."

"Yeah. You're welcome."

Lame! He could do better than that! Zack took a deep breath
and glared at the pink heart icon in the corner of his OptiGlasses.
This was his chance. Get a girlfriend. Win the game. Get back to
Star Fury.

Ask her out.

"Yeah, so, anyway," Ashley said, trying to fill in dead space.

Zack gritted his teeth. He could do this. For Star Fury. "Hey, do
you want to go out sometime?"

The car driver caught his eye in the rearview mirror and
grinned. Zack smiled back weakly.

Ashley was silent. Crap. She was going to say no. Now things
would be awkward between them, and he'd have to find another
woman to do conversation quests with, and—

"Yeah, I'd like that."

"Really? I mean, um, cool!"

The driver flashed him a thumbs-up.

Zack grinned back. "How about tomorrow?"

The sooner he completed this quest, earned unlimited game
time, and ended his ridiculous affiliation with DaEvo, the better.

"I work tomorrow," Ashley said. "Then I promised to stay with
Amber in the evening. And I have to study. Sorry, I—"

"Your lunch break then," Zack said. No way was he letting

something as stupid as a job get in the way of this date. "I'll bring you lunch. What do you like?"

After a pause, Ashely said, "Yeah, okay. Yeah, that will work. Um, whatever you like is fine. Just no Space Rations?"

Zack laughed. Space Rations were the standard-issue MREs given to Armada pilots in Star Fury. According to game lore, they were disgusting. The company behind Star Fury had sold some real-life versions as a limited edition promotion a few years ago. Zack had bought some. They had indeed been disgusting. A notification flashed up and Zack dismissed it, focused on the conversation.

"You've been reading up on Star Fury!" he said.

"No, just listening to the gamers in the common room. Hey, I've got to go. See you at noon tomorrow?"

"It's a date."

Zack hung up the call and slumped back into his seat. He had done it. He had a date. After tomorrow, he would be a free man. The driver gave him another thumbs-up as they reached his condo.

Zack smiled back and walked slowly to his room. Very slowly. His legs were trembling with adrenaline as well as fatigue now. Thank goodness all this would be over tomorrow afternoon.

He reached his apartment and collapsed into his gaming chair. Dirty laundry, boxes full of clothes, and a puddle in the middle of his floor from the interrupted pedicure surrounded him. The hamster darted past Zack's feet. The watch had fallen off it at some point. He would need to track that down later.

But right now, he was basking in his success. DaEvo was still flashing a pink heart in the corner of his OptiGlasses, so Zack pulled up the notification he'd received earlier.

Achievement Unlocked! Get a Date!
+360 minutes for unrestricted internet privileges

Relationship Milestones!
You have unlocked Relationship Milestones. Gain bonus points and progress your relationship by completing any of the following:

- *first significant physical contact*
- *in-depth exchange of history*
- *your first kiss*
- *schedule a second date*
- *take her out to an exciting and memorable event*
- *your first [Dev Note—are we even allowed to suggest this? Ask Legal]*
- *become an [#select_variable: relationship type: exclusive;primary;secondary; pair-bonded; metamour]*
- *get engaged*

Each milestone completed will fill your Lovemeter and increase your progress in the game.

Engaged? DaEvo was apparently not messing around with these relationship quests. But none of those mattered right now. He had a date.

A date that had already given him significant game time. Add that to his repeatable conversation points and a bonus for giving the gift, and he was set.

Zack logged into his Star Fury account. His teammates had already logged in and sent him rendezvous coordinates. He set a course to join them. He had more than enough time to train. More than enough to game all night.

Things were finally looking up.

Chapter Eighteen

Quest Failed!
Get a good night's sleep.
Physique -0.1

ZACK GLARED at the debuff notification on his OptiGlasses and silenced the blaring alarm clock app. Yeah, he had stayed up late, but not any more than usual when he was training with his team. Why had he set the alarm to wake him so early?

He turned off the alarm, buried his face in his pillow, and went back to sleep. DaEvo's cheerful chiming woke him what seemed like a few minutes later. He swore as he put on his OptiGlasses so he could silence the notification.

Relationship Milestone in Progress
First Date with Ashley Barnes

The date!

Zack sat up in bed, groaned, and fell back against his pillow. He was still sore from that stupid Physique quest. If anything, he felt worse today.

He checked the time on his OptiGlasses. He had set an alarm for ten in the morning to give him plenty of time to get ready and fulfill any bonus quests that DaEvo popped up. But since he had slept in, he only had forty-five minutes to prepare.

No time to waste.

Zack opened the quest notification and read through it as he brushed his teeth. He wasn't taking any chances with this. Everything had to be perfect. Given how buggy DaEvo was, there was no telling what might set it off.

Quest! Relationship Milestone: First Date

The first date is your only chance to make a first impression. Make sure your style is on point and you do something special to make it memorable.

Crap. How was he supposed to do that when he was just bringing her lunch at work and had overslept? Maybe he should have waited until he had time to do something really special.

No. This needed to happen now. He could do this.

Quest!

Breakfast is the most important meal of the day. Eat a healthy breakfast to level up your Physique.

Zack glared at the notification. Fat chance. He had learned his lesson about health food yesterday. He opened his fridge to grab a slice of pizza and frowned. The fridge was empty. He didn't even have an energy drink left.

Right. He had eaten everything last night while gaming.

"No time for that anyway," Zack said.

DaEvo chimed and offered a list of healthy options near him, including the gym café.

"Fat chance."

Eating healthy is easier than ever! You don't even have to leave your room!

That was followed by an advertisement for the café's delivery service. All the options listed looked much more appetizing than the smoothie he'd had yesterday, but Zack still wasn't interested. He swiped away the notification.

"Why are you so pushy today?"

Congratulations! You have been upgraded to DaEvo 1.2.0a. Our developers are constantly working to improve the system and make it more effective.

"I have a date, okay? After I get through this, I won't need your stupid quests anymore."

It's important to keep improving yourself even when you're in a relationship. Keep leveling up your life to get better results!

That was followed by an animated emoji showing a man lifting weights.

Zack rubbed his forehead, trying to push away the headache he felt building. "Will you shut up if I order something?"

DaEvo remained silent. Zack took that as a yes and used the condo's app to order the first breakfast item on the menu and have it delivered. Then he pulled off his OptiGlasses and took a shower. Yesterday's workout, hospital incident, and gaming session had not done his hygiene any favors. As DaEvo had happily reminded him. The only good news was that somewhere during his hospital stay and the ruckus with the ambulance, the condo had found out about his leaky faucet. They had sent someone in to fix it, leaving his floors dry for once. It was surprising how such a little change made the entire showering experience so much better.

He heard a scratching in the living room. The hamster had found a pizza crust by the gaming chair and was gnawing on it. Zack poured some seeds on the floor in case the pizza crust wasn't enough and set a bowl of water on the floor for good measure. He'd catch the thing later, but right now, he had more pressing matters.

His stomach growled, and he wondered if there were any more

pizza crusts around. As if answering his question, the condo app chimed to let him know his food was waiting outside his door.

His health food. That was how they got you. Starving you until you were short on time and desperate.

Zack retrieved the tray of food from the hallway and studied it suspiciously. It looked harmless enough. At least, the omelet filled with grilled vegetables did. The glass of green juice was suspicious.

Zack took a bite of the omelet and chewed experimentally. Not disgusting. But was he missing some kind of trick? There had to be a catch. He finished the omelet almost without realizing it and stared at the glass of green juice. DaEvo hadn't offered a notification, so apparently he had to finish everything on the tray to get any points.

It seemed a shame to leave the quest unfinished. It bugged him that it wasn't done, like an unfilled cell in his spreadsheet. And really, what kind of min-maxer would he be if he didn't finish what he'd started?

It was just like his dad had said, "If you're going to start something, you'd better..." Zack pushed the thought aside and focused on the plate.

Right. Juice. He picked up the glass, fingers slipping a little on the condensation, and raised it to his lips.

It wasn't disgusting either. He wouldn't exactly call it good, but it wasn't as disgusting as the smoothie. A little chunky, but it was cool and only left a bit of a bitter aftertaste. Zack took a deep breath and drained the glass.

DaEvo chimed.

Quest Complete!
Eat a healthy meal.
Physique +0.2

Zack grinned in satisfaction and turned his attention to choosing his clothes. The boy next door look had worked well with Ashley before, so he dug through the boxes stacked around his living room until he found jeans and a polo shirt. He added the limited edition sneakers and frowned. He was missing out on jacket and accessory points.

But it was way too hot to wear a jacket. Zack slashed open more boxes, piling clean clothes on top of dirty ones until he found a hat he had bought on a whim during his shopping spree. It was a baseball cap with the Corsair skull and crossbones on it. Apparently, limited edition or designer or something. Whatever. It added Style points.

Zack checked the time and swore. A quarter to twelve. Had he really spent half an hour getting ready?

Stupid DaEvo.

He adjusted his cap and shook his head. Just a little longer. Get through the date, then he could burn the clothes and get back to sweatpants and Star Fury.

He might burn the OptiGlasses while he was at it. Maybe those luddites who refused to wear smart tech had a point.

Zack called a ride and searched the map for takeout restaurants near Gord's. He settled on a Chinese place with good reviews and ordered a few things he could pick up on the way. DaEvo chimed, and Zack gritted his teeth.

Relationship Milestone: First Date
Suggestions
Keep it casual but make it special. Try bringing your lady a gift or some other token of your affection.

Another gift? Didn't the food count?

Apparently not. DaEvo didn't offer any points when Zack stopped by the restaurant to pick it up. It was one of those hole-in-the-wall places that catered to the lunch crowd with takeout food more than a sit-down experience. Worn metal-and-plastic chairs pushed up against the store window and a long counter met Zack's gaze as he waited for his order.

He looked at the clock. Only five minutes until noon. There wasn't time to stop anywhere else and buy something. Zack's eyes fell on a display of items at the end of the counter. That bamboo folding fan was pretty. Would Ashley like it?

Even if she didn't, it would earn him bonus points with DaEvo.

"How much for the fan?"

The cashier, a gangly kid who looked as if he was still in high school, gave Zack a weird look as he finished packing Zack's order, tossing in fortune cookies and chopsticks. "It's just there for decoration."

"Okay, but can I buy it?"

"I'll have to ask the manager."

Zack tapped his fingers on the counter, running through weapon fire sequences to relieve stress. He was running out of time. "I'll give you a hundred dollars."

The cashier's eyes widened. "I can't just—"

"Two hundred."

"What? Yeah, all right."

Zack paid the extra with his OptiGlasses, grabbed the bags of food and the fan, and hurried out of the restaurant.

DaEvo chimed.

Relationship Milestone: First Date begins in 1 minute
Don't be late

Chapter Nineteen

HE WAS LATE. Zack blamed the traffic, although it wasn't any worse than usual. He was late, and DaEvo wouldn't stop nagging him about it. Zack grabbed his bags and tipped the driver with a swipe of his eyes. A wave of heat swept over him as he stepped out of the car.

Hygiene Levels Lowering
Consider taking a shower and changing into a clean pair of clothes.

"Really? You've never bugged me about that before."

Congratulations! You have been upgraded to DaEvo 1.2.0a. Our developers are constantly working to improve the system and make it more effective.

Zack swore as he rolled his eyes and swiped away the notification. It looked as though the new version included a lot more nagging. Just what he needed in his life.

Anyway, he wasn't that sweaty, and there was no time to change.

What if Ashley thought he had ditched her? What if DaEvo didn't count the date because he was late?

He burst into Gord's in a flurry of takeout bags. Ashley waved at him from the counter, where she was checking a customer into a room. Zack stood by the door and wiped his palms on his jeans, waiting for her to finish. Oddly enough, the sweating hadn't stopped now that he was in the air-conditioned interior. His palms, in particular, refused to stay dry. Maybe he should take Phil up on that physical after all.

"Hey, I'm taking my break now," Ashley said to another Gord's employee.

Then she crossed the room and grinned at Zack. DaEvo chimed.

Quest in Progress
Relationship Milestone: First Date

The notification was followed by a flood of pink hearts. Zack returned Ashley's smile, feeling suddenly cheerful. Just a little longer, and he would be a free man again. He couldn't help but sweep his gaze over the brunette, idly noting how the black and khaki uniform really didn't flatter her. Well, it didn't flatter anyone, but her especially.

"My break's kind of short," Ashley said, "but there's a park around the corner where we could eat."

"Sounds great. I hope you like Chinese."

Zack waved the bags as he followed Ashley out of Gord's and to the park. They found a table in the shade, and Zack spread out the food. It covered most of the table. He had bought more than he realized.

Ashley laughed, her eyes twinkling with mischief. "How much do you think I eat?"

Zack surveyed the spread and laughed as well. "I wasn't sure what you liked, and don't forget half of this is for me. Chopsticks or fork?"

He offered both, and Ashley took the chopsticks. She selected a takeout box filled with stir fried vegetables and ate. Zack chose some lo mein but realized after the first bite he wasn't hungry. The combination of a late breakfast, heat, and nerves was getting to him.

DaEvo chimed.

It's important to make a good impression. Don't forget the gift!

"Oh, right. This is for you." Zack pulled the fan from his pocket and handed it to Ashley.

DaEvo chimed in triumph, and Ashley gave Zack a strange look. He swallowed. Maybe the gift had been a bad idea.

"You know. Because it's hot out." He waved vaguely at the park. It was cooler in the shade, but still hot as Phobos VII.

Ashley opened the fan and fluttered it. "Thanks. And thanks again for the flowers yesterday."

Zack shrugged and took a bite of food so he wouldn't have to respond. Unfortunately, that meant he had to chew the food. It tasted fine, but his stomach was not excited about it. He swallowed and stirred the noodles in silence for a few moments. Normally DaEvo would chime to encourage him to keep the conversation going, but apparently the rules were different for dates.

"How's your training for the tournament going?" Ashley asked.

Zack sat up straighter. "Great. I'm almost done going through the latest updates. There's this new laser cannon I really like, but it puts off EMPs and—"

DaEvo chimed.

Don't talk about yourself too much. Get to know your lady better by asking about her interests.

"And it's going great," Zack finished lamely. "How are your classes?"

Ashley smirked. "Do you really want to hear about Management Economics and Principle-Centered Leadership?"

"Maybe start with a definition of what that is?"

She laughed, and DaEvo flashed a thumbs-up emoji along with the bonus notification. That was new. And annoying.

Stupid update.

"Math and philosophy rolled into one delightful package."

"Why?"

Ashley's expression grew serious. "Because sometimes why and how you do something is just as important as what you actually do."

Zack nodded thoughtfully, trying to look less confused than he felt. Apparently, he didn't do a good job, because Ashley laughed and continued her explanation.

"I'm getting an MBA with an emphasis in Medical Technology Management. I've spent a lot of time in hospitals with Amber, and some of them are pretty awful. They have the resources they need, but they aren't being used properly. Or they're missing just one thing that would make the difference between success and failure, but no one bothers to find out what that thing is."

"You want to level them up," Zack said, understanding.

"I guess that's one way to put it."

"So what do they need? What's that one thing?" Zack leaned toward her eagerly. If Ashley had the secret to improving hospitals, Zack could tell Phil and have the trust buy it for them. Maybe Phil would be so impressed that he'd release Zack from DaEvo and stay off his back for a while.

But Ashley shook her head. "It's different in each situation, and medical technology is always changing and improving. You have to consider patient needs and doctor training to evaluate which technology would be most efficient in your facility. And you have to balance your budget so you can afford the new equipment while still keeping care affordable. It's—"

"It's like Star Fury," Zack said.

"What?"

"They release updates constantly. The meta-game is always changing. So players have to adapt as well if they want to remain competitive."

Ashley tilted her head and looked at him for a moment. Then a smile spread slowly across her face. "Yeah, you're right. It's like Star

Fury. Only I wish everyone got as excited about new medical scanners as they do about drones."

"Drones?"

She shrugged and fanned herself with Zack's gift. "Some Armada guys in the common room have been talking nonstop about a new drone build."

Zack leaned forward even more, until he was practically climbing over the table toward Ashley. "Really? What did they say? What's so special about them?"

"I don't remember the details, but apparently, these ones have a few tricks up their sleeves."

"If you hear anything else—"

DaEvo chimed a warning that he was boring his date again, and Zack leaned back in his seat and stuffed a single noodle into his mouth. He needed to stay focused on the mission. Have a successful date and earn unlimited game time. Apparently, that meant he shouldn't talk about Star Fury.

"You want me to spy for you?" Ashley said.

She seemed amused, and Zack swallowed. "No, you don't have to—"

"I'll keep my ears open. After all, I am a Veridian."

She raised her hand for a fist bump, and Zack grinned. DaEvo chimed points for physical contact, and Zack relaxed a little.

"So other than asking Veridians to spy for you, how do you keep up with all the new updates?" Ashley asked. "Honestly, it sounds exhausting."

With a grin, Zack launched into a detailed explanation about his gaming strategies, starting with his big picture goals and working down to his stat spreadsheets. He had honed the process over several years until he had it down to an art. It was nice to talk to someone who appreciated it.

DaEvo chimed.

Don't talk about yourself too much. Get to know your lady better by asking about her interests.

Crap, he had done it again. Zack cut off mid-sentence. He needed this date to be a success. He couldn't afford to get side-tracked and anger DaEvo.

"But I'm sure you don't care about all that," he said instead. "Tell me more about medical tech."

Ashley blinked at him. "No, you're right. Keeping up with game updates sounds really similar to hospital management. I wonder if I could apply some of your systems to evaluating new medical tech?"

"Really?"

"Yeah, I—" An alarm sounded on Ashley's phone. She pulled it out and made a face. "Ugh, my break is over and apparently they're swamped in there. I'd better get back to work."

"Oh, okay."

Ashley stood and picked up the fan. "Um, yeah. So, thanks for lunch!"

"Yeah."

Zack wasn't sure what else to say, and DaEvo didn't offer any help. The time had flown by, and he hadn't prepared any plans for how to end the date.

Before he could think of anything to say, Ashley waved the fan and walked away.

DaEvo chimed.

Quest Complete!
Relationship Milestone: First Date
Relationship Milestones Updated!
Unlocked: Lovemeter
Unlocked: Unlimited non-essential internet privileges (per Lovemeter rankings)
Notifications for non-essential electronics time disabled {---! T- Make sure to delete this code for the actual version!

K- Maybe we can sell a premium version? Then all this extra coding doesn't have to go to waste. -----!}.

The notification was followed with an animated graphic of a

thermometer filled halfway with sparkling pink hearts. The heart-shaped bulb at the bottom had a picture of Ashley's face pulled from her social media stream and the word "Lovemeter" scrawled across it.

Zack grinned. He had done it! He had gone on a date and unlocked unlimited game time!

He was finally free from DaEvo.

He opened his messaging app.

Zack: *Ha! I beat Phil's game. Who's up for a raid tonight? Anything scheduled?*
  Greg: *Yeah, way to go!*
  Jenny: *I'll check the postings in Corsair's Cross.*
  Faz: *Already done. We're taking on Starboard Outpost at six. Be there or be square.*

Zack grinned as he gathered the leftover food and stuffed it back into the bag. There was quite a bit left since he hadn't eaten much, but no worries. It would give him enough leftovers to get through several days of gaming as he made the most of his newfound freedom and prepared for the next tournament round.

His OptiGlasses chimed with a message. Phil.

Phil: *Doctor Jones had an unexpected opening in her schedule. You're meeting her for coffee today at 3:00 to discuss the foundation. Don't be late.*

Zack shook his head. He had gone on a date and won. He didn't have to cater to DaEvo anymore.

Zack: *Sorry, I'm busy. Plus, I beat your stupid game, so I don't need the points anymore. Have one of the trust members fly out to meet with her.*

. . .

Phil didn't respond immediately, so Zack took that as victory. He called a ride and was halfway back to his condo before the trustee answered.

Phil: *I just spoke to the developers. You have made progress, but they assure me you are still miles away from winning DaEvo. The new version adds more robustness to their system and a better user experience, but I'd be careful.*

Zack stared at the message. Miles away from winning? More robustness? What was that supposed to mean?

Zack: *But I went on a date! I won!*

He opened the app and checked his stats. They looked normal to him. Still far lower than they should be, but that was nothing new. DaEvo chimed and flashed a notification.

Lovemeter Ashley Barnes: -0.1%

Zack opened the Lovemeter and checked it. The thermometer was still filled with pink hearts, but the number beside it now read "54.9%."

"What the heck? I didn't do anything," Zack said. "Why did it go down?"

DaEvo chimed.

The Lovemeter tracks your relationship progress with your date. All new relationships begin at 50%, with bonus hearts given for bonus objectives completed on dates. Fill your Lovemeter by completing Relationship Milestones and spending quality time with your partner.

To reflect real-world relationships, the Lovemeter will decrease due to a

*variety of factors including loss of contact, unhappiness on your part-
ner's side, verbal and physical disagreements, and the like. In addition,
length of relationships and relationships where social status levels are
vastly different will affect the speed of decay in your Lovemeter.*

Fill the Lovemeter completely to enter a stable, healthy relationship!

Zack glared at the notification. So Phil was right. He wasn't free
yet. Still, keeping the Lovemeter full couldn't be any harder than
doing Physique quests or constantly trying to repeat the conversation quest. He could check in with Ashley at Gord's, bring her gifts
or whatever DaEvo thought necessary to maintain a healthy relationship, and still have plenty of time to use his unlimited game time
for Star Fury.

His OptiGlasses chimed with another message from Phil.

Phil: *I have already set up the meeting with Doctor Jones, and I am not
canceling on her now. If you skip this meeting or set one foot out of line during
the meeting, I will enact the budget clause in your contract and cut off your
funds. It would be a shame if you missed the tournament because you couldn't
afford the plane ticket to Vegas.*

Chapter Twenty

ZACK ADJUSTED his tie and leaned back against the seat as he rode
to the coffee house to meet Dr. Jones. He had showered and
changed into slacks and a button-up shirt that he'd bought during
his online shopping spree. The outfit had high Style points and
hopefully was the right thing to impress a doctor. The tie counted as
an accessory, and DaEvo had assured him it worked with the rest of
his outfit. It was less pleased that he had paired the slacks with his
sneakers, but Zack had been unable to find his new dress shoes in
the mountain of boxes in his apartment.

On the one hand, he wasn't sure why he had bothered to make
such an effort. He could discuss the foundation without being
dressed up, and he had unlimited game time now thanks to his date
with Ashley. Still, it wouldn't hurt to bank a little extra time just in
case DaEvo went haywire or updated again. Both of those things
were more likely than not. Plus, he needed this to go well so Phil
would leave him alone. Successfully recruiting Dr. Jones to work
with the foundation would finally give Zack some leverage to use
when bargaining with the trustee.

The car pulled up to the coffee house, and Zack adjusted his tie
once again. He entered the building and glanced around. The

coffee shop was on the corner of the block. Its large, expansive windows let in natural light. It had a patio, and inside were a ton of tables perfectly sized for a laptop and a half. The smell of good coffee wafted through the air, mixing with the smell of lemon scones and donuts. He was a few minutes late, which probably meant that Dr. Jones was already there. Hopefully she didn't report his tardiness to Phil.

He should have asked Phil what she looked like. It wasn't as if doctors automatically looked different than everyone else. The coffeehouse was bustling with students, local medical personnel, and the occasional hospital visitor. How was he supposed to find her in the crowd?

DaEvo populated stats for the women as Zack looked around the room. He scanned the names. Jones. He needed someone named Jones. A few of the women had their backs to Zack. DaEvo pulled information from their smart devices and offered their names and levels.

Well, it did that for almost everyone. The space above one woman's head remained stubbornly blank. Just a question mark floating in a pink heart. She had dark hair tucked under a sunhat and sat alone. Was she the one he was supposed to be meeting?

Zack walked casually across the dining room so he could give DaEvo a good look at her face and get her name. She was looking down, swiping at a tablet. Zack sat at a corner table, watching her and waiting for her to raise her head.

She finally looked up, and DaEvo chimed.

Cassie Jones (Social Level 65)
Physique: 81
Style: 59
Reputation: 34
Occupation: 87

Jones. Cassie from the park was Dr. Jones from the hospital.

Damn it! Why hadn't he noticed that earlier? Apparently, he hadn't been paying attention to her last name.

Zack felt his face go red, and he stayed in his chair in the corner, trying to make a plan. This was bad, but maybe he could play it cool. Maybe she wouldn't recognize him now that he had leveled up his Style.

Cassie looked up, and Zack quickly looked away to hide his face. He needed more time to make a plan. When he glanced over, she was looking down again, but her head was at a strange angle. Was she watching him from under the brim of her hat?

Breathe. Zack stared at the wall and focused on breathing until he hoped his face was back to a normal shade. He needed to stay calm, and he needed a plan. Retreat or attack? He couldn't hover in neutral space forever.

If he faced her, he had a chance of success. She might not recognize him. Even if she did, he was offering her a job and extra money for her department. Who wouldn't be happy about that?

If he bailed, Phil would cut off his funds.

Zack forced himself to stand and approach her table.

"Dr. Jones?" he said, offering his hand and using his best professional voice.

Cassie looked up, and her eyes narrowed with suspicion. "So it is you. I saw you watching me, but I was hoping I was wrong. What are you doing here?"

Damn. So much for not being recognized. Zack tried again. "Dr. Jones, I'm Zack Moore. My trustee arranged for us to meet to talk about—"

"You're Zack Moore? Is this some kind of joke?"

"Um, no?"

Cassie stood and pointed an accusing finger at Zack. "You've followed me in the park, at work, and now here?"

People at the tables around them watched the exchange with interest. Zack loosened his tie, trying to get more air.

DaEvo chimed.

Quest: Your Lady is Upset
Find out what's bothering her and make her feel better to earn bonus points.

For once, Zack knew exactly why the lady was upset. He offered Cassie what he hoped was a reassuring smile. "Dr. Jones, this whole thing has been some terrible misunderstanding. I'm sorry we got off on the wrong foot. Can we start again?"

It sounded like something Phil would say, and Zack hoped it was professional enough to do the job here. He offered his hand again. Cassie stared at him for a moment, then her face relaxed a little. She shook Zack's hand and sat back at the table. DaEvo chimed bonus points for physical contact, and Zack sank into his chair with relief.

"You're really Zack Moore? *The* Zack Moore?"

Cassie's eyes swept critically over Zack, and he flushed. There was no need for her to look so surprised, but that wasn't the point right now. He needed to be polite. Win her over. He could do this.

DaEvo chimed, reminding him to compliment her for bonus points.

"Yes, I'm Zack Moore. I really admire your work at the hospital. You do a great job with your patients."

Bonus Objective Completed: Bonus Objective Completed! You complimented her. For additional bonus points:

- *Give her a gift*
- *Ask her about her interests*

"How have you been following my work? Those files are confidential."

Crap. She looked suspicious again. Zack's mind raced.

"Of course, but your reputation is flawless, and several patients have mentioned being very satisfied with your work." He hoped that was true. Ashley had said something about Dr. Jones being good, so that was basically the same thing.

Cassie didn't question his explanation. DaEvo gave him extra points for making his lady feel better, and Zack relaxed back into his seat. He could do this. He was doing this.

"So why increase the budget now?" Cassie said. "And why put me in charge of it?"

Zack flushed as he searched for a professional, adult way to explain it. "I admire the work your hospital does with the foundation's funds," he said, trying to compliment her while also not making it clear he had no idea what she did, "and Phil thinks you'd do a great job managing the extra funding."

"You admire the work," Cassie said dryly. "The two-million-dollar mural in the children's wing, for example?"

"Two million dollars?" The other patrons of the coffee house stared in alarm at his shouting, and Zack forced himself to lower his voice. He still couldn't keep the incredulity from his voice though. "That monstrosity cost two million dollars?"

If that was true, Phil had no right to complain about Zack spending a few grand on new clothes. Zack could finally have some leverage.

"Not such a fan of the work after all?" Cassie said.

"Apparently, I haven't followed the reports closely enough."

Zack felt a strange anger building in his chest. This foundation was his parents' legacy. Helping sick kids had been their pride and joy. He had poured money into it to honor their memories, and this was where it had gone? Into badly done redecoration projects?

"I doubt you've been reading them at all. I checked up on you when your trustee called and offered me the job, Mr. Moore. Your reputation isn't exactly stellar."

"Damn Reputation."

He'd meant to mutter that to himself, but Cassie heard and raised an eyebrow. "As I said, there were a lot of red flags about you. I was willing to give you the benefit of the doubt and hope that you had matured since those articles were written. Apparently not."

"What does that have to do with anything? You'll get the money either way. You don't have to deal with me."

Cassie's eyes narrowed. "Working with you would mean our names would be linked. I'm not willing to stake my professional reputation on someone who doesn't even bother keeping up with his foundations projects." She frowned. "Speaking of that. If you haven't been reading the reports, how did you know my name that day in the park?"

Zack tried to stay calm, but it was getting more difficult. Why couldn't she just let the park incident drop? "Why does any of that matter? I'm offering you a ton of money!"

That caught the interest of the people sitting around them again.

Cassie glared. "So you think you can just buy me with funding? Is that it?"

"What? No! Why on earth would I want to buy you?"

She leaned across the table, her eyes sparking. "Look, I've tried to be professional and give you the benefit of the doubt. I'd love to have the funding. I'd love to work with your foundation. But unfortunately, that would mean working with you. Giving you access to even more of my time and personal information. And no amount of money is worth my personal safety and peace of mind."

"Personal safety? You think I'm threatening you?" Zack looked at her, entirely befuddled. Cassie wasn't bad looking, not at all. But it wasn't as if he didn't already have more than enough on his plate with Star Fury and DaEvo. And, frankly speaking, she was incredibly annoying.

"I think you're stalking me. I don't know why. I don't know how. I am very careful with my privacy settings and personal routines. But you keep showing up. You know things about me that you shouldn't know. What other explanation is there?"

She seemed to be hanging onto her temper by a thread. DaEvo flashed a warning that she was upset, and Zack swiped it away.

Cassie scowled. "There! That's why I hate OptiGlasses. You just sent a command. I saw your eyes swipe. What did you do?"

"I-I got a message from a friend and was swiping it away."

"You're lying."

Zack protested but flushed red. This was not going nearly as well as he had hoped. In fact, it was not going well at all. Cassie stood, and Zack scrambled to his feet.

"We're done here, Mr. Moore. If I hear from you or your trust again, I'm calling the police."

"I'm not stalking you! You're the last person I would want to stalk!"

Reputation -0.1

A few people around the coffee shop had pulled out phones and were filming the incident. More were probably discreetly recording the interaction with their OptiGlasses. They watched Zack and Cassie as if they were watching a tennis match, their heads swiveling to follow the conversation.

Crap. They would probably post those videos online. That meant this would get back to Phil, which would mean even more trouble. The worst part was, it wasn't even Zack's fault. He hadn't done anything but be in the wrong place at the wrong time.

That was if Cassie didn't tell Phil everything first. But what other explanation would she offer for turning down the job and the extra funding?

"Dr. Jones, please just take the money."

"Explain how you knew my name that day."

DaEvo chimed, helpful as ever.

Reputation -0.1

Zack's mind raced. There was a perfectly good reason for his behavior but explaining it would mean explaining DaEvo and the conversation quest.

Cassie watched the thoughts play across his face. When it became apparent he wasn't going to provide an answer, she huffed in disgust and hurried out of the coffee shop.

Quest: Your Lady is Upset
Your lady has left, upset! We recommend you:

- *buy her a gift*
- *follow her to explain your position*
- *wait for her at her house when she has calmed down*

Yeah. Zack was pretty sure none of those ideas would help. In fact, Zack was pretty sure they'd make things worse.

DaEvo chimed again, and Zack realized it had been running a conversation timer during the whole interaction. Well, at least this wasn't a total loss.

People were still staring at him and snapping more pictures. Zack glared at them and hurried out the door.

Cassie was already gone. That was probably for the best. People leaned their faces against the glass to watch him out the windows, so he crossed the street and called for a ride.

Reputation -0.2

As he suspected, people had already posted videos of the incident. Great. Just great. He could only hope no one had heard his name. Zack walked down the sidewalk, putting more distance between himself and the coffee shop and searching for some shade to provide relief from the pounding sun.

Reputation -3.1

Please note, due to your decreased social level (17.52), your active Lovemeter results will decrease at a faster rate. Raise your social level to be further in-line with active relationships!

Lovemeter Ashley Barnes: -0.1%
Current Level: 47.3%

Zack groaned internally. The damn Lovemeter had been dropping all through the night and now it was supposed to drop even faster? How was that even fair?

"What the hell? Why is my Reputation still dropping?"

Reputation scores are taken from negative and positive interactions with others in public and other social situations as well as the overall reputation of an individual in greater society.

Individual results from posted content online, including highly public and viral information, might result in a greater-than-normal reputation drop in the short term. Short-term effects from viral posts will, eventually, decrease depending upon further public interactions.

What the hell did that all mean? Luckily, all of it was followed by a link. Zack clicked on it and gritted his teeth when the page loaded.

It was a blog post.

On Cassie's blog.

About him.

Zack gritted his teeth and read.

"The Modern Stalker: How OptiGlasses Make Privacy Violation Easier than Ever."

I wrote this post a few days ago but decided against posting it because I wasn't sure that my suspicions were founded. It turns out, this incident was part of something much bigger and more alarming. I'm posting now so you all know what to watch for. Even if you aren't using any smart technology, people can still access your information and use it to violate your privacy. This latest incident—

Zack stopped reading and scrolled down to the comments. Maybe nobody read Cassie's blog. Maybe—

She already had thirty-five comments. Most of them also decrying the evils of OptiGlasses and those who used them. Even as he watched, he noticed another share of her blog and another comment.

Damn luddites.

Zack's car arrived. He got into it as Phil called. Zack stared at the incoming call, gathering his nerve. Then he answered and spoke quickly before Phil could launch into his lecture.

"I'm not stalking her, okay? Whatever she said, it's not true. I tried to win her over. I really did."

"You mean you didn't have your medical charity spend millions of dollars to support hospitals as a conspiracy to get a coffee date with a stranger?"

Phil was laughing. He could even hear the man slapping his knee over the call!

"You think this is funny? I lost major Reputation points in DaEvo over this!"

Phil laughed harder and Zack hung up. His OptiGlasses flashed a notification from his condo.

Reminder: Your cleaning service is scheduled to resume today. Your maid is on schedule and will arrive in thirty minutes.

The cleaning service! Zack sighed in relief. Cleaning the apartment would give him more points and hopefully repair some of the damage Cassie had caused to his stats. He pulled up the quest information quickly and nodded. Just cleaning his clothing would improve his reputation points—probably by removing the negative debuff for looking like a hobo.

Shouldn't it already have disappeared? Or was that just bad code, forgetting to remove what it had deducted when he got his new style points? If it was, Zack wasn't going to tell DaEvo.

Best part of the cleaning services was that it would take no effort at all on his part.

The car arrived at his building, and Zack ran out and rushed up the stairs. He wanted to oversee this appointment to make sure the housekeeper did everything DaEvo would give points for.

Workout detected: Keep it up to earn Physique points.

Zack swiped away the notification. Even after that disaster, he wasn't desperate enough to accept another Physique quest.

Chapter Twenty-One

"HOUSEKEEPING!"

The voice was muffled through the door, but definitely a woman's. Zack grinned. He could get points for cleaning and points for conversation all at once. Score.

Wait. He didn't need more game time, not really. He had unlimited gaming time with Ashley now. Though he wondered if the gaming time was banked or used concurrently? It was probably concurrent. No reason why DaEvo wouldn't screw him.

He pulled open the door. A gray-haired woman in a staff uniform smiled at him. She looked more like a grandmother than a potential date, but DaEvo popped the conversation clock into the corner anyway, ready to start as soon as she spoke. Zack shrugged. For all the app knew, he was into older women. Maybe he could use that to his advantage somehow. Would volunteering at a nursing home and talking to residents improve his Reputation?

He pushed away the idea. He had unlimited game time from his date with Ashley. No need to go overboard.

Rosa Perez (Social Level 52)
Physique: 54
Style: 39
Reputation: 76
Occupation: 37

Zack glared at the stats. How the hell did a cleaning woman have better stats than him?

"Stupid bugs," he muttered.

Your alpha test bug report has been logged.
Thank you for your help in making DaEvo a success!

"You have bugs in there?" Rosa asked, wrinkling her nose.

Her eyes widened as she leaned around Zack and got her first look at the apartment. Zack followed her gaze. Yes, it was a bit of a mess, but that was why she was there, wasn't it? To clean the mess?

"What? No, there are no bugs," Zack said.

"Because I only clean. I don't do vermin."

"There aren't any bugs, lady."

"It looks like there could be bugs." She crossed her arms and scowled at him.

Zack sighed. "I promise, there aren't any bugs. Just some dirty laundry."

And the piles of boxes from his online shopping spree. And an assortment of pizza boxes, takeout containers, and bottles sprinkled over the floor.

Zack stepped aside and held out his arm to welcome her into the apartment. "You can start right away."

"Ha!"

Bonus Objective Completed! You made her laugh.
Good going! Laughter is highly regarded as a method of achieving a strong relationship.

That wasn't a laugh. Even Zack knew that. But obviously DaEvo didn't. Well, it wasn't as if Zack hadn't been exploiting bugs already. He just shouldn't mention them to Rosa. She might leave.

"This is why you shouldn't cancel cleaning services," Rosa said, gesturing to a particularly tall pile of dirty clothes.

"It isn't that bad," Zack said defensively. "I've been busy."

"Too busy to blink and schedule an appointment?" She nodded toward his OptiGlasses.

Zack scowled. "OptiGlasses don't operate by blinks. It's a highly precise sequence of—"

"I'll have to charge extra for this. We charge extra for extra messy apartments."

"Since when?"

DaEvo chimed to let Zack know he had been speaking to Rosa for two minutes.

It felt a lot longer.

"Since now. Oh! Was that a mouse?" Rosa shrieked and jumped back.

Zack squinted at the corner of the room she was pointing at. Something small and furry darted out from behind the gaming chair and burrowed into a pile of laundry.

"No, it's a hamster."

"There are even droppings." She looked at the floor with disgust, toed a candy wrapper with one foot, then shook her head and backed into the hallway. "Bugs and mice. This place is disgusting. Get the exterminator in here first, then we'll clean. I'll bring a team next time."

"What? Where are you going? You can't leave."

"I certainly can, young man! My contract exempts me from working in unsanitary conditions."

"Unsanitary? It's not that bad."

"This apartment is the very definition of unsanitary. Call us after you've had the exterminator in." She grabbed her cleaning supplies and hurried down the hallway.

Zack watched her go and swore under his breath. DaEvo chimed, giving him gaming time. Which he didn't need. What he needed was more levels.

Zack groaned and shut the door and let his head bang on it. Gently. He wasn't going to damage his best piece of equipment. Pushing against the door, Zack turned around, reminded once more that the apartment did not smell good.

Veobos the hamster darted across the room, stuffed his mouth full of the seeds on the kitchen floor, and disappeared underneath the couch once more.

Zack stared at the mess. No points for cleaning.

DaEvo chimed.

Reputation -11.4

Zack flinched and pulled up the associated link. It looked like Cassie's blog post really had gone viral. Worse, while Cassie hadn't named him directly, others had put together the videos of them and his name was being bandied around.

Lovemeter Ashley Barnes: -0.1%
Current Level: 40.0%

Zack's jaw dropped. How had it dropped so fast? He'd been ignoring the twinkling lights on the Lovemeter for the most part, since he didn't have time to go poking at it. But now that he had the entire thing pulled up, he noticed another notification appear.

Lovemeter Ashley Barnes: -0.1%
Current Level: 39.9%

Notice: Due to lost Lovemeter relationship points with Ashley Barnes, your Unlimited Internet Privileges have been revoked once again.
Increase your Lovemeter levels to improve your relationship with Ashley Barnes!

"What the hell?"

Zack pulled up the full log for the Lovemeter and saw how it had dropped again and again during his ride back, during the conversation with the cleaning lady, and had sped up the moment his Reputation points dropped his Social Level even further. The pink hearts twinkled at him, taunting him with just how close he was to freedom.

"You've got to be kidding me! You said I had unlimited game time!"

Quest!

Your elevated heart rate suggests you're exercising. Keep going to level up your Physique stats.

Zack huffed. His elevated heart rate had nothing to do with exercise. "How do I refill the Lovemeter?"

To fill your Lovemeter, please complete your Relationship Milestones! In addition, there are repeatable relationship actions that will increase your Lovemeter level. These actions include:

- *communicate with your relationship target regularly*
- *get her to laugh*
- *give her gifts*
- *increase the intimacy index (calculated via touch, eye contact, smiles, and positive expressions of interest)*
- *express thanks for her time or what she has done for you*
- *practice active listening*
- *use terms of endearment*

Your current Relationship Milestones include:

- *first significant physical contact*
- *in-depth exchange of history*
- *your first kiss*
- *schedule a second date*
- *take her out to an exciting and memorable event*
- *your first [Dev Note—are we even allowed to suggest this? Ask Legal]*

- *become an [#select_variable: relationship type: exclusive;primary;secondary; pair-bonded; metamour]*
- *get engaged*

Each milestone completed will fill your Lovemeter and increase your progress in the game. Additional completed Milestones will also reduce the rate of decrease in the Lovemeter.

Zack sighed. It looked as though he wasn't quite as set as he'd thought he was. Still, it was a simple enough fix. He just needed to talk to Ashley. Maybe go on a date. That'd give his entire thing a bump. After that, maybe he'd focus on raising his overall level so it wouldn't drop so quickly.

He dialed Ashley's number and reviewed some of the suggestions for how to keep the Lovemeter full. Some of the suggestions like eye contact and physical touch wouldn't work for a phone call, but others would. He could express thanks and listen. Hopefully that would be enough.

The call went to voicemail, and Zack found himself stammering a message that he hoped would check all the right boxes.

"Hey, Ashley! Uh, it's Zack. Just wanted to call and say thanks for the date. Yeah. It was great listening to you. Um, I mean, it was great that you listened to me. I mean, thanks. Yeah. Thank you. That's what I called to say. Thank you. I appreciate you."

Zack hung up the call before he could embarrass himself further and waited for DaEvo to chime and refill his Lovemeter.

But nothing happened. Apparently, he had to deliver the message to Ashley directly. He called her again and once again ended up in voicemail. He hung up without leaving a message and prepared to dial her number a third time.

DaEvo chimed.

Relationship Hint: Frequent Contact is Good, Desperation is Bad

We noticed you've attempted to contact Ashley Barnes repeatedly. While frequent contact can improve your relationship, no love interest wants a desperate individual. Consider holding off and giving your target time to reply.

Forget appearances, he was desperate! Zack called Gord's just in case Ashley was working and not able to answer her personal phone. But the worker who answered said she was finished with her shift.

So much for the Lovemeter. He needed a backup plan fast. Preferably one that did not involve talking to anyone new. He wasn't willing to risk it after the disaster with Cassie. Sure, he had some time thanks to Cassie's and Rosa's conversations, but that wouldn't be enough. It wouldn't fix his real problems.

He didn't want to be cut off in the middle of a mission with the team. Not to mention he had promised them he had this under control. He was still trying to earn back their trust after the tournament incident and he definitely did not want to tell them why his stats had suddenly taken a turn for the worse. Faz was already having a field day with chore jokes. If he found out about the stalking and dating incidents, Zack would never hear the end of it.

He opened the available quests menu and stared at it. Reputation was a lost cause. So was Occupation. Style was pretty close to being maxed out with his clothing and he'd failed the cleaning option already. If he wanted to get it any higher, he needed to work on Physique.

The last thing he wanted to do was work on Physique.

But what other choice did he have?

Zack opened the Physique quest menu and chose meals. He ordered the highest point value meals and smoothies from the gym's restaurant to be delivered to his apartment. Then he scanned through the other quests. There were all the repeatable quests for working out, but he was definitely not doing those.

Zack flipped open the style quests just in case he had missed something easy. He could order more clothes online, but he had more than enough clothing. He could just swap clothing and get higher style points, though he was already very high unless he wore his WesterNeon outfit again.

No. He wasn't that desperate. And it wasn't a long-term solution.

He flipped through the different salons offering at home appointments for manicures and pedicures. No luck. He gritted his teeth and checked appointments for manscaping. Thankfully, that was booked out as well.

Zack pushed away his chagrin at the knowledge that the service was that popular and returned to the problem at hand. He needed to level up, and he needed to do it now.

That left cleaning. It would increase his Style points, depending on what he threw away or wore, but most importantly, it would increase his Reputation score. Maybe he could schedule another cleaning service to come tonight. He opened the app to see what appointments were available.

Error! Your apartment has been flagged for unsanitary conditions due to vermin. Please schedule an exterminator visit first.

Damn it! Rosa must have written him up. Zack flipped through the app menu to schedule an exterminator visit, but the service had nothing available that evening.

He was on his own.

Greg: *Hey, guys! You ready for the raid? Two hours to go!*

Jenny: *Yeah. I've got some new EMP shielding that just made its way onto the market. I'm going to test them out on my drones.*

Faz: *Great! I've got a new booster combo I want to try. I think it will be even faster than my last one. Zack, you in? Or do you have to finish your chores first?*

Zack swallowed and stared at his apartment. At the piles of laundry and garbage covering the floor. The discarded plates and, Zack hated to admit, the smell that he kept being reminded about. A thin layer of dust and grime coated everything. The place hadn't been cleaned in months, and it showed.

He pulled up the quest information again and noted the improvement in Reputation points for cleaning his clothing. In addition, there was the improvement in Physique and Reputation for cleaning the entire apartment.

Damn it. If he wanted game time for the raid, he would have to clean it himself. The raid was important. They needed to test out new tech combinations, needed to work on their tactics. If nothing else, they needed to practice taking out bases because there was certain to be other base attacks in the tournament rounds.

He gritted his teeth. If he could no-hit run the entire Aluada asteroid belt encounter, he could beat DaEvo.

Zack: *Yeah, I'm in.*

Chapter Twenty-Two

Two hours. He had two hours to make this happen.

The condo app chimed to let him know his food had arrived. Zack spread the assortment of salads and smoothies over his grimy counter. He swept a gaze over the meals and sighed.

Zack shoveled salad into his mouth as he scrolled through the available quests and made a plan. Laundry was an easy place to start. He would get points for washing clothes and throwing away worn and torn items. Cleaning would help too.

Zack finished a salad and grinned as DaEvo gave him +0.1 Physique for it. Then he shoved the smallest pile of dirty clothes into the empty Fit Life box and dragged it to his laundry room. He dumped the clothes into the washing machine and stared at it. He had never actually run the machine. Where did you start? Probably with soap. There should be some sort of detergent somewhere.

Zack rummaged through the cabinets until he found laundry detergent, poured some into the machine, and pressed start. The machine's screen lit up, and it vibrated as it spun the clothes. A timer lit up. It would take an hour to wash the clothes.

That was way too long.

Zack canceled the cycle and selected the "quick wash" option.

That one would only take twenty minutes. That would give him enough time to wash six loads before the raid. Well, he would probably only get through five. It would take a few minutes to change out the loads.

DaEvo chimed cheerfully.

Quest Begun!

Congratulations, you've started a load of laundry! Cleanliness in your home and hearth is important in forming relationships and creating a healthy mindset.

Additional cleaning quests are available and will provide bonuses in attributes, unrestricted internet privileges access, and special accolades. Bonus points if you can improve your olfactory stats.

Home Cleanliness Objectives

- *Clean your kitchen*
- *Clean out your fridge*
- *Mop floors*
- *Clean the bathroom*
- *Vacuum the carpets*
- *Make your bed*
- *Take out the trash*

Zack scanned through the list. Yes, this could work. He could make this work. This was easy, just like min-maxing a series of quest runs. Figure out which parts could be done concurrently. Like stacking a bunch of quests on a single run. And he'd get an accolade, which was perfect. The only issue was that he only had two hours.

"Play high energy music," Zack said.

His smart home responded, pumping music with deep bass beats through his surround sound speakers. The new speakers were perfect, a definite upgrade over the ones he'd replaced only weeks ago. Zack grinned. That was more like it.

Zack changed into his Fit Life clothes so that he'd be at a higher social level. It might not make a difference since he was alone, but he wasn't certain. And with how buggy DaEvo was, you never knew.

He grabbed a smoothie off the counter, sipping it as he hurried into his bedroom. His entire bed was highlighted red, where the crumpled sheets and blankets were beckoning his attention. Swearing to himself that Faz would never know about this, Zack made the bed, smoothing out the sheets. He had to do it again, because the damn app kept highlighting a rumpled corner.

Home Cleanliness Objective—Make your bed completed!

Zack waited for a second for more information, but whatever accolade or bonus attributes or time he was getting, it looked like he'd have to finish everything before he got it. Shrugging, he chugged the rest of the smoothie.

DaEvo chimed in satisfaction.

Physique Quest Complete!
+0.05 Physique

Sweet. Zack grabbed a grocery store bag from the kitchen and filled it with the trash strewn around his bedroom. DaEvo chimed again, showing him a percentage completion bar. Zack put the bag of garbage by the door and paused to gather his thoughts.

DaEvo chimed.

Quest Begun!
Based on your elevated heart rate, you're exercising! Keep it up to earn fitness points.

Perfect. For once, Zack accepted the fitness quest, which as far as he could tell involved keeping his heart rate elevated for twenty minutes. Easy. He could earn points in multiple categories without having to leave the house.

Zack stared at the piles of laundry scattered around his living room. Even six loads wouldn't be enough to get through all this.

And the dryer was empty right now. That seemed like a waste.

Zack stuffed another pile of laundry into the Fit Life box and dumped it into his bathtub. He stopped up the drain and let the water run while he grabbed the laundry detergent and poured some into the tub.

The faucet blasted water out, soaking Zack as he stirred the laundry. He hastily turned down the water flow, ignoring the puddle on the floor and focused on the murky gray water in the tub. Had his clothes really been that dirty? It was kind of disgusting.

DaEvo apparently didn't recognize his genius, because it didn't chime the start of a new laundry quest. If this didn't work, Zack was definitely filing another bug report.

Not that those had helped at all so far.

He drained the water, wrung the clothes as much as he could, then stuffed them in the dryer and put it on the highest setting. DaEvo chimed recognition of the latest load of laundry, and Zack grinned. He just might be able to pull this off.

Next step, remove all the trash.

Zack stuffed empty drink bottles, used tissues, and candy wrappers into every takeout bag he could find. Bending over to pick everything up off the floor was enough exertion that he began to sweat.

DaEvo chimed.

Wow, you're really going for it! Keep this up, and you'll be fit in no time! You've completed fifteen minutes of elevated exercise.

Fifteen minutes gone already? Zack groaned and doubled his pace. He hauled the bags of trash to the garbage chute in the hallway and stuffed them in. Then he stacked the pizza boxes and carried them out as well.

That took two trips, and a rogue slice of pizza fell out of a box and stuck to his shirt. Zack pulled it off and rubbed out the grease stain as best he could. A notification warned him about hygiene, but he had more important things to deal with. He'd change later.

The washing machine chimed that it was done, and Zack rushed to the laundry room. The dryer was still running, so he stuffed in both loads and restarted the cycle. Then he filled the Fit Life box with another pile of dirty clothes and poured them into the washer. DaEvo chimed.

Don't forget! You can level up style points by getting rid of worn and torn clothing.

"What counts as worn and torn?" Zack muttered.

He wasn't expecting a response, but DaEvo chimed. New stats appeared in Zack's OptiGlasses. A frowning face emoji hovered over every pile of clothing on the floor.

"They're not that bad!" Zack protested.

DaEvo stayed silent. Zack pulled a pair of sweatpants from a pile and studied them. Sure, they had a few holes, but that didn't matter. No one saw him when he wore them. There was no reason to get rid of them.

No reason except he needed game time for tonight.

Crap.

Zack threw the pants into the kitchen trash can, which he had never bothered to put a bag in since he never used it. DaEvo chimed in triumph.

Zack blinked at the trash can. It was cleaner than most places in the apartment. He could throw clothes in there, get marked for completion of the quest, then retrieve them later as needed.

Zack grabbed a T-shirt off the nearest laundry pile and threw it away. Veobos the hamster scurried across the room as Zack disturbed his hiding place. DaEvo chimed again.

Apparently, the app considered everything Zack owned to be substandard. Well, he could use that to his advantage. Zack tossed clothing into the trash can until it was full, working in time with the music and gaining points for each action. Occasionally, once he finished a pile and the completion rate filled, he'd get a new notification telling him he'd gained points in Physique, Reputation, and unrestricted electronic time. All he had to do was keep this up and he'd have enough for the evening and raise his overall level. Just a little more, and he would have game time and a high enough level to slow the Lovemeter's depletion once he refilled it.

He scanned through the list of house cleaning quests. He didn't own a mop or vacuum, so those were out. The trash and laundry situations were vastly improving though, and he could easily clean the fridge.

The dryer chimed, and Zack sprinted across the apartment to remove the clothes. He shoved them into his dresser, which he hadn't used since he first emptied his suitcase into it when he moved in. He didn't bother to fold anything, but DaEvo still gave him points when he closed the drawer.

The washing machine cycle still had fifteen minutes. He had forgotten to select the quick wash for the second load.

Too late now, but there was no point leaving the dryer empty. Zack dumped another load of clothes into the bathtub, poured in some detergent, and started the water.

His condo app chimed.

Noise complaint: Your neighbor has filed a noise complaint. Please turn down your music.

"Fat chance."

Filling the tub would take a while, so he rushed back to the kitchen and quickly removed the half-eaten takeout. He put it into a bag that had been used for a massive order of Thai takeout a few months ago and stuffed it down the garbage chute.

DaEvo chimed, but only marked the objective as half completed. Apparently, he and the app had different standards for what counted as cleaning the fridge.

Damn it.

Zack leaned against the kitchen counter to catch his breath and surveyed the room. He had made progress. There was no doubt about that. Only a few piles of laundry remained, and the trash piles were gone. He had shoved all the unopened boxes of clothes into the various closets around his apartment to make things look tidy and fool DaEvo into thinking he had put them away. Things were still a little dusty, but the cleaning service could take care of that.

The washing machine chimed, and Zack hurried to fill the empty dryer. As he stuffed the clothes into the machine, Zack became aware of the sound of running water under the pulsing beat of his music.

Damn it all!

He rushed to the bathroom, where the bathtub had overflowed and created a small lake on the bathroom floor. A small lake of soapy water, thanks to the detergent he had added. Zack slipped and grabbed the sink for balance as he reached to turn off the water.

DaEvo chimed and started the objective for mopping the floor.

Sweet. He wondered if he grabbed some of his soaked shirts and wiped things down if he could even finish that objective.

Focus! Zack drew a deep breath as he pulled the drain, listening to the gurgle of draining water for a second. He hurried back to add the clothes from the bathtub to the dryer load.

Only forty-five minutes until he was supposed to be online. This was going to be close.

Zack removed the last of the clothes from the living room floor and shoved them into a small pile in the corner of the laundry room. There was no room to walk there now, but he had cleared the floor in the main room, and DaEvo gave him points for it.

The apartment seemed a lot bigger now. It actually looked pretty nice without all the trash strewn about. Zack leaned against the wall, taking a moment to catch his breath and feel pride in his accomplishment. He was drenched, soapy, and sweaty, but he had done it. He had brought his apartment up to standard and earned enough time to join tonight's raid on the Armada base. He had also received bonus Physique points for eating the health food and keeping an elevated heart rate for almost two hours.

A glance at the total amount of internet time he had showed

Zack had just over five hours. More than enough time, even if it was a maze or grind.

His condo's app flashed another noise complaint notification, but Zack swiped it away. Whoever was complaining could just deal with it. He had bigger worries right now.

DaEvo flashed a reminder suggesting that Zack improve the olfactory stats of his apartment for even greater points.

Not a bad idea.

Zack rummaged through his supply closet, looking for air freshener. Nothing. He settled for the lemon-scented cleaner he had used before and ran around his apartment, spritzing everything in sight until the bottle was empty.

The condo app flashed again, and Zack swiped it away. He didn't want to deal with annoying neighbors in his moment of triumph.

The smell of sweat and old food mixed with the scent of lemon as it settled. Zack wrinkled his nose, not sure this was an improvement. But DaEvo chimed and gave him points anyway.

Apparently, it was close enough. Thank goodness. He leaned against his counter and checked the clock.

Ten minutes to go. He had leveled up and earned game time with ten minutes to spare.

Zack sank into his gaming chair. He was drenched with sweat and soapy water. His heart rate was still elevated, and he was breathing hard.

DaEvo chimed.

Your heart rate is settling. If you're done working out, complete a cool down to earn +15 minutes unrestricted internet privileges and +0.1 Physique.

Zack raised an eyebrow. That was pretty damn good. He opened the quest log. All he had to do was stretch for five minutes. DaEvo suggested a list of simple stretches he could complete.

Why was it almost as much Physique for stretching as all the exercise he'd done before? He shook his head, muttering about bug reports, and got up out of his chair. He even ignored the bug report notification.

Zack stood in front of a mirror as DaEvo suggested and bent forward to touch his toes. At least, he tried to touch his toes. His fingertips stopped somewhere around his calves.

Still, DaEvo started a timer, and Zack held the stretch until DaEvo chimed and prompted him to try the next exercise. The five minutes of stretching felt a lot longer as sweat poured from his face and his breathing ached. Still, the bonus time was important and the increase in Physique all added up.

The condo app chimed again. Zack swiped the notification away and sent his team a message as he sank into his gaming chair.

Zack: *Logging in now, you ready?*

Faz: *Great! You got your chores done on time!*

Zack: *Ha, ha.*

Greg: *Seriously, Faz. Even I think that's getting old.*

Faz: *Whatever. You just don't appreciate good comedy.*

Jenny: *Glad you're here, Zack. Can you arm your new laser cannon so I can test my EMP inhibitor?*

Zack: *With pleasure. Let's go blast some Armada scum!*

The Star Fury theme music blasted through his speakers as he powered on his gaming console and spawned at the nearest station. He set autopilot on a course for the rendezvous point and started arming all the weapons he wanted to test with Jenny's setup. If she had found a way to make her drones immune to the EMP, maybe Zack could strengthen his and take out enemy drones who were less prepared.

His OptiGlasses chimed with another notification from his condo app. Zack pulled them off his face and threw them onto his couch. Notifications could wait. Right now, all he cared about was the game.

Chapter Twenty-Three

"YOU GUYS READY FOR THIS?" Zack called.

"Born ready," Jenny said.

They were in formation and waiting just out of range of the outpost's sensors. Zack had made it to the raid with two minutes to spare and was taking advantage of the extra time to brief his team.

"I've set up five different laser cannon configurations to test with Jenny's new EMP dampener. We'll also keep an eye out for the unusual drones or anything else out of the ordinary." Zack had splurged and hired a mechanic drone so that he could pull out and swap out configurations in the middle of the battlefield without flying all the way back to base. It was expensive, but they didn't have time for him to fluff around flying back and forth.

"Yeah, if the Armada found an Easter egg, there's no telling what was in there," Greg said.

"Nothing we can't handle," Jenny said. She closed one of her boosters for a moment, giving the impression that her ship was winking, then circled around to settle into her place behind Greg.

"Hey, it's time," Faz said. "Let's go!"

They stopped talking as they focused on their roles and flew forward. Other teams of Corsairs and solo players materialized around them, all converging on the Starboard Outpost, a collection of Armada waystations and hangouts.

Zack's screen lit up as explosions and lasers filled the space around the outpost. The whine of engines and deep booms of hits landed blared through his surround sound speakers. A lucky hit by one of the Armada drones slammed into his ship, and Zack's chair shook from the reverberating aftershock.

"Pull back!" Zack shouted as the Armada launched a counterattack.

Jenny released a wave of drones as the team put some distance between themselves and the base. She dropped mines and distracted Armada ships while Zack blasted them with his laser cannon. Faz darted in and out, disabling ships for Zack to destroy while neatly avoiding the crossfire. Greg provided cover for everyone, disintegrating any Armada scum that got too close.

The other teams had pulled back too, pulling the Armada ships out of formation, while the base raid team waited in the wings for an opening.

"Still a little EMP interference," Jenny said. "It's better, but not perfect."

"Let's try a different cannon," Zack said. He flipped a few switches, diverting power. He had set up for two different cannons with different configurations on them, all before he had to head back and reconfigure his ship. "Faz, can you lure a few ships closer so we can test this on them?"

"You betcha." Faz let out a war cry and plunged his ship into the heart of the battle. He emerged a few seconds later with a crowd of ships on his tail, whooping in triumph.

"He said a few," Greg said. "Not the whole fleet!"

"Had to account for the mines," Faz said.

Sure enough, Jenny's mines webbed and disabled many of the ships before they were within range, breaking up the formation. Zack put the second laser cannon through its paces while Jenny fiddled with settings.

His OptiGlasses chimed with a message notification. Since he had taken them off, the sound echoed through his surround sound speakers. Zack ignored it. Whoever was trying to contact him could wait.

"Hey, let that ship through," he said. "I think I recognize it."

Jenny pulled her drones aside, making a small opening that would let the ship through but not be obvious about it.

Zack grinned. "Yeah, that's the Armada scum that had the unusual drones in my PvP. Jenny, keep everyone else away. Let's see if he has any other tricks up his sleeves."

Zack suspected that Steve would recognize his ship from their previous round, but he took the time to hail him with an emoji sticking out its tongue just in case the Armada player was too busy in the heat of battle to notice who he was fighting.

Steve responded with a skull and crossbones and several rude gestures. Zack grinned. Looked as though he remembered after all.

Zack's smile disappeared as something landed a hit on his tail.

"What the hell?" Greg said. "Something just hit me, but nothing showed up on my sensors."

"Same!" Faz said. "Cripes, what's going on here?"

Zack upped his shields so the surprise hits would cause less damage and flew toward Steve's ship, engaging him in a close quarters dogfight that would make it more difficult for the other player to concentrate on manually commanding his drones—or whatever the heck he was doing.

It didn't seem to do much good. Zack kept taking damage even though Steve didn't land any obvious hits.

"It's drones," Jenny said, "But they're slippery. I'm sending you some sensor settings to try."

The string of numbers from Jenny flashed across his screen. Zack pulled back from the dogfight and typed them into his sensor settings.

"Nothing," he said.

Jenny swore. "Keep him busy then. I have a few more ideas."

Someone knocked on his door. Zack flinched and missed the timing on his evasive maneuvers, allowing the Armada scum to land a hit. His chair shook and his shields flashed yellow.

Who would possibly be knocking at his door? Phil usually called ahead unless he was planning some kind of sneak attack. Sweat beaded on Zack's brow. He really hoped it wasn't Phil.

The knocking continued, growing more and more insistent. Zack wondered if it was possible to soundproof a door so you couldn't hear knocking. That would allow him to ignore it as easily as he ignored digital notifications.

Greg's initial pull finally managed to catch up, having dealt with Jenny's mines and the webbing drones slowing them down. She'd even managed to destroy a few, but now the team had a swarm of Armada ships to deal with. The sharp ping of laser fire intensified, interspersed with the hum of additional missiles. They should have dealt with Steve by now, but those damn stealthed drones were taking out Jenny's drones and forcing them to divert power to shields rather than lasers.

Well, crap.

"I know you're in there," a female voice yelled from the hallway. "I can hear you. I've been hearing you all night!"

DaEvo's familiar chime sounded through the speakers. Had it started the conversation timer?

Zack tried to squelch his curiosity and focus on the fight, but he couldn't help wondering who was at his door. Was it Dr. Jones? Surely she wouldn't come to his condo in the middle of the night. But maybe she wanted to apologize? That would be great, but it seemed unlikely.

Ashley didn't know where he lived and seemed equally unlikely to track him down. Those were basically the only women he knew.

Unless it was Zoe Cross.

No, that was ridiculous. Why would a supermodel be at his door?

The knocking continued and got even louder. The mystery lady seemed to be battering the door with some kind of hard object.

Zack missed another input, and Steve landed a hit that sent Zack's shields into the red. Seemed as though Steve had swapped out from lasers to mass drivers, which gave him a higher rate of fire and lower energy draw. Of course, there were issues in terms of range, but Zack was in a middle of a dogfight.

Rather than push matters, Zack swore and pulled back to take cover behind Greg.

"Fancy meeting you here," Jenny said.

"What is that noise on your end?" Greg said. "I can't focus with that going on."

"You can't focus? How do you think I feel?" Zack said, keeping his voice down so that the woman at the door wouldn't hear him. "Some lady is trying to knock my door down."

"Seriously?" Greg said. "Why?"

"I hate to pass up the comedic gold of this situation," Faz said, "but in case you haven't noticed, we're kind of in the middle of something right now. Either get your head in the game or let Greg cover for you while you answer the door."

"I'm sure she'll go away eventually."

The knocking intensified until it was an insistent pounding.

Zack sighed. "Fine. I'll be right back."

He pulled away, hitting the boosters and killing his recharge for his lasers. A quick set of commands had him headed to dock and swapping out his weapons. They had enough data for these two, so he might as well make use of the time. And the autopilot could deal with the simple commands.

Then Zack stood slowly and limped toward the door. His muscles were still sore and sitting for so long had made him stiff. He grabbed his OptiGlasses off the couch and slid them on.

A flood of notifications rushed past. The condo app had sent him a message from the exterminator, confirming his appointment for tomorrow; a notice from the building's management that the cleaning service had registered a hygiene complaint; and five noise complaints from another resident. The noise complaints were accompanied by messages from the app's resident messaging service, which Zack had not known existed until that moment. Apparently, you could send messages to the other residents via private chat rooms.

Handy if you knew your neighbors, which Zack didn't. But whoever was in room 615 was seriously ticked about his music choices and the reverb his laser cannon produced. Zack pulled open the door and froze.

A very angry woman stood in the hallway, her strawberry-blond hair mussed and her attractive face settled into a scowl.

Kayla Taylor.

She held a stiletto heel in each hand and had apparently been beating the door with them. Kayla's face was flushed from the effort of pounding down his door with her footwear. Her blue eyes glistened with a fury that made Zack swallow and wish he had checked the security camera before answering the door.

DaEvo flashed Kayla's stats, but Zack didn't need a reminder that she was a swimsuit model.

"You!" Kayla said. "What the hell is wrong with you?"

DaEvo chimed and restarted the conversation timer.

"Wait, it really is a girl?" Faz's voice echoed from behind Zack.

"Zack's got a girl trying to break into his apartment?" Greg whistled.

"Focus!" Jenny said.

Their voices rang through the speaker, definitely loud enough for Kayla to hear.

Zack quickly muted the console with a swipe of his eyes and smiled at Kayla, trying to ease the tension. "Sorry about that."

"Sorry? I've been sending you messages for the past three hours. What is your problem?"

Zack swallowed. "Yeah. Sorry. Didn't see them."

"Didn't see them? You honestly expect me to believe that your OptiGlasses and smart house system didn't let you know you had messages? I'm trying to film a makeup tutorial for my vlog. You're killing my vibe with your lame music and video game sound effects. This is unacceptable." She pursed her lips again.

Zack felt sweat beading on his brow. "Kayla—"

She raised an eyebrow and glared even harder at him. "Have we met?"

Damn, he had done it again. Stupid DaEvo. The last thing he needed was for another woman to accuse him of stalking and further ruin his Reputation.

"I, um, recognized you in the gym the other day. Look, I'm sorry."

Quest: Your Lady is Upset
Find out what's bothering her and make her feel better to earn bonus points.

His lady? That was a stretch, but maybe he could score some bonus game time here. Zack stared at Kayla. He had leveled up. Maybe she wasn't so far out of his league now.

"Oh, you're a fan. That's different. But still, you need to keep it down. Some of us have important things to do."

Important things to do? She had some nerve. Before Zack could respond, Kayla tossed her strawberry-blond hair over her shoulder. Zack caught a whiff of floral perfume that distracted him from the rant he had been about to start. She smelled a whole lot better than his now overwhelmingly lemon-scented apartment.

Success!
Based on our scan of her facial expression and voice tone, your lady is feeling better. Now seal the deal and ask her out!

Social Status Bonus: +60 minutes of unrestricted electronic time

Ask her out? That was crazy, wasn't it? Then again, maybe not. DaEvo's advice had been mixed so far.

Zack decided to chance it. "I-I really am sorry. Let me m-make it up to you."

Kayla crossed her arms, and he clamped his mouth shut, embarrassed that he had even tried. She looked him up and down as if she might be quizzed on him later and needed to notice every detail. Her gaze flickered to the inside of his apartment. It looked better since he had cleaned it, but her expression said it was still far from satisfactory.

"Let me take you to dinner?" Zack wasn't sure why the words

came out as a question. He wasn't sure why he was bothering to speak at all, except that DaEvo was giving him conversation points.

"The gym," Kayla said finally, uncrossing her arms. "You were working with a trainer. I remember now."

"Yeah? I mean, yeah. I got a little out of shape after my injury, but I'm getting back into it now."

Zack struggled to breathe and prayed Kayla would accept the excuse and not ask what injury. He was still wearing his FitLife clothes and drenched. Granted, he was mostly wet with laundry water, but the effect was largely the same. As far as she knew, he worked out all the time.

DaEvo flashed another notification, once again encouraging Zack to ask her out.

Why not? He had nothing to lose at this point.

"So you probably work up an appetite burning all those calories," he said. "I could treat you to lunch in the gym café sometime. You know, to make up for ruining your makeup. Just don't try the smoothies. They're really gross."

Kayla stared at him for a moment. Then she laughed. DaEvo chimed bonus points.

"They really are disgusting, aren't they?" she said. "I did a commercial for those once. Drink them and smile. It was one of the toughest shoots I've ever done."

"That sounds awful!" Zack said.

DaEvo chimed a warning, scolding him for insulting her work.

"I mean, that sounds cool!" he added quickly. "That you were in a commercial, that is. Really awesome!"

DaEvo chimed points for the compliment.

Kayla smiled. "It was all right, I guess. So what do you do? Sit around and play video games all day?"

Zack swallowed, the desire to impress her warring with the desire to defend Star Fury. He glanced at the conversation timer and bonus points and decided now was not the time to argue about the validity of professional gaming as a career.

"Oh, that? It's just something I picked up to pass the time while I recovered from my injury. Usually I'm busy managing my charitable trust…" Seeing she seemed a little interested, Zack added the only pertinent detail he could think of, "In New York."

"Really? What does your charity do?"

"It helps hospitals."

Zack hoped Kayla wouldn't ask more questions. He really wasn't prepared to answer them. Lucky for him, she was starting to look bored by the conversation. Or not so lucky. He was getting conversation points, but the date would get him some serious game time.

"We should do coffee sometime," he said. "Since we're neighbors, you know? It's crazy how no one knows their neighbors these days."

Kayla looked over Zack consideringly once more. Her eyes strayed into his apartment then stopped at his OptiGlasses and clothing. "All right."

"All right?"

"Yes, all right. I'm meeting with some friends tonight to discuss a charity event. If you're into that sort of thing, we can go together. It might make you both happy."

Both? Zack wondered who the other person was but discarded the stray thought. Better to focus on the agreement. "Perfect! I'll take all of you. Wherever you want to go. My treat."

Zack's voice was little more than a wheeze. DaEvo chimed something about a date, but he swiped away the notification. Hopefully DaEvo wouldn't take the points away when it realized this date was more of a group thing. If he could get points for the date tonight, it would go a long way to getting him enough time for the tournament. And if Kayla didn't think it was a date, that was fine—so long as DaEvo did. Though she had started eyeing him again after he offered to pay for everyone. Maybe he had pushed it too far?

Faz: *Hey, we're dying here. Finish up with your lady and get back here.*

. . .

Zack swiped the notification away and kept his attention on Kayla. She smiled at him, looking more like she was posing for a camera than actually experiencing happiness.

"All right, then. Alfonso's at ten thirty. It's black tie. I already have a reservation under my name."

"Great!" Zack hated that his voice cracked a little. Not exactly the impression he wanted to create. But

Kayla didn't seem to notice. "We'll meet you there. What was your name?"

"Zack."

"See you later, Zack."

She gave him another smile and walked away. Zack stumbled back into his apartment and closed the door.

DaEvo chimed.

Conversation Quest (On-going) Succeeded
Rewards: +30 minutes unrestricted internet privileges
Bonus Achieved: Cheer her up +45 minutes
Bonus Achieved: Make her laugh. +30 Minutes Use Time

Zack found himself grinning. Her higher level meant that she gave him a ton of points.

Main Questline Progress: Get a Date!
Against all the odds, you've managed to get another date. Congratulations!

Reward: Additional 2.5 hours of Unrestricted Electronic Access

Bonus Reward: Date a woman over level 50 levels above you—+4 hours

Bonus Reward: Increased Reputation ($variable—date Reputation status)

Successfully completing a date will unlock the following:

Spend some one-on-one time with your special lady by asking her out on a date. Completing this quest will unlock Relationship Milestone bonuses and additional quests.

A successful date will unlock the Lovemeter and unlimited access to non-essential internet privileges.

Zack's jaw dropped a little at the notifications. First, the additional play time. And then, the fact that he could unlock the Lovemeter with more than one woman. That would come in handy. Ashley still hadn't called him back. Maybe she hadn't enjoyed their date as much as Zack had. Maybe DaEvo was right and he shouldn't have talked so much about gaming.

He opened the phone app to call her, but DaEvo flashed a warning.

Relationship Hint: Frequent Contact is Good, Desperation is Bad

We noticed you've attempted to contact Ashley Barnes repeatedly. While frequent contact can improve your relationship, no love interest wants a desperate individual. Consider holding off and giving your target time to reply.

Penalty: Increased Lovemeter diminishment

Zack sighed. If he couldn't call and Ashley didn't call back, he had no way to refill her Lovemeter. He needed a backup plan. Kayla lived in his building. She was higher level and easier to reach. Even if he didn't manage to get the Lovemeter going, maybe he could bank enough time via casual conversations to keep training.

Zack checked the time. He had a few hours until he was supposed to rendezvous with Kayla and her friends. It sucked that he'd have to cut out of the raid early, but at the least, he could finish destroying Steve and test out the lasers and the EMP issues. He would have to explain things to the team, but he was sure he could figure out a good excuse. Worst case, he'd meet up with them tomorrow and run another set of tests.

He dove back into his gaming chair and picked up his joystick and shifted the keyboard closer. Some of the other Corsair teams had noticed the large group of Armada gathering around them and had swung by to provide backup. A tap of the button had Zack undocking and boosting back to the main fight.

Time to get this over with and test out the weapons. Maybe if they figured out what these new drones were, the team wouldn't be too angry with him when he cut out early.

Chapter Twenty-Four

NOTHING TO WEAR. How could he have boxes full of new clothes and still have nothing to wear? As soon as the raid ended, Zack had logged out of Star Fury and searched what black tie dress code meant. Apparently, it was more than just the tie. He would be expected to wear a tuxedo jacket, cufflinks, and cumberbund.

Whatever the hell that was.

Maybe he should have ordered that custom tux from the store in the mall after all. What were the odds that he could get all those things in the next twenty minutes?

His OptiGlasses chimed, and Zack answered the call as he rummaged through the online shopping boxes searching for something that might be appropriate for his dinner date with Kayla. A series of cheers and war cries assaulted his ears. His teammates were in full celebration mode.

"Dude, why did you log off?" Greg said. "There's an insane celebration going on in the Corsair's Cross!"

"He probably has to wash the dishes," Faz said.

"Oh my gosh, please stop making jokes about chores," Jenny said. "Are you out of game time, Zack? I thought you'd figured that out."

Zack sighed. Corsair's Cross was a popular digital hangout for Star Fury players. The party was probably great. The chat would be buzzing, and people would be running silly dares and missions, with drone and mine layers setting up impromptu courses all night long.

"Sorry, I can't make it tonight. I've got a date, and I need to figure out what to wear."

"A date?" Greg said. "With the girl who was breaking down your door?"

"No, with Zoe Cross, stupid," Faz said. "Don't you remember? Zack talks to her all the time."

Jenny giggled, and Faz laughed so loudly that he maxed out his microphone, turning the sound into digital distortion. Zack glared at the mountain of clothes around him. He had undone all his cleaning efforts in his search for something appropriate and was still no closer to having black tie apparel.

He only had fifteen minutes to figure out a solution, and his teammates' laughter was not helping his concentration. "It's not Zoe, but she is a model."

He was trying to shut them up, but Faz and Greg laughed even harder.

"Who is it then?" Greg said. "Anybody we know?"

"Shut up."

"So what are you wearing?" Jenny asked.

Zack hesitated, trying to decide if he was walking into another joke. He glanced at the clock again and swallowed. If he was going to pull this off, he needed help. "Black tie, but I don't have a tux. Any ideas?"

"You're serious?" Jenny said.

"Dude, that's taking it too far," Faz said. "Just let it go."

"You're one to talk about taking it too far," Greg said.

"You need more than a tux for black tie," Jenny said. "How much time do you have?"

"Ten minutes."

Jenny swore, and Zack winced. Apparently, he was in more trouble than he thought.

"Seriously, guys. I need ideas."

"Wait, do you actually have a date?" Faz asked.

"If you can't meet the dress code, your best bet is to be edgy," Jenny said. "Wear something unusual and call it avant-garde."

"Avant what?" Greg said.

"You could look at the latest editions of fashion magazines for ideas," Jenny said. "Maybe you could pull off hobo-chic? It's a little tricky, because if you do it wrong, you'll just look homeless, but you probably have everything you need already."

"How do you know all this?" Greg asked.

"What? You think I can't be a gamer and follow fashion at the same time?"

Zack ignored their bantering, left the piles of clothes and boxes on his floor, and went to his closet. The WesterNeon jacket hung there, the fringe rustling as it swayed on the hanger.

"So something from a magazine?" he said weakly. "Something edgy?"

"Yeah. Some places are still pretty strict about black tie, but it's your best bet. Do you have anything like that?"

"Of course he doesn't," Faz said. "This is Zack we're talking about. He doesn't have any avant-garde clothes, and he definitely doesn't have a date with a model tonight. He's just trying to cover for the fact that he's out of game time and has to wash the dishes before he can join the party."

Zack stayed silent and stared at the WesterNeon jacket. The memory of Ashley laughing at him ran through his mind, and he winced.

"Is that true, Zack?" Jenny said. "If you're trying to distract us, you could come up with a better story than that."

"I think you mean a worse story," Greg said. "That's a great story. A little too great."

"At least some good came from it," Faz said. "We learned that our Jenny is a fashionista."

"Shut up, or I'll have drones follow you all night in Corsair's Cross and steal your drinks."

"Don't you dare! You cost me the hundred-drinks-in-a-day achievement the last time around."

Jenny snorted and Zack's lips twitched. Like most achievements, that one was utterly useless except as a nice little trophy on the wall. It was also incredibly hard to get since the avatar's coordination got worse each drink. Along with the stumbling came an increased chance of fainting. More than one player had been booted and forced to either choose to reenter sober—resetting their counter—or stay logged off till the system woke them.

"Zack, you still there?" Greg said.

"Huh? Yeah, I've got to go. Thanks for the help, Jenny. You guys have fun."

Zack hung up the call and pulled the WesterNeon jacket off the hanger. He only had five minutes to get ready for the date. He pinged the rideshare app, making sure the car was on time, and gulped.

This had better work.

Chapter Twenty-Five

ZACK SWALLOWED as his ride pulled up to Alfonso's. The place was ritzy to say the least. Gold, black marble, and dark brown hardwood accented the outside of the building. The doormen were dressed in expensive tailored uniforms, and the patrons were dressed in black tuxedos or gorgeous evening gowns.

Crap.

Zack opened DaEvo and looked over his Style stats to remind himself that some circles considered the fringed jacket and neon jeans fashionable. Hopefully these people were in those circles.

Kayla should be. She was a model. She was so stylish that he was going to earn Reputation points just for going out with her. They'd errored out the amount—or maybe it'd depend on how public this was?—but DaEvo had definitely mentioned it. As long as DaEvo recognized it as a date, this would start another Lovemeter and give Zack a backup plan for unlimited game time. He might even get more Reputation points to cover the damage from Dr. Jones.

"You getting out, buddy?" His driver, a tired-looking Hispanic man, was looking back at him with raised eyebrows.

Zack swallowed. "Yeah. Thanks."

He stepped out of the car, repeating to himself all the reasons this was a good idea and ignoring the attention that his neon clothes attracted. He was fashionable. Cutting edge.

He hoped.

Zack walked up the steps to the door and smiled at the hostess. As he treaded the stairs, he couldn't help but notice that there was a light floral scent in the air, something pumped to the exit. It actually smelled nice and made him a little hungry. The hostess was clad in a formal, black and white uniform that DaEvo gave high points for Style.

She gave him a haughty stare and wrinkled her nose when he made his way to her. Apparently, she didn't subscribe to *Fashion* magazine. "Can I help you?"

She sounded as if she would rather throw him down the stairs than let him into her restaurant.

"Yeah, I have a reservation. I'm with Kayla Taylor's party."

"You know Kayla Taylor? The model?" She raised an eyebrow, her voice filled with skepticism. She looked him up and down rather obviously. "I'm sorry, sir, but we have a very strict dress code. I can't let you in dressed like that."

"But this is—"

Someone gasped behind Zack, and he turned to see a short, slight man wearing large tortoiseshell OptiGlasses and the same fringed jacket as Zack. Actually, they were wearing the exact same outfit, down to the neon yellow cowboy hat.

"WesterNeon!" the man said. "You're wearing my work!"

"Um, yes?" Zack said.

"And it looks fabulous on you!" He walked around Zack, studying him with a critical eye.

Zack studied him as well. The man had curly dark hair covered by an enormous cowboy hat. Zack hoped his own hat didn't look that ridiculous. The whole outfit looked extremely out of place in such a swanky setting.

The man was either unaware of the scene he was causing, or completely aware and enjoying it immensely. He gave Zack a final sweeping look and beamed in approval.

"Yes, this was my vision! Fashionable apparel for the modern cowman. It suits you perfectly!" Before Zack could respond, the man turned to the hostess and tipped his hat. "David Davidson at your service, ma'am. I'm in Kayla Taylor's party."

The hostess's eyes widened. "Oh, of course, Mr. Davidson. Welcome to Alfonso's!"

"I'm with Kayla too!" Zack said quickly. If the hostess was going to let David in wearing the fringed jacket, she had to let him in too. At least, Zack hoped that was the case.

The designer tipped his hat again, this time in Zack's direction. "I should have guessed. Kayla always finds the most fashionable people wherever she goes. Shall we?"

He offered his arm. Not quite sure what else to do, Zack took it. They walked past the stunned hostess and into the restaurant.

Alfonso's was decorated with minimalist luxury: white walls and dark wood floors with a few gold accents and leafy green plants. Other than Zack and David, everyone in the restaurant looked equally elegant in their dark suits and jewel-toned gowns. The diners spoke in soft voices punctuated by the occasional clinks of forks and wine glasses. It reminded Zack of the board member dinners Phil had forced him to attend. That had stopped after Zack had spilled red wine on a particularly dull board member. It had been an accident. Sort of.

Zack had been glad to get out of the dinners at the time, but now he wished he had paid more attention to them or taken that deportment class DaEvo had suggested. How was he supposed to impress Kayla when he didn't know which fork to use?

"Kayla! Where are you?" David Davidson called.

Reputation -0.1

David's voice pierced the restaurant, as out of place as his neon jacket and hat. The room went silent as everyone stared at them, and Zack wondered if he should have stayed home and partied at Corsair's Cross after all. This evening was not off to a good start.

"Dave! David, over here!" Kayla's voice rang from a corner of the room, and the designer pulled Zack along with him. Kayla laughed as she kissed David on both cheeks. "Causing a scene again?"

"I can't help it if I'm the only thing worth looking at in this place," David said. "And look who I ran into at the door. Your very stylish, fashion forward friend."

"You came!" Kayla said, studying Zack with a critical eye before nodding in approval.

He let out the breath he had been holding. She wasn't laughing in his face. Thank goodness.

"And wearing WesterNeon. That's bold. Is Dave paying you to promote his line?"

DaEvo alerted him that he was on a date, and Zack breathed a little easier. It seemed that DaEvo was going to count this as a date. After dismissing the notifications, Zack realized Kayla was still waiting for an answer, so he mutely shook his head. Kayla's blue eyes gleamed as she copied her greeting to Dave and kissed both Zack's cheeks. He flushed, and DaEvo chimed to inform him the date was going well.

"I would never bribe someone to wear my work," Dave protested. "Your friend simply has excellent taste."

"In clothes, but not in music. Zack's treating us to dinner to apologize for making too much noise and ruining my makeup tutorial filming," Kayla said, pursing her lips in a fake pout.

"Fabulous!" David said. "Where is everyone?"

"Running late as usual," Kayla said. "Smile. This will be great exposure for your collection, Dave."

She wrapped her arms around the two men and smiled at a woman holding a camera. Zack was too distracted by Kayla's arm around his shoulder to process what was happening. Then the camera flashed, and Kayla pulled away.

"Sorry we're late!"

A small crowd of people swept toward them, and Zack found himself surrounded by a well-dressed, elegant group of strangers. Kayla grabbed his arm and dragged him to a chair next to hers at a round table. Waiters poured wine, and Zack surveyed the table.

There were at least fifteen people there. DaEvo chimed and put hearts with stats over the women's heads. Zack glanced through the provided information. Most were also models or fashion industry experts, although one worked as a dermatologist and one was a psychologist.

"Who's your friend, Kayla?" a woman asked. "Did you rope him into helping with the gala as well?"

She was seated to Zack's left and blocked from his view by David Davidson's enormous cowboy hat. When Zack selected the pink heart above her head, DaEvo chimed.

Social Status information currently unavailable. Please acquire a full view of subject's face and/or request access to individual's social profile for further information.

{----! Dev note—Due to concerns about DaEvo's data collection methods raised by a number of alpha users, we have adjusted data collection methods to only publicly facing data collection methods. ----!}

"The gala?" Zack asked, leaning forward and trying to see her face. She sounded familiar, but he couldn't quite place her voice.

"The benefit gala," Kayla said. "That's what we're here to plan. You should come! Everyone who's anyone will be there."

"Yeah? Yeah, sure. Sounds great," Zack muttered.

It sounded like a date, so DaEvo would give him points for going. Right? He tried to find some enthusiasm in his soul for it, but really, hobnobbing wasn't his thing. He'd done a few galas as a teen when Phil had forced him to go. And, Zack had to admit, he'd thought it might have been a good chance to meet women. In the end, he'd just felt stifled and bored.

Kayla grinned at him and turned her attention to someone across the table, talking about which filter to use on the photos taken at the gala and what the official hashtag should be. Zack, forgotten, sipped on the wine the waiter had poured him. Apparently, someone had ordered for the table at some point, because the waiters brought out appetizers and bread without any sign of a menu.

Zack chewed on a piece of calamari and leaned back in his chair. He had to admit, the food was good. Better than his usual diet of pizza and Chinese takeout. It was good enough, in fact, that DaEvo was highlighting aspects of the dishes as a healthy meal. Not the calamari of course. Deep fried was bad...

The woman hidden behind David Davidson's hat seemed to be in charge. She checked in with each person at the table, asking about details for the gala or their latest fashion projects. Boring. This was just a board meeting with a different kind of board.

Zack flipped open his messaging app. Doing that discreetly with his OptiGlasses was easy enough. His teammates had sent him screenshots of the digital afterparty at Corsair's Cross. It looked epic. Someone had set up an obstacle course, and everyone was racing around the outpost. They were all using disposable pods, so when they crashed into the mines, the explosions were extra spectacular.

Maybe he should ditch this dinner. Yes, Kayla was hot, but he'd rather be celebrating the successful raid and seeing what his fellow Corsairs knew about the mysterious new drones.

DaEvo chimed, and Zack opened the app. A *Quest in Progress* notice showed that in spite of the strange circumstances, the app was still counting this as a date. It was even giving bonus points because Kayla was doing most of the talking rather than him. For once—okay, more than once—the buggy app was working for him.

Reputation +1.3

What? How had his reputation improved so much? He was just sitting here.

Beside him, Kayla giggled. "I told you this would be good exposure for your collection, Dave. Check it out."

She held a tablet toward the designer, and Zack gaped at it. Kayla, or more likely the assistant who had taken the picture, had uploaded the picture of them to Kayla's social media profiles. Kayla looked stunning. David Davidson looked eccentric. Zack looked—well, he looked like himself in a neon, fringed cowboy jacket, surprised to have his picture taken.

But over two thousand people had already liked the picture. DaEvo chimed.

Social media can be a great way to improve your Reputation and show people who you really are. Nice job, influencer!

Holy crap! He had improved his Reputation score without any effort on his part! Apparently, Kayla was Reputation gold.

"Did you mention the gala in the post?" the woman behind David's hat asked.

"Oops! Slipped my mind," Kayla said, shrugging. "I'll catch it next time and put a link to buy tickets."

"This is about more than selling tickets to a party and boosting brands, Kayla," the woman said. "If we truly want to help our cause and improve access to technological education in underprivileged communities, we need grassroots support. Real change happens when communities get involved, not just celebrities."

She leaned forward, and Zack dropped his fork in surprise. It clattered to the floor, and a waiter scurried to pick it up and give him a new one. Not that Zack really noticed. He was too busy staring at the woman.

Zoe Cross.

He was sitting three feet away from Zoe Cross.

Zoe looked amused by his staring and turned her attention to the person next to her, asking for details about press coverage or something.

"People are asking about you in the comments," Kayla said, nudging him. "They're wondering if we're an item."

"Huh?" Zack dragged his gaze away from Zoe and turned back to Kayla.

Her blue eyes had turned steely, and DaEvo chimed.

**_Your lady is upset because you're not being atten-
tive. Make her feel better by paying her a
compliment._**

Tip: You probably shouldn't ogle other women while on a date.

*{--Dev. note: Is this tip really necessary? Surely nobody would be that
stupid.--}*

Ogle? He hadn't been ogling Zoe exactly. Just staring in surprise.
Surely Kayla wasn't upset about that?

Zack studied her face. She was smiling brightly. Quite brightly,
with big teeth. He probably should answer her question, but now,
he'd forgotten it.

"I haven't responded to the comments yet. I thought it might be
fun to keep them guessing." Kayla leaned forward slowly to put her
wine glass back on the table, giving Zack a prolonged look down her
low-cut dress.

"Oh, yeah. Sure? Guessing. Good."

He could feel his face getting red, but Kayla didn't seem to
notice. Or at least, she didn't seem to care.

"You know, I don't have a date to the gala yet. We could go
together."

"Yeah?" Zack's voice had gone a little scratchy, but at least it
wasn't squeaking.

"Yeah. What do you think?" Zack nodded, and Kayla turned to
the woman who had taken their picture. "Karen, my friend Zack
wants to buy two gala tickets. Send him an invoice?"

Karen tapped on her tablet, and a purchase request popped
onto Zack's OptiGlasses. He swiped the confirmation and took a
drink of water, trying to ease the dryness in his throat. It didn't help.

Kayla seemed to be expecting him to say something, so Zack
cleared his throat and did his best to speak. His voice came out in a
rasp. "Gala. Cool."

Bonus Achievement! Use a sexy growl.

Sweet. This evening was going even better than planned.

Zoe leaned around David's hat and smiled at Zack. "Thanks for that. It's generous of you to support the cause."

"Um, yeah. The cause."

Zack stared at Zoe, still feeling dazzled. There seemed to be a little twinkle in Zoe's eyes when she looked at him, then she darted her gaze over to Kayla beside him. Before he could think of something else to say, an enormous yellow cowboy hat obstructed her from view.

"You'll wear WesterNeon, of course!" David Davidson said.

"Um, sure."

"He'll do no such thing," Kayla said. "You don't have a Wester-Neon line for women yet, and we need to coordinate. He's wearing a tux."

"I'll make him a tie then."

"Only if you make matching shoes for me."

"Deal."

Kayla grinned, and that seemed to settle the matter. She leaned back in her chair, and conversation once again turned to planning the details of the gala. Kayla turned her attention to her phone, tapping furiously.

Zack blinked, wondering what had just happened. He'd talked to Zoe Cross and gotten a second date from Kayla. DaEvo had even given him bonus points for setting up a second date before his first one. However, there wasn't any indication that he'd unlocked the Lovemeter yet, which was odd. Was it because the first date wasn't over?

Silence can be good, but not if your date is no longer interested. You've spent 83% of the current date not speaking to one another. Keep the conversation going!

Zack leaned closer to Kayla so the rest of the table wouldn't hear and whispered the first thing that came to mind. "I don't have a tux."

She blinked at him in surprise, then shrugged and set her phone on the table. "So we'll go shopping tomorrow. The moving company lost half my clothes when I came here, so I don't have anything to wear either."

Her breath was warm against his skin, and Zack's heart rate increased as she leaned in closer and put a hand on his shoulder.

Workout Detected

Your increased heart rate indicates that you're working out. Accept an official quest to level up your physique.

Quest in Progress: First Date

Good job! We've detected a significant and frequent amount of physical contact between you and your date. This is a common indicator of interest.

For once, Zack didn't need DaEvo to tell him that she was flirting. At least, he was pretty sure that was what was happening. His mind raced. Shopping. What would shopping with a supermodel look like? Would they stick to dresses or—

Zack stopped himself from following that particular train of thought. He couldn't afford to get distracted right now. Not if he wanted to satisfy DaEvo and gain unlimited game time. "Really. That's… a pity. We'll have to fix that."

"So shopping tomorrow?"

"Yeah. Sounds good."

DaEvo chimed, giving him further accolades for scheduling a third date. It flickered for a second before changing to second, probably updating as it registered timing. Either way, this looked amazing. So long as he didn't mess up, he was guaranteed to get the Lovemeter unlocked.

Kayla winked at him and turned to answer a question Zoe had asked about the gala. Zack leaned back in his chair and smiled. This had gone way better than expected. Apparently, he had just needed to level up a little to find the right woman. Much as he hated to admit it, maybe Phil had been right. DaEvo was just what he needed.

Chapter Twenty-Six

ZACK WOKE with a massive headache and his OptiGlasses chiming a message notification. He slipped them on, grimacing at his sore muscles and grateful that he could control everything with his eyes.

Ashley: *Hey, so sorry I missed your call! Amber's back in the hospital, and I forgot my charger. Anyway, I had a great time. Thanks again for lunch and the fan.*

Zack grinned as DaEvo congratulated him on the message and added a full heart to Ashley's Lovemeter. A 10% increase for a single message. He needed one more to earn unlimited game time though, as it'd kept falling all through the night. He blinked as he noted that the damn app had updated itself. Again.

He read the message again and swiped his eyes to reply. He didn't need DaEvo to tell him that Ashley was probably upset to have her sister back in the hospital, but he wasn't quite sure what to say to make it better. The familiar feelings of dread and helplessness hovered at the edge of his mind, and he kept the text short so he could finish and push them away.

Zack: *You're welcome. Hey, is Amber okay?*

He left the messaging app open in case she answered right away. When she didn't, Zack settled back in his pillow and closed his eyes to block out the morning sunlight.

He opened them again as memories slowly surfaced. Dinner with Kayla. Meeting Zoe. Had all that really happened?

He opened DaEvo and checked his stats to make sure the evening hadn't been a dream. Sure enough, he now had two Lovemeters up and running. He still wasn't sure if that was supposed to happen, but if this was a dating game, then maybe? He knew dating more than one person was common. Because really, it was the modern world. Multi-dating was a thing, right?

Looking more closely at the Lovemeter, Zack winced. Ashley's was flashing red, warning him that he had lost unlimited game time until he refilled it. DaEvo must have considered the expensive dinner worth more points than the picnic lunch, because the pink hearts in Kayla's thermometer were three quarters of the way to the top. If spending money was the key to keeping the Lovemeter full, he had no problem making the sacrifice.

Zack grinned as he replayed the evening's events. Zoe had been all business, but Kayla had been into him. Apparently, DaEvo was actually right about some things. His Style upgrade had paid off, and he had a second date with a model. Multiple dates if you counted the upcoming gala. That should be plenty to keep the Lovemeter full and give him unlimited game time.

Plus, he was earning Reputation points and—

His OptiGlasses chimed, interrupting Zack's scheming.

***Potentially fraudulent activity detected. Did you
make this purchase?***
Alfonso's Restaurant. $3,932.12

Good grief, that dinner had not come cheap. Zack scrolled
through the itemized list, then gave up and swiped away the receipt.
He had scored a date with a swimsuit model and a ton of points.
Worth it. He sat up and stretched his arms over his head. They were
still sore from cleaning his apartment the day before. And now, he'd
made a mess of it again.

His OptiGlasses chimed again.

***Potentially fraudulent activity detected. Did you
make this purchase?***
Zoe Cross Charity Gala. $40,000.00

Zack collapsed back onto his pillow. Forty grand? Maybe he
should have asked a few more questions before agreeing to buy
those tickets. Then again, his foundation gave way more than that to
hospitals on a regular basis. Those ticket purchases were supporting
two good causes: a charity and his love life.

Three good causes if you counted the Reputation points he
would earn from attending such a high-profile event with Kayla on
his arm.

Zack scrolled through his appointment calendar. What time had
he agreed to meet Kayla for shopping? Not until two o'clock in the
afternoon. That left plenty of time to eat and train first. Jenny had
collected some interesting data on the new Armada drones during
the raid and sent the team some settings to try that might make it
easier to detect them.

Zack pulled himself out of bed.

DaEvo chimed.

Health Quest Failed!

You did not get enough sleep last night! Adequate rest improves one's health and appearance.
Effect: -0.1 Physique

Recommended Quests:

- *Facial*
- *Application of makeup*
- *Nap time*

The suggestions were new. Must be part of the update. Zack rolled his eyes and stumbled toward the bathroom. His OptiGlasses chimed just as he finished brushing his teeth.

Phil.

Zack sighed and accepted the call. The trustee's eyes were bugging out of his head even before he started speaking.

"What the hell? Forty-thousand dollars for gala tickets? Four grand for dinner? I'm enacting the budget clause. The trust will cover your bills, but I'm freezing the rest of your accounts."

"What? No, you can't! I have a shopping date today."

"Your dates have very expensive taste. You know a real relationship isn't based on spending money, right?"

"She's a model!"

"And that justifies spending thousands of dollars in a week? I thought we were over this phase!"

Zack said, "It's not like I spend it on anything else. The app is working. This is what you wanted!"

"This is most certainly not what I wanted! You're rich, but even you have limits."

"A few nice dinners aren't going to bankrupt me."

"They will if you make them a habit, and I won't sit here and watch you buy your way into a relationship. This isn't healthy behavior. You were warned. As of today, you've been cut off."

"That's not fair!" Zack whined. "I've done so many stupid things for this app, and you're going to cut me off for spending money? I even cleaned the apartment!"

"You mean you hired someone to clean the apartment. You bought that just like you're trying to buy everything else."

"No. I literally cleaned the apartment myself."

Phil was quiet at that. He seemed too surprised to speak.

Zack saw an opening and took it. "I threw out all the garbage, put away my clothes, even did my own laundry! Come on, don't cut me off. I'll do anything."

"Anything?"

"Well, not anything. I mean—" Phil's eyes narrowed, and Zack quickly backstepped. "Fine, anything. Look, she's into me, and I got carried away trying to impress her. I should have paid attention to the ticket prices. I'll watch my spending from now on, but I can't date without any money. Do you want me to beat this game or not?"

"Hmm."

Phil seemed to be considering that, and Zack forced himself to stay quiet and wait for the trustee's verdict. If Phil cut him off, he wouldn't be able to get a suit for the gala or buy Kayla new clothes or—

"Fine," Phil said. "I'll give you back access to your accounts on one condition."

Zack swallowed. The trustee was giving him what he wanted, but the glee in Phil's voice suggested that Zack wouldn't like the condition. "What's the catch?"

"You will complete every Physique quest DaEvo suggests. That means you eat what it tells you to eat and complete the workouts it suggests. You get enough sleep. You—"

"What!"

"The doctors at the hospital were concerned about your health, and I have to agree with them. You're overweight and showing early signs of some chronic conditions. You need to turn this around."

"I'm fine! I feel fine!"

"That's my deal. Take it or leave it."

Zack leaned against his sink, staring in the mirror as he tried to process the implications of Phil's offer. Sure, he had gained a little weight since college, but didn't everybody do that? It was perfectly natural. "You're killing me, Phil."

"More like saving you. So what will it be? Your pizza or your bank account?"

Zack gritted his teeth and gripped the edge of the counter. "Fine. You win." He spat the words with as much venom as he could muster.

Phil's grin widened. "Great. I'll be in close contact with the developers to make sure you don't step out of line. Have fun on your date."

Phil ended the call, and Zack collapsed against the counter. Every Physique quest. He would be dead by the end of the week. This couldn't be happening. It had to be a bad dream.

Physique Quest!
Breakfast is the most important meal of the day. Eat a healthy breakfast to level up your physique.
Reward: +0.1 Physique

Crap.

Chapter Twenty-Seven

ZACK SHOVELED the omelet into his mouth as fast as he could and downed the green juice.

DaEvo chimed.

Quest Complete!
Eat a healthy meal.
Physique +0.1

There. He had satisfied Phil's requirements and eaten a healthy breakfast. Now, he needed to log into Star Fury and train before anything else interrupted him. He had unlimited game time thanks to Kayla's Lovemeter, and he didn't want to waste it.

Someone knocked on the door, and Zack swore under his breath. What now? He pulled open the door without checking the security camera. Whatever this was, he wanted to deal with it as quickly as possible and get back to training.

A man in brown coveralls and a baseball cap stood in the door-way. His hat had a dead roach embroidered on it, and he held a basket filled with an assortment of bottles with brightly colored labels. "Hi, I'm Rob. I'm here to spray for bugs."

Your alpha test bug report has been logged.
Thank you for your help in making DaEvo a success!

"Crap. I mean yeah, come in."

Rob entered the apartment and surveyed it with a critical eye. Thanks to Zack's frantic search for black tie apparel, the apartment was once again covered with scattered clothing and boxes. "Yeah, I can see why you'd have a problem. You'll need to throw away any food and wash all your dishes after I'm done."

"Sure. Not a problem."

Considering that Zack was out of food and didn't own any dishes, that wouldn't be a problem at all.

"You have a pet?" Rob said, gesturing to the hamster cage on the counter.

"Yeah. He's roaming free at the moment."

"You let a rodent run free around your apartment?"

"Not on purpose. He kind of escaped."

"You'll have to catch him before I spray. There's a pet-sitting service on the first floor where you can leave him until the fumes die down."

Zack glanced at the clock. Just past ten. Still plenty of time before his date with Kayla, but this exterminator was seriously eating into his game time. "Right. I guess we'd better find him then."

But Rob didn't seem inclined to help search for the hamster. He unpacked his basket then turned his attention to his phone. Zack rolled his eyes and surveyed the room. Veobos didn't have quite as many hiding places since Zack had done the laundry and cleaned. Where was the hamster most likely to have gone?

Zack knelt on the floor and peeked under the couch.

Beady black eyes stared back at him.

Success.

He reached under the couch, but the hamster darted out of his reach and all the way across the room. By the time Zack pulled his arm out from under the couch, Veobos had found some pizza crumbs on the floor and was chewing contentedly. The missing fitness band sat a few inches away from Zack's knees under the couch.

Physique Alert!

It's easier to track your results with accurate data. Put on your fitness band to provide more accurate Physique quests.

Crap.

Zack ignored the band and crept toward the hamster. Veobos kept chewing on the pizza. When Zack got close enough, he bent over to scoop up the creature. The hamster easily darted away. Zack sighed, picked up the fitness band instead, and put it on his wrist.

DaEvo chimed.

Physique Quest has Begun!

Your elevated heart rate suggests you're exercising. Keep your heart rate elevated for 30 minutes to level up your physique stats.

Damn it! Now he had to complete the physique quest or Phil would cut him off. He needed to be more careful about triggering those things. Zack wiped away the beads of sweat gathering on his forehead and continued to stalk the tiny rodent. This should be easy. A retrieval quest like in Star Fury. He just needed to surprise it.

Zack lunged toward the hamster. It scampered off and looked back when it was a safe distance away.

He would swear that thing was laughing at him. As was Rob the exterminator, although he quickly looked at his phone when Zack glared at him.

Okay, time to regroup. He wasn't faster than the hamster, but he was smarter.

It obviously liked pizza. Zack retrieved a half-eaten slice from the floor, set a Fit Life shipping box sideways, and placed the pizza inside. After that, he cleared the floor of any other crumbs or pizza slices, dumping them into a garbage bag. Best not to mix things up too much. Once he was done, Zack stood behind the box as quietly as he could and waited.

Slowly, Veobos crawled over to the box. With bulging eyes, the hamster studied the pizza, then darted into the box.

Zack bent over and scooped up the box. "Ha!"

His OptiGlasses chimed a notification through the condo's app.

You have been flagged multiple times for noise complaints this week. Please refrain from jumping and shouting.

"Yeah, yeah."

Zack swiped away the message. The noise complaints had led to his date with Kayla, so everything had worked out all right. Veobos scurried around the box, not pleased to be trapped. Zack opened the door of the hamster enclosure and shook the Fit Life box until the hamster tumbled into the sawdust at the bottom of the cage. Veobos glared at him, then scampered over to his wheel and ran.

"You'll need to stay out of your apartment for a few hours," Rob said.

"But I need a shower."

"Use the one at the gym. I'm already behind schedule thanks to that thing."

Zack glared at Veobos. If he went to the gym, DaEvo was sure to suggest further Physique quests. Plus, the trainer he'd hired was probably on the lookout for him since he had skipped out on his weightlifting routine.

"Or I can come back later," Rob said. "I've got another opening next week."

Zack gritted his teeth. If he wanted to raise his level and slow down the Lovemeter's emptying, he needed that cleaning service to resume. He couldn't afford to delay this. "No, I want you to do it today. Give me a minute to get some clothes."

Zack reserved a room at Gord's for the afternoon and evening, just to be safe. Then he threw his gym clothes and one of his higher-level casual outfits into a backpack left over from his college days, grabbed the hamster enclosure, and stalked out of the condo.

Chapter Twenty-Eight

Quest Alert!
Your heart rate has slowed. Finish your workout to level up your Physique.

ZACK SWIPED the notification away so he could pay for the pet sitting service, then he sighed as he took the elevator back up to the gym. He jogged in place to raise his heart rate back to a level that DaEvo considered acceptable. He couldn't risk angering Phil by failing a Physique quest one day after he had agreed to complete all of them. As soon as Zack entered the gym, the condo app chimed.

Welcome back! Your personal trainer has programmed a workout for you. Would you like to begin it?

Zack stared at the notification. It had come from the gym, not DaEvo. That meant he didn't have to accept it, right?

He swiped no and flinched, waiting for DaEvo to tell him he had failed a quest. But nothing happened. Zack sighed in relief and opened his quests-in-progress menu. He just needed to keep his heart rate elevated for three more minutes. He could do that.

Zack shoved his backpack of clothes into the nearest locker and started walking around the track. DaEvo chimed and congratulated him on his elevated heart rate. Zack watched the countdown timer as he moved, determined not to walk a step further than necessary.

Quest Complete
Keep your heart rate elevated for 30 minutes. Physique +0.1

Thank goodness that was over. Zack had timed his walk so it ended in front of the locker room and he didn't waste any time. Now he just needed to take a shower, get dressed, and get to Gord's. DaEvo chimed.

Quest!
New workout detected: weightlifting routine. Working with a personal trainer is a great way to maximize your workouts. Complete the workout assigned by your personal trainer to level up your Physique!

"No!"

Zack only realized he had screamed the word when everyone in the gym turned to stare at him. He mumbled an apology while he stared at the quest notification and tried to think of a clever way around it.

When nothing came to mind, he hurried to the weight machines in the farthest corner of the room. If he had to do this, there was no point delaying the torture. The condo app chimed, directing him to his first machine, changing the settings for him automatically, and showing him a brief animation reminding him how to use it.

Zack groaned as he settled in and moved the weighted bar up and down. This was the worst. The literal worst.

It was almost lunchtime by the time he had finished the workout, showered, and changed. Throughout the morning, he'd noted the constant decrease in Kayla's Lovemeter. Her higher social status was really harming their love life, with it dropping at a rate nearly triple Ashley's. He really needed to close the distance between the two of them.

His clothes were wrinkled from being stuffed in the backpack. Not that Zack would normally have noticed, but DaEvo chimed a warning and deducted Style points, so it was hard to miss.

Whatever. He had two hours until he was supposed to meet Kayla, and he still hadn't completed any training for Star Fury. He didn't have time to waste ironing his clothes. Also, he didn't own an iron.

Zack entered Gord's and grinned when he saw Ashley at the counter. She smiled and waved between serving customers.

DaEvo chimed.

Relationship Quest!

You had a successful first date, but follow-up is key. Consider pursuing one of the following relationship milestones to fill your Lovemeter and level up:

- *first significant physical contact*
- *in-depth exchange of history*
- *your first kiss*
- *schedule a second date*
- *take her out to an exciting and memorable event*
- *your first [Dev Note—are we even allowed to suggest this? Ask Legal]*
- *become an [#select_variable: relationship type: exclusive;primary;secondary; pair-bonded; metamour]*
- *get engaged*

Zack scanned through the list. Most of those would be difficult to accomplish during a casual interaction at Ashley's place of work. They could exchange their history, although he wasn't exactly eager to give anyone an in-depth look at his past. That left scheduling a second date as an option.

Worth a try.

"Hey!" Ashley said. "How's it going?"

DaEvo chimed, and Zack noticed a new thermometer floating in the corner of his vision. He groaned, wondering if it was something new. A quick glance showed that it was new, and a way to tell how well a date was doing. Well, it could be worse.

Zack's smile widened as he focused on Ashley. "Not bad. You?"

"Busy. I thought things might slow down around here after the first tournament round, but we're busier than ever."

"Yeah, everybody who qualified will be practicing harder than ever before."

"Even the scum." Ashley cast a significant glance at the corner of the room where Steve and some other Armada players were practicing, and she made the Corsair sign, crossing her fingers and putting them over her heart.

Zack laughed and made the sign back to her. "I'd be careful about flashing that around here. You'll tick off the Armada."

"Oh, I already have. But I'm a Veridian, remember? They don't dare cross me anymore." She laughed, and DaEvo's thermometer shifted up.

Zack grinned. "I'm glad that worked."

"Like a charm. I only told one guy, but I guess word got around. You want your usual for lunch?"

She tapped on her computer, and Gord's flashed an order on his OptiGlasses for pizza and coffee. Before Zack could answer, DaEvo chimed.

Quest
If you eat better, you'll feel better! Consider one of the following healthier lunch options available at Gord's to level up your Physique.

- *Caesar Salad with Light Dressing*
- *Rotisserie Chicken Wrap*

Crap. Zack stared at the options for so long that DaEvo flashed a warning on the thermometer, making it drop.

"You okay?" Ashley asked.

"Huh? Yeah, fine. I'm actually going to take the chicken wrap today."

"Okay, cool. You still want coffee? We just got a fresh batch of raptor cow milk in."

Zack inhaled slowly, waiting for DaEvo to tell him he couldn't have the coffee, but the app remained silent. He smiled with relief. "Yeah, that sounds great."

Ashley turned her attention to making the latte and wrap. DaEvo flashed a conversation hint and suggested he ask about her interests. Zack opened his mouth to ask about her studies, then closed it again as he remembered the text she had sent that morning.

"Hey, how's Amber doing?" Zack said. "You said she was back in the hospital, right? Is she okay?"

Ashley's expression tightened a bit, and Zack wondered if he had misstepped. Maybe that hadn't been the right thing to say. Or maybe things hadn't gone well. What if Amber had suffered serious complications or—

"She's fine," Ashley said, and Zack's racing mind breathed a sigh of relief. "It's just going to take a while for things to get back to normal. It's hard, you know?"

"Yeah," Zack said softly.

The truth was, he had no idea. His parents had been killed instantly, so he had been spared long waits in hospital rooms and the slow recovery process. It was a mercy that they'd gone quickly and hadn't suffered. At least, that was what he told himself whenever he thought about it.

Almost without realizing what he was doing, Zack took Ashley's hand. He barely noticed DaEvo's thermometer going up as she met his gaze. Her eyes were brimming with tears that she refused to cry, although a few spilled over when Zack squeezed her hand.

"It will be all right." He had no way of knowing if that was true. Hell, he didn't even know what Amber was being treated for or how serious it was. But right now, he really wanted it to be true. He really wanted everything to be okay.

"Thanks."

Someone across the room shouted, interrupting the moment,

"Hey, I ordered a pizza twenty minutes ago! You going to bring it over, or are you too busy talking to your boyfriend?"

Ashley quickly let go of Zack's hand and wiped her tears. She glared at the gamer and flashed him the Corsair sign. "Cool your engines, Steve. You'll get your pizza." She winked at Zack as she handed him the coffee and wrap. "Armada scum."

Zack laughed.

Reminder: Relationship Milestones Unfulfilled!

To increase your Lovemeter ratings, you should complete additional Relationship Milestones. While frequent contact is important in establishing a relationship, you should be looking to progress the relationship. Push ahead with the relationship before things get too comfortable!

Zack spoke in a rush before Ashley walked away or he could second-guess himself. "Hey, do you want to go out again sometime? I could bring you lunch again or something."

"Yeah, I'd like that."

"Really?"

"Yeah. But right now, I'd better get back to work. That guy is a jerk, but I really can't afford for him to lodge a complaint with the manager."

"Yeah. Sure. Yeah. I'll see you later then."

Zack hurried away before he could say something stupid and ruin the moment. He was only vaguely aware of DaEvo playing cheesy music and filling Ashley's Lovemeter with pink hearts thanks to the conversation and second date.

Notice: Due to lost Lovemeter relationship points with Kayla Taylor, your Unlimited Internet Privileges have been revoked once again. Increase your Lovemeter levels to improve your relationship with Kayla Taylor!

Relationship Milestone Achieved! Schedule a Second Date

You have scheduled a date with Ashley Barnes. You have gained +20% to your Lovemeter with Ashley Barnes.

You now have sufficient Lovemeter levels with Ashley Barnes to access Unlimited Internet Privileges.

Zack dismissed the notifications. Thank goodness Ashley had been at work so he could ask her out. His date with Kayla that afternoon should fill her Lovemeter back up, and so long as he kept in contact with her, he should be able to keep it high enough.

He logged into Star Fury and set a course for the nearest battle royale to train.

Chapter Twenty-Nine

IT SEEMED as if only a few minutes had passed before a notification sounded on Zack's OptiGlasses. He took a deep breath and checked it, a little paranoid that DaEvo had come up with another Physique quest for him. But it was just his calendar app reminding him that he was supposed to meet Kayla in an hour.

That was followed by a reminder that his Style stats could be improved and probably should be if he wanted to make a good impression. Zack glanced at his shirt. It wasn't that wrinkled. And he couldn't go back to his apartment now because of the fumes from the bug spraying.

So there was nothing he could do about it. Besides, he was in the middle of a dogfight with two other ships. They had been exchanging fire for a while, none of them able to gain an advantage. If Zack timed this right, maybe he could finish the battle before he needed to leave for the date.

He lost himself in a blur of laser fire. His opponents were also Corsairs, and they had a few tricks up their sleeves. Tricks he needed to fight through so he would be prepared for the next tournament round.

His calendar app sent another reminder, and Zack swiped it

away. He had plenty of time, and he wouldn't get the kill rewards if he left the fight now. One of his opponents released a wave of drones, and Zack swore softly. What was it with drones these days? He needed to find a way to deal with them.

Zack grinned when he realized he already had. Since Jenny had managed to identify the EMP frequencies that disabled her drones, Zack had been able to amplify them. Maybe that would work to disable this guy.

He swooped into the cloud of drones and blasted one with his newly modified laser cannon. The resulting explosion caused five percent damage to his shields and fried the drones' navigation systems. Zack grinned with satisfaction as the drones drifted aimlessly through space.

Now he could move in for the kill, and—

His OptiGlasses chimed with a message.

Kayla: *See you soon. ;)*

The message was accompanied by the address of a formal wear store in the Gaillardia Mall. Zack looked at the clock in his Opti-Glasses frame and swore. Where had the time gone? He was going to be late.

Zack fired a few blasts from his laser cannon as a farewell, then he withdrew from the fight. The other ships sent a few missiles after him, then turned back to fighting each other. He sent a quick GG to the other Corsairs, grateful they hadn't chased him. With a flick of his fingers, Zack set his ship on a course for the landing dock and logged out.

Ashley was busy with a line of customers at her counter, but she waved as Zack sprinted through the lobby, calling a car. Once the car came and he got inside, he sent the address to the driver and settled back to catch his breath. A message chimed on his Opti-Glasses.

. . .

Kayla: *Where are you?*

Zack glanced at the estimated arrival time in the ride app and groaned. It was time for the date, and he was still twenty minutes away.

Zack: *Sorry, I got caught up in some work things. See you soon.*
    Kayla: *Fine, but I'm starting without you. What do you think of this one?*

That was followed by a picture of Kayla in a form-fitting black dress with a slit up to her thigh. Zack swallowed. He wasn't sure his initial response was appropriate to send, so he settled for:

Zack: *You look amazing!*
    Kayla: *Just amazing? I'd better try a few more then. ;)*

Zack tapped his foot impatiently as the car drove through the city. Hopefully DaEvo wouldn't take away points for his being so late. He needed to fill Kayla's Lovemeter so he had a backup for unlimited game time. He would complete Relationship Milestones with her, and that should give him a second life. Hopefully being seen with her would boost his Reputation as well. That would mean slower Lovemeter depletion and more time for gaming.

He had the plan. He just needed to execute it.

To distract himself during the drive, Zack pulled up an analysis from a trusted blogger about the latest Star Fury weaponry release. The next thing he knew, the driver was clearing his throat to let him know that they had arrived. Zack paid and hurried into the sleek shopping center. The mall's app guided him to the formal wear store, putting glowing purple arrows on the walkway in his vision while DaEvo kept filling in social stat information for every eligible woman he passed.

Once he arrived, Zack hurried inside, slightly out of breath and shaking from the strain on his already taxed muscles. Luxurious gowns on sleek mannequins filled the space. Softly pulsing music matched Zack's heartbeat as he surveyed the room looking for Kayla.

"Can I help you find something?" A silver-haired woman in black trousers and a crisp white shirt approached Zack. She looked immaculate, and her nose wrinkled slightly, as if she would rather help him find the door than something to purchase.

Zack caught a glimpse of himself in a mirror and sighed as DaEvo deducted style points. The hour of gaming had not done his already wrinkled clothes any favors, and he had spilled coffee on his shirt at some point without realizing it. "Yeah, I'm looking for Kayla Taylor."

It seemed like the kind of place where they would know a model by name, but the woman shook her head. "I'm afraid I don't know who you're talking about."

"But she said she was here."

"All of our client records are confidential, young man. Whatever you saw while stalking her on social media, it doesn't mean you can come barging in here, demanding to see someone."

Reputation -0.1

"Why does everyone think I'm a stalker?"

"Maybe because you look like one right now," Kayla said. "What are you wearing?"

Zack turned around to reply but found himself speechless. Kayla was wearing a sparkly red gown with a plunging neckline.

She struck a casual pose that accentuated the curve of her hips. "You like it?"

"You know him?" the store clerk said.

There was no need for her to sound so surprised. Kayla grinned and kissed Zack on both cheeks in a greeting. DaEvo chimed and his date thermometer that had started out cold increased.

"Of course. This is my date for Zoe's gala. He's going to help me pick out a dress."

Zack gave the clerk a smug look.

She studied him for a moment, then forced a smile and nodded. "Of course. So sorry for the misunderstanding, sir. Kayla insists on checking in and posting her location every time she shops here. We appreciate the publicity, of course, but it sometimes draws out the rabble trying to get close to her."

Zack chose to ignore the pointed way the clerk stared at him as she said "rabble." Instead, he focused on Kayla. "Is that the dress you're getting?"

"You like it?" She turned and walked the store aisle as if it were a runway.

Zack grinned. Yeah, he liked it a lot.

Kayla smiled back at him, taking his admiring gaze as an answer to her question. "I like it too, but I'm afraid it's a little too flashy for the gala. Zoe prefers for her events to be a bit more conservative."

"Oh. That's too bad."

Kayla laughed at the disappointment in Zack's voice and considered her reflection in a nearby mirror. "Maybe I should still get it. There will be other events."

"I'll buy it for you," Zack said quickly, before he could lose his nerve. Kayla raised an eyebrow, and he felt his face going as red as the dress. "You said they lost your luggage, right? Consider it a housewarming gift."

That sounded lame even as he said it, but Kayla grinned. "All right, if you insist. Thanks, neighbor." She turned to the store clerk. "I'll take this one and the black one I had set aside. Can you deliver them for me?"

"Of course."

Kayla turned back to Zack and smiled at him, placing a hand on his arm for a second. The clerk looked at Zack who just nodded absently. "Just give me a minute to change, then we'll do something about your wardrobe."

She disappeared into a fitting room, and Zack sank onto a nearby chair. Wow. This was going really well. Like, unbelievably well. Maybe DaEvo wasn't so worthless after all.

The store's app sent him a bill, and he blinked in surprise that two dresses could cost that much. Was that snooty clerk trying to overcharge him? A quick perusal of the store's online store and other similar sites told Zack that the prices were considered "normal" for women's gowns. Why anyone would pay thousands of dollars for a single dress was beyond him, but apparently it was a thing. DaEvo had better give him extra points for this. He approved the payment, then distracted himself by reading the Star Fury analysis until Kayla rejoined him. Zack grinned. She was wearing skinny jeans and a form-fitting tank top that was almost as revealing as the red dress.

Kayla pulled him to his feet and rested her hand on his arm, guiding him out of the store and through the mall. DaEvo chimed, doubtless to offer updates on the physical contact, but Zack swept away the notifications. He would sort through those later.

"I'll need accessories and a backup pair of shoes if David doesn't come through," Kayla said, "but first, we need to get you a tux."

She swept Zack into the custom tuxedo store he had noticed when he came to the mall to buy his WesterNeon outfit.

"Miss Taylor, welcome! You've decided to take up my suggestion to wear menswear to your next event? You'll make quite a splash."

Kayla laughed. "Not this time, Giacomo, but my date has nothing to wear to Zoe's gala. Can you fix that?"

Giacomo studied Zack from head to toe as if scanning him for custom battle armor. Not sure what else to do, Zack returned the stare. The tailor had salt-and-pepper hair and moved with a sort of studied casualness, as if he knew the world would wait for him to get where he was going and be glad when he did. If he hadn't been wearing purple crocodile-skin shoes and a measuring tape wrapped around his neck, Zack might have mistaken him for a banker or high-level CEO.

Or maybe a model. Giacomo's appearance was polished and his

suit was immaculate. Some sort of soft, gray material without a wrinkle in sight. He was perfectly groomed too, which reminded Zack he'd not shaved in a day. Or two.

Giacomo finished examining Zack and sniffed. "This will take some time, Miss Taylor. Perhaps you have some other errands you could run while I work?"

Kayla considered this, then turned to Zack. "I do need to pick up my shoes and accessories. I could do that now, unless you want to come? I can text you pictures of everything I find to make sure it will coordinate with your outfit. And we can go to dinner afterward."

She cocked her head, letting her red-gold hair fall down across her bare shoulder as she waited for his answer. For a moment, Zack found himself staring into her blue eyes, caught up in how pretty she was, even without filters. And then DaEvo chimed, letting him know that it wasn't polite to ogle his date for so long. Apparently, DaEvo just wasn't a fan of ogling in general.

"Yeah. Yeah, okay. And anything you buy is my treat, okay? I'm not sure dinner was enough to make up for ruining your tutorial."

Zack idly noted that Giacomo was smirking subtly as he watched the pair of them. Zack winced a little, trying to make himself look a little less awestruck. He was such a noob.

"Marvelous. Make him look fabulous, Giacomo." She kissed the tailor's cheeks and hurried out of the shop.

As soon as the door closed, Giacomo turned to Zack. "You can't go to dinner with Miss Taylor looking like that. I have a few ready-made things I can adjust for you."

"I just need a tux."

"My boy, you need much more than that."

The tailor rang a small bell sitting beside his cash register. Three young men rushed out from behind a curtain. They were dressed as impeccably as Giacomo, in different styles of suits made in different fabrics. Zack found himself surrounded by a blur of well-mannered activity as they took his measurements and held up different fabrics to see how they suited his complexion.

"Nothing that wrinkles," Giacomo said. "He slouches."

"How do you know I slouch?"

Giacomo simply sniffed and cast a pointed gaze at Zack's wrinkled clothes. "Try this on."

He held out a pair of gray slacks. Zack took them and waited for the tailor and his assistants to leave. They seemed to be waiting for him to strip.

"Um, where's the dressing room?"

"If you expect us to tailor things to your body, we need to see how they fit."

Zack considered protesting, then sighed as he removed his wrinkled pants and replaced them with the gray slacks. "Wow. These look good."

Giacomo smirked, looking like the cat that had gotten all the cream. Which, Zack assumed, was Zack's wallet. He made a mental note to himself to explain it as clothing for new trust meetings to Phil. Surely he wouldn't complain if Zack promised to come to a few?

"They'll look even better once we tailor them. Now stand still."

Zack obeyed and once again opened up the article about new Star Fury releases. If he was going to be flying into clouds of drones on a regular basis, a shield upgrade might be a good idea. Problem was, upgraded shields would cause a greater draw on his reactor, meaning his recharge times on his lasers would reduce. Maybe if he shifted to autocannons for his secondaries... Zack bit his tongue and did the calculations on his OptiGlasses, pulling out the spreadsheet that contained his ship's data and inputting several shield options to see which one would work best.

His OptiGlasses chimed. Kayla had texted a picture of her foot in a sexy red stiletto heel. Moments later, a store called Shoe Central sent Zack an invoice. He paid it without looking at the amount and debated what he should text Kayla.

Before he could decide on a response, Giacomo's assistant brought in a light blue button-up shirt. Zack sighed as he took off his own wrinkled polo and replaced it. At least the fabric was soft and comfortable. He had always found that sort of shirt to be stiff and itchy.

Giacomo nodded as if he could read Zack's thoughts. "Quality makes a difference, and we always use quality."

"Yeah. Sure."

Even if the clothes were impressive, that was as much praise as they were going to get out of him. Zack resigned himself to being pinned and prodded as the tailor and his team worked. Kayla sent more pictures followed by more invoices. Zack gave up on working on his ship because of the frequent interruptions, instead just pinning ideas for new builds as he skipped between articles on the latest weapon and ship updates.

Finally, Giacomo stepped away and nodded in approval. "Now you are ready for dinner, and your tuxedo will be ready in time for Miss Cross's gala. We will make sure of that. Would you like us to deliver your purchases to your home?"

Zack absently nodded, knowing his OptiGlasses would provide their courier the address and a one-time access code for delivery if he wasn't home. In the meantime, Zack looked at himself in the mirror and did a double-take. He looked nothing like himself. The gray slacks and blue shirt fit better than any other clothing he had ever owned. They made him look slimmer and more sophisticated. The team had also added some sort of product to his hair so it sat flat instead of sticking up. He was even wearing a tie.

DaEvo chimed. Rather than look at the single stat, Zack decided to pull it all up.

Physique: 35.65
Style: 72.4
Reputation: -33.74
Occupation: 0
Social level: 18.58

"Maybe I should try some different shoes?" Zack said. Even his upgraded, limited edition sneakers looked out of place with this classy ensemble.

Giacomo nodded solemnly. "But of course."

He offered some shiny black dress shoes, which Zack quickly put on. They weren't as comfortable as his sneakers, but they weren't horrible.

Style: 77.5

"Oh, Giacomo, you've outdone yourself!"

Kayla swept into the store, and Zack forgot all about his new look. She had changed as well and was wearing a short blue dress that coordinated with his new shirt. Had she been texting Giacomo as well, or was the color coordination a coincidence? She kissed the tailor's cheeks, then turned to study Zack.

"I'll have the rest of his clothes delivered to his apartment," Giacomo said.

"Marvelous. You're the best."

"The rest of my clothes?" Zack said, feeling a little behind. "You mean the tux?"

"And a few other surprises," Kayla said with a grin. "Come on, we don't want to be late for our reservation."

She took Zack's arm and pulled him out of the store. He followed her, paying the charges Giacomo sent to his OptiGlasses with only a small wince. Zack would have to put a cap on clothing purchases at some point, if for no other reason than to conserve space in his apartment.

Kayla led Zack into a waiting limo and poured him a glass of champagne. He took it, feeling as though he had skipped a few tutorial levels and found himself on a quest he didn't quite understand.

"Cheers," Kayla said, clinking her glass with his. "I'm having a really great time."

"Yeah, me too."

The lie slipped out easily. Shopping wasn't exactly Zack's idea of a good time, but that was universal, wasn't it? Girlfriends went shopping, and boyfriends humored them. Everything was a little expensive—hers more than his by far. But his hasty research seemed to indicate that this was normal. Women were just more expensive than men. He remembered hearing his college girlfriends complain about how expensive hair appointments and manicures were. And if he had to spend an afternoon shopping, at least it was with someone hot.

"Smile." Kayla held out her phone and leaned toward Zack to take a selfie.

He leaned in, smiling at the camera this time. Kayla tapped at her phone, then turned back to drinking her champagne.

A few moments later, DaEvo chimed.

Reputation + 0.3

That was followed by the picture Kayla had posted to her social media accounts. A flood of likes and comments was already pouring in.

Sweet.

Zack pushed aside his worries and settled into the limo seat. He realized he was slouching and sat up straight just to spite Giacomo. Slouching indeed.

The limo stopped outside a swanky-looking restaurant surrounded by a vineyard. Elegant couples checked in with the hostess and sat on a patio lit by lanterns hanging in the trees. The hostess greeted Kayla by name without bothering to check her reservation book, and they followed the waiter to their table. Kayla stood beside the table, staring at Zack as if she expected him to do something.

DaEvo chimed.

Treat your date like a lady to win her over. Try the following:

- *Open doors for her*
- *Pull out her chair*

Zack stared at the notification. That was a bit much, wasn't it? This was just dinner.

Then again, DaEvo had gotten him this far.

Zack walked around the table and pulled out Kayla's chair. She rewarded him with a bright smile as she sat. DaEvo chimed to let him know he had succeeded and added a burst of color to the date thermometer, and Zack grinned.

So far so good.

As soon as Zack opened the menu, DaEvo chimed.

Physique Quest Alert!
If you eat better, you'll feel better! Consider one of the following healthy options to level up your Physique.

- *Summer Kale Salad*
- *House Salad*
- *Red Snapper Slivers; Asian Pear, Akinori, Kimchi Emulsion*
- *Pan-Roasted Monkfish; Wild Mushroom Stuffed Cabbage, Bacon Jus*
- *Hangi potato, with Hen Yolk and Kaluga caviar*
- *more...*

"Damn it, why is it all seafood?" Zack muttered.

He realized he had accidentally spoken out loud and looked up to see if Kayla had noticed his outburst. But she was busy taking selfies from as many angles as possible. Zack sighed and turned back to the menu. He wasn't a fan of fish, and caviar tasted like slimy fish eggs. This restaurant had some great options, but unfortunately, DaEvo wouldn't let him have them. And he definitely needed to toe the line with the Physique quests after all the shopping.

Zack sighed. At least it wasn't a smoothie.

Chapter Thirty

ZACK GRUNTED as he pulled the bar toward his chest. The condo's fitness app added another rep to his count. Ten more to go for this set, then he would be done for the day. DaEvo flashed a thumbs-up as encouragement.

Stupid fitness quests. Zack had been working out for the past three days and was still struggling. Wasn't this supposed to get easier? The worst part was how much he ached everyday. He'd taken to taking warm and cold showers—at the prompting of DaEvo and his body—to help with the constant muscle aches.

"Hey, stranger." Kayla grinned and took the machine next to his.

Zack grinned back and released the bar, grateful for a distraction. He had been texting with Kayla since their date and sent her flowers at DaEvo's prompting, but between Physique quests, training for the upcoming PvP round of the tournament, strategizing with his team, spying on Armada scum at Gord's, and chatting with Ashley, he hadn't found the right moment to ask Kayla on another date yet. This could be his chance

"Hey."

Not exactly a brilliant response, but Zack found himself a little tongue-tied. He had forgotten how gorgeous Kayla was. Her workout clothes were skintight and had strategic cutouts that let glimpses of her skin peek through.

"Don't let me stop you," Kayla said.

She tucked her legs into her own machine and did extensions. Zack sighed as he grabbed the bar again and resumed his workout. He tried to make it look easy so he could show off for Kayla, but sweat beaded on his forehead as he struggled to pull the bar down again.

His OptiGlasses chimed with an incoming message.

Faz: *Hey, we're all logged in and ready to rendezvous for training. You coming?*

Zack: *Yeah, just finishing something.*

He checked the rep counter. Five more to go, then he was free. Zack gathered the last of his energy and powered through. The gym's app chimed to congratulate him on finishing his prescribed fitness routine, and DaEvo offered points for completing the physique quest. Zack toweled off his machine then his face. Thank goodness that was over.

"You're leaving already?" Kayla pulled her legs out of the machine and lounged against it, looking like an advertisement for fitness equipment or fitness apparel. Possibly both.

Zack caught himself staring and swallowed. "Um, yeah. I finished my routine for the day."

"That's a shame. I was thinking we could jog around the rooftop track together."

"The what?"

Kayla laughed. "You need to get out more. Come on, I'll show you."

She placed her hand on his arm, not seeming to care that it was drenched with sweat, and pulled him toward a set of stairs at the far end of the room.

DaEvo chimed.

Relationship Milestone!

Your lady has invited you on a date. Looks like you made a good impression! Don't worry, there's nothing wrong with women being the one to make the first move. It's a modern society!

Reward for completion: It's a third date. You can't have a relationship without a date!
+0.5 Kayla Taylor Lovemeter.

"Is something wrong?" Kayla released Zack's arm and pursed her lips in a pout.

He shook his head. "No, nothing's wrong! Let's go!"

Kayla took his hand and dragged him up the stairs. Zack texted Faz as he climbed.

Zack: *Sorry, something came up. Be there as soon as I can.*

Then he turned his attention to breathing, which was becoming more and more difficult. Kayla didn't seem to notice his struggle. She kept jogging up the stairs until she reached the top and pushed open the door.

Zack found himself on a rooftop lounge. The center was dotted with putting greens, hot tubs, and counters serving drinks and food. Zack moved toward the nearest chair. This was a great idea for a date. They could sit back and enjoy the view and a few drinks. Hopefully, there was something on the menu that DaEvo would consider healthy enough for him.

Kayla took Zack's hand and pulled him in the opposite direction of the counters. "This way, silly."

Zack realized with growing horror that she was leading him toward a track that looped around the edge of the building. Right, hadn't she said something about jogging? Several people in workout clothes were already moving around the track at a quick pace.

The city stretched out beneath them. Zack's head swam at the height, although a glass barrier stretched around the exterior to keep people from falling. It also seemed to block the wind. The rooftop terrace didn't have the usual Oklahoma gusts whipping past, although the morning sun still felt oppressive without any shade.

Zack grimaced as he stepped onto the track. This would be fine. They could walk a few laps together and—

Kayla jogged. Zack swore under his breath and forced his legs to move in rhythm with hers.

"We'll do a nice warmup first," Kayla said easily.

"Sure."

At least, that was what Zack tried to say. It came out as more of a wheeze. Warmup indeed.

DaEvo flashed a warning.

Highly elevated heart rate detected! Your heart rate is beating at 143BPM. This is approaching dangerous levels. Consider lowering the intensity of your current workout.

That was followed by another notification.

Relationship Quest Update!
Consider pursuing one of the following relationship milestones to level up your relationship:

- *first significant physical contact*
- *in-depth exchange of history*
- *your first kiss*
- *schedule another date*
- *take her out to an exciting and memorable event*
- *your first [Dev Note—are we even allowed to suggest this? Ask Legal]*
- *become an [#select_variable: relationship type: exclusive;primary;secondary; pair-bonded; metamour]*
- *get engaged*

Zack scanned the list, desperate for anything to take his mind off the burning in his legs. He wondered what exactly DaEvo would count as "significant physical contact." Fainting into Kayla's arms might do it, and he was closer to doing that than he wanted to admit.

Would that also count as an "exciting and memorable event?"

"Isn't this fun?" Kayla said. "I love it up here."

She seemed to be enjoying herself. Her hair streamed behind her, and she glowed with a light sheen of perspiration. Her eyes sparkled in the sunlight. She seemed like a different person from the studied socialite at dinner or the glamorous fashionista in the shopping mall. It looked as if she was enjoying the torture that was about to kill him.

Zack wheezed as much of a response as he could manage and steeled his resolve to keep moving. So Kayla was some kind of superhuman fitness freak. So what? He had a date with her and an opportunity to fill her Lovemeter. Three days of non-contact—even with the second date bonus he'd received—had depleted her Lovemeter significantly. He needed to fill it.

He wouldn't let something as trivial as breathing stand in his way.

Faz: *What do you mean, "Sorry?" Where the hell are you?*

Zack flicked his eyes to respond and nearly fell. Kayla slowed to check on him, and he did his best to smile and gave her a thumbs-up. Apparently, he couldn't manage texting and jogging.

Greg: *Where are you?*

Jenny: *Zack, are you okay?*

Was he okay? No, not really. Zack grimaced as more messages came pouring in. He could leave now, but that would mean leaving the date with Kayla unfinished. As much as he hated to miss training, he could catch up later. If he didn't keep his Lovemeters up, he wouldn't be getting any training at all.

And he might not get a second chance with Kayla.

Zack: *Going to be late. Sorry.*

Then he muted notifications and sprinted to catch up with Kayla, who had gained a lead while he stopped to answer the text and didn't seem to notice that she was leaving him behind. His lungs burned and his legs shook by the time they finished the first lap. Kayla wasn't even breathing hard.

———

"I can't believe you abandoned us again!" Greg said.

"I said I'm sorry!"

That was met by silence, and Zack sighed. The jogging date with Kayla had ended with protein smoothies on the rooftop lounge. Rather than taking a half hour or something reasonable, the date had stretched out. The whole ordeal had left Zack sore, sick, and sunburned.

And with a three-quarters full Lovemeter, but he questioned if it had been worth the cost.

He was currently lying flat on his couch, using his OptiGlasses to control Star Fury because he couldn't move his arms. Jenny and Faz had already logged out by the time he got back to his apartment, but Greg was still online.

"How can I make it up to you guys?" Zack said.

He was already buying them all the new gear on their team wish list. He'd had to transfer a ton of credits from his smurf account, but it was worth it. He almost considered buying more credits from a farmer but decided he'd gone far enough to the dark side with the smoothies. Hopefully, the gifts would be enough to smooth things over.

"You could stop disappearing and actually show up for training," Greg said.

"I told you, Phil pulled a fast one and—"

"And you told us you had it figured out. And we believed you."

Zack sighed. "I may not have it quite as figured out as I thought I did."

"No kidding. So, what was it this time?"

Greg didn't launch into a list of jokes about chores. Zack appreciated that. Faz would have been teasing him mercilessly by now.

"I unlocked unlimited game time, but I have to fulfill certain criteria to keep it. I was getting ready to log in when something popped up."

"We can't help if you refuse to share details," Greg said. "Why are you being so vague about everything?"

"Maybe because I don't want you mocking my every move?"

"That's more a Faz thing. Look, man, this tournament is my chance to go pro and have a career. I don't want to be bagging groceries for the rest of my life. But if we want to make it, we all have to show up and work."

"I am working!" Zack protested. "Honestly, I'm working harder than I ever have."

The fact that he was on the couch and unable to move proved that. Of course, Greg couldn't see the miserable, sunburned blob of pain Zack had become.

"I have something for you," Zack said, bundling all the gear he had purchased into a shipping container. He didn't have enough space to transport it otherwise. "Hang tight. I'll be right there."

While DaEvo wasn't offering bonus points to cheer up Greg, Zack was hoping the same principles for making someone feel better applied to friendships. Ashley had liked the food and the fan. Kayla had liked the clothes and flowers. Greg would like the new gear.

Zack turned on autopilot and set a course to rendezvous with Greg. His ship pulled away from the outpost, and Zack settled back against the couch and closed his eyes. Greg lived in Iowa, just a few quadrants over from Zack's area. The space between them was too populated to hyperjump, so the journey would take a few minutes.

The sound of an explosion rocked the apartment, and Zack's eyes shot open.

On instinct, Zack had the ship pull up and to the right, aiming to dodge the follow-up shots. Unfortunately, he was dragging the cargo container, which left him a lot slower than normal. His shields kept flickering as he diverted energy from his lasers to both his engines and shields. All the while, he scanned his sensors, searching for the problem.

Nothing.

A flick of his eyes had the sci-fi equivalent of chaff deploy. Not a moment too soon as he banked again, and the back of his craft lit up as unseen missiles exploded. Working on intuition, Zack pulled open the local solar system chat.

"*Noob! Walking right into an ambush. You're dead now!*"

That was followed by the Armada flag and a stuck-out tongue emoji.

"Steve…" Zack whispered. Idiot didn't even know how to do a proper ambush.

Now that Zack knew who he was fighting, he flicked over to the right settings for his sensors. The drones Steve had been using showed up as ghosts that flashed in and out, but it was enough for Zack to fire.

Another round of explosions rocked Zack's ship and he snarled. Even taking out the drones wasn't enough to get him ahead. He could run, he should run, but he wouldn't make it with the cargo container. In fact, towing it was costing him speed.

He bit his lip, trying to work out the best way to win. Another drone blew up as Zack targeted it with his lasers, and the EMP blast knocked out another pair that was hiding farther back.

A flicker in the corner of the sensors and Zack winced. It wasn't just Steve. He'd brought friends with him, and they were moving to cover all Zack's options for running away.

"*Real brave. Bringing your friends to the fight.*"

"*All's fair in love and war. Isn't that the Corsair motto?*"

"Just like Armada scum to be hypocrites."

Artillery shells rocked Zack's ship, the explosions forcing him to spin around. He lost hold of the container, and as he tried to swing around, he ran right into the railgun pellets. Shields died and damage notifications flared all across the ship.

Not having a choice, Zack pulled away, hitting his afterburners to dodge the next series of attacks. All of which pushed him away from the cargo container. A series of taunting memes showed up in the chat, baiting him to come back.

Zack snarled, fingers twitching by his sides as he twisted around and fired at more of the stealthed drones. If he had his joystick. If he wasn't ambushed. If… if he didn't leave now, he would lose his ship and the cargo container both.

"Where are you?" Greg sent.

"Getting ambushed!" Zack snarled. "I've got three Armada scum on me. And I lost the cargo container with the weapons and shields I bought."

"What!?!"

"I know! Now let me get out of here!" Zack muted the chat.

Slamming his fist into the couch, Zack burned fuel and darted straight for one of the surrounding Armada scum. He might not be able to save the container, but he might be able to do some damage as he ran.

And he'd have his revenge on Steve. Later.

Chapter Thirty-One

ZACK SPRINTED INTO GORD'S, once again late for his date with Ashley. He always seemed to be running late these days as he tried to squeeze dates, Star Fury training, and workouts into his schedule. It had taken a few weeks, hours of grinding—mining with his alt whenever he had a chance—but he'd managed to get enough credits to buy the team their improvements. It had helped—a bit—to assuage his guilt and their anger.

Now it was all about the team PvP fights, and he pitied any Armada scum that got in his way.

At least sprinting was easier now. Much as Zack hated to admit it, the working out and healthy eating was finally paying off. He ached a lot less every day, and even if he had to return a lot of clothing because he'd lost weight and bulked up, it was worth it.

He grinned at Ashley and held up the bags of food. This was part of his routine. Morning workout. Lunch date with Ashley when she was available. Afternoon training. Evening date with Kayla when she was in town. Late night training. Full night's sleep for Physique points.

Neither woman was available enough to satisfy DaEvo and keep their Lovemeters full, but so far Zack's careful balancing act was working. He had yet to run out of game time since the cleaning incident.

Ashley waved from the counter then turned her attention back to her customer.

Steve.

Zack forced himself to stay back and not confront the Armada scum. Steve and his team had also progressed to the next round, and Zack was hoping to take his revenge on the battlefield.

Unless, of course, Steve gave him a reason to act now. Zack narrowed his eyes, ready and eager to step in if the jerk gave Ashley any trouble, but she had the situation under control. She had proved a quick study and interested in Zack's rambling about Star Fury. She knew enough now to hold her own with the Gord's customers, and she used that knowledge to keep them in line.

She wasn't the only one who had learned something at their lunch dates. While helping Ashley study for her upcoming exams, Zack had picked up a lot of information about hospital management. He was saving the knowledge, looking forward to pulling it out at the next foundation meeting he attended. How far would Phil's eyes bug out of his head? Zack couldn't wait to find out.

"Ready?" Ashley asked, nudging Zack's shoulder to bring him back to the present.

"Yeah."

Zack wrapped an arm around Ashley's shoulder as they walked to their usual picnic table under the tree. An arm that, while not exactly muscular, was significantly less flabby than it had been when they first met. He wondered if Ashley noticed. If she did, she didn't say anything.

Out of idle curiosity, Zack pulled up his stats as they crossed the road to the park.

Physique: 48.45
Style: 63.5
Reputation: -12.74
Occupation: 0
Social level: 24.80

He smiled as he saw the improvements, and Ashley returned the smile, probably thinking it was for her. Seeing her smile, he returned it further, the pair of them sharing goofy grins as he set out their lunch. All healthy options, thanks to DaEvo. Today he had gone with a selection of Mediterranean salads. Ashley selected a container, sprinkled some feta over the salad, and ate.

"Hey, I have something for you," Zack said. He spun his fork in his fingers, not sure why he suddenly felt so nervous.

Ashley shook her head. "You don't have to give me a gift every time we hang out. I mean, I appreciate it, but you don't have to."

"Yeah, I know."

He didn't have to, but the bonus he got from DaEvo at the end of a date was well worth it. Besides, it was fun to surprise her. But today's gift was a little different from the trinkets he usually brought. Zack had spent hours working on this since their first date, and now he was rethinking his plan. What if she didn't like it? DaEvo had sent several prompts warning him that this wasn't exactly a romantic gesture.

"Hey, are you okay?" Ashley set down her fork, looking concerned.

Zack swallowed. Maybe he shouldn't have brought it up. Or he should have saved it for after they ate so things wouldn't be awkward if she hated it. But Ashley's lunch breaks were short. There might not be time left if he waited.

"Yeah, I'm great. Anyway, I… that is—I made you a spreadsheet!" The words burst out of his mouth before he could stop them.

Ashley tilted her head. "A spreadsheet?"

"Yeah, but it's probably lame. I mean, if you don't want to look at it, we can just finish eating."

"What does it do?"

She looked genuinely interested, so Zack wiped his sweaty hands on his legs under the table and pulled a tablet out of his bag. "It's to help with hospital management. I adapted it from the one I use to track Star Fury updates for my ship. I made tables so you can calculate stats for new hospital equipment and figure out which items would add the most value to each department."

"Really?" Ashley's eyes sparkled with interest. She moved from her place across the table to sit next to Zack so she could see the tablet. She leaned close against him and stared at the screen. DaEvo chimed bonus points for physical contact. "How does it work?"

She ate her salad while Zack explained his design and walked her through the basic functions of the spreadsheet. DaEvo chimed to warn him that he was boring his date by talking too much about himself, but he swiped away the notification. Ashley didn't look bored. She was leaning close, asking questions about the formulas he had used to calculate stats for the equipment and how to customize the spreadsheet for each department.

"This is amazing!" she said when Zack finished his walkthrough.

"Yeah?"

"Yeah."

Zack felt his face going red and looked at the table to hide his blush. DaEvo chimed.

Relationship Milestone!
You've managed to impress your date with your thoughtful gift. Keep this up and you'll be in a real relationship soon!
Reward: +10 to Ashley Barnes Lovemeter Level

"So yeah, I'll just email it to you then."

"Perfect." Ashley's phone chimed, and she made a face. "Break's over. Sorry, I have to go."

She really did look sorry, and Zack's mind raced. A real relationship. Wasn't that what he needed to finish DaEvo? And she looked really happy.

He spoke in a rush before she left. "Hey, do you want to go out for real sometime? To dinner or something?"

Ashley's grin widened. "I'd love to."

"Really?"

"Yeah. I'm free next Friday night."

"Okay. Yeah. Great."

Where was DaEvo when you needed it to suggest some kind of smooth comeback?

But Ashley didn't seem to mind. "And thanks again for the spreadsheet. This is awesome."

Before Zack quite knew what was happening, Ashley kissed his cheek. Then she grabbed her bag and hurried back to work. DaEvo chimed, offering a wave of points for the kiss and the date, but Zack hardly noticed. He was too busy watching Ashley retreat with a huge grin on his face.

Chapter Thirty-Two

"WATCH OUT!"

Zack pulled back and flushed his missiles, watching them arc from his ship, thrusters burning as they flashed toward his target. He was already switching targets, aiming for the next of the drones which were busy bothering Greg. His friend was tanking the majority of the drone fighters, but it was Zack's job to take them out.

They were floating in the middle of null space, just another random spawned location in the great, big galaxy with some pretty graphics, a warp gate, and a mini-station. The Braughtry Pirate Station run was one of the more common raid locations for people at their level, with decent rewards and a high variety of opponent types. Great for training.

In the corner of his vision, Zack noted their raid completion rate. Stage 3 of 5 in an hour and thirteen minutes. Not bad at all. If they kept up this rate, they'd beat their best time.

He triggered his lasers again, watching the combined fire between him and Faz burn through their target's shielding. At the same time, Jenny and Greg took out another drone fighter, leaving only four opponents.

"All right, I'm going for the objective," Zack informed the others, twisting his ship around and hitting the afterburners. If they took too long, the station would spawn another wave of adds.

DaEvo chimed.

Reputation -24.2

"Zack, watch out!"

Faz sent a blast of laser fire to destroy a drone closing in on Zack. Zack swore and set a course away from the objective.

"Sorry, guys. Let's try that again."

Reputation -1.2

"What the hell?"

"Everything okay, Zack?" Greg asked.

Reputation -1.15

Notice: Due to significantly lower Social Status levels, Lovemeter will decrease at a higher rate for Kayla Taylor and Ashley Barnes.

"Hang on," Zack said.

He swiped open DaEvo, checked his reputation stats, and swore under his breath. Cassie's blog post about him had been picked up by a news outlet and was apparently in the process of going viral.

Crap.

"Zack, focus!" Jenny said. "We're on track to break our record."

"I know that!" Zack growled.

Reputation -0.7

That article was causing a major debuff. Zack groaned as DaEvo ticked down for Kayla and he saw a partially filled heart drop off entirely.

Notice: Due to lost Lovemeter relationship points with Kayla Taylor, your Unlimited Internet Privileges have been revoked once again. Increase your Lovemeter levels to improve your relationship with Kayla Taylor!

Zack scrolled through his stats. He had lost unlimited game time with Kayla, and Ashley's Lovemeter had dropped as well. But the bonus he'd gotten from Ashley had her Lovemeter at a much higher level than Kayla's and hers was dropping slower too. Especially if their next date went well.

"Sorry. Trouble with Phil's app."

"You said you fixed that thing," Faz said.

"I thought I had. Okay, let's double down on the objective. Faz, you come in with me. Greg and Jenny, give us some cover."

"You got it," Jenny said.

She flew beside Greg and activated an army of drones. They hovered around her in a cloud of blinking lights.

The OptiGlasses chimed.

Kayla: *Hey, I'm back in town! There's a WesterNeon party tonight at Royal Texas. You in?*

That was accompanied by a picture of Kayla in a fringed mini dress the same brilliant orange color as Zack's WesterNeon jacket. Apparently, she had finally convinced David Davidson to make a few items for ladies. Zack shook his head. It was tempting, but he had training tonight with the team.

Zack: *Can't. Sorry.*

"Zack, watch out!"

Zack swiped away the picture of Kayla and realized he was

313

about to fly into a cloud of enemy drones. He swerved, and Jenny sent a swarm of her own drones to dispatch the enemies.

"Thanks," Zack said.

"Dude, can you focus?" Faz said.

Reputation -2.1

"Why is that blog post causing so much damage?"

DaEvo chimed and brought up an image. Not the blogpost, but a social media post of Kayla pouting in her WesterNeon dress.

When you're all dressed up, but he's busy. :(

She had tagged Zack's account in the post, and KayTay's fans were not happy with him for ditching her. The post was already getting a flood of comments about what a jerk he was.

Zack sighed. He couldn't afford two Reputation debuffs right now. Besides, going to the party with Kayla might boost his Reputation enough to counteract some of the damage caused by Cassie's blog post. After all, all of his recent gains in that arena had been from his—rather public—dates with her.

"One second, guys."

His teammates groaned as Zack pulled back from the battle to text Kayla.

Zack: *You're right. Let's go out tonight. Pick you up in two hours?*

Kayla: *I thought you'd never ask. ;)*

A few seconds later, DaEvo chimed.

Reputation +3.3

Kayla had deleted the sad post and replaced it with the picture of her in the mini dress and text saying how excited she was to go out with her man tonight.

Zack grinned and turned his attention back to Star Fury. "Okay, I'm back, and I fixed it. Let's finish this."

He swooped forward, then pulled back with a curse as the base spawned a wave of new drones. They had taken too long to defeat the first wave.

"Back to reverse diamond formation," Zack said with a sigh.

"So much for the new record," Faz said.

Reputation +0.1

They dispatched the new drones and continued toward the objective. Retreading the same ground was frustrating, but Zack took advantage of the situation and tried a series of new strategies. They finished the quest in decent time, but nowhere near their record. Zack sighed as they flew away from the explosions to a quiet quadrant to debrief the mission.

Kayla: *See you in fifteen minutes.*

Zack looked at the clock. Crap. He was going to be late. "Got to go, guys."

"What?" Faz said. "You can't leave now. We need to debrief."

"We'll have to do it tomorrow. I'm sorry."

Zack logged off and hurried to his closet to retrieve the Wester-Neon outfit from its place next to Giacomo's slacks, jackets, and button-up shirts. He briefly considered wearing a suit, but Kayla had said this was a WesterNeon party. Hopefully, that meant he'd get extra Style points for wearing WesterNeon.

DaEvo chimed to let him know that a shower would improve his olfactory stats, and Zack swiped away the notification. Doubtless the app was right, but he didn't have time for that. Hopefully, the cologne Kayla had given him would be good enough.

. . .

Jenny: *You said you'd figured out that app. You said you had unlimited game time now.*

Zack: *I do, but I still have to earn it. Something came up.*

Faz: *Emergency load of laundry.*

Greg: *Oh my gosh, Faz, please stop. This is serious. That app cost us a record.*

Zack: *They updated the app, and the calculations are a little different now. But a few more quests should take care of it.*

Jenny: *You mean like the last few quests took care of it? Zack, you have to fix this.*

Zack: *I am fixing it.*

He just wasn't willing to admit how. It was better to let them think he was doing laundry and making his bed. Anyway, he *was* doing laundry and making his bed since they were tied into his Physique quests. Something about good hygiene? Truthfully, he had skipped the explanation.

Well, he was having someone else do the cleaning, but DaEvo didn't seem to notice the difference. Zack's apartment was sparkling clean now, and that was what the app cared about.

Zack pulled on the WesterNeon jeans and studied his reflection. The pants that had fit perfectly when he bought them were now a little loose. He dug through his closet, looking for a belt to hold up the green jeans.

Jenny: *Okay, we can make this work. We can still debrief if you aren't online.*

Greg: *Yeah, that's true! I found out a few more things about that Easter egg build that might be useful.*

Faz: *Sweet.*

Zack: *I'll check in when I can, but I'm going to be busy tonight. I think our current setups should be fine.*

Faz: *You think?!?!?*

Greg: *What happened to inputting everything into your mega-spreadsheet and knowing for sure?*

Zack pulled off his T-shirt and sighed as he looked at the orange fringed monstrosity draped across his bed.

Zack: *I can't input things into the spreadsheet if I don't have the numbers. It's more important that I complete this quest so I don't have to worry about getting locked out before the next tournament round.*
Jenny: *What's the quest? Maybe we can help.*

Zack swallowed as he spritzed himself with the cologne and DaEvo chimed to confirm that his olfactory stats had improved. He hated lying to his team, but he still refused to admit to them that he was trapped in a dating sim. Besides, they wouldn't believe him anyway.

Zack: *Fitness. I have to go to an extra workout class to meet my quota.*
Greg: *Man, Phil is not messing around. So you'll be buff by the time we see you in Vegas?*
Zack: *Sure thing. You won't even recognize me.*

He paused, then he glanced at his bare arm and flexed. It made his biceps, which were now beginning to actually show, pop. A quick command sent the mini video to his friends, with a smirk emoticon along with it.

Faz: *Dude, you weren't kidding!*
Jenny: *Ugh. Just get to your workout class and leave us to debrief.*

· · ·

Zack waited for more texts to come in, but his OptiGlass screen remained blank. Apparently, they had moved their conversation to the Star Fury comms. He pushed aside his disappointment that he couldn't join them and muted his texting app so he wouldn't be distracted by the flood of teasing that was sure to follow as soon as they finished training for the evening. Then he pulled on the orange jacket and set the cowboy hat on his head.

DaEvo chimed.

Style: 93.4

Very Stylish!

You have breached 90 points in Style! It's not just dressing well but looking good in what you're dressed in that will have the women swooning, you stud.

Zack couldn't help smirking as he hurried out the door. His leveling up kept paying off. Yes, he had to leave training early, but he had a date with a model at an exclusive night club. On top of that, since he was dressed in the WesterNeon outfit, his social level had bumped back up and the Lovemeter wasn't dropping anymore. If he could get some good photos with Kayla, his Reputation points might go up a little too. He'd still be in the negatives, but he was on a date with a hot model.

Was that really something to complain about? There were certainly worse things Phil could have done.

The jacket's orange fringe swished as he sprinted down the hall, determined not to be any later than he already was. It was a good thing Kayla lived so close.

Chapter Thirty-Three

AT DAEVO'S PROMPTING, Zack hurried around to open the limo door for Kayla. She stuck out her legs first, giving everyone a good view of her stiletto cowboy boots, before she took Zack's hand and let him pull her up.

She kept hold of Zack's hand as they approached Royal Texas. The club was busy on a normal night, but it was an absolute madhouse now. A neon pink carpet covered with the WesterNeon logo led up to the door. Velvet ropes and bouncers held back the cheering crowd and reporters with flashing cameras.

Zack swallowed and wiped away the sweat trickling down his forehead. This was next level for sure.

"We love you, Kayla!" a group of fans screamed in unison so their voices rose above the chaos.

Kayla blew a kiss at them and spun in a circle so her fringe swished. Her outfit was a strange mix of flapper dress and cowboy vest that Zack didn't quite think worked, but clearly, he had no idea what was trendy.

They posed for pictures for reporters, took a few selfies with the crowd, then walked up the pink carpet. Well, Zack walked. Kayla strutted as if it were a runway, her fringe swishing with each step. The bouncer at the door glanced at the guest list on his tablet, then opened the door so they could enter. Zack's OptiGlasses chimed as the Royal Texas app prompted him to pay the cover charge and start a tab. He swiped permission and followed Kayla into the club.

Music blasted through the room. It was that same mix of country and techno that had played at the WesterNeon store, but the DJ on the stage was remixing it into more of a dance rhythm. Kayla swayed with the beat as she pulled Zack to the center of the room.

"KayTay!"

David Davidson spotted them and pushed through the crowd. He kissed Kayla on both cheeks, then did the same to Zack. The designer wore WesterNeon, but had traded the fringed jacket for a vest and added hot pink chaps.

Zack really hoped DaEvo wouldn't prompt him to wear those any time in the future. They looked both uncomfortable and ridiculous. Fashion or not, he had limits, and apparently pink chaps were where he drew the line.

Reputation +0.3

Zack grinned. It looked as though someone had already posted a picture of him from the event. It might have been Kayla herself. She seemed capable of posting selfies while doing other things. Multitasking at its finest.

"I told you the collection would look fabulous as women's wear," Kayla said. "Don't you agree?"

She twirled again. She seemed to really enjoy the fringe on her dress.

David Davidson nodded. "You were right, and you wear it beautifully. Now, grab yourself a drink, and let's celebrate!"

Kayla took Zack's arm and dragged him to the bar. He tried not to gape at the prices. This was an exclusive, fashion industry event. Exorbitantly overpriced drinks were probably normal.

The bartender, who was dressed in a variation of the outfit that the clerk at the WesterNeon store had worn, smiled at them. "Tonight, we have a special menu designed to go with David Davidson's collection. We've used all-natural ingredients to create cocktails that match WesterNeon's signature colors."

Zack seriously doubted that those colors could be achieved with all-natural ingredients.

DaEvo seemed to agree with him. It rejected most of the menu as unhealthy and offered him a few options.

Available Beverage Options:

- *Get Your Hand off My Butt, I'm Trying to Leave*
- *How Do I Get Rid of You If You Won't Go Away?*
- *Missing You is Horrible, It's Almost as Bad as When You Were Here*
- *A Couple More Whiskies, and You'll Be Good-Looking*

Great. Just great. Zack wasn't sure how he could say any of those names with a straight face. The menu informed him that they were the names of popular songs David Davidson had featured in his runway shows. Somehow, that only made it worse.

"The one with the whisky, I guess," he finally said.

Kayla raised an eyebrow but didn't comment. She considered the menu a moment longer, then smiled at the bartender. "I'll have whichever one matches my dress."

"An excellent choice."

The bartender busied himself fixing their drinks, and Kayla took that as an opportunity to take more pictures. She pulled her phone out of a garter on her thigh that looked like an old-fashioned gun holster and photographed Zack, the room, and the bartender in rapid succession. Then she pulled Zack in and kissed his cheek as she took a picture of them.

DaEvo chimed for the physical contact, then chimed again as Kayla posted the pictures.

Reputation +0.4

When their drinks were ready, Kayla handed her phone to Zack and sat at the bar. "Take some pictures of me. These color-coordinating drinks are genius."

She posed with the drink, changing positions and expressions after every shot like the professional model she was. Then she scrolled through them while Zack finally took a drink of his own. He made a face and set it back on the counter. Whatever natural ingredients they'd used to turn the drink neon blue were extremely sour and didn't mix well with whiskey.

Kayla looked at her phone with increasing disappointment as she scrolled through Zack's pictures. Then she turned to the bartender. "Would you mind taking some pictures of me?"

"Of course, miss."

Kayla worked through the exact same poses she had done before, then she pulled Zack in for a few shots together, instructing him how to pose and what expression to make for each shot. Apparently, the bartender was an acceptable photographer, because Kayla nodded with approval at his pictures and started typing captions and posting them.

Reputation +0.1

Zack sipped the blue drink, gagged again, and set it on the counter with a sigh. Kayla sipped her own orange cocktail. Apparently, it was more palatable, because she seemed to be enjoying it. Zack supposed that made sense. There were plenty of orange things in nature. Too bad that drink wasn't DaEvo approved. They sat at the bar, watching the pulsing lights and dancing couples. Zack wondered if any of the other approved drinks were any good. He wasn't sure it was worth sorting through the ridiculous names to find out.

DaEvo chimed.

To level up your date and receive bonus points:

- *Compliment your lady*
- *Give her a gift*
- *Ask her to dance*

Why was DaEvo so obsessed with giving people gifts? Zack wished the app had offered that suggestion before he was actually out on the date. Still, it was nothing that drone shipping couldn't fix. He scrolled through the jewelry DaEvo suggested as suitable for Kayla's style and level, selected a diamond bracelet, and ordered it shipped to Royal Texas as soon as possible. That resulted in an enormous shipping fee, but the app assured him it would be delivered by the end of the party. Zack wasn't sure if the bouncer would let a drone through the door, but he could always go out to meet it. He would do whatever it took to get the maximum points out of this date.

Now he needed to fulfill the other two suggestions. Zack looked at Kayla, trying to form the perfect compliment. The longer he looked at it, the less Zack liked the fringed flapper dress. But his opinion didn't matter with this sort of thing. And even if he didn't like the dress, Kayla looked hot in it. She leaned against the bar and stretched out her legs as if determined to show them off to best advantage. She was focused on her phone and didn't notice his staring.

Zack let his gaze linger a little longer before he spoke. "Hey, you look amazing tonight."

Not quite the truth, but close enough.

Kayla looked up from her phone and smiled at him. "Sorry, did you say something?"

"You look amazing tonight."

"I know. We're trending!"

She grinned and waved the phone in front of Zack to show him her social media dashboard. Zack had to agree, the numbers were good. It would do wonders for his Reputation. Now he just needed to complete DaEvo's bonus quests to get extra points for this date and slow down the Lovemeter's depletion.

"Do you want to dance?"

Kayla shook her head. "Not yet. We need to wait for my assistant to get here so she can get pictures."

"We can dance now and still take pictures later."

"And get all sweaty for the shots?" Kayla laughed as if Zack had said something extremely funny and turned her attention back to her phone.

Zack sighed and turned away as well. He knew by now what she was like when she got focused. In some ways, it reminded him of how he was when he was playing Star Fury. Blocking out everything as she watched her stats and responded to the flood of compliments from her fans with practiced efficiency.

Maybe this was for the best. If he danced, it would raise his heart rate, and DaEvo would offer a Physique quest. No need to exercise if he didn't have to.

He swiped his eyes across his OptiGlasses and pulled up his Star Fury spreadsheet and the blueprint information on the latest updates. Zack skimmed blogs and official release updates, inputting relevant data into his spreadsheet while the party raged around him. He could have done it automatically. Gotten a script set up, or even purchased some of the preset inputs others created and just copied it over.

But this way, Zack got a chance to read the stats themselves. More than once, he'd seen a wrong input, a line missed by others. Better to do it himself so he knew the data inside and out.

He kept a careful eye out for any information about cloaking devices or drones but saw nothing. There hadn't been any official new releases that explained the Armada's mysterious new builds. Online chatter was filled with rumors, including the Easter Egg find, but nothing substantial. Whatever they had found, they were keeping it to themselves.

Occasionally, Kayla pulled on his arm, dragging him into a pose or greeting as she spoke with another acquaintance. Zack would grunt and nod, even try saying something nice to get further bonus points.

He almost felt disappointed when Kayla's assistant arrived to photograph them dancing. He'd been making progress with his analysis and hated to be interrupted. But DaEvo offered bonus points for the dance, and Zack managed to move slowly enough that he didn't raise his heart rate and trigger the Physique quests.

He counted that as a win.

Chapter Thirty-Four

ZACK AWOKE to multiple notifications from his bank. He swiped them away, not really wanting to know how much money he had spent at the WesterNeon party or in the week after. Spending time with Kayla was expensive, but his Reputation had finally recovered from Cassie's blog post. He checked his stats to make sure nothing had happened overnight to wreck them and deplete his Lovemeter. He wouldn't call himself paranoid but….

Physique: 51.45
Style: 50.2
Reputation: -15.67
Occupation: 0
Social level: 21.50

Sweet.

He was now fitter than the average male, which was kind of cool. And he could easily boost his social level if he dressed in high style—but pajama bottoms and a T-shirt didn't do much for him.

He did wonder if they were ever going to adjust the Style stats so that it didn't bounce around so much, but that wasn't his problem. He just had to game the system.

Yawning, Zack dressed in his FitLife clothes and hurried to the gym, eager to finish his workout so he could get in some Star Fury training. Now that Kayla was back in town, his evenings hadn't had much time for gaming. Zack's suggestion that they play together had made her laugh so hard she'd cried.

Then she had complained about ruining her makeup and rushed to the bathroom to fix it.

Zack ran hard on the elliptical, releasing pent-up frustration and earning a compliment from DaEvo. He was even on track to get a higher bonus to his Physique.

His frustrations came from normal relationship stuff. He had checked forums and seen countless men complaining that their girlfriends cut into their gaming time.

Progressing the relationship with Kayla was a struggle though. Even with all the dates, her Lovemeter rankings kept dropping. But it was only temporary. He just needed to play along and keep the Lovemeters full until he beat DaEvo.

Zack let that happy thought push him through the rest of the workout. Freedom from DaEvo. No more pink heart notifications. No more fitness quests or healthy eating prompts. It would be like the first day of summer, free from school and teachers and responsibilities. He could play video games all day and eat whatever he wanted. He could cancel the cleaning service.

Actually, he might keep that. He was getting used to the lemony fresh scent in his apartment once again. He could still enjoy that even if he wasn't worried about maintaining his olfactory stats. And being able to walk around his apartment without tripping over pizza boxes or old plates was nice.

He finished his final set and wiped down the machine. DaEvo prompted him to order a healthy breakfast, and Zack swiped to have it delivered to his room. He skimmed through Star Fury blogs while he ate the veggie omelet that had become his go-to breakfast and downed the green juice.

A new wave of surprise releases had dropped, and it would take a while to go through them. Worse, some idiot had stumbled upon an alien artifact cache and, rather than keep the blueprints, had sold them off. Which had then flooded the market with copies, so now it'd become a thing.

Idiot noobs!

Zack even saw some sideswipes by the customer service and developer accounts in the main forums. It seemed that no one had expected the cache to be found or revealed so soon.

It also didn't seem to be related to the drone Easter egg. These newly released blueprints were all marginal improvements on various systems, with the major addition being a type of seeker missile. On the other hand, whoever had found the drone Easter egg was keeping information on those under wraps. Zack hadn't seen any sign of them since his last run-in with Steve. And Steve had been gaming in private rooms since qualifying for the tournament, so spying on him in person had become a lost cause.

Zack sighed. He'd just finished inputting and running the calculations on all the old-new releases, and now he'd have to do it all over again. Worse, some of the new lasers in particular might change the game. Lower power draw, higher penetration, but rate of fire took a small hit. That was balanced by the greater speed the turrets tracked.

They'd still need to test them out, see how much of a difference it actually made. Stats were one thing but seeing how it actually affected their formations was another.

Faz: *You see the new releases?*

Zack: *Yeah, just going through them now. You guys want to meet up tonight to test them out?*

Jenny: *Definitely. There's some good stuff in here. They have this new swarm drone that might make things interesting. Greg?*

Greg: *I'm in.*

The afternoon passed in a blur of stats and spreadsheets. Worse than the spreadsheets, Zack had to figure out how to acquire everything. Some of the necessary components for the new guns were only found in Armada space. Not a big issue normally, since the free market saw the materials transfer over eventually. But eventually wasn't good enough. Not now.

It looked like a raid was in order, but Zack wasn't eager to get caught in another trap. He didn't have the Credits to rebuild his ship, not with all the time he'd spent actually training.

He wouldn't be able to review all of the new releases before training tonight, so he turned his focus to the weapons that seemed most likely to suit his style. His teammates would do the same, then they could brief each other on what they'd discovered.

At DaEvo's prompting, Zack ordered a healthy lunch and made his final purchases while he ate it, moving with a well-practiced efficiency and complete disregard for budget. He winced at the total cost, but he even paid for a fast courier to deliver the goods to his station so that it'd be ready when he logged in.

Zack logged into Star Fury and flew to his local contested quadrant of space. A rematch with Armada scum would be just what he needed to test out some of these weapons and get his revenge.

Steve's ship was nowhere in sight, but Zack's sensors picked up a decently leveled Armada player in the neighboring quadrant of space that belonged to Texas. He set a course toward it and hailed the ship with the Corsair logo and an emoji sticking out its tongue.

The Armada scum ignored the emoji and sent a wave of the new seeker missiles instead. Apparently, not all Armada players were as easily taunted as Steve. Did this ship have the new cloaked drones? Zack kept a careful eye on his newly upgraded sensors just in case.

Sure enough, the jerk had sent a wave of drones circling around. They weren't cloaked though. At least, not with the same setup Steve and his buddies used, and this one was a lot less effective. Zack blasted them with the new laser, made a mental note about the laser's drain and how fast it took down the drones, then launched a proper offensive.

Hours passed as he fell into the familiar rhythm of PvP combat.

Once he beat the Armada scum the first time around—and they returned for a few more thrashings—he had to find more people to play with.

Some unfortunately did not have the new seeker missiles or the drones. Those he finished as fast as he could before moving on. Others were just bad at using the new tech. His latest opponent wasn't bad, but he seemed to be using some of the swarm drones that Jenny had mentioned and was just not very good at it.

Zack waited for his opponent to launch a new set of drones, then Zack began evasive maneuvers. They swerved after him, always a few steps behind. Zack lured them away and let them land a few hits to lull the other player into a false sense of security. Then he executed a full one-eighty turn and blasted the Armada ship with his main laser cannon. The EMP disabled the drones, and Zack flew closer to the ship as he fired targeted blasts at vital systems.

The ship tried to dodge, but Zack had caught him off guard. There wasn't enough time to recover. Zack alternated quickly between the different laser cannons he had purchased, testing how they did against the Armada ship's shields so he would have data to look through later. He scowled when the Armada ship exploded before he had a chance to test all the weapons. Just his luck. Now the data would be incomplete. He'd have to do even more math to balance out ship regeneration for the other ships he'd fought.

At least he had blasted some Armada scum into oblivion. He put himself on autopilot while he scanned for more opponents while he pulled up the damage log and exported it out of Star Fury. He then started inputting them into his spreadsheet. That would give him some great data to discuss with his team tonight.

His OptiGlasses chimed with a notification from the condo app.

There has been a problem with your payment to our Pet Sitting Service.
Please come retrieve your pet or update your payment information.

Pet sitting service? Why on earth was he paying the condo's pet sitting service?

Oh, right. The hamster. Zack had completely forgotten about it.

He hoped they were taking good care of Veobos. They were probably taking better care of the creature than Zack would have since he had completely forgotten the hamster existed.

Zack opened the condo app and skimmed through the payment information. His credentials had been entered correctly. Probably just a bug in the system.

DaEvo chimed, and Zack rolled his eyes. Speaking of bugs.

It's almost time for your date with Ashley Barnes. Take your relationship to the next level and earn Lovemeter bonuses by fulfilling one of these relationship milestones.

Relationship Milestones

- *first significant physical contact*
- *in-depth exchange of history*
- *your first kiss*
- *take her out to an exciting and memorable event*
- *your first [Dev Note—are we even allowed to suggest this? Ask Legal]*
- *become an [#select_variable: relationship type: exclusive;primary;secondary; pair-bonded; metamour]*
- *get engaged*

"Crap, that's tonight?"

Zack opened the calendar app and stared at it. His date with Ashley was tonight, and he didn't have anything planned. The exciting and memorable event seemed like the easiest milestone to complete, but that meant he needed to find an exciting and memorable event in a matter of hours.

Faz: *Dude, these new releases are awesome! You try out the new missiles yet?*
Jenny: *The new drones are really cool.*
Greg: *There's more to life than drones, Jenny.*
Jenny: *:p*

. . .

Zack stared at the messages. Training. He was supposed to train. Why hadn't he checked his calendar before promising to train with his team tonight?

Because Kayla had a photoshoot and had made sure to tell him she wasn't available. And his dates to Ashley thus far had stayed during the day or early mornings, due to her school schedule. He'd sent flowers to the photo studio at DaEvo's prompting and forgotten all about it.

He should cancel the date. He needed to train, and all the high-profile events with Kayla had given him plenty of points. His Reputation was better than ever, and Kayla's Lovemeter was nearly full. Ashley's was almost empty, and her lower level gave him fewer points.

Yeah, it made sense to cancel.

Zack opened the phone app on his OptiGlasses to text Ashley and cancel. He stopped, his gaze wavering from the texting app to the picture that his OptiGlasses had pulled from Ashley's social media to be her contact photo. She smiled at the camera, squinting a little from the bright sun. Her curls were chaotic as the wind swept through them.

Zack swallowed, unsettled by the realization that he didn't want to cancel the date. He was looking forward to spending time with Ashley. He wanted to hear her thoughts about the hospital spreadsheet and if it had helped with any of her classes. Maybe he could run some of the new Star Fury stats by her to see if she caught something he missed.

But he didn't want to cancel training with his team either. And he could always reschedule with Ashley for another night. That was the logical decision.

"How much would it hurt my stats to cancel the date?" he said.

Thankfully, DaEvo answered.

Canceling a Date at the Last Minute?

A gentleman doesn't cancel a date, not at the last minute. You'll have to

make it up to your lady.
Penalty: Make Up Quest! {----!Dev Note: Get it!?! Dev Note 2: We
need a ruling on puns in our Quests. Dev Note 3: They're Awesome.
Dev Note 4: No, they're not! Dev Note 5: Ask Marketing----!}
Penalty: Reputation -0.5
Penalty: Lovemeter -10 (1 heart)
Penalty: Increased Lovemeter depletion for two weeks

"What about rescheduling for later?"

Rescheduling a Date at the Last Minute?
A gentleman doesn't reschedule a date, not at the last minute. You'll have
to make the new date worth her while and will still incur a penalty.
Penalty: Reputation -0.4
Penalty: Lovemeter -10 (1 heart)
Penalty: Increased Lovemeter depletion until next date

Okay, think. There had to be a way around this. He was smart. A
strategist. The team always needed him to pull them out of the
hardest situations, to help their builds. This was just another
problem to solve. And the first thing he needed was more
information.

"How long does the date need to be?" Zack asked.

A date is a meeting of minds and hearts. As such, a date can be as long
or as short as the participants in the date require it to be.

Note: Increase in Lovemeter levels dependent upon final thermometer
level at end of date and overall average of level during your date.

Perfect. Zack did some quick calculations. He could pick Ashley
up from work, take her somewhere memorable for dinner, and make
it back in plenty of time to train with his team. The late night might
cause a Physique debuff, but surely that wouldn't be enough to
cause Phil to cut him off? He had done every other quest DaEvo
suggested.

He could make this work. Zack opened his app and texted Ashley. Maybe she had forgotten as well. That would let him off the hook, and they could reschedule for another night.

Zack: *Hey, are we still on for tonight?*
    Ashley: *Yeah! I'm looking forward to it.*

Crap.

Zack: *Great. I can pick you up after work?*
    Ashley: *I'll need some time to go home and get ready, unless you want to take me out in my Gord's uniform. ;)*

Other than the time they met at the hospital, Zack had only ever seen Ashley in her Gord's uniform. He swore softly. It hadn't occurred to him that she would want to change after work. That might throw off his entire plan. Kayla took hours to get ready for their dates. Or for anything, really.

Ashley: *It won't take long. I can meet you at the restaurant if you give me the address.*

The address. Zack swore again. He had been so busy with Star Fury and Kayla that he hadn't even picked a restaurant yet.

Zack: *Yeah, I'll send it to you.*

And he would—as soon as he knew what it was.

Chapter Thirty-Five

PIZZA.

Zack stared, the word alone enough to make his mouth water. He hadn't had pizza in over a month. While his waistline thanked him for it, his soul was starving for cheesy goodness.

But why was it here? Zack had asked DaEvo to suggest restaurants near his condo with options healthy enough to satisfy the fitness quests, and the word "pizza" stood out like an oasis in a desert of salads.

He selected Howie's Pizza and browsed the suggested menu options.

Howie's Pizza

- *House Salad with Grilled Chicken and Balsamic Vinaigrette Dressing*
- *Veggie Wrap with Fresh Mozzarella*
- *Cauliflower Crust Pizza with Veggie Toppings*

"Cauliflower pizza?"

Since when did they make pizza out of cauliflower? A quick

search showed Zack that it was a popular option for calorie conscious and gluten-free diners. Comments on forums showed a range of opinions from "Can't taste the difference" to "Worst idea ever."

Zack stared at the picture on the online menu. Pizza. He really missed pizza, but the idea of eating one made from cauliflower seemed wrong somehow. He returned to the list of restaurants near him that had options healthy enough to satisfy DaEvo. Salads, salads, and more salads. A few seafood places. The Mediterranean place where he got lunches to bring to Ashley most days. But it would be lame to take her to the place where they always got takeout.

Zack pushed aside his prejudices against cauliflower and texted the address for Howie's Pizza to Ashley. Then he tried to make a reservation with his OptiGlasses, but apparently, Howie's wasn't classy enough to do reservations. Zack swallowed. Maybe he should have picked one of the seafood restaurants and gone for pizza by himself another night. This was supposed to be a special date, and he had suggested pizza. If his experiences with Kayla had taught him anything, it was that women expected you to spend money on them during dates.

Zack opened his texting app to let Ashley know he had changed his mind, but she texted him before he could type the words.

Ashley: *Sounds great. See you at six?*
Zack: *Perfect.*

Six? That meant Ashley was only giving herself an hour to leave work, get ready, and meet him at the restaurant. That gave Zack way more time than he had planned on. He might be able to squeeze in a few more Relationship Milestones after dinner and fill the Lovemeter further. It wouldn't take them that long to eat pizza.

"Show me some exciting and memorable events happening near me tonight," Zack said.

DaEvo populated a list, and Zack scrolled through them.

Exciting and Memorable Events

Level up your relationship by treating your lady to one of these unique experiences!

- *Rodeo at the Stockyards*
- *Czech Society Dance Class and Social*
- *RiverWalk Whitewater Rafting*
- *Museum of Osteology*
- *Carriage Ride Downtown*
- *Oklahoma City Zoo and Botanical Gardens*
- *Oklahoma City Museum of Art*

Zack raised an eyebrow. He wouldn't have considered any of those as date options if left to his own devices. Frankly, he hadn't known any of them existed.

"Which ones are near my condo?"

Events Near You

- *Czech Society Dance Class and Social*
- *Oklahoma City Museum of Art*

Not great options. Zack dismissed the art museum. It might take hours to get through it, and it didn't exactly sound memorable. At least, not in a good way. He had taken field trips to the Metropolitan Museum of Art for school and wasn't eager to repeat the experience.

That left the dance class. Zack selected it and browsed the description.

Czech Society Dance Class and Social

Learn traditional Czechoslovakian dances in a friendly, supportive environment. No experience needed! The 30-minute dance class will be followed by a social dance with light refreshments.

DaEvo chimed.

The event Czech Society Dance Class and Social meets the follow quest requirements:

- *fitness: 30 minutes of elevated heart rate*
- *style: learn to dance (choose dance type)*

Sweet! The class started at seven, which would give them plenty of time to eat and walk the few blocks to the nearby building where the class was being held. Then they would dance for thirty minutes. Zack would receive points for another Relationship Milestone and two additional quests, and still be home in time to train with his team. He reserved two places in the dance class and paid for the tickets. His bank sent a notification marked with a red exclamation point, but Zack swiped it away. The dance tickets had been cheap, especially compared to the cover charges for the clubs Kayla liked to frequent. His bank had absolutely no reason to complain about this evening.

And he had a few hours before the date. Time to check out more Star Fury releases.

Chapter Thirty-Six

ZACK SAT at the table at Howie's Pizza, fidgeting with the bouquet of flowers he had brought and wondering if he should throw them in the trash instead. DaEvo had prompted him to bring a gift, but Ashley had said gifts weren't necessary.

But he wanted the bonus points for the quest.

The flowers had seemed like a nice compromise when he bought them, but now they seemed a little silly. Maybe he should have brought jewelry again. Kayla always liked jewelry.

Well, she usually liked jewelry. She had refused to wear the bracelet he'd had delivered to Royal Texas because it clashed with her WesterNeon outfit. Zack was still trying to figure out how diamonds could clash with anything. They were clear. Shouldn't clear go with anything?

The door chimed as someone entered. Zack looked up and forgot all about diamonds as Ashley walked into the restaurant.

She looked completely different than she did when dressed for work. Her hair was down and framed her face in a riot of auburn curls. She wore a dark green dress that showed how much the Gord's uniform had been hiding. It was criminal, Zack decided, making someone so shapely wear such unflattering clothes.

DaEvo concurred, flashing her latest social information. There were minor changes, but her higher Style bumped up her social level even more.

Ashley Barnes (Social Level 57)
Physique: 72
Style: 68
Reputation: 62
Occupation: 25

Ashley walked slowly across the restaurant, looking a little uncertain, and Zack became aware of how hard he had been staring. He blinked, trying to gather some sort of sense so he could say something clever.

"Wow," he said. "You look amazing."

Not exactly brilliant, but he was feeling a little tongue-tied. DaEvo chimed for delivering the compliment, and Ashley grinned.

"Thanks. You clean up pretty nicely yourself. No fringed jacket today?"

Zack laughed. He had gone with his usual dark jeans but dressed them up with one of Giacomo's shirts, a gray button-up with thin silver stripes. DaEvo had awarded him decent style points when he put it on, but it had also suggested that at the first opportunity, he purchase clothes that actually fit. For once, Zack agreed with the app. He had lost enough weight that his clothes were getting baggy. Phil wouldn't be pleased to see invoices from another shopping trip on Zack's bank statements.

DaEvo chimed.

Treat your date like a lady to win her over. Try the following:

- *Open doors for her*
- *Pull out her chair*

"Oh!"

Zack belatedly realized Ashley was still standing, although she didn't seem to be waiting for him to do anything. How long had he been staring into space? He was acting like a complete idiot.

He jumped up and pulled out her chair for her. "My lady."

Ashley rolled her eyes playfully as she sat down, but Zack thought she looked a little pleased. The thermometer bumped up. Then a reminder about the gift flashed up.

"Right, um, these are for you." He offered her the bouquet, feeling completely lame.

He should have gone with diamonds, even though they didn't go with everything. Or asked her what color she was wearing and picked something that matched. Emeralds were green, right? Maybe he could have some emeralds delivered.

Before he could search for nearby jewelers with drone delivery, Ashley took the flowers with a smile, brushing her fingers against his as she did so. DaEvo's thermometer flickered again for physical contact as Ashley pulled a daisy from the bouquet and tucked it into her hair.

"Thanks. This is nice." She gestured to the flowers and the restaurant.

Zack released a breath he hadn't realized he was holding. She didn't hate it. Thank goodness.

Ashley smiled at him, looking a little sheepish. "I, um, I actually have a present for you too."

"Really?" Zack didn't bother trying to hide his surprise, and Ashley laughed.

"Gift giving goes both ways, you know! It's probably lame. But, well—" She stammered out a few more excuses before pulling an official-looking envelope from her purse and handing it to Zack.

He turned it over in his hands, trying to guess what it might be. It was sealed with a Star Fury sticker. He realized Ashley was waiting for him to open it and broke the seal. Curiosity built up as he pulled out a single sheet of paper and unfolded it. What on earth had Ashley given him?

The top of the paper looked like the official stationery Phil always sent letters on, except instead of a company logo, it had the Corsair crossbones.

"Official Veridian Report."

Zack read the heading aloud, then he skimmed ahead, reading silently. The letter was short. Just a string of numbers and a list of a few materials. Zack looked at Ashley, who was blushing in embarrassment.

"It's probably stupid, but I overheard Steve and his buddies talking about a drone Easter egg build they found. Those are all the materials they mentioned, and some of the sensor settings they used to compensate for the cloaking."

"What? Really?" Zack dropped the paper and leaped to his feet in excitement.

Ashley laughed in relief. "Oh, good. I'm glad you like it."

"Like it? This is—you—" Zack realized he was drawing the attention of the other diners and quickly sat back down. No need to lose Reputation points over this.

Even if it was the answer to a problem that had been plaguing him and his team for months.

"This is amazing," Zack said. "You're amazing!"

Ashley brushed her hair back and smiled before looking aside at Zack's fixed gaze. They were interrupted by a waiter bringing them menus. Ashley seemed a little grateful for the interruption, focusing her attention on the waiter. Zack scanned the note with his Opti-Glasses to make sure the information was safe, then he tucked it in his pocket. The waiter took their drink orders then left them alone.

"Have you eaten here before?" Ashley asked.

She picked up a menu, browsing casually. Zack did the same, although he already knew what he was getting. The only pizza approved by DaEvo.

"No, I think it's new. Oh, pizza made from cauliflower. I wonder what that's like?"

He said it casually, as if he were just curious. He really hoped Ashley wouldn't make fun of him for ordering it. A few months ago, Zack would have mocked anyone who even considered eating such a thing, but DaEvo and Phil had left him with no other options.

Ashley pulled the menu a little closer, apparently reading up on the cauliflower pizza. "Only one way to find out. It's way healthier, so worth a shot."

"Really?"

"Yeah, let's try it!"

The waiter came and took their orders. Zack chose the DaEvo-approved cauliflower pizza with veggie toppings. Ashley ordered one with pepperoni and sausage.

"You've really been eating healthy lately," Ashley said.

Zack waited for the follow-up insult, but it didn't come. She just seemed to be making an observation.

"It just seemed like a good idea, you know?"

Fortunately, Ashley accepted that explanation. They chatted until their food arrived, discussing everything from Star Fury to the hospital spreadsheet to Ashley's latest exam.

"So you're done with classes?" Zack asked.

"We're on break for a few weeks. It'll be nice to have some time off, although I had to pick up a side job with a caterer to help cover the cost of books for next term, so it won't be quite as leisurely as it sounds." She made a face.

Zack laughed, fighting back the uncomfortable feeling he always had when money came up. The trust had covered his college tuition and all the ancillary costs, including the books. He had no idea how much they cost, but apparently, it was quite a bit. Enough that Ashley had to pick up another job to afford them.

"Hey, it's fine," Ashley said, noticing his discomfort. "It's a little crazy, but it's temporary. Everybody struggles while they're in school."

"Sure," Zack said, trying to sound as if he had experienced that struggle firsthand.

"So, what do you do for work?" Ashley asked. "I just realized I've never actually asked. Sorry about that."

"What? No, it's fine. I—" Zack's mind raced. He couldn't admit he'd never worked a full-time job after Ashley just said she was working two while going to school. He would sound like a complete slacker, even if it was the truth. "I'm a professional gamer." He kept talking, trying to soften the lie. "Well, more like semi-pro, but I'll get a spot in the pro league if I place well enough in the tournament."

"Really? Wow, that's awesome. No wonder you spend so much time playing Star Fury."

"Yeah, just trying to be the best."

"And your parents are cool with that?" Ashley asked. Zack felt the blood drain from his face, and Ashley looked at him with concern. "I'm sorry, sensitive topic? I was just joking. You don't have to—"

"They... they've passed away." Zack said, fighting to contain the flood of emotions the topic always brought up. He was pretty sure crying on a date would lead to a major debuff.

"Oh gosh. Zack, I'm so sorry. I didn't know. I didn't mean to bring that up."

She offered her hand, and Zack took it. He smiled a little too brightly, his usual way to push the negative feelings back down where they belonged. "It's fine. What about your parents? They must be really proud of how hard you work."

Now Ashley looked uncomfortable, and Zack wished he could take back the words. He had meant them as a compliment. Before he could find a way to backtrack, Ashley sighed.

"They're divorced," she said finally. "My mom moved to Texas, and my dad travels a lot for work. My grandma raised Amber and me, but it's hard for her to get around now that she's getting older."

"Oh."

No wonder Ashley had been spending so much time at the hospital with Amber. She was the only one available. Zack searched for something to say that would make it better, but he was no good at this sort of thing.

DaEvo chimed, and Zack opened the notification as fast as he could, hoping for a prompt that would show him what to say to make all these awkward problems go away.

Relationship Milestone Achieved!

- *in-depth exchange of history*

Zack swiped away the notification. He would rather not have had that particular exchange, although maybe DaEvo had a point. He did feel as though he understood Ashley better after that conversation. It was strange, but he'd never had that kind of conversation with Kayla. It was mostly about fashion or, occasionally, gossip about other models or celebrities she knew.

The waiter brought their pizzas, and Zack realized he was still holding Ashley's hand. He hastily let go so the waiter could set their food on the table. The man grinned at them like a proud father, and Zack felt his face going red.

"Would you like anything else?" the waiter asked.

There seemed to be some extra meaning to his words, and Ashley laughed.

"No, we're good." She picked up a slice of her pizza and nodded to Zack. "Ready to try some cauliflower?"

Zack grinned at the challenge in her tone and picked up his own slice. "Let's do this."

He took a bite and chewed thoughtfully. Ashley did the same.

After she swallowed, she said, "Not bad."

"Yeah," Zack said, smiling at her. "Not bad at all."

Chapter Thirty-Seven

THEY FINISHED the pizza and chatted a little more. Zack did his best not to sigh in disappointment when the waiter offered the dessert menu. There was no way DaEvo was letting him have anything sweet.

Ashley noticed his expression and shook her head. "No thanks. We'll have the check, please."

The waiter nodded and hurried away.

Zack checked the time on his OptiGlasses and winced. "Wow, is it really that late already?"

"Oh, do you need to go?" Ashley said.

She sounded disappointed and brightened when Zack shook his head. Yes, he needed to go soon, but not before he received full bonus points for stacking his quests.

"No, it's not that. I have something else planned for us tonight."

"Really? What is it?"

Ashley grinned, and Zack found himself smiling back. Her excitement was contagious.

"A surprise."

He really hoped she didn't hate it. But girls liked dancing, right? DaEvo had suggested it as an exciting and memorable event.

Then again, DaEvo had also suggested wearing WesterNeon.

Crap. What if she hated it?

The waiter brought the check, and Zack took it, ignoring Ashley's protests. It was an old-fashioned paper receipt, with a barcode for him to scan rather than an automatic OptiGlass integration.

Damn luddites.

Zack focused on the barcode until his OptiGlasses scanned it.

Error: Insufficient Funds

"What?" Zack scanned it again and received the same message.

"Is there a problem, sir?" the waiter said.

"I'm not sure..." Zack frowned.

The waiter walked off and returned with a small pad that showed the payment method Zack had been trying.

"I'm sorry," the waiter said as he looked at the tablet. "There seems to be a problem with your payment."

"That's impossible. There must be a problem with your system."

It had to be their outdated system. Their stupid, old-fashioned technology.

But the waiter made a few taps on his tablet and shook his head. "Our system is fine. It says your card has insufficient funds."

Zack remembered the notification from his bank and winced. Had Phil cut him off after all? Had he missed a Physique quest notification? He had been trying so hard to do them all.

"I-I just need to call my bank," Zack stammered, feeling his face go red.

The waiter raised an eyebrow. He had seemed to approve of the couple before, but now he looked like a father questioning if Zack was good enough for his little girl.

"Don't worry, I've got it," Ashley said.

She pulled an old-fashioned credit card from her purse and handed it to the waiter with a smile. Zack sputtered something about paying her back, and she shook her head.

"Don't. You've bought lunch every time we've met. It's my turn to pay, all right?"

Zack waited for the trap to spring. For her to add something to pile on the guilt. If this had happened while he was out with Kayla—

But Ashley wasn't Kayla, and she truly didn't seem to mind.

"You're sure?"

She laughed. "Yeah, it's only fair. I was going to suggest going Dutch for our lunches anyway. It's not fair for you to be spending all your money on me."

"All my money?" Zack sputtered, not quite understanding.

"Look, I've been overdrawn before. It sucks. We'll split costs from now on, all right? No big deal."

She thought he was spending all his money on her. That bringing her a few lunches had somehow contributed to his financial downfall. The girl who was working an extra job so she could buy a book was trying to save him.

Zack blinked, not sure what to say, but desperate to fix this so Ashley didn't think he was broke and she had to spend all her money on him. With a sinking feeling in his stomach, he watched her sign the paper receipt. He needed to come clean, but how? Maybe he could have Phil make it look as if she won the lottery.

But she was probably smart enough to see through that.

Zack swallowed. "Ashley, I—"

"You're not going to be old-fashioned and stubborn about this, are you? It's fine for women to pay for things on dates. I ate just as much pizza as you did."

Her eyes had a steely glint that Zack hadn't seen before, and her face was stern. He wasn't going to win this argument.

"Nope. No stubbornness here." Zack raised his hands in the air.

Ashley laughed. "Good. Now, where's the surprise you mentioned?"

"Not far. We can walk."

Zack gathered his composure and offered his arm. Ashley took it. DaEvo chimed bonus points for physical contact, and they walked as Zack followed pale purple arrows that his OptiGlass overlaid on the sidewalk to lead them to the dance. It was a nice night, with stars and streetlights sparkling overhead. Zack looked at Ashley and smiled. She caught him staring and winked.

Faz: *Dude, these new releases are insane!*
   Jenny: *I'll say. See you guys soon.*
   Zack: *Be there in 40.*

Then he swiped away the notifications and muted his messaging app. He hoped Ashley hadn't noticed that he had sent the text and was checking the time fairly often. They should be right on time for the dance class. And once that was over, he'd make the short walk back to his apartment and share the information his Veridian had recovered for him.

Ashley studied the building curiously when Zack stopped in front of it.

"The New Czech Dance Hall," she read.

"Yeah. I signed us up for a dance class."

"Really? That sounds cool."

Zack smiled. His initial impression had been correct. Girls liked to dance. He pushed open the door for Ashley and received bonus points from DaEvo for acting like a gentleman. He was finally getting the hang of this.

The sound of tuba music assaulted his ears as soon as he entered the room. Zack listened to the "oom-pah, oom-pah" with growing dread, his heart beating in time with the low brass. This was memorable, all right, but not quite what he had pictured for a romantic moment. Ashley pressed her lips together, clearly trying to not to laugh at his expression.

"You're here for the dance lessons?" a woman asked.

Zack nodded and managed to say his name. She checked her reservations and ushered them through a door into the dance hall. The tuba music intensified as they entered the room. A brass band sat on a stage at the far end. They were dressed in black pants, white shirts, and red vests, and playing what Zack considered to be the un-coolest music in the history of music. Tubas. Why hadn't DaEvo warned him that traditional Czech music involved tubas?

The room was filled with couples and singles of all ages. Some were dressed in traditional clothes like the band, some wore nicer dress clothes like Zack and Ashley, and a few wore jeans and T-shirts.

"Everyone onto the dance floor," one of the women in tradi-tional dress called, waving to silence the band. "Grab your partner, and we'll start with the polka!"

Zack looked at Ashley in horror. "I am so sorry. I thought a dance class would be, um, not this."

He gestured around, looking from the tuba players to the other couples, to the dance floor where he was expected to stand. At least the room itself was pretty. White walls decorated with painted murals of red flowers.

"It looks fun," Ashley said.

"Really?"

"Yeah. I don't know anything about Czech culture. Let's try it out."

She grabbed Zack's arm and pulled him onto the dance floor, where the instructor instructed them to clasp one set of hands and wrap their arms around each other's waists. Zack suddenly found himself in very close quarters with Ashley and thinking that maybe she was right, and the polka wasn't so bad after all. The instructor showed them the basic steps, a sort of double skip that didn't look too challenging.

"Easy enough," Zack said, suddenly grateful for all the fitness quests he had completed. He was much lighter on his feet than he might otherwise have been.

Then the music began again, and Zack found himself cursing the tuba for an entirely different reason. Did the blasted thing have to play so fast? He stepped on Ashley's foot and offered a quick apology. Before she could respond, she stepped on his toe. Zack stumbled and nearly fell over. Ashley caught him but nearly fell over herself.

"Sorry!"

They skidded to a stop and stood in the middle of the dance floor, laughing while the other couples, who were obviously not beginners, swirled around them in time with the rollicking music. Zack caught Ashley's gaze and was suddenly very aware of his arm on her waist. He leaned closer and she did the same, until their faces were almost touching.

"I see we need to go a little slower," the dance instructor said, rushing over and ruining the moment. "You two come with me. I'll show you the steps."

She pulled them to a corner of the room and walked them through the steps again, dancing with each of them in turn to make sure they understood before turning them loose to dance with each other.

Zack smiled with surprise as he and Ashley skipped and twirled with the other couples in the room. The booming bass of the tuba made it easy to keep time and stay together. He grinned, and Ashley grinned back as they moved across the dance floor.

DaEvo chimed.

Relationship Milestone Achieved!

- *first significant physical contact*

This wasn't exactly what Zack had pictured for that quest but holding Ashley for thirty minutes certainly did seem significant. By the time the class ended, Zack knew how to dance the Czech Polka, Czech Waltz, and a line dance whose name he couldn't quite pronounce. He reluctantly let go of Ashley as the dancers cleared the floor to give everyone a chance to rest before the social dance began.

"That was more of a workout than I thought it would be," Zack said. He wiped the sweat off his brow and grabbed a glass of water for himself, as well as one for Ashley.

"Yeah." Ashley was breathing heavily and also sweating a bit. She didn't seem to mind though.

Ashley collapsed into the nearest chair, pulled a fan out of her purse, and waved it at her face. Zack sat next to her, and she fanned him for a bit as well before returning to herself.

He looked more closely at the fan. "Is that the one I gave you?"

"Yeah. It comes in handy more often than you'd think."

Huh. Maybe DaEvo knew what it was doing with those gifts after all.

As if on cue, DaEvo chimed.

Physique Quest Complete!
Reward +0.1 Physique

Style Quest Complete!
Reward +0.1 Style

Zack stared at it. He still didn't get how dancing was a style quest, but he'd take it. Maybe there was a baseline or something for grace.

Either way, he had completed the bonus quests for learning how to dance and had gotten two relationship milestones at the same time for exchanging history and significant physical contact. The class was over. He could call a ride to take Ashley home and get back to his apartment in plenty of time to train with his team. He could see from the way the thermometer was glowing, he'd score a ton of Lovemeter points if he called the date done.

Except the band was playing again, and somehow the oom-pah of the tuba had become rather endearing. Probably something to do with the way Ashley's eyes glittered when she smiled.

She held her hand out to Zack. "May I have this polka?"

"Of course."

Zack wrapped his arm around Ashley's waist and swept her onto the dance floor. They joined the other couples, losing themselves in the music and each other. Zack learned quickly to keep his eyes on the dance floor so he didn't run into other couples, but he also sneaked glances at Ashley whenever he could. She seemed to be doing the same and winked whenever she caught his eye.

The evening passed in a blur of auburn curls, sparkling eyes, and tubas. By the time the band leader called for the last dance, Zack was drenched in sweat. He needed to step up his fitness routine, he decided. Maybe add some cardio.

Then again, maybe not. Everyone around the room seemed to be equally sweaty and didn't care a bit about it.

The last dance was a waltz. A slower one, as if the band leader knew everyone was tired. The more relaxed tempo gave Zack a chance to catch his breath and speak.

"Sorry this was kind of weird—" he said. "I—"

"I liked it," Ashley said. "It was different. I've never done anything like this before."

"Yeah, neither have I," Zack said.

They were drifting to one of the corners of the room, away from the other couples. Zack wasn't sure if he was leading them that way or Ashley was. Or if they were moving by some sort of unspoken agreement. Whichever it was, they ended up in the darkest corner of the room, not dancing anymore but still holding each other close.

"Hey, I…"

Zack couldn't remember what he had been going to say, but it probably wasn't important. He was tilting his head toward Ashley, and she was lifting her head toward his, and then they were kissing.

DaEvo chimed and the tubas played, but Zack was too caught up in the moment to notice.

Chapter Thirty-Eight

ZACK WOKE to the full afternoon sun glaring through his window. He rolled over to grab the glasses and groaned as his muscles protested. Why was he so sore? His trainer hadn't added any new weights to his routine.

Physique Quest Failed: Get sufficient sleep
Physique -0.1

Crap. Hopefully, Phil would let that one slide. Why had he been out so late?

Right, the dance class. Zack grinned as he remembered the evening. Apparently, polka people knew how to party. The dance had lasted until after midnight, although they hadn't exactly been dancing at the end, then he and Ashley had walked in a park until she remembered that she had to be up early to take Amber to a doctor's appointment and had reluctantly said goodbye.

The OptiGlasses chimed again. Zack slid them onto his face to check his messages.

. . .

Kayla: *Hey, want to go out tonight? I've missed you.*

That was followed by a picture of her pouting for the camera and another of her staring wistfully into the distance. It would have meant more, but Zack had seen the pictures before. He had subscribed to all her social media feeds to make sure DaEvo saw all the pictures of them together and gave him Reputation points, which had worked well over the past few weeks.

These particular shots were part of Kayla's latest advertising campaign for perfume. A perfume that Zack hated the scent of, but Kayla insisted she had to wear as part of her contract.

Zack: *Sorry, can't. I need to train for the tournament.*

Specifically, he needed to deliver Ashley's information to his teammates and see what they could do with it.

Zack grinned. Ashley. He still couldn't believe she had managed to get that information for him. She was like a real life Veridian. She was amazing. She was—

Kayla: *Training? *Yawn. Sure you don't want to skip? There's a sale at the mall. ;)*

That was accompanied by a picture Zack hadn't seen on any of Kayla's social media feeds. Kayla leaned toward the camera, smiling seductively and showing quite a bit of cleavage. Zack stared at it, feeling tempted to skip training after all.

Except he had already missed multiple rounds of training in his quests to keep the Lovemeters full. He was running out of time. His teammates—

Crap! He had missed training with his teammates last night!

Zack checked the conversation he had muted and groaned out loud. He had over a hundred messages from his teammates wondering where he was. They had even debated calling the police to check on him before remembering they didn't know his address.

Zack: *Guys, I am so sorry! Phil sprung another quest on me out of nowhere last night. But good news! I found information about the Easter egg! When can everyone meet today?*

They didn't answer. Zack hoped they were still asleep and not ignoring him.

Kayla: *Or we could skip shopping. Maybe go to the pool?*

She sent a picture of herself in a bikini and a link to buy tickets to a swanky spa located just outside the city. Zack wasn't sure which photo shoot had led to this particular photo of Kayla, but he was prepared to buy everything the advertisement was selling. He opened the link without thinking and clicked on the button to buy tickets.

Error: Insufficient funds. Please contact your bank.

Right, his card had been denied last night!

Zack called Phil and started talking as soon as his trustee answered. "Look, I've done all your stupid fitness quests. Every single one. Well, I missed one night of sleep. But that's nothing, and that happened afterward. So why isn't my card working? You said you wouldn't cut me off."

"I haven't." Phil sounded calm. Too calm.

Zack narrowed his eyes in suspicion. "Then what's going on? Why do you sound so smug?"

Phil laughed. "You reached your credit limit. Your account is set to automatically pay the balance every month, but you reached your limit, so your card is rejecting new purchases until you pay it off."

"My limit?" Zack hadn't realized his card had a limit, or that it wasn't tied directly to his bank account. Apparently, it did, and he had never spent enough for it to matter. "So how do I fix it?"

"Go into the credit app and give it permission to pay the balance early. I'm sure your bank has sent you notifications about this. Didn't they cover that in your finance classes in college?"

They probably had. Zack had skipped all the lectures in that class. They hadn't seemed relevant to him.

"Thanks," Zack said.

"So how are your dates going? You meet anyone special yet?"

Zack hung up. Then he opened the credit app, digging around in the menu until he found the button needed to pay his balance. He gulped at the number. Had he really spent that much in a month? Maybe Phil had a point about his spending after all. His OptiGlasses chimed with a message before he could go back to buy the tickets.

Greg: *We agreed last night to train PvP this afternoon at 2:00.*

Zack waited for more, but nothing else came. He sighed. Much as he would love to spend the afternoon with a swimsuit model actually wearing a swimsuit, he really needed to train. He opened the spa's website again, purchased a single ticket, and forwarded it to Kayla.

Zack: *I have to train, but have a good time.*

Kayla responded with an emoji of a kissing face.

Reputation +0.1

Kayla had already posted about his gift on her social media. Comments from her fans poured in, saying how lucky she was to have a boyfriend who spoiled her. Zack rolled his eyes. Those were the same fans prepared to attack him at the first sign of inattentiveness. Kayla's popularity was a double-edged sword.

Zack congratulated himself on avoiding a disaster and rolled out of bed. DaEvo chimed, reminding him to work out and eat a healthy breakfast, and he settled into his now-familiar morning routine. After he ate, he put his dishes in the sink and changed into his FitLife clothes.

At DaEvo's prompting, Zack had bought real dishes, and the cleaning service came every few days to wash them and tidy up the apartment. Zack looked around, appreciating how clean it was. The granite countertops sparkled. The floor was clean. His laundry was washed and put away. His gaming system gleamed. It even smelled nice. Perfect for inviting his lady over, as DaEvo constantly reminded him.

Except Kayla never wanted to come over. She either needed beauty rest or had to be out late for an industry event. Or she was out of town. In truth, it was getting rather frustrating. So much so that he even occasionally hit the gym in the evenings after a night out with her.

And Ashley—Zack grinned. He had actually considered inviting Ashley over last night, before she had remembered that she had to be home in the morning for Amber. He glanced around the apartment again, wondering how he would explain this place to her when she saw it. She thought he was broke.

He shrugged. He would think of something. Maybe say he was housesitting for a friend.

Zack walked to the gym, settled into his first weight machine, and began his reps. His breathing settled into a steady rhythm as he pulled the bar down and let it back up. He increased his speed a little, eager to finish this and log into Star Fury so he could put Ashley's information to work.

The condo app chimed.

Based on your rep speed and heart rate, it's time to adjust your weights! Congratulations!

Crap. Zack tried to swipe the notification away before DaEvo sensed it, but the dating app was too fast for him.

Physique Quest Alert!

You've leveled up your Physique! Congratulations! Accept your personal trainer's new routine to receive additional Physique points.

Zack sighed as he accepted the quest and gave the condo app permission to raise the weight on the machines. This deal with Phil was a pain. Literally a pain. The weight machine clicked, and suddenly the bar was more difficult to move. Zack grunted as he pulled it down.

DaEvo chimed and showed his latest stats.

Physique: 52.1
Style: 63.2
Reputation: -15.54
Occupation: 0
Social level: 24.94

It amused Zack once again how some stats, like Reputation, could keep going up or down as public posts like Cassie's blog or Kayla's incessant social feeds affected them. And how Physique could inch up a little at a time before taking a sudden jump as it decided he'd made enough progress to show. Like the first time he'd taken a proper look in the mirror with his OptiGlasses on.

As he mused, Zack realized that DaEvo had another notification for him.

Relationship Hint!

Make sure to follow up with your date to keep the good impression going!

Zack grinned and texted Ashley as he moved to the next machine.

Zack: *Hey, I had a great time last night. And thanks again for the info! I'm putting it into practice today.*

Ashley usually texted back pretty quickly. Zack watched his Opti-Glasses as he worked his way through the machines, but the only notifications that came in were a selfie of Kayla at the spa and a few Reputation points once she posted the selfie to her social media.

Zack had worked up a sweat by the time he finished the workout. He followed DaEvo's prompting to make a recovery smoothie at the bar, nodding at the other gym users as he blended his potion. He had figured out a more palatable recipe, thanks to some of the bodybuilders. They were actually decent guys once you got to know them.

Sometimes he hung around to chat with them, but today he made the smoothie to go and hurried back to his apartment to shower and get started with training.

He tossed his dirty clothes into the laundry hamper the cleaning service had placed for him, toweled his hair dry, and considered the clothes in his closet. He now had a collection of high-end suits, WesterNeon apparel, and other clothes by up-and-coming designers Kayla had assured him were both stylish and worth the investment. So far, DaEvo had agreed and given Zack significant points for wearing them, so he had gone with it.

But he wasn't going out with Kayla today. He was gaming.

Zack slid into some sweats and a T-shirt and settled into his gaming chair. He logged in and smiled when the Star Fury music filled his apartment. He opened up his ship's map system and marked all the coordinates that contained the materials on Ashley's list. Calculating the properties that resulted in combining those materials could provide some valuable clues in how to get around the drones.

"Dude! You found something about the Easter egg?" Faz's voice echoed through the speakers. He sounded as if he had drunk a few too many coffees and was bouncing off the walls.

"Yeah! I have materials and some sensor settings! I'll send them over."

Faz let out a low whistle as he read through the list. "You sure about this info? Could be a trap. If we use these settings and they're wrong—"

"No, I trust the source."

Their sensors pinged as Jenny came online.

"Nice of you to join us, Zack."

"Look, guys, I'm so sorry about last night. I—"

"Save it," Faz said. "You'll be fine as long as you read the notes I typed for you. We figured out some cool stuff last night."

Zack opened his email and groaned. His teammates had indeed sent him notes last night. Pages and pages of notes. Unfortunately, he had no time to review them now. "Yeah, thanks!"

They couldn't have discovered anything too radical in one training session, right? He could wing it for today, then review the notes later.

"Whoa," Greg said as he came online. "That's a lot of materials. Whose shopping list is this?"

"Ours, apparently," Jenny said. "Where did you get this info, Zack?"

"Oh, a friend gave it to me."

"A friend?" Jenny sounded skeptical. That was fair.

"It was Zoe Cross, wasn't it?" Faz said. "She's got the inside hookups because she's the tournament spokeswoman."

It was less ridiculous than it sounded, given that he had met Zoe and had dinner with her, but Zack laughed along with his teammates.

"It will take a lot of time to collect all this and analyze it," Jenny said. "I vote we do PvP training right now as planned."

"Do we have to?" Greg said. "I want to see if Zack's top secret information pans out!"

"No, Jenny's right," Zack said. "This will take time to put

together. A quick round of PvP won't hurt anything. Let's do the usual. Fight each other to look for weaknesses and offer feedback. Greg, you'll take Faz first. I'll face off against Jenny so we can see how her EMP shields are coming along."

"But Jenny—"

"Shut it, Greg," Jenny said. "Let's just go with Zack's plan."

Jenny's ship came into view as Zack reached her quadrant of space. She had already activated her army of drones around her. Zack grinned and armed his laser cannon. Jenny was great in the team battles, but weaker in PvP rounds because she relied so heavily on her drones. She was definitely going to be in trouble once he revealed how he had turned up the EMP on his laser cannon. Zack swooped closer, trying to draw away some of Jenny's drones and find an opening.

Jenny hailed him on the comms. "So, you and Kayla have been spending a lot of time together lately."

"What?" Zack was so surprised, he didn't notice a drone planting a bomb in his path. It exploded, delivering 1% damage to his shields. "Hey, no fair!"

"All's fair in love and war. You seem to be gaining experience with both."

More drones circled around him, and Zack had the strange feeling he had walked into an ambush on multiple fronts. "How do you know about Kayla?"

Zack turned up the settings that caused the EMP and fired a rapid succession of blasts into the cloud of drones. It blew up a group of drones in Jenny's outer defenses, and the resulting EMP blast knocked out even more around the explosion. They turned upside down as their navigation systems fried, making them look like dead fish floating belly up in a pond.

"Social media posts are public. Or had you forgotten that?"

"Of course I know that."

He just hadn't realized that any of his friends followed Kayla's feed. Zack continued to blast the laser cannon, disabling more and more of Jenny's drone defenses. She used his focus on that as an opportunity to circle more drones around and land a few blows of her own. Zack ignored them. They were weak attacks, and his regeneration could deal with it. He even had a shield booster ready if necessary. It was an old build, but it worked well with his setup. Just one of many modifications he had made over the past few weeks.

Actually, the shield booster had been Ashley's idea. She had mentioned how some of the older machines were actually still better for hospitals than the latest build and he'd...

A blast rocked the ship and he focused on launching a series of missiles at Jenny. Of course, Jenny's droids got in the way, but it meant he'd thinned her swarm.

Zack frowned. Did Ashley follow Kayla's social media feeds? He wouldn't want her to think—

To think what, exactly? Zack and Ashley weren't exclusive or anything. Last night had been the first time they had officially gone out. Although he had completed a lot of Relationship Milestones with Ashley last night. That seemed significant. Her nearly full Lovemeter said DaEvo agreed.

So where did that leave Kayla?

Zack's ship rocked with an explosion, and he swore loudly. Jenny laughed and launched missiles at him as Zack checked his readouts. His shields were down 50%.

"What the hell? How did you do that?"

"I'll tell you after I beat you."

"Fat chance."

Zack flew closer, dodging the disabled drones floating around Jenny. Even floating dead in space, they were still a fairly effective defense, as any shot he fired would hit them instead. The drones bounced off his hull as he tried to get close enough to her ship to get a clear shot.

"I haven't told Greg and Faz yet. What do you think they'd say if they knew you were actually dating a model?"

"Who knows?" Zack refused to let himself be distracted again.

Jenny released a few heat-seeking missiles and dodged deeper into the sea of disabled drones. It was almost as bad as driving through an asteroid field. Weirdly, the field of broken drones seemed to be getting thicker. There must have been more drones behind Jenny than Zack realized. Those swarm drones everyone had been talking about must be these things. He hadn't seen anyone use them in this manner.

He felt a strange urge to turn on windshield wipers to clear his view. It was like driving through heavy rain.

"Or maybe I should tell them you've been skipping our training sessions to go out to clubs with her. Expensive clubs in designer clothes. Does she buy them for you so you'll be better arm candy?"

"Very funny. I told you guys, I've had to cut back on training because of this thing Phil tricked me into."

"Your former guardian is forcing you to date a model? That seems a little strange."

The cloud of drones had gotten even thicker. Zack supposed it was natural for them to be drawn to his ship. It had mass, so gravity would attract them. Still, they seemed to be actively floating toward his ship. Of course, that was impossible. The EMP had disabled them.

"Zack, I know what those clothes cost. What those clubs cost. There's no way Kayla's paying for you, which means you must be paying for her."

Jenny sounded angry, which raised Zack's defenses. This was why he never talked finances with his friends. It always got awkward. "Yeah, so?"

"Look, I get that you don't need money, but you're hurting the whole team by blowing off training. We need you to be on top of your game! Maybe it doesn't matter to you, but the rest of us could actually use the prize money and contract!"

"What? What are you talking about?"

The disabled drones now completely blocked his view. He could still see through his various scanner and sensor outputs, but it was still annoying. Unfortunately, he didn't have any rapid-fire lasers anymore, not since they'd chosen to swap it out for his main laser.

"You're rusty, Zack. You've let yourself get distracted."

"I'll show you distracted!"

Zack located Jenny with his scanner and blasted her with his sniper laser. She dodged, but not before taking some damage.

"Does that look rusty to you?"

Jenny sighed. "You know, good gamers don't let themselves get arrogant."

"What's that supposed to mean?"

There was a moment of silence, then the drones covering Zack's main viewscreen lit up as they came back online. He fired up his boosters and engaged evasive maneuvers, trying to escape, but they clung tight. His ship's engines groaned from the extra weight. The drones' lights changed from yellow to flashing red as they began a self-destruct sequence.

"Hey! I disabled these." Zack tried to increase his speed to shake the drones, but nothing worked.

Jenny chuckled. "If you'd actually bothered to come to training or read the report Faz made, you'd know that I perfected my EMP shield. We tested it last night."

"What? Jenny, don't—"

"Bye, Zack."

The red lights flashed faster, and Zack's ship exploded. The sound reverberated through his apartment, and every screen of his gaming setup went white.

"Jenny? Jenny, are you there?"

Nothing but static in response. He would have to respawn before he could talk to her through the game system. Zack swore and punched the necessary buttons. Why had Jenny taken it so far and actually blown him up? He would have to completely restock now. And while he could afford it—he had enough in his main account for the tournament—it was still expensive. He didn't have his usual cushion anymore.

Kind of like in real life.

His ship spawned, and he set autopilot to take him to the rendezvous spot.

"What the hell, Jenny? Did you have to blow me out of the sky?"

She didn't respond.

Zack swallowed. "Hey, guys. You done yet?"

"Still going," Faz said. "I'll get back to you after I win."

"You wish!" Greg said.

"Stop distracting them," Jenny said. "Maybe you can pass the time reading your report and seeing exactly how I beat you."

"You beat Zack?" Greg said. Then he yowled as Faz landed a hit on him.

"Focus," Jenny said.

"So, is that a yes or a no?" Faz said.

Zack sighed. Better to admit to it than to have Jenny brag about it. "Yeah, she beat me. That was a neat trick with the drones. It caught me by surprise."

"By surprise?" Faz said. "We planned that strategy last night! I wrote all about it in the notes I sent you."

"He didn't read it," Jenny said. "You'd better get reading, Zack. Leave Greg and Faz alone so they can focus. I'll look at these coordinates and try to figure out if the information is good or not."

"It's good," Zack said.

"Yeah, I'm not exactly in the mood to trust what you say without checking it out first," Jenny said.

She had transferred their conversation to a private channel so they wouldn't distract Greg and Faz from their match.

Zack swallowed. "Are you going to tell them?"

"About Kayla? I'm not sure yet. I think they deserve to know, but I don't want to distract them from the tournament."

"I didn't have a choice," Zack protested. "Besides, I wasn't out with Kayla last night."

"Oh, that makes me feel so much better," Jenny said. "Nice to know you're blowing us off for multiple reasons and not just your new arm-candy girlfriend. You're supposed to be leading this team. Get your priorities together and do it."

She signed off, leaving Zack to the laborious task of reading through the notes and rebuilding his ship. Hopefully, he'd figure out a way to balance all these priorities at the same time.

Chapter Thirty-Nine

DaEvo's all-too-familiar chime interrupted Zack's concentration. He scowled as he turned away from the spreadsheet he was making. How was he supposed to analyze all these materials with constant interruptions? Once they'd checked out the mining operations indicated, they'd confirmed that the Armada had been busy hogging those spots. So it seemed as though the new drones definitely needed a specific material build.

Now, they just had to figure out the ratios or get the blueprint, then they could disseminate the information and put a serious cramp on Armada production. That'd make a big difference in the tournament—not just for themselves but everyone else.

He closed the spreadsheet with a sigh and opened DaEvo.

Relationship Notification: Kayla Taylor's Lovemeter has dropped to 50%

"I've been sending her gifts!"

He really had. Ever since she'd been back in the last week, she'd been wanting to go out constantly. But Zack hadn't had time to meet up with her, not since the team needed him more on point as they were headlining the material search. Now that they were past the dungeon rounds, PvP training was all the more important and needed his full attention.

Please note due to low level of Relationship Milestones with Kayla Taylor and a disparate social level, Lovemeter amounts reflect the fast depleting consideration between yourself and your date.

Meet your Relationship Milestones and reduce social status variations to reduce decrease in your Lovemeter!

Yeah, yeah. Zack was well aware of that fact. He gave up on his analysis and flipped through his DaEvo stats. He hadn't seen Ashley since their polka date, but her Lovemeter was still pretty full since they had hit so many relationship milestones. And it didn't deplete as quickly since Ashley was closer to his level. He grinned. DaEvo might have gotten those levels a little wrong. Going dancing with Ashley was way more fun than dancing with Kayla.

Fun. Zack blinked in surprise at the realization he'd had fun with Ashley. He actually enjoyed her company. He wanted to see her again.

He brushed aside the desire as a matter of practicality. Why go to the trouble of keeping two Lovemeters full when you could focus on one? Ashley's depleted slower. She was the logical choice.

Feelings had nothing to do with it. And his social media stats were doing much better.

Kayla's constant stream of social media posts had repaired the damage from Cassie's blog and more, but he didn't need them anymore now that traffic to the blog post had slowed. He could let Kayla's Lovemeter drop and go out with Ashley. Maybe put a little more care into planning their next date to maximize points. The polka class had worked out fine, but he wasn't going to take any more chances. He started to search for things to do in Oklahoma City, then realized he needed to know when they were going out before he decided what they were going to do.

"Let's not put the oxidizer before the pump," he muttered as he opened his texting app.

Zack: *Hey, do you want to go out again this weekend?*

Then he turned back to his spreadsheet, swiping away notifications about Kayla's Lovemeter as fast as they came in. An hour passed, and Ashley still hadn't answered. Zack stared at his message.

"Did I say something wrong?" he wondered.

DaEvo did not offer any help, so he typed another message.

Zack: *Or I could bring you lunch if you're working.*

Another hour of planning, and still no answer. DaEvo chimed to let him know that Kayla's Lovemeter had dropped below the level he needed for unlimited game time. Not the worst thing in the world, except Ashley's would continue to drop as well if she didn't text him back.

Why wasn't she texting him back?

Zack tried to push the matter out of his mind and get back to planning, but he couldn't shake it. He stood and called a ride to Gord's almost before he knew what he was doing. Even if they couldn't do a Memorable Event or a lunch date, he would still get points for chatting with her at work.

But Ashley wasn't at the cash register.

"Hey, is Ashley working today?" Zack hoped he sounded casual.

The man at the desk shrugged. "Should be here in thirty minutes."

"Okay, cool. Can I get a private room?"

The cashier tapped on his tablet, then shook his head. "They're all booked up. Will the common room be okay?"

"Yeah, sure."

Zack paid with his OptiGlasses and searched the busy common room for a place to sit. He picked a spot between people who weren't playing Star Fury—to make sure he wouldn't be spied on—then opened his spreadsheet and resumed his analysis.

"Where is he?" a woman screamed.

Everyone in the room turned. A tall, thin woman clad in the green apron and white smock of the local grocery superstore stood in the doorway, her face flushed with fury. The flushed face did nothing for her freckled complexion and red hair. She clutched some kind of paper and waved it as if it were some kind of weapon.

"Where is Steve?"

"Ma'am, I—"

"Shut up and tell me where my no-good, lying boyfriend is! I know he's here!" Her tone said he probably wouldn't be her boyfriend much longer. She searched the common room, then shook her head in disgust. "He's in a private room, isn't he?"

"Ma'am, please calm down. I can't just tell you where a customer is."

"No? I'm his emergency contact, and this is an emergency. Check your system." She stalked over to the cashier and flashed her ID.

He checked it and sighed. "He's in room twenty-three."

"Thank you." She stalked up the stairs. Zack and the rest of the gamers in the lobby watched in a kind of horrified fascination. Room twenty-three was at the top of the staircase, so they had a great view as the woman pulled the door open and screamed, "You lowlife scum! How dare you?"

The high-pitched whine of lasers echoed out from the room. "Hey, babe! I'm kind of in the middle of something right now. Can this wait?"

"The only thing you're supposed to be in the middle of is job hunting! How can you afford a private room? I've been working overtime to cover rent, and you're gaming in their best room?"

An explosion reverberated through the room, and Steve swore. "Can you let me finish this first? Then we'll talk, I promise."

"No, we're talking now. Where did you get the money for all this? Are you selling drugs?"

"What? No. Do I look like a drug dealer to you?"

"You look like a lying, cheating, good-for-nothing layabout! Put that controller down this moment and explain this to me, or we're through."

"Babe, I just need a few more minutes," Steve said, not putting the controller down. "Then we'll talk. I promise."

It was the wrong answer. Zack didn't need DaEvo to tell him that.

The woman unleashed an impressive string of profanity, slammed the door, and sprinted down the stairs. She stopped at the bottom, suddenly realizing everyone was staring at her. She glared at the other gamers as if they'd had a hand in this, then she turned to the cashier. "Sorry to disturb you. Please take me off his emergency contact list."

Then she left, leaving everyone staring at the door. Zack could practically picture her Lovemeter dropping to zero. Maybe even lower. Maybe exploding. He rubbed his forehead, trying to push the image away. Just another way DaEvo was getting in his head. He was starting to picture all relationships by its terms.

Steve stuck his head out a few minutes later, glanced around as if expecting she might be waiting for him, then disappeared back into the private room.

Slowly, everyone returned to what they had been doing before. Zack looked at the clock. Over an hour had passed. Ashley was late for her shift. He glanced at the cashier, who shrugged to say he hadn't heard anything from her.

Zack called Ashley almost without realizing he was doing it. After that display, he wasn't going to take any chances. The phone app rang.

And rang.

Just when he had given up on her answering and started to think about what he should say in a message or how he could check to make sure she was all right, she answered the call.

"Hello?" Her voice sounded a little strange. Slightly shaky, and with a hum in background that the noise-canceling software on her low budget phone couldn't erase.

"Ashley! Are you all right? I'm at Gord's, and they said you were scheduled to work. But you're not here."

Ashley swore. "I completely forgot I was scheduled to work today. Hang on. I need to call them."

She hung up on Zack, and the phone at the cash register rang. The cashier picked it up, had a short conversation, then shrugged at Zack.

What was going on?

A call from Ashley came through, and Zack answered it as fast as he could. It was weird that he was so worried. Probably leftover anxiety from watching Steve's breakup.

Ashley wasn't breaking up with him, was she? Was that why she hadn't come to work? That seemed a little extreme.

"Hey, what's going on?" Zack asked. "Are you okay?"

"Yeah, I'm fine," Ashley said.

Quest! Your lady is upset.
Find out what's bothering her and make her feel better to earn bonus points.

Zack blinked at the notification. Why did DaEvo think she was upset? Ashley had said she was fine.

But she was skipping work. Obviously, something was up. He wasn't sure how to cheer her up over the phone when he had no idea what was wrong, so he stuck to the original plan. Maybe a date would make her feel better.

"Hey, do you want to go out this weekend?" Zack said.

DaEvo chimed, giving him a heart in the Lovemeter for asking her.

"I can't."

Crap. So much for keeping the Lovemeter full. Zack regrouped and tried to hide the panic creeping into his voice. "Okay, that's cool. I can bring you lunch then when you come back to work."

Ashley sighed. "I'm not going to be at work for a while. They had to transfer Amber to a hospital in Houston for another procedure. I'm driving there now."

"Oh."

Not a great answer. DaEvo sent him a notification to make sure he knew it and reminding him that he should make his lady feel better. At least now he knew what was wrong.

"I can come with you," Zack said. "I can help…"

Help with what exactly? He froze up at the sight of a hospital room. He'd be no help at all.

"It's fine," Ashley said. "I'm staying with my mom. Hey, I've got to go. I'm sorry, Zack."

She hung up the call. DaEvo chimed, rubbing salt into his wound as it pointed out that he hadn't even cheered her up. Or gotten his date.

Zack watched in dismay as DaEvo removed a heart from Ashley's Lovemeter. The sparkling pink thermometer that had looked so full and comforting before now seemed rather precarious. Ashley was out of town and refusing to accept help. He couldn't take her on dates if she was out of town. Not even lunch at the park while she was on break. And really, it wasn't his fault he couldn't cheer her up.

"Stupid buggy app."

He pushed aside the app notification, though for once, he hoped someone would actually fix it. This wasn't a laughing matter.

Talking about fixable, Zack had a brilliant idea for Ashley. He typed a message. It would be easy enough to set up a new gaming system there or find another Gord's. He could train anywhere. It would be a short flight. He could work on the materials analysis while in the air.

Zack: *Hey, I meant it. I'll come to Houston and help however I can.*

DaEvo chimed before he could send the message.

Relationship Hint: Frequent Contact is Good, Desperation is Bad

We noticed you've attempted to contact Ashley Barnes repeatedly. While frequent contact can improve your relationship, no love interest wants a desperate individual. You just failed to make her feel better. Recontacting her at this time would likely exacerbate matters.

Desperate? This wasn't sounding desperate. This was offering to help. Zack sent the message anyway and turned back to analyzing the list of materials. Ashley responded sooner than he expected.

Ashley: *Thanks, but it's fine. I'm not sure when I'll be back, but we'll hang out then, okay?*
Zack: *Okay.*

What else could he say? Zack stared at the text, trying to figure out where he had gone wrong.

DaEvo chimed.

Ashley Barnes Lovemeter: -10

He glared at the little love icon for DaEvo. He could almost swear it was mocking him, telling him "I told you so" as it took away a full heart. Worse, with her out of the city, there was no way to replenish it, especially since it didn't sound as though she wanted to talk at all.

Damn it. He had been so close. What had he done wrong?

An unfamiliar ache settled in Zack's chest. Disappointment? Hurt?

Whatever it was, he didn't like it. He stared at the Lovemeters a while longer. Ashley's was depleting. His team was preparing for the PvP rounds of the tournament and he was already on thin ice with them. He couldn't risk losing game time and leaving them hanging.

Well, that was what backup plans were for. It looked as though his original strategy had been a good one after all.

Zack: *Hey, do you want to go out tonight?*
   Kayla: *I thought you'd never ask. ;)*

Chapter Forty

JENNY: *Semi-final tournament round in two days! Is everyone ready?*
   Faz: *Yeah!!!!!!!!!*
   Greg: *Lay off the coffee, Faz.*
   Jenny: *You've got everything sorted, Zack?*
   Zack: *Yeah. I'll be ready.*

And he would be. He'd spent the past week juggling dates with Kayla, PvP tournament rounds, their competitor equipment analysis, and training.

Once they'd confirmed the material requirements for the drone, they'd spread the information to the Corsairs. That had gone over well, and the Armada mining sectors had seen a significant increase in privateer activity. It'd gotten so bad, supposedly the price for some of the ore had quadrupled. There had been a definite drop in the number of stealth drones running around during non-tournament fights.

Zack was rather proud of that. He just wished he had more of a chance to gloat and let Ashley know. Still, Kayla's Lovemeter was full and he had continued to level up his Physique and Reputation, so the Lovemeter between he and Kayla was depleting a little slower every day.

He was ready.

Zack: *Hey, how are you? Just wanted to say hi.*

He typed the text to Ashley but waited to send it until DaEvo gave him a thumbs-up. They'd been texting intermittently since she left and had even done a few phone calls so that Zack could quiz her for upcoming exams.

DaEvo gave him the go-ahead that he wasn't being clingy, and Zack sent the message. Their interactions weren't enough to keep the Lovemeter full or even stop its continued drop, so Zack wasn't sure why he kept up with them. As backup plans went, this wasn't a great one. He occasionally got bonus points for cheering Ashley up and making her laugh, but that didn't go very far. His biggest win was when he'd told her about what her little note had brought about. She'd laughed for ages.

Making her laugh felt good. Maybe that was reason enough to keep contacting her.

Jenny: *You've got enough points in DaEvo to get through this tournament round, right?*

That was sent as a private message rather than to their group text. Since Jenny had called him out on dating Kayla, Zack had told her a little more about the app.

Zack: *Yeah, the Lovemeter is almost full, and I've got another date tonight. And we've got the gala in a few days, so she's not going out of town until after that.*

Jenny: Good. Get me the analysis on the L33t D3m0ns before you go. I want to go over it with the boys.

Zack: Yeah, I'm almost done.

Jenny texted him a thumbs-up, and the app chimed to let him know that another message had come in. Zack opened it quickly. What if Ashley—

Kayla: Ready to do some shopping tonight?

Zack swallowed his disappointment and tried to muster some enthusiasm for the evening ahead. He was really tired of shopping, but Kayla loved it. And she usually got so into it that he could work on Star Fury tactics without her noticing. That was a plus.

Zack: Yeah! I've got a reservation for dinner after.

Kayla: Great! Don't forget that your final tux fitting with Giacomo is tonight. You can do that while I pick out jewelry.

Crap. Zack had completely forgotten about the tux fitting. Focusing on the battle records of the L33t D3m0ns would be difficult while he was being poked and prodded by the tailor and his entourage.

It was too bad somebody else couldn't stand in for him.

Zack grinned as a genius plan formed in his mind. Who was to say that somebody couldn't? Kayla would be busy shopping. The tailor needed a body to fit. But it didn't have to be Zack's.

He made a few quick calls and purchases, then logged into Star Fury. Everything was ready for the date. Now he needed to make sure that everything was taken care of for the tournament.

By the time Zack had to log out and prepare for the date, Ashley still hadn't texted back. He typed another text to her but deleted it after DaEvo warned him he was being clingy. He couldn't afford to lose Reputation points. Or annoy her.

He packed the supplies and a list of instructions for his master plan into a box and called a car to take them to the airport and pick up the other part of his plan. Then he knocked on Kayla's door. She smiled at him, looking perfect as always. She kissed Zack's cheeks in her usual greeting then took his arm. DaEvo chimed for physical contact, and Zack's mood lifted a little. He was dating a model. He had unlimited game time.

He really had no reason to complain.

———

Two hours into their shopping date, he was remembering reasons. Kayla had decided she needed new shoes for their upcoming dates and was asking Zack's opinion about each pair. Every time he opened battle videos and started watching the fights, she asked him a question. He forced a smile and offered a vaguely complimentary opinion. His OptiGlasses chimed with the latest message.

ZD: I'm here and dressed. Where do you want to meet?
Zack: Wait in the food court. I'll be right there.

He checked the time and grinned. Twenty minutes until his fitting. Everything was falling into place.

Kayla came out to model a pair of shoes that looked almost identical to the last ten pairs. Zack absentmindedly wondered if they were the same ones and she was testing him. He offered another of the compliments he was cycling through, and Kayla seemed satisfied.

"Hey, I have to get to my fitting," Zack said. "See you in an hour?"

"Wow, is it that late already?" Kayla said. "Yeah, go ahead. I've still got a lot of things to try on."

Zack hurried away, taking the long way round so he bypassed Giacomo's store on his way to the food court. The tailor had only seen him once, but he didn't want to take the chance of being recognized.

His meetup was waiting at a corner table, wearing the clothes and OptiGlasses Zack had sent him. He smiled and waved when Zack slid into the booth next to him.

"Thanks for flying out," Zack said. "I know it was short notice."

The body double—ZD or more correctly, Tim—grinned. Years ago, Zack had used a facial recognition algorithm to search acting agencies until he found someone who could go to trust meetings and sign papers for him. The resemblance between them really was uncanny, but that had been ages ago. Now…

"You've lost weight," Tim said. "Will that be a problem?"

Tim gestured toward his own body, which filled out the clothes that now hung loosely on Zack. Zack looked over his ex—current? —doppelganger and frowned. Had he been that out of shape before?

"I was still your size the last time I saw these people, so it should be fine. I've only met them once."

"All right. So what's my angle?"

"You're getting fitted for a tux for a gala hosted by Zoe Cross."

Tim raised an eyebrow. "Man, you're living it up these days! You do know, you're going to get a bad fit, right?" Zack eyed Tim then shrugged. It wouldn't be that much of a difference. "Your call, man. So, you need me to attend the gala in your place? I'll discount my rates."

He laughed, but Zack considered the offer. Would it be possible for Tim to fill in for him on dates? Kayla was usually focused on her phone and rarely looked at him. Would it work?

Probably not. He'd have to fool DaEvo as well, and the app was tied into his OptiGlasses, which scanned his retinas periodically to make sure he was actually the one wearing them. Zack had bought OptiGlasses for Tim to complete his look, but they weren't running any of his apps.

"If I figure out a way to make it work, I'll let you know," Zack said. "You shouldn't need to say much at the fitting. You're taking Kayla Taylor as a date."

"KayTay!" Tim said. A few people turned to look at them, and Tim ducked his head. "You're dating KayTay? Man. You're living the dream."

"Something like that," Zack said. "Okay, you've got five minutes until your appointment starts. I'll listen in via the OptiGlasses and offer help if you need it. I'll be at the internet café across the mall, so I can jump in pretty quickly if needed."

"You got it, boss!"

Tim slid out of the booth and hurried toward Giacomo's. Zack let him get a head start, then walked in the opposite direction toward the internet café. He checked into the private room he had reserved and sorted through his materials.

"Mr. Moore, welcome back!" Giacomo said.

Zack held his breath as he listened to the conversation being broadcast through his OptiGlasses. Would it work? Or would Giacomo realize what was happening?

"Thanks," Tim said. "So, let's get this over with."

Zack laughed. The body double had studied his mannerisms before they attempted the signing stunt, and he did a great job imitating Zack's voice. Zack tapped into the visual feed Tim's Opti-Glasses were broadcasting and watched for a few minutes as Giacomo and his crew tried the various parts of the tux on Tim, pinned, sewed, and pinned some more.

Tim looked bored, and Zack wasn't sure he was acting.

Oh well. He was being paid well for his time.

Zack left the channel open in case Tim ran into trouble and logged into his Star Fury account. He booted up his alt and set it up to run a bunch of mining operations to get him some credits. While it did that, he loaded the latest set of videos and watched his opponents for their tells.

Chapter Forty-One

ZACK BOUNCED IN HIS CHAIR, DaEvo and his messaging apps all muted. It was the semi-final tournament round and he did not need to be distracted. As the Star Fury music played in the background of the announcements being made, he stared at the wire diagram of his ship. In the corner of his eyes, he saw the viewer count ticking up as fans slid in to watch the upcoming battle.

"You sure you did all your chores?" Greg teased Zack.

"Not now," Faz snapped, tense.

"Yeah, not now. What's the plan, Zack?" Jenny said. "You've been cagey about it."

"We're going with the Jen-special," Zack said. He really wished he had a better name for it, but he hadn't managed to find anything that worked. Or wasn't cringe-worthy like Faz's suggestions. Thankfully, all their talk was muted from the public.

"Are you sure?" Jenny said. For once, she sounded unsure.

"Definitely. We start with you. Faz, you're next, then Greg. I'll anchor," Zack replied.

The way the PvP rounds worked, the survivor from each duel stayed in the ring till the next duel. In most battles, that let the vast majority of the players fight, which was considered more thrilling for the fans.

"All right, if you say so..." Jenny said.

She began tapping away, as did the rest of the team. They didn't need to alter their configuration much for the plan, but eking out every little advantage was the way they were going to win.

In a few minutes, Star Fury announced the start of the battle. Zack ignored the introduction and muted the public chat, knowing there was nothing of value in there. Even voice chat was silent as the team allowed Jenny to focus as her ship appeared in the arena. The ring was just a blank spot in the map, devoid of anything interesting like mines, asteroids, or moons to mess up navigation and flying.

"Decent draw," Faz muttered.

Zack had to agree. It would have been better in a crowded location, but at least it wasn't a near-planetary fight. Those would have made their initial plans a mess, with the way the planet would draw Jenny's drones and mines.

The moment the countdown ended, Jenny launched her drones. Each went on their routes, dropping proximity and laser mines in a pre-set pattern around her. In the meantime, Jenny was booting as many drones as she could while launching mine missiles, each of which would litter the space ahead.

Not that her opponent was going to give her any time to set up the battlefield. He hit his afterburners, shooting straight toward Jenny.

"I knew it," Jenny crowed.

The N00bs had led with the Max Destroyer in the last three PvP fights, relying on the bigger, stronger craft to wear down their opponents. Unlike Zack's team, the N00bs ran an artillery and laser heavy team, with the Max Destroyer the equivalent of Greg's heavily armored ship and three medium, all-rounder craft making up the remainder of their team composition. In team battles, the Max Destroyer was the linchpin attacker, with tactical flexibility offered by the all-rounder ships. But in a PvP, the Destroyer was only useful for figuring out the opponent's plans due to its slower speed.

All that meant was that Jenny was able to keep out of its weapon range for quite a while. Unfortunately, Jenny's drones were great for harassing fire and laying out the wide grid of mines and sensor jammers, but they weren't the best at dealing damage.

"All right, that's it… I'm going in," Jenny said.

Already, the public chat was filled with boos as Jenny ran circles around the Destroyer, picking up some damage whenever it got near enough to land a hit with its massed artillery.

"You're at 84%. More than good enough," Zack said.

Hooting and hollering, the team cheered Jenny on as she twisted her ship around and burrowed into the massed fire. Her quick switch left the Destroyer flummoxed initially before it got its bearings and targeted her. Shields failed, warnings lights flashed constantly on Jenny's shared screen as missiles, massed drivers, and lasers hammered into her.

In the meantime, Jenny had her drones drive straight into the Destroyer's rear as it targeted her, making its shielding fail at the back where the drones self-destructed. Rapid fire on her own close-range point defense pinked off the Destroyer's shields, making her opponent choose between destruction or crippling as his shields failed.

A lucky shot, and Jenny's already frail shields gave way as an artillery shell landed right on the ship. A flash of white and Jenny was sent back to respawn, while the remainder of her drones disappeared.

But unlike her drones, the sensor jammers, the mobility webs, and the proximity mines stayed behind. The now heavily tilted environment was the heart of the Jenny-plan and would guarantee their win.

Grinning wolfishly, Faz's fast, light ship teleported in even as the Destroyer's shields were auto-refreshed by the tournament round.

"Now, let me show you how a real pilot does this!" Faz said. A tap of his fingers had his ship burning fission materials as he ducked into the heart of the minefield.

Zack grinned, leaning back, and watched. This was going to be fun.

"Damn cowardly Corsairs," Steve growled, his ship weaving in and out of the remainder of Jenny's minefield. "Using mines and drones."

Three enemy ships later, the initially populous minefield had been stripped bare. The Destroyer and the other two had each taken quite a bit of damage in the fight, while the ship before had taken out Greg's ship at the last moment with a surprise dark matter bomb. It'd destroyed his own ship and left a giant gravitic anomaly that had swept another third of Jenny's mines into it.

"Look at the Armada scum who's talking," Zack taunted as he pulled his ship into a tight turn. Thankfully, the details about the stealthed drones allowed him to keep track of Steve's favorite new tactic, which meant that Steve was on the ropes, unable to sneak in shots or lead Zack into ambushes. "But it's okay. You can just go home and cry about your losses when we're done."

Zack bit his lip, deciding not to add in a bit about if he had a home. There were lines you didn't cross, and he wasn't going to taunt Steve about his love life. Especially considering his own was mixed.

What was the Lovemeter anyway? An actual gauge of his relationships? Because it felt like his Lovemeter, his relationship with Kayla, seemed to hit hot and cold patches all the time. And he and Ashley were... weird. Good, but she wasn't around and was always busy. Busy in a good way, of course, with her courses and jobs. But busy. Unavailable.

"Pay attention, Zack!" Greg shouted as a trio of missiles slammed into Zack's ship, making his shields flash even as he tried to dodge them.

"What! Where did that come from?" Zack's eyes narrowed. He hadn't seen them until the last second and his dodge should have worked, but they'd managed to follow him.

"That looks familiar..." Jenny muttered. He heard her tapping on her keyboard.

"I bet you thought you were the only ones with a surprise," Steve crowed.

Intuition had Zack hit his afterburners as he dodged the next set of missiles that flashed into existence a short distance from him. He managed to dodge them, but he was forced to dodge around a trio of still-working mines as he did so, pulling out of the remnant of the minefield.

"They're a mixed seeker missile with the stealth drone shielding!" Jenny cried. "You'll need to adjust your sensors a bit. I think he swapped out some of the settings. Try using settings—"

Zack's fingers flew as he tapped in the data while he boosted away from Steve, following Jenny's instructions. He kept one eye on the sensors, another on Steve's ship, and a third non-existent one on the data he input. Again and again, they tried sensor settings.

"Yes!" Zack hissed as data populated. He now had both stealthed drones and the missiles.

A flick of Zack's fingers killed his afterburners, letting it refuel and get ready as he let both ship and drones get close again. Already, his ship was rocking, his shields flaring as damage accumulated. A twitch of his fingers diverted energy to his main laser cannon while he ignored Steve crowing about how Zack couldn't run anymore.

"Zack..." Faz's voice was low, concerned. "Are you sure you know what you're doing?"

"Oh yeah, I know this idiot," Zack said.

After dueling him multiple times, Zack knew exactly what Steve was going to do. Steve was impatient, arrogant, obsessed with Star Fury. Once he thought he had a win, he wouldn't let go, always headed for the fastest and easiest solution.

Which meant with only a little maneuvering, Zack had Steve almost directly behind him. Zack's rear shields were flashing, almost gone, and another pair of seeker missiles were nearly on him.

And it didn't matter.

A flicker of fingers cut his engine output. Another series of quick taps sent Zack's ship spinning, doing a complete one-eighty turn in space that would be impossible in atmosphere. It was one reason why Zack loved the game. It kept true to real-world physics in certain things, like the ability to turn around entirely, flying backward.

"Say hello to my little gun!" Zack crowed. He stabbed his finger down, seconds before the seeker missile would have impacted. The main laser fired, the EMP blast washing out the missiles and disabling their explosives.

More importantly, he hit Steve head-on with his laser. The damage Zack had already done was enough to let his main laser cut-through Steve's front shields. Follow-up shots from Zack's secondaries were enough to finish the battle.

"That's how Corsairs do it, baby!" Zack shouted, throwing his hands in the air as Star Fury blared his victory.

On the battle chat, Steve was cursing and screaming about cheating, but Zack ignored it.

They'd won. Now, all they had to do was sweep the next round and they'd be guaranteed a seat in Vegas. As he accepted his friends' congratulations and cheers, Zack couldn't help but open up his messaging app to tell Ashley.

And stop, when DaEvo warned him he was getting a little clingy once more.

Damn it.

Chapter Forty-Two

"You look awful."

Zack sighed, trying not to let Kayla's words get him down. They'd won the semi-finals match last night, but Kayla had looked less than interested when Zack mentioned it. On the other hand, Ashley had sent him a congratulatory message late last night. He'd only noticed it when he woke this morning, but it had made him smile.

Kayla wrinkled her nose as she studied Zack from head to toe. In spite of the manicure, pedicure, and haircut quests he had completed in preparation for the gala, DaEvo had also not been impressed when Zack put on the tux that had been delivered that morning. Even the tie that Davison had provided did little to help with the situation, even if it did match Kayla's shoes.

Apparently, having Rob fill in at the final fitting session with Giacomo had been a bad idea.

A really bad idea.

"You look like a teenager who borrowed his dad's suit for prom," Kayla said.

"At least my dad has good taste," Zack said, trying to salvage the situation with a joke.

Kayla's stare said he was making things worse.

DaEvo chimed.

Quest! Your lady is upset.
Find out what's bothering her and make her feel better to earn bonus points.

Zack rolled his eyes at the notification. He could tell Kayla was upset, and for once, he even knew why. Judging by the Style debuff DaEvo was giving him, this tux was pretty far from acceptable.

"Look, there's nothing we can do about it now. It will be fine."

"Fine. You think this is fine?"

"What do you want me to do about it? Change into WesterNeon?"

Kayla looked horrified. "Ew. Do you have any idea how much that would clash with my dress?"

Zack bit his lip to keep from replying that her dress was black and should go with anything. It was the diamonds all over again. "Fine. We don't have to go if you don't want to."

Zack had actually been looking forward to the gala, but if it was going to be like this the whole night, he'd rather stay home and work on analyzing the results from the last tournament round. They were close to qualifying, but it wasn't guaranteed. They needed to nearly sweep the next team to be guaranteed a spot.

"Of course we're going." Kayla sniffed. "Come on. We're already late. We'll just tell everyone you're starting a new trend. Hobo formal."

The thought seemed to cheer her, and she was halfway down the hallway, strutting as if it were her runway, before Zack realized she had left. He hurried after her, admiring the view. That gown had been expensive, but worth every penny.

Kayla spent the limo ride taking pictures of them, applying filters, and posting to her social media about how much she was looking forward to the gala. "Your hashtag is #hoboformal. Make sure to use that with any pictures you post."

"Sure," Zack said.

He hadn't been planning to post any pictures. Kayla posted enough for the both of them, and she had way more followers.

"Oh good, it's trending," Kayla said. "I don't know what Giacomo was thinking. He's not usually such a risk-taker with his designs. This is a bold new direction for him."

She seemed to believe that. Zack let out a slow breath, relieved he was off the hook for using a body double. Kayla relaxed a little and leaned back against the limo's leather seat.

DaEvo chimed.

Relationship Quest in progress: Take her out to an exciting and memorable event

You're taking your lady out on an exciting and memorable event. You should make it more memorable by:

- *giving your lady a compliment*
- *buying or giving her a gift to remember the event by*
- *ensure that she is enjoying herself at the event*

"Hey, you look amazing."

Zack meant it. Kayla's outfit was more reserved than her usual trendy style, but the black dress showed off her body from every angle. The otherwise conservative ensemble was made less so by the thigh-high slit on one side and stiletto heels. Zack wasn't sure why it had taken weeks to find those particular shoes or what made them so special, but he liked them. Her strawberry-blond hair was pulled back in a way that emphasized her bright blue eyes. Or maybe that was the makeup.

He was clearly no fashion expert. But he could appreciate the overall effect.

Kayla smiled at the undisguised admiration in his voice and expression. The smile softened her face in an imperceptible way, made her look less the perfect model and more personable. It made her even more beautiful to Zack. "Thank you."

She leaned closer and put a hand on Zack's shoulder, but the limo stopped before they could get any further. Kayla winked at him and pulled back, waiting for the chauffeur to open her door. Then she exited legs first, giving the crowd a show and clearly loving every moment of it.

Zack swallowed and slid out of the limo with significantly less style and enthusiasm. The gala was being held in the Devon Tower in downtown Oklahoma City. It was the tallest building in the skyline, and looking up at it made Zack a little dizzy. Or maybe that was the flashing bulbs from photographers gathered behind the roped-off press areas on either side of the red carpet.

"Over here, Kayla!"

"KayTay! Who are you wearing tonight?"

The questions poured over them in a rush of barely intelligible words. Kayla took Zack's arm and pulled him toward the crowd. He realized with a jolt that some of the questions were aimed at him.

"What inspired you to mix hobo chic with formal wear?"

"Is this the start of a new venture for Moore Enterprises? How long have you been planning to start your own fashion line?"

His own fashion line? Zack blinked into the pulsing lights, too surprised to answer.

Kayla pulled him close and smiled at the crowd. "Zack is always on the cutting edge. He wanted to push the envelope tonight and try something new."

All traces of her earlier anger were gone. She was such a good actress that Zack almost believed the story himself. Kayla elbowed him in the ribs, and he found himself nodding as she spun a story about his fashion inspirations.

Reputation +0.3

Sweet. Maybe he should consider starting his own fashion line. It would earn him points and annoy his board of trustees.

Another limo arrived, and Kayla guided Zack up the red carpet and into the building. She took a few selfies with him in the lobby, an enormous open space made of glass and towering white beams, then pulled him to an elevator while she posted the pictures.

"It's working," she said. "Look at this!"

She shoved the phone in front of Zack's face. He wasn't exactly sure what he was looking for, but whatever graph Kayla was showing him was definitely trending upward. He hoped #hoboformal didn't get so popular that any of his friends saw it. Jenny knew about the gala and was doubtless watching and laughing her head off. That was bad enough. It would be worse if Greg or Faz found him out.

Or Ashley.

Zack swallowed. Ashley. What would she think if she saw him?

He had missed her call, and she hadn't returned his. Maybe it was over.

"Reservation?" a security guard at the elevator said.

Zack looked straight ahead so his OptiGlasses could complete a retinal scan for security, and the guard nodded and let them through. Kayla stayed occupied with her phone on the long elevator ride up to the fiftieth floor. Zack amused himself by watching the numbers click up, then checked his notifications on his OptiGlasses. He was receiving a steady stream of Reputation points as the pictures flooded social media.

DaEvo chimed.

Style +11.2

"Why the sudden increase?" Zack muttered softly, turning his head away from Kayla so that she wouldn't hear him.

Style calculations are amalgamated from crowd-sourced opinion polls, social media images, influential bloggers, and fashion magazines. #Hoboformal is currently designated as a new style trend created by Zack Moore. Style calculations might alter depending on long-term trend forecasts.

Jenny: *Hobo formal?*

She followed her message with a steady stream of laughing emojis and gifs of people cracking up. Zack muted the conversation. He didn't need Jenny's commentary distracting him this evening.

The elevator chimed to let them know they had reached their destination. Kayla looked up from her phone and took Zack's arm. They walked into an open space lit with minimalist light fixtures. A string quartet played softly, and Zack was distracted by the panoramic view from the wall of windows that stretched as far as he could see. Then he was distracted by the crowd of well-dressed people. He slumped a little, feeling self-conscious about his ill-fitting outfit.

"Confidence," Kayla hissed. "Don't you dare wimp out now."

Then a woman separated from the crowd to greet them, and Kayla smiled as if nothing were wrong. Zack stared as his Opti-Glasses chimed, filling in social details. Not that Zack needed any of that information. He recognized the woman. She was more of a constant in his life than Kayla or Ashley.

Zoe Cross.

"Thank you both so much for coming!"

Zack tried to speak, but his throat had gone dry. It was Zoe Cross, in person and looking more gorgeous than ever. She wore a deep blue gown with something sparkly in the fabric, and her black hair hung loose in waves around her shoulders. She smiled and offered her hand. Zack blinked at it for a moment before taking it and shaking it.

He was shaking hands with Zoe Cross.

"You're Zack Moore, right?"

Zack nodded, still not quite able to speak.

"I hear your medical trust is interested in expanding its reach. Perhaps our foundations could work together. I would love for the students in my tech program to complete internships and see how they can put what they've learned to practical use."

"Work? Together?" His mouth was moving, but he had no control of it. Zack was vaguely aware of Kayla taking his arm and squeezing it, but he was too starstruck to do anything else about it.

"Zack's too busy for things like that right now," Kayla said. "He's training for the Star Anger tournament."

"Star Fury," Zack and Zoe corrected together.

They laughed, sharing a bemused look. Kayla didn't.

"I'm hosting that tournament," Zoe said.

"Yeah. I know." Zack's brain was still working overtime, trying to process the fact that he was speaking to Zoe Cross. That it was going well.

DaEvo chimed.

Relationship Hint: Pay Attention to Your Date
No one wants to play second fiddle on a date. Make sure to keep your attention on the individual you are on the date with to increase intimacy and your Lovemeter.

Quest! Your lady is upset
Find out what's bothering her and make her feel better to earn bonus points.

Kayla Taylor Lovemeter -0.1

Zack swiped away the notification with annoyance and looked at Kayla. She didn't look upset. She was smiling brightly at Zoe and complimenting her outfit. Zoe returned the compliment with equal warmth. Once again, DaEvo had it all wrong. If he wasn't right in front of Zoe, he'd make a bug report.

"Your foundation does great work at the hospital," Zoe said.

"Yeah, if you forget about that nightmarish redecoration job in the children's wing."

She laughed. A genuine laugh that made her eyes crinkle. Zack laughed with her.

Kayla pursed her lips. "What's wrong with new decorations? I'm sure doctors like to work in nice spaces as much as anyone else."

"It's not nice," Zack said. "It's awful. I was trying to recruit a local doctor to help manage the new funding, but she wasn't interested."

"Was it Doctor Jones?" Zoe said with a hint of a twinkle in her eyes. "I follow her blog."

Zack's eyes widened and Zoe's smile grew even wider. He felt his heart rate increasing but swiped away the notifications. Why was DaEvo so verbose today? Did they reset his settings again? They kept running updates on the damn thing.

"We should go," Zack said, suddenly eager to get away before Zoe mentioned anything more about Cassie's blog. "Kayla's right. I'm too busy with Star Fury right now to do any work with the foundation. My team is one round away from qualifying for Vegas."

"Then hopefully I'll see you there. And good luck expanding your foundation. I'm sorry you're not interested in collaborating."

Zoe turned to greet new guests arriving, and Zack let Kayla pull him away as he tried to sort his thoughts. Zoe knew about the blog. She knew he was a stalker. No, she knew that Dr. Jones thought he was a stalker. It wasn't the same thing, and Zoe hadn't seemed to mind talking to him. Maybe she didn't believe Dr. Jones. She wouldn't have offered to work with someone she thought was a stalker, would she?

Zoe had offered to work with him. Zoe was sorry he didn't want to collaborate. Had he said he wasn't interested in working with Zoe? He was pretty sure he hadn't said that. Why would he have said that?

Reminder! Your lady is upset.
Find out what's bothering her and make her feel better to earn bonus points.

Kayla Taylor Lovemeter -0.1

Zack looked at Kayla, but she looked fine to him. Maybe she was gripping him a little tightly, but she had a tendency to do that when his mind wandered. What did she have to be upset about anyway? The evening was going fine. A quick glance at the social stats and that bar graph she'd sent showed they were still trending.

"Let's dance," Kayla said.

She led Zack to a dance floor where couples were gracefully twirling to the soft music of the string quartet. The marble floor reflected the muted lights above, highlighting Kayla's dress as she and Zack made their way to the edge of the dance floor. Kayla made sure to position herself against the backdrop of the city, skyscraper lights twinkling. Then she hailed a nearby photographer, handed him her phone, and gave him detailed instructions about the shots she wanted.

"You can dance, can't you?" Kayla said. "I forgot to sign you up for a class ahead of time."

"Yeah, I can dance," Zack said. "Well, I can polka."

"Polka?" Kayla looked so horrified that Zack couldn't help laughing. That made her look even more scandalized.

"Yeah, it's cool. Although I'm not sure this music works for it. You think Zoe would mind bringing in a tuba?"

"This is unbelievable. Just follow my lead, all right?"

Then Kayla smoothed over the anger in her features, putting on what Zack recognized as her modeling face, and guided his hand to rest on her waist. The fabric of her dress was cool and smooth to the touch, but thin enough that he felt the heat of her skin underneath. Zack's heart beat faster again and he had to swipe away another notification as Kayla took his other hand and pulled him close.

"Look into my eyes," she directed. "Just step forward and back. We need some movement for the pictures."

Zack stepped forward and landed on Kayla's foot. She swore and tightened her grip on his hands.

"Sorry."

"I said follow my lead. That means you go backward first."

"Yeah, okay. Sorry."

DaEvo chimed, suggesting that he buy his lady a gift to make her feel better. Zack swiped away the notification and focused on following Kayla's directions. Step back and step forward. Smile for the camera. Now look serious. Now stare into her eyes.

Zack stared, noticing a few flecks of hazel that he'd never seen in the blue before. Kayla was studying him with equal intensity as they leaned closer and closer together, lips almost touching. And then they were kissing. Zack's heart raced as he tightened his grip around her waist and—

"Okay, I've got all the shots you wanted, Miss Taylor."

Kayla pulled back, breaking the spell. She smiled at Zack while he tried to catch his breath, then she reached for her phone.

Chapter Forty-Three

ZACK STARED AT KAYLA, his mind still whirling from the kiss. She was focused on her phone once again, typing furiously to add the hashtags.

"Hey, do you want to take a break from posting and just dance?" Zack said. "We don't have to polka. You could teach me something else."

He moved closer and put his hand around Kayla's waist, trying to distract her from that blasted phone so that they could enjoy the evening.

"Later," Kayla said. "If we're going to make hobo formal a thing, I need to keep posting."

Zack sighed and hailed a nearby waitress with a tray of drinks. Thankfully, it looked as though the gala was sticking to wine rather than the trendy but undrinkable cocktails of the WesterNeon party. DaEvo put small pink hearts over the acceptable drinks. Zack grabbed one and nodded at the waitress to thank her.

She froze and stared at him. "Zack?"

"Ashley?" Zack blinked as the waitress's face suddenly came into focus.

Ashley was in the same nondescript black uniform the rest of the staff wore, and her auburn curls were slicked back in a tight ponytail. Dressed like that, she was practically invisible in the glamorous crowd.

DaEvo chimed.

Lovemeter Subject: Ashley Barnes located...

Would you like to start an informal date with Ashley Barnes?

{Error! --- Conflict in Relationship Date Protocols.
Subject is currently on date with Kayla Taylor.
Error report sent to Developers}

Would you like to cancel your date with Kayla Taylor and begin a date with Ashley Barnes?

Ashley looked confused and surprised to see Zack. He angrily swiped away the notifications, finding the last one refused to swipe away till he made a decision. He declined the option, then glanced at Kayla, who was still busy typing hashtags.

"Hey," Zack said as the silence dragged on. He was suddenly very conscious of his hand on Kayla's waist and pulled it away, face flushing.

The sudden movement distracted Kayla from her phone, and she paused her typing to look at Zack. Then she spotted Ashley holding the tray of drinks. "I don't need anything right now."

Satisfied she'd figured things out, Kayla turned back to her phone. Ashley gritted her teeth, and Zack winced at the condescension in Kayla's voice. This was not good.

Reputation +0.3

"They love this one," Kayla said, moving closer to Zack and showing the picture of them kissing. "Look how many likes it has already."

"Yeah, great." Zack's face flushed further when he saw the

picture. Had Ashley seen the kiss? Or was she just confused to find him at the gala? For that matter, why was she at the gala?

He didn't need DaEvo to tell him this was a messy situation.

Even as, when he looked at Ashley, the damn app gave him the same option to cancel his date with Kayla and go on one with her.

"Zack, why are you dressed like that? What's going on?" Ashley's voice had grown colder as she continued to stand there. There was a tightness around her eyes that DaEvo picked up on.

Quest! Your lady is upset.
Find out what's bothering her and make her feel better to earn bonus points.

"It's hobo formal," Kayla said, not taking her eyes off her phone. "Look, I know it's tempting to talk to celebrities at events like this, but we'd appreciate our space. I'm sure you have work to do."

"Celebrities? Zack, what is she talking about?" Ashley said.

"I thought you were in Houston," Zack said, desperate to find something to say.

"I had to come back for a few days to work this event. I called, but you didn't answer." Ashley said, shaking her head as if dismissing the change of topic.

Zack swallowed. He'd been so busy with the tournament... he kept meaning to get back to her, but they'd missed calls, and he'd been too busy to really follow-up. And maybe he was a little notification shy with DaEvo always bugging him. Anyway, their Lovemeter levels hadn't dropped that far.

"How are you a guest at this gala?" Ashley asked. "Tickets are, like, ten thousand dollars. Your card bounced when you tried to pay for pizza. Are you her guest?"

"Twenty thousand," Zack corrected absently, his mind spinning as he tried to work out how to get rid of her and salvage the situation. Then he mentally kicked himself. Why was his first instinct to correct Ashley on the price?

She was looking more confused than ever, and the corners of her mouth drew down.

Quest! Your lady is upset.
Find out what's bothering her and make her feel better to earn bonus points.
Ashley Barnes Lovemeter -0.1

"Wait, do you actually know this person?" Kayla said, finally looking up from her phone and giving Ashley a quick once-over. She then plastered on a smile, sliding an arm around Zack's waist.

He twitched, unsure if he should pull away or lean into it.

"I don't normally do this, but I can make an exception for a friend of Zack's. Do you want a selfie with me? I'd use your left side. That's your better side." Kayla held out her phone and activated the camera, using the phone to beckon Ashley over.

Ashley stared as if Kayla were speaking a foreign language. Then she turned to look directly at Zack. "Who is this? Why does she think I want a selfie with her?"

"I'm his girlfriend. Didn't he tell you?" Kayla shrugged. "I guess you're not that close a friend then. It's fine, we can still do the selfie."

Zack continued to work his jaw, trying to figure out what to do or say. DaEvo kept glitching, struggling to figure out what to do when both of his Lovemeter prospects were on the same page.

Kayla kissed his cheek, presumably to bring him back to the present.

Ashley no longer looked confused. She looked furious. Her face flushed, and she was leaning forward rather aggressively. Zack half expected the tray of drinks to spontaneously combust in her hands.

"That's funny," Ashley said. There was absolutely no humor in her voice. In fact, the heat in her voice could rival a Class I Anti-Base Nuke. "I thought I was his girlfriend."

Quest! Your lady is upset.
Find out what's bothering her and make her feel better to earn bonus points.
Ashley Barnes Lovemeter -0.1

Quest! Your lady is upset.
Find out what's bothering her and make her feel better to earn bonus points.
Kayla Taylor Lovemeter -0.1

Both women turned to look at Zack. He twitched and stepped away from Kayla's arm around his body. She didn't even try to stop him from moving away.

Kayla Taylor Lovemeter -0.1

"We never talked about being exclusive..." Zack said, desperate to find a way to get out of this. "We were just dating—"

"Me," Kayla said.

"I didn't think we had to say it!" Ashley said at the same time. Zack winced.

Quest! Your lady is upset.
Find out what's bothering her and make her feel better to earn bonus points.
Ashley Barnes Lovemeter -0.1

Quest! Your lady is upset.
Find out what's bothering her and make her feel better to earn bonus points.
Kayla Taylor Lovemeter -0.1

"So that's it? You just decided to date some celebrity while dating me because we didn't have the talk?" Ashley snapped.

"That's not—"

"You mean you really dated this... this... nobody?" Kayla said, raking her gaze over Ashley. "I'm not surprised you chose me over her."

"Chose?" Ashley's voice grew colder.

"I didn't—" Zack said.

DaEvo sent another notification to inform Zack they were both still upset. This time, it was offering him choices of things to buy— an outfit for Ashley and a diamond bracelet for Kayla.

As he dismissed the notification, Kayla squeezed his arm. "Stop looking at your app. Tell your *friend* you're done and to get back to her job."

"Yes, Zack. Tell me, are we done?" Ashley's voice had gotten hoarse and DaEvo showed another drop in her Lovemeter. "Tell me why you started dating someone else."

"You were in Houston," he said lamely.

"So you cheat on me as soon as I leave town?"

"I needed to keep my points up. You weren't answering my calls," Zack said desperately. He needed her to understand it wasn't on purpose.

Ashley's face was crimson, and the drinks on the tray rattled as she shook with fury. "My sister was having surgery, and I was trying to patch things up with my mother, who I haven't spoken to in five years. Excuse me for being unavailable for a few days!"

Kayla dropped her hand from Zack's arm, looking at his face then Ashley's. Her studied indifference disappeared. "Enough. Tell her to go, that you were done with her once you started dating me. Then you and I will have a talk."

Zack shook his head, the gesture eliciting another set of declines in both their Lovemeters.

"Are you seriously saying you're choosing her over me?" Kayla preened a little, unconsciously running a hand down her dress.

"I'm not saying that!" Zack said desperately.

Kayla smirked while Ashley flinched.

Zack turned to Ashley. "No, I didn't mean I wasn't choosing you. I like you!"

"And you don't like me?" Kayla's voice grew colder.

"No, I like you! I need you," Zack said. DaEvo chimed and he gave up, muting the entire app. He saw Ashley's face twist in hurt and he shook his. "And you too!"

"Really," Ashley said without any intonation.

"Yes! I need you both. You get it? Kayla, you go out of town so often, and your Lovemeter drops really fast. I needed a contingency plan. Ashley, you understand that, right?"

"So I'm your backup plan now," Ashley said.

"Well, I was dating you first. So Kayla's actually the backup," Zack offered.

"What?" Kayla's shriek rang through the room.

Silence descended as the string quartet stopped playing and everyone turned to look at them. Zack could almost feel the way DaEvo was taking away his Reputation points. Now Kayla was angry, her full lips pressed thin.

"That's not what I meant..." Zack tried, but that made him aware of the way Ashley twitched. Every time he tried to explain to one of them, the other got upset.

Somehow, things had gone south really fast. He'd already mentioned the Lovemeter. Maybe he should just tell them the rest of it. People always said the truth would set you free. Maybe it'd help now? It was better than whatever he had been doing. If he explained the app, maybe they'd understand that he hadn't had a choice. They knew how much Star Fury meant to him.

He took a deep breath. "Look, let me explain..."

"Stop." Kayla took in the glances, looked at her phone that was blowing up, and shook her head. "People are watching."

Kayla grabbed Zack's arm and pulled him along, her grip possessive. Ashley followed mutely, still holding the tray of drinks. She was no longer trembling.

That was a good thing, right?

———

Kayla dragged him to one corner of the open space of the ballroom, using the press of bodies among the standing tables to hide them. It wasn't out of sight by any means, but there was really no place to hide. At least with his back against the window, the crowd was only staring at him from one direction. Kayla had dropped his arm the moment they arrived. And along the way, DaEvo had turned its notifications back on, showing him their Lovemeters already deeply red.

"So, Zack. You said you have an explanation?" Kayla began the interrogation.

"He'd better," Ashley said.

Zack swallowed around their tones. He struggled to find a place to begin, a way to make all this make sense. "Ashley works at Gord's. You know, the gaming center? That's how we met." Kayla only narrowed her eyes, so Zack pressed on. "And Kayla is my neighbor. We met at the gym."

"And?" Kayla's voice dropped.

"I started dating Ashley first, then I met you." Zack said. "I didn't... well, I dated you both because I needed you both. For the game. To keep my points up."

"What does Star Fury have to do with this?" Ashley asked, sounding puzzled. Not angry anymore, which was good. Better than angry.

Zack shook his head. "Different game." Zack pushed ahead before they could bombard him with questions. "My guardian tricked me into alpha testing a dating app, and I had to go on dates to earn points. But you're always gone"—Zack nodded to Kayla—"and our relationship wasn't hitting the milestones we needed. And Ashley was too low leveled. I had to date both of you to be sure."

"Low level?" Ashley exploded. "What does that even mean?"

"I think it's pretty obvious." Kayla gave Ashley a condescending look. "But it's still the stupidest excuse I've ever heard for cheating. A dating app forcing you to date two women? You might as well just tell the truth."

"No, it's true! It's called Dating Evolution. Look it up."

Kayla glared at him, then tapped on her phone. Zack really hoped DaEvo was far enough along to have a website. This was his last hope of convincing them that he was telling the truth.

"It's a thing," Kayla said finally, holding her phone over so Ashley could read it. Somehow, that didn't make Ashley look any happier.

"'Relationship gaming with a real-world twist,'" Ashley read in a flat voice. "'Level up your love life and earn real life rewards.' What real life rewards were you earning, Zack?"

Both Lovemeters dropped again, the ticks seeming to come faster now. Much faster.

Zack was sweating, his chest constricting as breathing grew harder. He couldn't help but wonder if he was having a heart attack. That'd probably be better than this. The look in Ashley's eyes made him want to curl up in a ball.

"Access to my Star Fury account," Zack said. Truth. He had to do the truth. He'd already gone this far. "My trustee tricked me into this because he thought I was spending too much time gaming and should get out more."

"Your trustee?" Kayla said. "Aren't you a little old to have a guardian watching over your money?"

"What money?" Ashley asked, looking at Zack in his ill-fitting tuxedo.

Kayla sighed as if Ashley had asked an extremely stupid question. "He's one of the richest bachelors in the city. Did you think that I'd date just anyone? Unlike some people, I have standards."

"You lied to me," Ashley said softly. "Was anything real?"

"It was!" Zack protested. Ashley's Lovemeter was flashing red, the little thermometer barely filled at all. How did it drop so fast? "I just left out a few details."

Ashley's eyes were brimming with angry tears, and Zack's heart twisted unexpectedly at the sight of them.

"Ashley—"

"Well, that settles that." Kayla brushed her hands as if getting rid of dirt. "It's obvious he doesn't care enough about you to tell you the truth. You were a nice diversion till I came along, but he's found someone better. Go serve your drinks before they get warm."

Ashley flinched as if she had been struck. Zack reached for her, wanting to comfort her, and she moved back again.

"Don't!" Ashley warned him.

Zack winced, dropping his hands. Dropped, like her Lovemeter. "I didn't mean to lie. To hurt you."

"Oh. If you didn't mean to…" Ashley said. "The stupid thing is that I actually liked you."

Ashley let the tray of drinks drop. It landed at his feet, shattered glass and spilled beverages ruining his trousers. The people at the party who had begun to look away looked back, drawn by the sound of shattering glass and the metal tray hitting the floor.

"I liked you, and it made me too stupid to see what was happening! It was always about the game, wasn't it? That first day, when you were trying to talk to me and help me out? You were just using me for points."

"No!" Zack said. "It wasn't like that! You aren't the backup. It was Kayla! She's the one I used for her level!"

Kayla's Lovemeter flashed another notification of a drop.

"You and your stupid games." Ashley said, clearly heartbroken.

The next moment, Ashley swung, slapping him so hard that Zack felt he was watching a hyperspace jump. As his ears rang, he heard her stalk off.

Notice! Ashley Barnes Lovemeter: 0%
Relationship is considered annulled. Please begin a new relationship to reacquire relationship privileges.
Better luck next time, sport! Remember, there's always more fish in the sea!

As she crossed the ballroom, headed for the employee entrance, she was intercepted by an angry older man in an attendant's uniform. He gripped her arm, dragging her off the floor as he berated her under his breath.

As Zack moved to follow, Kayla grabbed his arm. She jerked him to a stop, leaning close as she said, "You're not going anywhere. Not until you explain and make good on what you did."

"Make good?" Zack said. "What? You want more diamonds?"

Kayla flinched a little, her eyes narrowing. Murmurs from the crowd snapped her attention to the public, and she hesitated. Caught between preening for the crowd and wanting to avoid the public embarrassment. "Is that all you think of me?"

"Isn't that all we do? Shopping trips, diamonds and photographs, and access to places like this?" Zack waved his hands.

"If that's what you think, then so be it." Kayla raised her phone.

Zack's stomach dropped and dropped even further when she took a photo of him. She smirked and stepped back as he reached a hand out to her, her fingers flying across the keys. She paused and looked up, meeting his eyes as his face burned.

"You know, I would have given you another chance. I'm the forgiving type."

Her finger depressed the button and she let her hand drop. Zack hesitated, then realized that Ashley was gone from the ballroom. He started off after her again, only to be pulled short by Kayla's voice.

"Where do you think you're going?"

"I'm going to find Ashley and apologize."

Kayla laughed. "Good luck with that. I doubt that girl will ever speak to you again."

She gave Zack a little wave and turned her attention back to her phone. Zack shook his head and sprinted away.

As he ran, DaEvo flashed him further notifications.

Kayla Taylor Lovemeter: 0%
As all active relationships are no longer active, all relationship privileges have been revoked. Please begin a new relationship to reacquire relationship privileges.

Better luck next time, sport! Remember, there's always more fish in the sea!

Reputation -11.3

Style Update -14.7

#Hoboformal is no longer trending and has been tagged as a failed haute couture attempt by Zack Moore.

Chapter Forty-Four

Notification: Lost Unrestricted Non-essential Internet Privileges
Lost title: Stylish
Lost access to Royal Texas, etc.
Reputation: -4.3

ZACK WATCHED his Reputation sink lower and swiped away the notifications with a grim sense of resolve. All his good work to get it up, all his effort was disappearing. Added on to all the old news reports and his Reputation as a useless trust fund kid was being reinforced.

On the fiftieth floor of the Devon Tower, Zack was waiting for the elevator. Unfortunately, the lobby opened into the main room, so he was still in view of the party. He tried to ignore the fact that people were watching him. Laughing at him.

When he saw Zoe Cross come around the corner and look his way, Zack gave up on the elevator. He darted to the nearest set of stairs and sprinted down them.

Elevated heart rate detected. Begin workout?

Damn it! Zack accepted the quest and continued down the stairs. There were a lot of them, and he was drenched in sweat and gasping for breath by the time DaEvo prompted him to end the workout and cool down. He ducked out of the stairwell and pressed the elevator button so it could take him the rest of the way down.

Warning! Current chosen wear does not meet minimum hygiene standards.
Please change to an article of clothing that has been freshly laundered or has an olfactory factor < 0.8

Zack entered the elevator and glared at the notification. Lucky for him, he wasn't in his condo. DaEvo couldn't lock him in here.

At least, he hoped it couldn't. He really didn't want to end up trapped in this elevator.

But that meant he couldn't go home. The moment he stepped through that door, DaEvo would lock it until he completed the basic quests.

After all that work, he was back where he had started. It was like rebuilding his ship after it exploded in a dogfight. Except this was worse. He wouldn't have a ship to rebuild if he didn't fix this and fast.

The elevator reached the lobby, and Zack hurried through the building. Well, he hurried as much as he could after his impromptu workout on the stairs. The security guard and staff stared at him as he walked through the building. Zack stopped at the glass door, staring down the red carpet at the handful of photographers and journalists still gathered outside the Devon Tower. If he waited for a ride outside the building, he was bound to catch their attention. He would probably catch their attention regardless, since he had gone from hobo formal to just plain hobo over the course of the evening.

Zack pushed open the doors and sprinted down the red carpet. His legs burned, but he forced himself to keep going full speed until he reached the Myriad Gardens across the street. A flurry of questions followed him, and a few intrepid reporters even followed him into the park, searching for answers. Luckily, the park had plenty of nooks and crannies to hide in.

Zack found a bench under a low hanging tree and collapsed onto it. He stayed still until the reporters' voices faded, then he sighed deeply. The night air was cool and washed away some of the heat and frustration he had built while descending the stairs, although he was still drenched with sweat. DaEvo flashed another Reputation debuff, and Zack swept it away.

Stupid app. Stupid Phil. Stupid world.

In that moment, Zack wanted nothing more than to disappear into Star Fury and never come out. To lose himself in the world of stats and explosions and carefully planned strategies. No feelings. No reputation. No responsibility.

When the blood pumping in his ears stopped being so deafening, Zack became aware of another sound. Something other than traffic and the wind rustling in the leaves overhead.

Someone was crying.

Zack peeled himself off the bench and limped toward the sound. He wasn't sure which he was hoping to find more: Ashley so he could try to explain further, or some random stranger so that he would be off the hook and could honestly say he had tried to find her.

It was Ashley.

DaEvo chimed.

Relationship Hint!

Your lady left upset. Help her see the best side of you by showing her your best side. Remember, you need to be genuinely sorry to have a chance at this.

Ashley Barnes Relationship Note

Please note: As the Lovemeter between you and Ashley Barnes has reached zero, you will need to reestablish a relationship with Ashley Barnes to activate the Lovemeter again. This requires you to go on a successful date to resume the relationship.

Zack swept away the notifications and focused on Ashley. She was curled up on the park bench, crying. When she noticed Zack, she uncurled and wiped the tears. She stood with her hands on her hips, as if she were posturing to make herself bigger and hide the fact that she had been crying.

That would take a lot more work than aggressive body language. Her eyes were red, and her makeup had run down her face in dark streaks.

Zack felt an unexpected twisting in his heart at her distress. "Hey."

"Go away."

"Ashley, I'm sorry."

Current Quest!

Hold a one-minute conversation with a woman face-to-face!
Restrictions: In-person. Non-VR generated. Unpaid interaction.
Difficulty: Variable
Reward: Access to electronics and internet

So they were back to the conversation quests? Zack sighed. Short of offering her the diamond jewelry that DaEvo so often suggested, apologizing was the only thing he knew to do.

Ashley scowled at him. "I don't want to talk to you."

"Look, I didn't mean for any of this to happen. I just got caught up in the game."

She scoffed. "I just got fired, and you're worried about the game?"

"You got fired?" Zack repeated her words, trying to make sense of them.

"Yeah. It turns out catering companies don't like it when their waitresses cause a scene at high-profile events. So excuse me for not feeling bad that you lost love points or whatever."

"I'm sorry," he said again.

Now would be a really convenient time for DaEvo to offer some help. Of course, the app remained silent.

"I didn't mean to hurt you," Zack said. "I was just trying to win the game."

"That's what's so bad about this. You don't see anything wrong with your actions since they were all for the game."

"I didn't have a choice! I like you, but you were always busy! And I needed points!"

"Well, excuse me for having responsibilities. I'm sorry I couldn't drop everything to go out with you every night! I'm sorry I actually have to work for a living!" Ashley didn't look sorry, and Zack didn't need DaEvo to tell him that this wasn't actually an apology.

"I said I'd come with you to Houston."

"Sometimes couples spend time apart. You don't own someone just because you're dating them."

"I didn't mean it like that. I'm sorry."

She flinched at the last word, as if it had an actual physical form. "Stop saying that! You don't care about me. I was just an NPC in your stupid game."

"NPC?" Zack echoed. "You mean a non-playable character?"

His confusion only seemed to anger Ashley further. "Don't look so surprised that I know what that means. You're not the only gamer who felt the need to explain things to me at Gord's."

"I—" Zack swallowed the words, curious about the other gamers who had been teaching Ashley gamer terms at Gord's. Had they been hitting on her?

"You acted like I didn't have any feelings," Ashley said. "Like I was some programmed bit of pixels that only existed for your entertainment. I don't disappear when I'm out of your sight."

"I never thought that," Zack said. "I said I'm sorry. I don't know what else to do. How can I make this right?"

DaEvo chimed, and Zack's gaze flew to the app automatically. It was just another Reputation debuff, but Ashley noticed him checking his notifications, and her scowl deepened.

"Trying to decide which apology will earn you the most experience points?"

"It's not like that!"

Zack pulled off the OptiGlasses and stuffed them in his pocket. That meant he probably wouldn't get points for whatever happened next, but this conversation wouldn't earn him enough points to train or complete the final tournament round anyway. His overall level had dropped so low that he would barely get any points at all for anything he did. His best chance was to resume a relationship quest with Ashley and make sure her Lovemeter stayed full.

Ashley rolled her eyes. "Taking off your OptiGlasses. Bold move. Is that supposed to be some sort of grand gesture to show me you don't care about the game?"

"No," Zack said, ignoring that she had pretty much guessed his thoughts. Ashley crossed her arms and glared at him, and Zack felt his face flushing. "Look, I know I messed up. How do I make it better?"

"You leave me alone. You don't call me. You don't talk to me if you come into Gord's."

"What?"

"You used me, Zack. I don't want to talk to you. I don't want you to apologize. I just want you to go away."

"Ashley, wait!"

But she had already gone. Zack tried to follow, but running down all those stairs in dress shoes that he'd never worn before had taken a toll on his legs. He stumbled, blisters throbbing, and he grabbed a nearby tree for balance. By the time he got his balance again and looked up, Ashley had turned the corner again, disappearing into the night.

Chapter Forty-Five

ZACK WOKE to silence and sunshine. He blinked at the ceiling as his sleep-addled brain tried to figure out where he was, why the silence seemed so strange, and why every muscle in his body was sore.

The reason for the pain surfaced first. Zack groaned as he remembered the events of the previous evening. Ashley and Kayla. Racing down the stairs to escape the gala. Ashley's tearstained face as her Lovemeter dropped to zero and she told him to leave her alone.

Lovemeters.

DaEvo.

Crap.

The shot of adrenaline cleared Zack's head, and he realized why the silence felt strange. He hadn't heard from DaEvo yet. The app should have chimed by now to remind him to go work out or to tell him that he was locked in his condo until he took a shower and put on acceptable clothing. He also expected it to scold him for breaking his ladies' hearts and suggest ways to make it better. Ways that would probably involve buying expensive gifts, which Zack was totally willing to do if it would help.

The silence continued until it became unbearable. Zack reached for his OptiGlasses, groaning as his entire body protested the motion. Maybe the glasses had broken. Maybe the battery, which was advertised as being able to go a year between charges, had died.

Maybe he had died, and his subconscious was carefully reconstructing familiar surroundings to ease him into the afterlife.

Zack dismissed that idea as ridiculous. No way would his subconscious create this much pain for him if he was dead. Throbbing muscles and a strange ache in his chest wouldn't be included in his preferred afterlife, and if someone had designed a personal hell for him, then DaEvo would definitely be involved.

The OptiGlass screen lit up when Zack put on the glasses, showing him that it was well past noon and he had missed five calls from Phil.

And none from Kayla or Ashley.

Zack sighed and flicked his gaze to DaEvo's pink heart logo. Maybe after last night, the app had decided he was hopeless and given up on him. Maybe Phil was calling to say that he had changed his mind and decided to let Zack off the hook after all.

Instead of the usual animation of pink floating hearts, DaEvo displayed a basic white screen with black text that read:

DaEvo v1.2.7a has been taken offline for maintenance. All previous user functionality and access to internet and other accounts has been restored. An update on the new version of DaEvo will be provided when available.

{L—we're taking this down until we can reconfigure some of these relationship meters and data. Between Z's and B's recent flameouts, we need to work on how those scores are being calculated.

M—Yeah, I don't think it's our scoring. That was an epic flameout.

I—No doubt. Look at this {memeZackface.gif}

L—I feel bad for Ashley. I liked her.

M—Bah. He deserved it. He could have stayed with Kayla, but he chose not to. What a loser.

I—Ashley was way too good for him. }

Zack read the notification again, scowling at the developer notes. Just how closely were they observing the users for the alpha test? He had never been concerned about his privacy before, but maybe the luddites like Dr. Jones had a point. How many people had been watching his dates?

He pushed concerns about that aside and turned his attention back to the beginning of the announcement. Offline?

Zack stared at the word. Maybe he had died and gone to heaven after all. A smile crept across his face as the knowledge sunk in.

DaEvo was offline. He was free.

His mind raced with the possibilities. That was likely the reason for Phil's calls. To tell Zack that even though DaEvo was offline, he still had to toe the line to keep access to his bank accounts.

But could Phil really expect Zack to follow his rules if he never told Zack exactly what the rules were? If Phil never made contact, Zack could simply claim ignorance and do whatever he wanted.

Zack made a few quick swipes with his eyes, placing orders to be delivered to his apartment, then pulled the OptiGlasses off his face and stuffed them in a drawer. Then he pulled them out, wrapped them in a discarded T-shirt to muffle any sounds they might pick up, and stuffed them back in the drawer.

He was free. He didn't have to shower. He didn't have to wear stylish clothes. He didn't have to eat healthy or exercise. He didn't have to leave his apartment at all. He could spend the whole day playing Star Fury and eating junk food. It would be just like old times. No ridiculous romance quests. No worries.

Zack jumped out of bed, eager to start the day. His legs buckled, and he found himself facedown on the floor. He swore as he pushed himself up. Stupid stairs. Stupid muscles. Maybe he should add more stairs to his workout routine.

Stupid Ashley.

A wave of guilt swept through him, and he retracted the thought. Better not to think about Ashley at all. That was over. DaEvo was offline, and he didn't need a girlfriend. Today was all about Star Fury.

Zack pulled himself off the floor and peeled off the ill-fitting suit he hadn't bothered to take off the night before. The luxury fabric was unrecognizable after being soaked in sweat and slept in. Zack kicked it under the bed. Rosa could deal with it the next time she came to clean the apartment.

Although now that DaEvo was offline, he could cancel the cleaning service. There was no need for interruptions.

He grimaced, remembering how his apartment had looked before DaEvo had forced him to clean it. And how it had smelled. Maybe it was better to keep the cleaning service. Canceling it would be more trouble than simply letting it continue, and there was nothing wrong with living in a decent place. The lemony fresh scent would help him focus while playing Star Fury.

Zack found clean sweats and a T-shirt folded neatly in his dresser drawer and put them on. They were too big, and he pulled the drawstring tight until the sweats gathered around his waist enough to stay up. His skin was sticky and itchy from sweating so much last night, but he skipped showering on principle and settled into his gaming chair, taking satisfaction in the knowledge that no one was measuring his Style stats.

He held his breath as he started his console, but the screens sprang to life and the Star Fury theme music filled his apartment. Zack wondered if Kayla would complain about the noise but dismissed the thought. He didn't have to worry about his Reputation stats anymore. It didn't matter what Kayla thought.

Although if he wanted to know, he could easily find out. She had posted at least one thing on social media last night. Judging by how quickly his reputation had dropped, it was nothing good.

Zack's eyes darted up to the corner where he kept his social media apps before he remembered that he wasn't wearing his Opti-Glasses. If he wanted to see Kayla's post, he'd have to put them back on. Was he curious enough to risk it?

No, it didn't matter anymore. Zack pushed away his curiosity, along with lingering guilt. DaEvo had gotten into his head, and he would have to fight to get it out. He wasn't worried about his Reputation stats or his former girlfriend or anything else but Star Fury.

He sent a quick message to his teammates through the game's messaging system.

Zack: *Having trouble with my OptiGlasses, so I'll have to communicate here. I'm free all day to train!*

Greg sent him back a thumbs-up and coordinates for his current location, an asteroid field that doubled as a nesting ground for space vipers. The perfect place to try out new weapons. Zack set his autopilot on an interception course and settled back to go over his ship's latest upgrades. He needed to decide which combinations he wanted to test in training.

Jenny sent him a private message, interrupting his focus.

Jenny: *So you have time for us now that you broke up with KayTay?*

Crap. That meant Kayla had definitely posted something about last night. Zack swallowed and raced through a few options before settling on his reply.

Zack: *That got out of hand, but it's over now.*

. . .

Silence stretched on as Zack waited for Jenny's reply. He sent a follow-up message just in case.

Zack: *Things got crazy, but I'm back now. How can I make it up to you guys?*

Jenny: *You can stay focused until the tournament and help us win. We're a team.*

Not exactly an acceptance of his apology, but it was a start. Zack's ship chimed to let him know he was approaching his destination. He turned on voice comms and hailed his team.

"Incoming, guys! And again, I'm sorry I've missed so many training sessions lately. The app is offline for maintenance now, so I can make Star Fury my top priority again."

"Again?" Jenny said, her voice dripping with annoyance. "Nice to hear we're so far up the list of priorities. Nothing like dating a model to change our priorities, is there?"

"Wait, you actually were dating Zoe?" Greg asked. "I thought that was a joke."

"Of course it's a joke," Faz chimed in as he came online. "There's no way Zack was dating a model."

"Then why does he keep ditching us?"

Zack stayed silent, weighing his options. Would telling his teammates the real truth help to win back some of their trust? Or would it simply push them further away? He'd been doing better making it to training sessions and hadn't missed an actual tournament round, but he also knew he wasn't doing his best for them. And it showed, in the margins. Which was where he used to eke out gains for the team.

A private message from Jenny popped up on his screen.

Jenny: *Well? Are you finally going to tell them?*

. . .

Zack: *It's over now. Do they really have to know?*

Jenny's silence was answer enough.

Zack swore softly under his breath. He bit his lip, glancing back to his OptiGlasses and the computer. Ashley's face flashed into his mind, accusing him of lying. Of hiding the truth. "Okay, I haven't been completely honest with you guys, but you deserve the truth."

"Dude, we didn't actually think you were dating Zoe Cross," Greg said. "You don't have to make up some elaborate story to cover it up."

"Actually, I'd like to hear that elaborate story," Faz said, a mixture of amusement and annoyance in his voice. "I'd love to hear how our team captain explains his repeated absences as we're preparing for our biggest tournament yet."

"Go on, Zack," Jenny said, cutting the guys off.

Faz's ship blinked into view as he reached the asteroid field. That created a pulse of energy that stirred the space vipers from their nests. They darted toward the ships, mouths open and fangs extended.

"Rendezvous at the nearest neutral moon," Zack said, engaging evasive maneuvers to avoid getting swallowed by a particularly large space viper. "I'll tell you everything, but you have to promise not to laugh."

———

They laughed.

A lot.

Zack gritted his teeth and pressed on with the story, finally muting their comms so he could focus. But they had turned on video for the call, so he could still see them shaking with laughter and wiping tears.

Greg had leaned forward, doubling over with laughter until his face all but disappeared from view. He was built more like a line-backer than a gamer, and his screen showed the top of his blond head and his broad shoulders shaking as he struggled to rein in his amusement.

Jenny was a little more successful at keeping a straight face, but her petite frame still shook whenever Zack told them about Cassie mistaking him for a stalker. She pressed her lips into a thin line to hold in the laughter and brushed back her long, dark hair.

Faz wasn't even trying to hold back. Tears ran down his face, and his turban was tilted and in danger of falling off. Zack suspected Faz had missed at least half the story since he was laughing too loudly to hear it. That meant Zack would probably have to repeat details later. Or maybe Faz would be too busy cracking jokes to ask questions.

"A dating sim?" Faz said between laughs when Zack finally finished his story. "You've been trapped in a dating sim?"

Zack took a bite of the pizza that had been delivered while he told the story. It tasted amazing after all the health quests, but it was getting harder and harder to enjoy it as his teammates laughed. He finished the slice of pizza, turned his attention to the half-finished donut balanced on the pizza box, and washed it down with an energy drink from the case he had ordered.

"There's still no way you were dating a model," Greg said. "If that dating sim helped you date a model, sign me up."

"Believe me, you don't want to sign up for this," Zack said.

"If it's real, count me in too," Faz said.

"Oh, it's real," Jenny said.

Her eyes sparkled with mischief as she started a screen share. A picture of Zack and Kayla from the WesterNeon party at Royal Texas popped onto the screen. Zack winced. The brightly colored outfit looked even more ridiculous than he remembered, as did the neon drink in his hand. Kayla, as always, was perfectly posed for the picture and showing off her legs to their best advantage.

"Damn," Faz said. "Definitely sign me up for that."

"Is she into cowboy clowns or something?" Greg said. "Because that's what you look like, and I can't think of any other reason someone that hot would date you."

"I'd dress up like a cowboy clown for her," Faz said. "Where'd you get that outfit?"

"Um," Zack hesitated, sharing a look with Jenny.

"No worries, I'll look it up," Faz said.

"Man, she's really famous!" Greg said as he scrolled through Kayla's social media feed. "How did you even meet her? Did the dating sim pair you?"

"Cripes!" Faz said. "These cowboy clown hats cost two grand! How did you afford the whole outfit?"

"You cheated on her?" Greg yelled, outraged. "How could you cheat on KayTay? You broke her heart!"

He waved his phone at the screen, blurring the image, but Zack saw enough to know that it was a picture of Kayla crying.

"KayTay?" Jenny said. "So you're a fanboy now?"

"She seems cool," Greg said defensively.

Jenny narrowed her eyes, and Greg turned red as he stashed his phone out of sight.

"Let me get this straight," Faz said. "Somehow this dating sim managed to get you two girlfriends, one of which is a super hot model, as well as designer outfits that cost thousands of dollars?"

"There's no need to sound jealous," Zack said. "It's been a nightmare. You've seen what it did to my Star Fury training. Anyway, it's over now. I'm back."

"Something still doesn't add up," Jenny said. "WesterNeon is an extremely exclusive fashion line, and Giacomo doesn't make bespoke suits personally for just anybody. And I know how often you've been out with her. Exactly how did you afford all that, Zack?"

"How did you know Giacomo made that suit?"

Jenny rolled her eyes. "I have interests outside of Star Fury. Apparently, I'm the only one on the team who does."

"I like fashion now," Greg said.

"You're just saying that because you have a crush on KayTay," Faz said.

"You're one to talk. I see you've followed her page as well."

They glared at each other through the screen, and Zack laughed.

"Can we get back to training?" he said. "Those space vipers won't hunt themselves."

"Don't avoid the question," Jenny said. "What else are you keeping from us? Are you a drug dealer or something?"

She crossed her arms and stared at the camera. Zack recognized that look. It was her game face, and it meant she wouldn't budge until she got what she wanted. She had an inkling of the truth. Probably more an inkling really. All those social media feeds, all the newspaper articles. If she had put in any real effort, she'd know.

Which meant she was likely letting him come clean the rest of the way.

Greg and Faz stopped fighting over Kayla and turned their attention to Zack as well. His mouth grew dry, and all the sugar from the donut he'd eaten suddenly seemed like a bad idea. Fingers clenched on the leather gaming chair, feeling the smooth material. This was bound to come up sooner or later, and there was no way his team would trust him again if they felt he was keeping something else secret.

"Okay, but promise this won't make things weird."

They nodded their agreement. Zack remembered their promise not to laugh about DaEvo and grimaced. Hopefully, they'd do a better job of keeping this one. His stomach churned—possibly from all the junk food. Maybe eating two whole pizzas and a dozen donuts hadn't been the best use of his newfound freedom.

Still, no turning back now. His teammates were waiting.

Zack took a deep breath, trying to decide where to begin. "Okay, you guys know Phil? Well, he's more than just my former guardian. He also manages my accounts."

"Like bank accounts?" Greg said.

"Yeah, something like that."

Chapter Forty-Six

ZACK HELD the sweatpants at arm's length, wondering how they managed to smell so bad when all he had done was sit in a gaming chair for three days. He had gone months without doing laundry before without a problem. Why did the olfactory stats bother him now?

Stupid DaEvo. Even now that he was free, the app was still ruining his life.

Zack shoved the smelly sweats into the clothing hamper and dug through his dresser for something else to wear. His gaze settled on the FitLife clothes, and he ran his hand over the fabric. He definitely wasn't planning to work out, but the outfit was soft and breathable. Perfect for gaming.

The FitLife clothes smelled fresh, making Zack aware that the stench wasn't coming completely from his sweats. He hadn't showered since DaEvo went offline. It had seemed like a good way to spite the app by doing the exact opposite of what it would have wanted, but maybe he was being a little juvenile. It's not as if the app really cared if he bathed or not. And he did stink.

Zack shook his head as he carried the FitLife clothes to his bathroom. There was no harm in taking one shower. It wasn't a sign that he was giving up. Rather, it showed that he no longer cared about DaEvo enough to even think about the app. He would do whatever he wanted regardless of what DaEvo might have commanded in the past.

Besides, the hot water was just what his tired muscles needed. Zack took an extra long shower, enjoying the feeling of being clean again. This would definitely help his Star Fury training session. He felt relaxed and alert and ready to play.

Zack dried off and pulled on the FitLife clothes. They were tighter than he remembered. Maybe it was just him though. They were stretchy clothing after all. They probably just seemed tight because he had been wearing such baggy sweats for the past few days. There was no way he had gained weight in three days. That was absolutely ridiculous.

Then again, he had been eating a lot of junk food. Nothing but junk food actually. Mostly pizza and energy drinks. He had a sudden craving for his usual breakfast of the veggie omelet and green juice. He always felt great after eating that. Almost without realizing what he was doing, Zack found himself in front of the condo's smart home interface by his door and looking at the food delivery options. Maybe—

No. Absolutely not. He would not eat that food. He wouldn't let DaEvo win.

His stomach rumbled, and he walked to the fridge and pulled out an energy drink and a box of leftover pizza. For some reason, the pizza didn't look quite as appealing as it had for the past few days.

Zack took a bite and chewed. The crust was a little dry, the cheese a little too cold and oily. The pepperoni had shrunk and dried out in the fridge overnight, leaving a slightly furry taste in his mouth. But the sauce was good, and cold pizza was the food of choice for gamers everywhere.

Right?

Maybe he was just tired of it after eating the same thing for the past three days.

Zack shook his head and took another bite of the pizza. He couldn't help but think that it'd be nice to have some veg on it. Something green, and with more protein. The veggie omelet and green juice came to mind again.

But that was DaEvo talking, and he was determined not to let the app get to him. He didn't need health food. He didn't need exercise.

The harder Zack tried not to think of all the things DaEvo had made him do, the more images flashed into his mind. Working out. Chasing Cassie through the park. Dancing the polka with Ashley.

Zack clenched his fists and took a deep breath. No. He was not going there. He definitely didn't need Ashley.

But what if she needed him?

For the past three days, Zack had been fighting the urge to check his OptiGlasses to see if Ashley had sent a message. If he checked them, Phil or DaEvo might trap him somehow. It was much safer to stay offline and focus on his gaming. The semi-finals were only a few days away. He needed to stay focused.

Had she found another job? Had Amber's surgery gone all right? Was she still mad at him?

No, he didn't need to worry about that!

Still, he wondered what Ashley was doing. Kayla hadn't stopped by to complain about the noise Zack was making, so he assumed she was out of town for a photoshoot. But what about Ashley? Was she still working at Gord's? Had she started her next round of classes yet? She probably needed help studying for them. Maybe she had found a new study partner.

Or a new boyfriend.

Zack stuffed the rest of the pizza into his mouth, nearly choking as he chewed and swallowed it. But at least the struggle to breathe pushed the image of Ashley out of his mind. He didn't care about her. He didn't care about anything but Star Fury.

Speaking of Star Fury, he was going to be late for training. Zack grabbed a few spare energy drinks and settled into his gaming chair. Time to get down to business. He pressed the power button on his console.

Nothing happened.

Zack blinked at the black screens and fought back panic. There was no reason to panic. There was a perfectly logical reason why they weren't working, and it had nothing to do with DaEvo.

He checked the plugs to make sure everything was connected. It was.

Sweat beaded on his forehead. This couldn't be happening. There was no way this was happening. DaEvo was offline. He had broken the app. He was free.

There was another way to test it.

Zack hurried to his front door and tried the knob. Locked. He punched the code into his smart home console, and a message flashed across it.

Error. User does not have access to door.

No. No way.

"This can't be happening," Zack muttered.

He shook the door and turned the knob, but the lock wouldn't budge. Zack swore. He should have deactivated the smart house apps as soon as DaEvo went offline. What had he been thinking, leaving everything online after what happened last time? He had let himself be lulled into a false sense of security, and that was always when the enemy chose to strike.

He walked slowly to his room, pulled the OptiGlasses from the drawer, and put them on. A flood of messages from Phil came through first, but they were blocked with pink heart-shaped locks.

Crap. This really was happening. He took a shaky breath and opened DaEvo.

Familiar cheerful music and a flood of pink filled his senses. The developers had finished the animation and music while the app was offline. It concluded with a cheerful flourish and an animated cupid flying past. It shot an arrow toward Zack, winked, and flew away.

Zack gritted his teeth. That was even more annoying than he remembered. Not to mention he was now late for his training session with his team and couldn't use his messaging app to tell them why.

He was getting major déjà vu.

Chapter Forty-Seven

Dating Evolution has updated. You are now using DaEvo v1.3.0a.

We have a wide array of updates in the latest update. This includes a significant upgrade in Reputation, Style, and Physique algorithms as well as an update to how the Lovemeter works.

We have also included multiple new hints on how to manage hints, including details on how to ethically manage multiple relationships at the same time, definitions of casual and non-casual relationships, and further updates on the kind of relationships users might be able to achieve and "win" the game.

ZACK SANK onto his bed in dismay and stared at the pink hearts filling his OptiGlasses. DaEvo was back online, and its timing was even worse than before. He needed to get online for the upcoming semi-finals qualifying round to get into the Vegas. And if they could beat the other team in the finals in the qualifying round, they'd have a leg up in the actual tournament with a higher buy rate to arm their ships. There was no way his team could make it into the actual tournament without him, not with the way the PvP rounds were set up. The teams they were all fighting were really good.

He gritted his teeth and pounded his fists into his mattress. He had just started to figure everything out! He had earned back his teammates' trust, and this would ruin it again! He would miss the training session! Possibly the entire tournament!

DaEvo chimed.

Statistics for Zack Moore have finished processing.

Zack Moore
Physique: 50.35
Style: 32
Reputation: -14.3
Occupation: 0
Social Level: 22.01

Current Relationships: 0
Previous Relationships: 2

Conversation Quest Found!
Hold a one-minute conversation with a woman face-to-face!
Restrictions: In-person. Non-VR generated. Unpaid interaction.
Difficulty: Variable
Reward: unrestricted internet privileges

Accept Quest?

Zack's mind spun. He needed access to the messaging app before anything else. At least he had washed and dressed, so he wasn't locked out because of that. It had just been a glitch while DaEvo was updating. He still needed to tell his team what was happening. He skimmed through his stats. As usual, Style would be the easiest to upgrade.

Crap.

Zack opened his closet and pulled out the WesterNeon outfit. It had been ages since he'd put it on. He blinked as he touched the gap that showed up as he put on his jeans. When he was dressed, he looked in the mirror.

Style Points Increased!
Style: 72
Social Level Increased! You have gained access to online communication functionality!

Zack opened the messaging app before DaEvo could change its mind.

Zack: *I'm so sorry I'm late! DaEvo came back online and reset all my stats! I'm locked out of my account again!*
Jenny: *Okay, I know this isn't funny. But also, it's kind of funny.*
Greg: *It's totally funny! Does this mean you're getting back together with Kay Tay? Don't forget to dress like a cowboy clown!*

Zack glared at his reflection. That was closer to the truth than they knew, but there was no need for them to know he was actually wearing WesterNeon at the moment.

Zack: *I'll figure it out and be there as soon as I can.*
Faz: *Maybe if you level up enough, the app will set you up with Zoe Cross.*
Zack: *Very funny. It doesn't work like that.*
Jenny: *Just get here as soon as you can.*

Zack hung up and checked his messages from Phil. There were a lot of them. He skimmed over the ones that were just ranting and swearing and pieced together the one-sided conversation he had missed over the past few days.

. . .

Phil: *Zack, I just heard what happened at the gala. Call me.*

Phil: *Just talked with the Dating Evolution developers. You're right. They're idiots. I'm surprised this didn't blow up sooner.*

Phil: *I've looked back over the logs of your progress in Dating Evolution, and this is not exactly what I had in mind when I signed you up for the program. Kayla was a complete disaster. It explains why you were buying her love like one of your space hookers.*

Phil: *Ashley was kind of nice. You two had something there, though you can't just buy your way into relationships.*

Phil: *Well, the recordings of the gala were even worse than what I heard. DaEvo really has no idea about human relationships. But neither do you. I'm willing to let you out of this if you want.*

Phil: *Really? You're going to ignore me again? It's been two days. Are you okay? Are you taking drugs? Crying in the corner like when Mandy turned you down for prom? Seriously, call me.*

Phil: *God damn it. This is exactly the kind of garbage you pulled the last time. Call me.*

Phil: *Dating Evolution is going back online tomorrow. The developers assure me that they've worked out the bugs, and it will be better this time. If I don't hear from you in an hour, I'm leaving you in the program. I thought you had learned something, but I guess I was wrong.*

Zack broke out in a cold sweat. Phil had tried to let him off the hook, and he had missed the memo.

He swore while he stripped out of the WesterNeon clothes and traded them for an outfit that DaEvo had classified as "Boy Next Door." Lower stats, but it would work better if he was going to talk to a woman. He remembered Ashley laughing when he wore WesterNeon to Gord's and grinned. She had laughed so hard, she had barely been able to stand.

Then he shoved away the memory. He could go to Gord's for a conversation, but he preferred something with less potential for drama. He could try the gym, but that would mean explaining to his personal trainer why he had been skipping workouts. That wasn't a conversation Zack was eager to have, no matter how many points it was worth. Besides, seeing the gym equipment would probably trigger a fitness quest, and he didn't have time for that.

The condo app chimed, and Zack saw that he had missed ten messages. Apparently, a lot had happened while his OptiGlasses were stuffed in a drawer. He opened the app and scrolled through them. One was a confirmation that Rosa was coming to clean tomorrow. Another was an update about the window cleaning service coming by next week. Routine messages.

The rest were from the pet sitting service. Apparently, Veobos the hamster was over the limit for long term stays and needed to be picked up.

The pet sitting messages were all signed by someone named Tina. Zack grinned and hurried out the door. It looked as though he wouldn't have to go far to have his conversation after all.

Chapter Forty-Eight

Tina Evans (Social Level 45.25)
Physique: 54
Style: 44
Reputation: 52
Occupation: 31

ZACK SMILED AT TINA, doing his best to look charming and approachable. "Hi. I got a message about my hamster?"

"Oh, hamster guy. Thank goodness."

DaEvo chimed and started the conversation timer. Since everything had reset, Zack only needed a minute of conversation to complete the quest, but he was hoping for much more so that he could earn enough game time to complete the training he had planned today.

"Veobos is three weeks over the maximum stay," Tina said. "I was starting to think you had forgotten about him."

Zack laughed nervously as Tina turned around to search for Veobos. Rather than let the conversation quest time out, Zack made small talk. Thank goodness, the weather was always around. Of course, Zack had to pull up a weather app to find out what the weather had been the last few days. It wasn't as if he actually looked out his windows.

He kept up a steady stream of conversation about how hot it had been while Tina pulled Veobos's cage from a shelf and set it on the counter. The hamster glared at Zack then burrowed in his bedding and ignored both humans.

Tina leaned over the cage and grinned at the hamster. "I told him that nobody could forget such a cute hamster. Isn't that right, Veobos?"

The hamster didn't acknowledge her at all.

Tina looked back at Zack. Her bright smile slipped as she crossed her arms and glared at him. "It's distressing for pets to be away from their people for so long. Look how heartbroken he is."

"Yeah, sorry. I was in the hospital for a bit."

"Oh, gosh! I'm sorry. Are you all right?"

Tina looked so concerned that Zack felt a little guilty. It wasn't technically a lie. He *had* been in the hospital. It had even been Veobos's fault, in a way.

"I'm fine," he said, waving away her concern. "Nothing serious."

"Well, that's good. I just need you to sign this paperwork to show that you've picked up Veobos, and you're ready to go."

"Right. Paperwork." He tried to keep his voice from going too dry, but he must have failed because Tina laughed good-naturedly. As always, DaEvo gave him points, which was kind of nice.

Zack glanced at the conversation timer. He had passed the minute mark and was receiving bonuses for the longer conversation. He just needed to keep this going, and he might get enough game time for the training session without having to find another woman.

He pretended to be reading the text on the tablet Tina had given him to sign. DaEvo flashed a warning that they had been silent for too long, and Zack's thoughts raced as he tried to think of something to say.

"So, you like hamsters?" Zack threw out.

It was an inane question. But Tina smiled. "Of course! They're so cute! You should see Veobos running around the hamster habitat during playtime. Adorable."

She kept going, talking about why she liked the small rodents. Zack listened with a smile pasted to his face and his eyes glued to the conversation timer.

The door opened behind him with a cheerful chime, and Tina stopped gushing about hamsters to greet her new customer. "Miss Cross, welcome! And hi, Bella! How are you today, you cute baby?"

Tina continued to baby talk Bella. Zack turned, and DaEvo chimed.

Zoe Cross (Social Level 91)
Physique: 94
Style: 85
Reputation: 95
Occupation: 91

The app didn't give points for the small white dog in Zoe's arms. On the other hand, Zoe was gorgeous, even dressed down like she was today. Of course, dressed down for her was still stylish, trendy clothing that Zack was sure would grace some gossip rag's front page.

"Hi, Tina. I'm going out of town in a few days, and I'll be gone a week. Are you available to watch Bella for me?"

"Of course!"

Zoe signed the dog into daycare for the day and worked out the details for Tina to watch Bella during the trip. Tina signed the papers then gathered the dog and carried her into a back room. DaEvo flashed a notification to warn Zack that his conversation with Tina had lagged too long, then ended the quest and awarded him points. He hardly noticed. He was too busy staring at Zoe.

Zoe Cross. What were the odds he would run into her again? Especially in his condo's pet sitting service. Admittedly, he knew they were open for everyone in the building, but still…

She was so high level that one conversation with her would set him up for the day. Maybe for the week. But he was feeling starstruck and couldn't organize his thoughts enough to think of anything to say.

Zoe noticed him staring and gave him a brilliant smile. "I'm sorry. I just cut in front of you, didn't I?"

"Um." Zack didn't even notice when DaEvo chimed.

"Is this one yours?" She gestured toward the hamster cage. When Zack nodded, Zoe leaned over to look into it. "Cute. What's his name?"

"Veobos?" It came out as a question, and Zack mentally kicked himself. What kind of idiot didn't even know his own hamster's name?

The kind of idiot who forgot he even owned a hamster.

"Oh, you're a Star Fury fan?" Zoe said. She looked from the hamster to Zack, and her eyes sparked with recognition. "Wait a minute. I know you, don't I?"

"Um. Kind of?"

Zack mentally kicked himself again. What was wrong with him? Why was he suddenly incapable of answering in complete sentences? This was the opportunity of a lifetime, and he was blowing it.

He knew the moment Zoe remembered who he was. Her eyes flashed with amusement, and she covered her mouth with her hand to hide her smile. "Oh, gosh. You're Zack Moore! We met at my gala."

"Yeah, sorry about that. I hope the rest of the event went okay?"

Zoe shrugged. "It's not the first time Kayla has caused a scene at one of my events. Did you two work things out?"

Zack laughed. "No. I haven't talked to her since."

"And the waitress?"

Zack's smile slipped at the mention of Ashley. "I haven't talked to her since either."

His voice broke, and he scolded himself for sounding so lame in front of Zoe.

Tina returned and noticed Zack's distress. "Oh gosh, is everything okay! Is something wrong with Veobos? Are you sick again?"

"You're sick?" Zoe said.

DaEvo chimed.

Relationship Quest Update!

Due to previous incidents, you must select your conversation partner. Setting up such conversation and relationship targets will then carry forth for all interactions.

Further confirmation once your first Relationship Milestone (that is, access to the Lovemeter after the first date) on your relationship goals and status will be required for the proper functioning of DaEvo.

Please choose if you are intending to pursue a relationship with:

- *Tina Evans*
- *Zoe Cross*
- ~~*Both*~~ *(Please enter Relationship Settings and answer* <u>*Ethical Polyamory Questionnaire*</u>*)*

Zack swiped to select Zoe's name and turned back to the conversation. "Just a minor health scare. I'm fine now."

Zoe studied his face, then nodded. "Are you busy right now? I have a few hours before my first appointment, and I meant what I said at the gala. I think our foundations would collaborate well. I'd love to get coffee and chat about the possibility."

"Really?" Zack's voice squeaked, and DaEvo chimed.

Achievement Unlocked! Get a Date!

+60 minutes for non-essential electronics

Bonus: +180 minutes for non-essential electronics due to Social Level disparity

"Unless you're busy," Zoe said.

"Nope. Not busy at all." He would be late for training, but it would be worth it if he got enough points to set him up for the tournament round.

Plus, she was Zoe Cross!

Zack hurried to open the door for Zoe and received bonus points from DaEvo for acting like a gentleman.

"Wait! You forgot Veobos!" Tina called. She held up the hamster cage.

Zack glared at it. No way was he letting the hamster get in the way of a date with Zoe Cross. "Do you think you could keep him a bit longer? He seems to really like you, and I haven't got his habitat in my apartment completely set up yet."

Tina considered that, then nodded. "Technically this can count as you picking him up since you came to see him. If you're sure, I can reset the—"

"Awesome, thanks!"

Zack smiled at Tina and hurried to catch up with Zoe. He followed her to the coffee house on the first floor of the condo, ordered the black coffee with a splash of almond milk that DaEvo suggested as a healthy option, and sat at a small table.

Incredible. He was on a coffee date with Zoe Cross.

Zoe had ordered an Earl Grey latte, and she sipped it thoughtfully as she studied Zack. He took a sip of his latte and gagged at the bitter taste. Stupid fitness quests. Stupid almond milk.

He set it aside and smiled at Zoe. He wanted to say something. Anything. He was on a date with the woman of his dreams. This was the time to say something brilliant and clever to impress her. But his mind was absolutely blank. Zack filled the empty space in his head with swearing, venting his frustration to himself as he flashed another smile that hopefully showed no trace of his inner frustration.

"So tell me about this dating app."

It was a good thing Zack wasn't drinking his coffee, because he would have spit it out all over Zoe. "W-what?"

"At the gala, you mentioned something about a dating app. I'm curious about any kind of technology that causes so much chaos. And I'm curious why it would encourage you to cheat on Kayla."

Zack waited for DaEvo to chime and tell him not to talk about it. He had always assumed it was something like fight club. First rule of dating app, don't talk about dating app.

But DaEvo remained silent. Apparently, this topic was fair game.

Crap. He was on a date with Zoe Cross, and she wanted to know about DaEvo and his exes. Now would be a fabulous time to change the topic, but Zack couldn't think of anything else to talk about.

"It wasn't my idea," he said.

Zoe raised an eyebrow. "So you were completely innocent, and this was all a big misunderstanding? I suppose the waitress just misread your actions and assumed your relationship meant more than it did?"

There was an edge to Zoe's tone, and she shifted in her chair as if she were going to stand and leave.

"Ashley," Zack said defensively. Even if it drove Zoe further away, he couldn't let her talk about Ashley so dismissively, as if she were a minor character in the drama that had unfolded. "Her name is Ashley, and I never meant to hurt her. I never meant to hurt anyone."

An NPC. Ashley had accused him of treating her like an NPC. Zack sagged in his chair as the memories of the evening washed over him. He had messed up. He had hurt Ashley.

He might never see her again.

"So what did happen?" Zoe leaned forward in her chair, seeming very interested in the story.

Zack swallowed. "You said you wanted to talk about our foundations. I'm sure you're not interested in my relationship drama."

"I like to know the people I collaborate with. I like to know that they're reliable, and I can trust them. I think your foundation does great work. I think we could do a lot of good together. But I need to know more about you before I'm comfortable moving forward with this. What exactly happened at the gala?"

Her words reminded Zack of Dr. Jones refusing the job at the foundation because she didn't want to work with Zack. He had thought his actions didn't matter, but apparently, they did. Apparently, he had hurt his parents' legacy more than he realized. He wondered absentmindedly if his actions had affected his parents' company as well. Phil had never mentioned it.

Or maybe he had. Maybe Zack just hadn't listened.

He took a deep breath and looked at Zoe. She was unbelievably gorgeous and giving him her full attention. She was well out of his level. He was getting a ton of time for the conversation.

But more than that, she seemed willing to listen, and he needed that. He needed it more than he had realized. Because as much as he hated to admit it, he had messed up. He had hurt people, and he had hurt himself.

"Okay," Zack said. "It's kind of a long story."

Zoe nodded for him to continue, so he did. Almost without meaning to, he told her everything.

Chapter Forty-Nine

ZOE DIDN'T LAUGH. She smiled a few times and had a few suspicious coughing fits, but she didn't laugh. She didn't comment either. She let him finish his story, listening with a sympathetic interest. Even when he was done, she remained silent.

DaEvo chimed to warn him that the conversation was lagging, so Zack said the first thing that popped into his head. "How do I fix this?"

Zoe raised an eyebrow. "What do you want to fix?"

Zack considered. That was a fair question given how complicated everything had become. Never mind the girls and DaEvo and the tournament, there was…

"The foundation," he said since technically Zoe was there to talk about their charities working together. "I still think Dr. Jones is the right person to run it."

"Then you need to show her you can be professional. Make her realize how much good she could do by working with you."

"That makes sense." Zack's mind raced as he tried to think of ways to prove he was professional.

While he thought, Zoe sipped her latte and watched him.

DaEvo pinged, warning him that the conversation was lagging again.

"Kayla," Zack said. "I should probably make all this up to her somehow."

DaEvo flashed a notification warning him that he shouldn't talk about ex-girlfriends on dates, but Zack swiped it away. This didn't feel like a date, although he was happy to let DaEvo think it was so he could get points for it.

Zoe didn't seem to mind the subject. "Kayla was pretty upset. What did you have in mind?"

"Usually I'd just buy her something." Zoe frowned, and Zack felt his face go red. "That's what the app said to do! I got lots of points for giving her jewelry."

"I think it will take more than a diamond bracelet to fix this."

Zack shook his head. "She doesn't like diamonds anyway. They don't match her clothes."

Zoe pressed her lips together, and Zack was pretty sure she was trying not to laugh.

"I don't get it either," he said. "They're clear! They should go with anything!"

Zoe did laugh then, and Zack joined her. Suddenly the whole situation seemed ridiculous. He stopped laughing as thoughts of Kayla brought him back to the fight at the gala.

"What about Ashley?" he asked.

"That's the waitress? What about her?" Zoe leaned back, looking casual.

A little too casual. Zack had a sneaking suspicion she was actually very interested in the whole thing.

"I need to apologize to her at least. I need—"

He needed her back. He missed her.

Zack gritted his teeth at the realization. He missed Ashley. He wanted to see her again. Wanted to have lunch dates with her and go dancing and—

Stupid DaEvo. The app had managed to make him fall for someone, but it had also made him lose her.

Could it help him get her back?

Zoe was pressing her lips together in that suppressed smile.

Zack quickly backtracked. "She lost her job because of me. I can't just sit here and pretend that didn't happen."

It seemed like a decent enough excuse to see her again.

If Zoe didn't buy it completely, she went along with it. "That's a little trickier, but it sounds like it's worth a try." Zoe's phone chimed with a notification. She checked it and made a face. "Sorry, I've got to go. I enjoyed talking to you."

She offered her hand, and Zack shook it. DaEvo chimed points for the physical contact and flashed another notification.

Relationship Quest!
Ask her out!

Spend some one-on-one time with your special lady by asking her out on a date. Completing this quest will unlock Relationship Milestone bonuses and additional quests.

A successful date will unlock the Lovemeter and unlimited access to non-essential internet privileges.

Zack looked from Zoe to the notification, then rejected the quest. The conversation had given him enough time to get through the final round of the qualifier tournament, and he wasn't eager to jump into another relationship after the previous two disasters.

And although the conversation had gone well, it hadn't felt romantic.

Zack shook his head as he walked slowly to the elevator. Zoe was gorgeous. His dream woman. Was he thinking of her as just a friend?

He really needed to keep this from Faz. He'd never hear the end of it.

As he entered his elevator, Zack broke into a laugh. How did he end up even thinking that someone like Zoe Cross could be his friend? She was an internationally renowned model and actress. And he was, well, him.

Zack sank into his gaming chair and pushed the conversation from his mind. The conversation hadn't given him unlimited game time, but Zoe was so high level that it had given him a lot.

His teammates already had their comms open, so Zack joined them as soon as he logged in.

"Hey, Zack," Faz said, "I've been thinking. Now that we know you're super rich, does that mean you can get us a cool suite at the tournament?"

"Faz!" Jenny said, sounding scandalized. "Zack does not have to buy us anything."

"No, Faz has a point." Greg's voice dropped as he wheedled Zack. "I know I've been very hurt by Zack's actions lately. A luxe suite at the hotel in Vegas would totally make me feel better."

"Don't listen to them," Jenny said. "You don't have to buy them things to make them feel better. That's ridiculous."

"But he can afford it," Faz pointed out. "And we'll play better if we're well rested."

"And he has let us down a lot lately," Greg said. "Trapped in a dating sim or not, he's been kind of absent. He should make it up to us somehow."

"Hmm?" Zack said. He was still thinking about Zoe and Ashley and Kayla, and it took him a moment to pull himself back and realize what his teammates were talking about.

"They're joking, Zack," Jenny said. "You don't need to—"

"No, I think it's a great idea." Zack's brain finally caught up with the conversation thread, and he grinned. "I totally owe you guys. Cancel whatever lame rooms you have reserved. We're doing Vegas in style."

He knew he was buying his way out of trouble again, but this felt different. Maybe because Greg and Faz were blatantly asking with little true expectation of getting anything.

Greg and Faz cheered as they guided their ships into the formation. Jenny stayed silent. Zack could practically hear her rolling her eyes. Why did girls have to hold grudges for so long? Why couldn't they just accept a simple apology and let it be?

"Come on, Jenny," Greg said. "It will be awesome."

Jenny zapped him with one of her drones, but she joined the team in laughing at Greg's outraged protest. Zack grinned a little, grateful to see that at least with his team, things were getting better. Now if only the rest of his life was as easy to sort out.

Chapter Fifty

ZACK FIDGETED WITH HIS TIE, resisting the temptation to loosen it. Giacomo had assured him this was the proper way to wear it and that he looked professional. If leveling up his style with DaEvo had taught Zack anything, it was that he needed different outfits for different situations. Kind of like outfitting his ship with different armor for different dungeons.

And right now, he needed professional armor.

Zack was so distracted by his fashion-as-armor analogy that he didn't notice Dr. Jones come in until DaEvo chimed. He looked up, seeing DaEvo populate the information for her.

Cassie Jones (Social Level 61)
Physique: 80
Style: 41
Reputation: 36
Occupation: 87

Doctor Cassie Jones looked as though she would rather be anywhere else in the world than meeting him in the hospital cafeteria on one of her few breaks. She was dressed for work in tribal print scrubs with her dark hair pulled back in a tight ponytail, dark bags under her eyes.

Zack stood and offered his hand. She shook it, and he tried to remember every handshaking tip he had read in his crash course research on being a professional adult. He felt more like an actor playing a part, but hopefully he could play it convincingly.

DaEvo gave him bonus points for physical contact, and Zack swiped away the notification. The points earned for this conversation would buy him more time for the tournament. Hopefully, it would boost his Reputation stats as well.

But that wasn't why he was there. At least, that wasn't the whole reason.

"Thank you for agreeing to meet me," Zack said.

"I don't have much time." Cassie sank into her chair with her arms crossed.

Zack hastily sat as well.

DaEvo flashed a notification.

Your lady is upset. Try the following to make her feel better:

- *Flowers*
- *Chocolate*
- *Apology*

Zack sincerely doubted Cassie would appreciate chocolate or flowers at the moment. That left the apology. Good thing that was the plan anyway.

He swallowed, wishing it was Ashley sitting across from him. She was the one he really wanted to make things right with. Maybe he could, in a roundabout way, if this went well.

"Doctor Jones, before we go any further, I'd like to apologize." Zack did his best impression of Phil, trying to imitate the trustee's formal tone and professional manners. Cassie said nothing, so Zack kept talking. "We got off on the wrong foot, and I haven't handled the situation well. I never meant to make you feel uncomfortable."

"Do you have a point, Mr. Moore, or did you come here to ramble and waste my time?"

Zack gritted his teeth as DaEvo flashed another warning that the lady was upset. This wasn't going well. Then again, she was still there. She looked angry enough to stab him, but she was still there.

"I came to apologize and ask you to reconsider helping us with the foundation's new budget. We need help. More than that, another person has expressed interest in donating funds and expanding the trust's reach even further. But she agrees that we need someone competent in charge before that happens."

Zack gave himself a mental high-five for that speech. It sounded very business-like. But would it be enough? Cassie's expression had changed from one of complete disgust to one of mild disgust. Did that mean it was working?

"Why did you double the budget?"

"What?" That wasn't the question he had been expecting, and his response came out as more of a yelp than anything.

Cassie's lips twitched into the hint of a smile. "Why did you double the budget? Why put so much of your money into this cause?"

"If not to stalk you, you mean?" Zack mentally kicked himself. Why did he bring up the stalking? She seemed to have forgotten about it, and he had brought it front and center. He charged ahead, hoping to distract her from the topic. "I just wanted to help. This foundation was my parents' pride and joy, and I want to grow it for them. Plus, it really ticked off my board. They wanted to cut funds to the foundation, so I doubled them instead."

"You added millions to a charity budget as an act of rebellion?"

"Maybe?"

Cassie laughed, and Zack slumped into his chair in relief, losing the professional businessman posture he had been working so hard to maintain. The tension of the conversation had finally broken, and Cassie relaxed as well. She leaned forward with her elbows on the table and studied Zack's face. He swallowed and straightened back up, feeling like a student caught cheating. But he wasn't cheating. He was trying to make things right.

"I may have misjudged you," Cassie said finally.

Zack stayed silent and waited for her to continue. He was finally making progress. He didn't want to open his big mouth and ruin it.

"Phil told me more about you when he called to set up this meeting," Cassie said. "I'm sorry about your parents. I think they would be proud that you want to honor their memory by helping people."

Zack's throat was swollen with emotion, so he barely managed to choke out, "Thanks."

"But that doesn't give you an excuse to act like a jerk and disregard other people's feelings," Cassie continued. "Phil also mentioned some kind of app as an explanation for your behavior, but technology isn't a valid excuse either. I hate when people use technology as a crutch. You should be able to function without it."

Damn luddites. Zack sat up straighter and forgot about his plan to keep his mouth shut. "You say that, but would your job be possible without technology? Would you be able to save as many lives? You use technology every day. It's part of your life whether you like it or not!"

Yelling at your lady is not the way to win her heart. Consider the following instead:

- *chocolate*
- *flowers*
- *apology*

"Sorry," Zack muttered.

He waited for Cassie to storm away, but she didn't. Instead, she leaned forward, looking interested. "So, you think the extra money should go to additional technology? Is that a requirement for hospitals to accept funding?"

"Of course not, but even you have to admit it would be better than spending the money on nightmare fuel murals. In fact, maybe redecorating would be a good place to start. How are kids supposed to feel better when they're surrounded by creepy caterpillars?"

She grinned. "I can't say I love working in a place decorated like a knockoff *Alice in Wonderland* theme park. Did you have something in mind?"

"Video games," Zack said without thinking. "We could decorate some of the wings to make it look like they're from video games. Maybe we could put gaming consoles in the rooms so the kids have something to do while they recover."

Cassie raised an eyebrow.

"It's a good idea," Zack insisted. "They would love it."

"Maybe. Do you have any other good ideas?"

Zack couldn't tell if she was mocking him or genuinely interested. He swallowed his enthusiasm for the video game idea and tried to recover his professional demeanor. "We need a system for evaluating what new equipment will have the biggest impact. We can't just go buying random things."

Cassie raised her other eyebrow. "And do you have a suggestion for how to make these evaluations?"

"Yeah, actually, I do."

Zack pulled his computer from the leather briefcase Giacomo had insisted was a perfect accessory for the suit and pulled up the spreadsheet he had made for Ashley. She had already filled in stats for some of the equipment she thought might benefit the hospital Amber frequented and added a few notes about the results from Zack's calculations. Zack's heart ached as he stared at it and remembered all their lunch dates at the picnic table outside Gord's.

He had been an idiot.

"Is something wrong?" Cassie's voice was still business-like but had softened a little.

"Here," Zack said, spinning the computer around so she could see. "It's a spreadsheet to calculate the potential value of new equipment in your hospital. There are an overwhelming amount of options and constant updates. The spreadsheet helps you sort the data and see what would make the most difference with your current lineup."

Cassie's eyes flickered over the computer screen, and she remained silent. Zack alternated between watching her and nervously playing with his cufflinks. They were one part of the outfit he actually liked. Somehow, Giacomo had found silver cufflinks stamped with the Star Fury logo. The designer had promised to look for some ties to match Zack's interest as well, and Zack had to admit he was intrigued.

"This is good," Cassie finally said. "This is very good. You have a surprising talent for hospital management." She pushed the computer back to Zack, a newfound respect in her eyes.

He shook his head. "It wasn't just me. My, um, friend did most of the work. She's working on a master's in Medical Management. Actually, I think she'd be perfect to work for the foundation."

If Cassie noticed how he stumbled over the word "friend," she didn't comment.

"If we grow this foundation as much as you want to, I will need additional staff," Cassie admitted. "Do you think she'd be interested in a job?"

"Yeah," Zack said. "I think she might be."

"Excellent. Have her send her resume over, and I'll take a look at it."

"Wait, does this mean you'll take the position?"

"There are still some details we need to work out, but I'm willing to consider it."

"Awesome!" Zack reached across the table for a high five, then pulled his hand back as he realized his mistake.

Cassie laughed. "I look forward to working with you, Mr. Moore."

"And I look forward to working with you, Dr. Jones."

Success!
Based on our scan of her facial expression and voice tone, your lady is feeling better. Now seal the deal and ask her out!

Social Status Bonus: +60 minutes of unrestricted electronic time for making her feel better.

For once, Zack agreed with DaEvo. This felt like a victory. He breathed in through his nose, taking in the over-recycled air of the hospital, the way it was a little too sterile. For once, it didn't send him spiraling back. In fact, it smelled even... well. No. It still smelled bland.

Cassie pushed her chair back a little. "Was there anything else you wanted to discuss in person?"

Zack swallowed, wondering how far he should push his luck. He decided to push it a little further. "Actually, there is. Your blog posts accusing me of stalking have damaged my reputation. Would you be willing to take them down?"

Cassie laughed. "Yes, that seems fair. Although it's a shame. Those are the most popular posts on my blog."

Zack winced. "I believe it."

They stood and shook hands again. DaEvo chimed bonus points for the long conversation and more physical contact.

Zack waited until Dr. Jones left the cafeteria before he let out a victory cry. The other diners gave him bemused looks as he hurried out to the hallway. He voice-messaged Phil the good news as he walked. Then he sent a message to Zoe for good measure. Now that Dr. Jones was on board, they could talk further about how their charities could work together.

Zack checked the time on his OptiGlasses. He hadn't been sure how long this meeting would go, so he wasn't scheduled to train until this afternoon.

And he knew exactly how he wanted to spend the extra time.

He called a ride and gave the app the address to Gord's.

On the way back to Gord's, DaEvo finally chimed.

Reputation Change!
Reputation +4.3

Sweet. He knew that in time, he'd regain more of his lost reputation as links to the now deleted blog posts were broken and more time passed. Zack grinned and crossed his fingers.

He had successfully managed one apology today. Maybe he could keep the streak going. Besides, he needed to ask for Ashley's resume.

Chapter Fifty-One

GORD'S WAS DECKED out with promotional posters advertising both local events and the special Star Fury booth they would have at the Vegas convention. Zack ignored them, more concerned about the way a few of the gamers were staring at him. He wondered if Ashley had told them what happened, then he realized they were probably staring because of his suit. It looked almost as out of place in the gaming center as the WesterNeon outfit had.

Maybe he should have changed first.

Before Zack could decide what to do about that, Ashley came out of a private gaming room with an empty tray. Her eyes widened with recognition when she saw Zack. Then they narrowed, and she turned away from him and hurried to the counter.

Zack swallowed. No turning back now.

He walked slowly to the counter and did his best to smile. It was difficult.

Ashley's expression was a mixture of anger and professional distance. When she smiled at him, it was more of a sneer that made Zack want to run for cover. "How may I help you?"

DaEvo chimed and started the conversation timer. It seemed that DaEvo did not have an ex-relationship side quest or relationship milestone since it was treating her like any other potential love interest.

Ashley's voice was overly bright and cheerful with a sharp edge that cut straight through Zack's soul. That wasn't what he wanted. He hated seeing her this upset.

"Hey." He tried to sound casual and failed miserably.

Ashley continued to glare. "We have a few private rooms available right now if you'd like one, or I can get you a console in the common room."

"Ashley—"

"And we have new items on our menu if you're hungry. Or thirsty. I highly recommend the caramel latte."

An advertisement for the new drinks appeared on Zack's Opti-Glasses, and he swiped it away. "I'm not here for a damn latte."

"Then why are you here?" Ashley's tone was still civil, but her eyes flashed with fury.

DaEvo chimed.

Your lady is upset. Try the following to make her feel better:

- *Flowers*
- *Chocolate*
- *Apology*

Maybe he should have brought flowers. Or chocolate. Or diamonds. Or his head on a platter, from the way she spoke.

Well, he had come with a job offer. That didn't seem quite right either, but it was what he had.

"I'm sorry," he said. "I came to say I'm sorry."

Ashley crossed her arms. "We also have a new green tea latte if that's more your style. It will go great with that pretentious suit."

"I hurt you, and I never meant to do that," Zack pushed on, not entirely certain what else he could do.

She laughed, and the sound sent a shiver down Zack's spine. DaEvo chimed.

{*!---Bonus: make her laugh +($_social_stat_value) minutes*
I: this is just wrong. We need to adjust the valuation of laughter.
Z: You think? I told you the social cue variation matrix is only at 84%
fidelity right now. We need more time to deal with edge cases like this.
B: You said that three updates ago.
Q: Can we please close the notations—Z's seeing this.
I: What...?" ----}

"So you never meant to cheat on me with a supermodel? Or to stalk that poor doctor? Those things happened completely by accident and were out of your control?"

"Wait, what?"

"Oh, didn't you know? You're famous. And rich. That means people write about you and post it on the internet."

"You've been reading about me?"

In spite of Giacomo's assurances that the suit was lightweight and breathable, Zack was sweating. This was bad. Really bad.

"Your girlfriend Kayla has a lot to say. As does Doctor Jones."

Zack swore. The blog posts. Ashley had read the blog posts. "I didn't—"

"Didn't what? Didn't take Kayla out for lavish dinners while you brought me takeout?"

"No. I mean, yes, but... I—"

"You didn't buy her diamond jewelry while you brought me a paper fan?"

"I thought you—"

"And you didn't stalk another woman while dating both of us? You're a psychopath, Zack."

"I wasn't stalking her!" Zack didn't mean to yell, but that accusation really was unfair. He hadn't been stalking Cassie. Even she had finally admitted it and taken down the blog posts. But it looked as though the damage was already done.

Their conversation was loud enough that the gamers in the room took notice. Some of them had removed their headsets and were listening.

DaEvo chimed.

Reputation: -0.1

"I wasn't stalking her," Zack said, lowering his voice to a frantic whisper. "That was a misunderstanding because of the app. She's taken the posts down now. Check her website. You'll see."

"And I suppose all those events with KayTay were misunderstandings as well? You just happened to run into her at the club while wearing matching outfits?"

Before Zack could protest that they had never worn matching outfits, Ashley pointed at a poster across the room. Zack followed her gaze, confused by the change in topic but hoping it meant that his pleading was working and Ashley was coming around.

He swore when he saw the poster. It was a full spread of Kayla Taylor dressed in a sexy version of the Star Fury Corsair uniform. She leaned toward the camera, giving a generous view of her cleavage as she winked playfully.

Crap.

"I have to stare at her stupid face every day," Ashley said. "Every. Day. Is that why you dated her? Did the app give you extra points or something because she was working for Star Fury?"

Zack dragged his gaze away from the poster. "I didn't know about that. I had no idea she was modeling for Star Fury. I just needed points for DaEvo, and Kayla was high level. You have to believe me."

"Why? Why should I believe a single word you say?" She was yelling again.

More gamers took off their headsets to watch the fireworks.

"Because I'm sorry. Because I never meant to hurt you. Because I like you. A lot."

"Oh, very good. Why don't you add a few more of the standard phrases? You'll never do it again. It was all a big misunderstanding. You're not that kind of guy, but you got carried away and didn't think it through."

"How did you—"

"You think every cheater in the history of dating hasn't tried the same lines?" she said. "You think you're clever or special because

459

you're saying these things and wearing a nice suit? You think you get a pass just because you're rich and run a charity?"

"I—"

"Because you don't."

"It was the app!" Zack said. "I didn't have a choice."

"Is this guy bothering you, Ashley?"

Zack looked up and found himself face to face with Steve. A few of his Armada scum buddies stood behind him scowling.

"We're just talking," Zack said.

"I think maybe you're done talking," Steve said. He wasn't a large man, but he puffed out his chest and leaned toward Zack in a way that suggested he was hoping for a fight.

"I don't need your help," Ashley said. "I can handle this on my own."

"Of course you can," a female gamer said, sliding between Zack and Ashley and pushing Zack away from the counter, "but you don't have to."

DaEvo flashed a Reputation warning as more gamers gathered around. He looked from them to Ashley with dismay. How had his apology attempt gone so horribly wrong? How had he ended up the bad guy while Steve was the hero? Zack swallowed and took another step back.

"I'm sorry," Zack said, painfully aware of how little those words accomplished. "I never meant to hurt you, and I'm sorry."

The other gamers scoffed, but Ashley's face remained stoic. She didn't look hurt or angry anymore. She just looked done. Not sure what else to do, Zack turned and left.

DaEvo chimed.

__Quest Complete! You spoke with a woman for 5:47!__
__You have earned non-essential electronics and__
__internet privileges!__
Reward, easy difficulty—+15
Bonus Achieved – Make her laugh. +20 Minutes Use Time
{!--- Z RelDeb Logged---!}

Zack swore. The app was worthless. He was halfway home before he realized he had forgotten to tell Ashley about Doctor Jones's job offer. He briefly considered going back but dismissed the idea. Ashley wasn't in the frame of mind to listen to anything he had to say.

But the job would be a good opportunity for her. He didn't want his mistakes to ruin her future any more than they already had.

He opened his messaging app and sent a quick message to Phil.

Zack: Worked out the details with Dr. Jones, and she's agreed to work with the trust. She's interested in interviewing this person as a possible assistant. Maybe you could set something up?

He followed up with Ashley's contact information, then settled into his seat for the rest of the ride. It was almost time for his training session, then they had the final qualifier round. Maybe that would help take his mind off Ashley.

He doubted it would, but what other choice did he have? He couldn't just shut away the world. He had responsibilities.

Chapter Fifty-Two

ZACK SNARLED, booting his ship into a spin and turn, bringing his lasers in-line with the pursuing ship. His opponent was an interceptor like Faz, which meant great speed, great maneuverability but lousy shields. Zack had to feint and let his opponent get in close. After two other opponents, his rear shields were burnt out and his ship itself was on its last legs.

Finger depressed and his main laser fired. Zack grinned. The lock-on was perfect, burning through shields and damaging his opponent's weapon systems. Unfortunately, that spin had killed Zack's forward momentum and the missiles he'd been dodging caught up.

Shields flared and whited out, his ship destroyed. He sighed, leaning back as Star Fury logged him out, leaving him to stare at the planet and stars flying past.

"Right on! This is the Zack we've been missing," Faz crowed.

"Focus! We don't need another Greg," Jenny said.

"Hey! I told you, my joystick froze up," Greg complained.

Zack made a face, remembering how Greg had been doing okay as the first player. And then, he'd suddenly stopped dodging for a few long seconds. Long enough for his opponent to tear through his shields and kill his engines. That'd left them one down.

Zack said, "Don't worry, I got you."

Luckily, Zack grinned viciously, he'd pulled it off. Even if the action was all bits and photons, the thrill of tearing apart his opponents had been everything he'd needed after his disastrous conversation with Ashley. For a few minutes, during the rounds, he'd been able to stop talking and just focus.

"I know, I know, I got this." Faz's ship hyperjumped in and the team shut up, not wanting to distract the man.

Zack knew some other teams cheated, using the secondary views to feed information to the player fighting. It was against the rules and a few stupider teams had already been caught. They'd never tried it, of course, because during the actual tournament, no cheating was allowed.

Anyway, they didn't need it.

Faz went in fast, afterburning to close the distance before his opponent could escape. Like a coward, the other ship had turned tail and fled while using repair drones to try to fix what he could. It wouldn't be enough, but it was the smart play.

Unfortunately for him, he didn't realize that Faz had switched over to a series of long-range missiles with boosters. All that running just gave Faz more opportunities to hammer away at him.

The entire battle was rather lackluster in that sense. By the time the interceptor had figured out what was going on, it was too late. Missiles hammered and dropped his shields, armor was ripped apart, and once they closed, the dogfight hadn't lasted long at all.

Zack grinned as Faz came out of his battle with only a mild amount of damage. "Nice! One last opponent and we'll be in."

"So damn sweet, man." Greg crowed.

"Good job," Jenny said. "But don't get distracted just yet."

"I won't, I won't..." Faz said, already doing pirouettes and spins through the void as he waited.

"Oh no..." Jenny whispered as Faz's ship stopped, explosions rippling across the lightly shielded ship. "Those damn drones..."

Zack could only nod. Faz had gotten too confident, darting in and out, playing with his opponent more than trying to actually win. He'd done damage of course, but he'd lacked that killing edge, the need to keep driving in. And carefully positioned stealthed drones had caught him.

"Come on, come on, come on," Zack chanted. He'd turned off the mic rather than distract Faz.

Faz's interceptor twisted and turned, afterburners kicking in. He dodged the third wave of attacks, leaving him free to harass his opponent. But it wasn't enough, not with his engines damaged, not with his shields at a fraction of their strength. He kept fighting, chipping away at his opponent, forcing him to use up missiles and drones. But it wasn't enough.

"Sorry, guys, I should have done better," Faz said, dejected as he was kicked back into the team chat, his ship destroyed.

The tournament chat scrolled, backseat pilots all harassing Faz. Zack's fingers itched, wanting to rebut them. Get into it, call them all losers who had no chance of getting as far as them. But he held back.

Not the right time.

"It's fine. Jenny can do it," Zack said. "Right?"

"I don't like the doubt in your voice there," Jenny said. But she was already being hyperjumped in, so the rest of the team only offered her short recommendations.

Zack bit his lip, hoping she could pull it off. The other opponent was the worst kind for her—a heavy fighter with big shields and space enough for a ton of shields and missiles. He'd used both, along with the drones he'd secreted, to take out Faz. Jenny, with her drones, was used to wearing down her opponents. Not taking them out in a direct fight.

Zack leaned forward, his hands clenching and releasing. He couldn't do anything but feel helpless. Kind of like how it was with him and Ashley. Everything was in someone else's hands and all he could do was sit back and wait.

Over the voice channel, he heard Jenny's fingers flying as she launched drone after drone. She'd taken to running immediately, moving away from her opponent. It was her only chance to lay out a minefield to grind down her opponent while her combat drones filled the space in between. The balance of mining drones and webbers and combat drones to do damage would matter.

Long minutes passed. In the chat, Zack saw calls for her to stop running, to make things more interesting. Viewership numbers dropped, everyone bored with what they were seeing. This wasn't an exciting dogfight but a game of chess as her opponent bulled through minefields and had his shields chipped away, while Jenny dodged attacks.

"Ignore them, you got this," Greg muttered over their comm channel.

"The chat idiots? Of course she's ignoring them," Faz said. "She's got this."

"Both of you, shut up!" Jenny snapped, spinning her plane in another tight spiral dodge. She snarled as her shields dipped when a trio of missiles tore away her defenses and lasers melted her armor.

"Come on…" Zack muttered, drumming his fingers then clenching them. He twisted his chair too, anything to bleed off the tension. It wasn't enough of course, but it was all he could do.

Wait.

Drone after drone shut down, high-powered lasers stabbing out as EMP shocks took out her drones. She spun, drawing the opponent into the thickest part of her minefield.

Zack's eyes darted across the screen, then he grinned… "Oh, you evil woman…"

Only to watch her reenact her humiliating drubbing of Zack as she engaged her drones and sent them all spiraling into her opponent on a kamikaze course. Just as Zack had done, her opponent tried to dodge, but he was slow and cumbersome, trapped in the center. Space lit up as her self-destructing drones took down shields, armor, and finally, her opponent.

"YES!" Faz screamed.

Zack was surprised he was echoing the man, Greg also

screaming a wordless yelp of joy. After they'd congratulated Jenny, they fell silent—except for Faz's crowing.

"We're in! We're in for sure!" Faz said. "I just checked; the other team lost. We've got our spot!"

That set off another set of screams and shouts as the team celebrated the end of a long road. And the start of a new one as they headed to Vegas.

Zack shouted along with them, but he couldn't help but feel as though he was missing something without anyone else to celebrate it with.

Chapter Fifty-Three

"THIS PLACE IS AWESOME!"

Faz ran around their Las Vegas suite. His long, lanky frame was dressed in a wrinkled T-shirt and jeans, a sharp contrast to the immaculate turban. He looked everywhere, opening drawers and poking his head into bedroom doors like a hamster checking out a new tunnel system.

Zack winced at the thought of hamsters, feeling a little guilty. He'd dropped off Veobos at the pet sitting service again before he left, and Tina had once again given her speech about how much the hamster missed him when he was gone. Zack seriously doubted that. He didn't exactly spend a ton of time with the hamster. Maybe he should fix that. Take him on walks or whatever you did with hamsters. At least buy him a new wheel.

Well, he was in Vegas for the next week. The hamster would have to wait. And waiting in the pet sitting service wasn't exactly a hardship. Tina had sent Zack videos of Veobos playing in the hamster habitat, which was a full room desert oasis complete with levels of tunnels that stretched up to the ceiling. It was hamster luxury at its finest, and Veobos seemed to be enjoying it.

"It's epic," Greg agreed. The portly gamer was a little more subtle in his admiration for the suite, but not by much. Like Zack, he was dressed in a limited edition Star Fury Corsair T-shirt and jeans, though Greg's looked to have grown one size too small.

Zack smiled at Greg's cautious optimism, basking in his friends' happiness. It wasn't the penthouse, but it was one of the larger suites located at the top of the hotel, with multiple rooms and floor-to-ceiling windows as well as a balcony that stretched all around the suite. The windows looked out over the glowing Strip beckoning them to pay a visit.

This was much better than buying Kayla diamond bracelets. And about as expensive.

"There's a pool!" Faz said, yelling from the expansive balcony.

"Really?" Jenny said.

She had been sitting on one of the many gold couches and playing it cool, but the mention of a private pool made her scamper out to join Faz. The short woman, dressed in a pretty cream blouse and black slacks, had claimed her room immediately before sitting on the couch in the living room and perusing the convention materials they'd been given upon checking in. Now she was outside, bouncing around the pool and muttering about swimsuits. Meanwhile, Greg found a grand piano at the other end of the suite and played a lyrical version of the Star Fury theme.

"I didn't know you played piano," Zack said.

Greg shrugged.

"Hey, I know how to play piano!" Faz said, returning from admiring the hotel's "public" pools below. He joined Greg at the bench and played a very bad rendition of "Chopsticks."

Jenny laughed. "This place is awesome. Thanks for setting this up, Zack."

DaEvo chimed and began the conversation timer. It had been doing that ever since Jenny arrived in the hotel lobby, and it kept prompting him to ask her out and complete Relationship Milestones. Zack didn't know how to correct DaEvo and tell it that Jenny was just a friend, and he wasn't sure he should. Thanks to the software's lack of perception, he was banking a lot of game time. He had plenty for the tournament and beyond.

"Yeah, you're welcome," Zack said. "It's the least I can do after ditching you guys so often."

"You couldn't help it," Greg called from the piano, where he was adding a lively accompaniment to Faz's version of "Chopsticks."

"Yeah, you were looking for love!" Faz added, only a trace of sarcasm in his voice. "I still want to sign up for that app once it goes public. If it can set you up with KayTay, who knows what it could do for me?"

"Believe me, you don't," Zack said.

"No, he really does," Greg said. "He won't stop talking about it. I wouldn't mind trying it out myself. KayTay—"

"All right, enough girl talk," Jenny said. "Let's go check out the vendor booths!"

"You want to leave?" Faz said. "We just got here. I never want to leave this room again!"

"Greg, didn't you want to see if they had the 1:125th scale rendition of the Marauder v7.2 at the booths?" Jenny said. "We won't have time tomorrow once the competition starts."

"Right," Greg said, running his hands over the piano keys. "Yeah, let's go. We can hang out here tonight."

"Fine," Faz said, throwing his hands in the air. He spun around on the piano bench, tucking in his feet as he did

Zack laughed and slipped his VIP badge over his head as the group walked down the hall and into the elevator. He was glad they were having a good time. For that matter, he was having a good time. All their hard work was paying off. Their last few practice sessions had gone perfectly, and DaEvo was finally under control. Yes, it would likely prompt him to work out in the hotel gym in the morning, and he would definitely need to comply with that so Phil had no reason to complain when he got the bill for the suite, but other than that, everything was perfect.

Well, almost everything. Zack couldn't shake the lingering ache in his chest from Ashley's rejection. He shook it away and laughed with everyone else at some joke Faz had made. Zack didn't need a girlfriend. He needed to forget about that mess and focus on the tournament.

The elevator doors opened, and the team hurried to the ballroom that housed the Star Fury convention displays. The entire tournament was being combined with the annual convention, so the first day was entirely competition free. But from tomorrow onward, they'd have to fight to keep their spot.

In the meantime, the convention was running its usual seminars, autograph sessions, and vendor halls to keep the public happy. Of course, the schedule was light the first day, with only a few boring seminars, so as to give everyone a chance to settle in. The big events were always held on the weekend, when things like new ship announcements, new factions, or a new solar system showed up.

As they joined the flow into the convention hall, Zack craned his neck and looked around, flashing his VIP badge as they scooted down the special VIP line before they entered the main hall. Judging by the crowded room, lots of people had the same idea and intended to go shopping now.

With a determined expression, Greg guided the group toward one of the official merchandise booths. Worming their way through the crowd, they reached the booth and Zack hurried inside, eager to see what new merch was available.

And found himself face to face with a life-sized cardboard cutout of Kayla in the Corsair uniform.

Crap.

Zack froze as he stared at his ex in all her glossy glory.

"She's hot, right?" the store clerk said. "They definitely picked a good replacement for the last model. She's doing a signing tomorrow. Buy that, and you could get her to sign it for you."

"She's here?" Zack's voice rose a few octaves in alarm.

The clerk laughed. "Tomorrow."

Damn. This was bad. So much for his strategy to forget about his love life.

Zack backed away from the cardboard cutout and looked for his teammates. Kayla was everywhere. Posters. Mugs. Keychains.

"She's the new face of the Corsairs," Jenny said. Zack jumped at the sound of her voice, and Jenny laughed. "Of course, there's still plenty of Zoe Cross merchandise over on the Armada side."

Greg and Faz appeared, their arms overflowing with purchases. Thankfully, being VIPs guests, they all had RFID-coded badges that could deduct purchases directly from their accounts rather than making them stand in line like luddites and peons.

"This place is awesome!" Greg said. "I just need to run these things back to the suite, then I want to see the rest."

"I'm sure we can have them delivered," Zack said.

He logged into the hotel's app and ordered a delivery service for their packages. A few moments later, a hotel employee appeared and whisked away their bags.

"Epic," Faz said. "Let's see what else is around."

They worked their way through the room, stopping to check out different booths along the way. Zack was having a great time hanging out with the team. He would be having a better time if DaEvo didn't flash a notification every time Jenny laughed, but that was a minor inconvenience.

"Oh, this one looks interesting," Jenny said.

She pulled the group toward a booth hidden by black curtains with the word StarFashion printed over them. They ducked into the curtains and found themselves in a sort of tent decorated with minimal black and white accents. High-end clothing with silhouettes reminiscent of the Star Fury uniforms hung around the tent. The room was split between men's and women's wear, with distinctive lines that stood out on the shirt, jacket, and trousers combination for the men and the sleek dresses for the women.

The curtains made the booth dark, and it was lit by tiny lights hanging in the ceiling that were probably meant to be stars. Zack blinked in the sudden darkness and stared at the clothes. Something about them seemed familiar.

"Welcome to StarFashion! Innovative clothing for the fashion-conscious gamer. StarFashion is the newest vision of world-renowned designer—"

"David Davidson," Jenny said with disbelief. "You're David Davidson!"

She squealed in excitement as David Davidson appeared from behind a rack of clothes. Zack tried to hide behind a mannequin, but he was too slow.

"Zack?" the designer said. "Imagine meeting you here! Have you come to upgrade your look? Neon is out. Finished. My latest collection is inspired by the cold, empty vacuum of space and the brave pioneers who travel it to search for meaning in the void."

"You know Zack?" Greg asked, looking around in confusion as he tried to figure out what was going on.

David Davidson beamed at him. "Of course! Zack is a dedicated patron of my art. And who are you all?"

Zack introduced Jenny, Greg, and Faz as his Star Fury teammates. Greg and Faz disappeared to the corners of the room to observe the conversation from a safe distance. Jenny examined the clothes, gravitating toward a sleek black dress.

"You don't usually do women's wear," she said.

"Ah, you know my work! I usually prefer menswear, but ladies are some of the foremost pioneers in the world of Star Fury, and I couldn't bear to leave them out of my new fashion universe. These clothes are functional as well as fashionable. For example, this dress has hidden pockets to carry portable gaming consoles. The pockets provide wireless charging and are lined with shock absorbent material to protect your devices. The men's jackets have the same."

"Really?" Faz inspected the jacket, intrigued in spite of himself. He sputtered when he saw the price tag. "Holy smokes! Is this really the price?"

Greg hurried over to join him. Before they could get too worked up about the cost, the curtains parted and let in a beam of light that temporarily blinded the group.

"David! Is my dress ready yet? I'm due on set in an hour."

Zack winced, recognizing the voice before his eyes cleared enough for him to see the speaker.

"Kayla Taylor," Faz whispered in disbelief. "It's KayTay."

Chapter Fifty-Four

"HELLO, ZACK."

Kayla's voice was icy, and her eyes were even colder. She ignored Greg and Faz, who were gaping at her over a display shelf.

DaEvo chimed.

Relationship Quest Update!

Due to previous incidents, you must select your conversation partners at the same time. Setting up such conversation and relationship targets will then carry forth for all interactions.

Further confirmation once your first Relationship Milestone (that is, access to the Lovemeter after the first date) on your relationship goals and status will be required for the proper functioning of DaEvo.

Please choose if you are intending to pursue a relationship with:

- *Jenny Romero*
- *Kayla Taylor*
- *~~Both~~ (Please enter Relationship Settings and answer Ethical Polyamory Questionnaire to unlock this option)*

Note: Kayla Taylor's Lovemeter is currently at zero, and as such, a new relationship must be completed to begin acquiring Relationship Milestones and for you to proceed with the relationship once more.

Zack flicked over confirmation that he was continuing to talk to Jenny, refusing to start the conversation with Kayla. There was no need to go down that path again.

"What are you doing here?" Zack asked. "You aren't supposed to be here till tomorrow."

It wasn't a great question. It wasn't even a good question. But it was all he could think of at the moment.

Kayla's eyes narrowed. "I'm wearing Dave's latest line in my interviews to help promote it. I'm here to pick up my clothes."

"But you're not a gamer," Jenny said. "Aren't these clothes designed specifically for gamers?"

Kayla turned and gave Jenny a head-to-toe look. She wrinkled her nose in mild disgust, and Zack wondered if he should jump in and defend Jenny. She was dressed in loose-fitting slacks and a Star Fury T-shirt. She was also much shorter than Kayla and had to tilt her chin up to meet the model's gaze. Jenny couldn't compare with Kayla's looks, but that wasn't the point. Jenny had a decent personality and life skills other than smiling for a camera.

Jenny gave Kayla an equally disgusted look, and Zack held his tongue. It looked as though Jenny could defend herself, and he wasn't eager to dive into a fight if he didn't have to.

"No, I'm not a gamer," Kayla said. Her tone was frosty and condescending. "That doesn't matter. It's about the fashion, not the features."

Jenny scoffed with equal condescension. "Of course it's about the features. Any designer can make a little black dress. It takes special talent to make a chic dress that also includes wireless charging. Only a gamer will truly appreciate that."

"I appreciate the wireless charging," Kayla said. "It'll be great for my phone."

Jenny laughed and turned to David Davidson. "If you want

gamers to take your clothes seriously, you need gamers to wear them. And you should consider making a more affordable line."

The designer looked taken aback and didn't respond.

Kayla rolled her eyes and turned back to Zack. "Is this your new girlfriend? You really do get around."

"She's my teammate," Zack said, his voice chilly.

"So you're the new face of the Corsairs," Faz said, edging toward Kayla. "I think that's awesome. They definitely made the right choice."

He gave Kayla what was probably supposed to be a sexy look. Greg was close behind him, pushing Zack aside in his eagerness.

Kayla rolled her eyes and stepped to the left to follow Zack as he stumbled to the side. "It's been like this since they made the announcement. I don't know how Zoe has done this for so long. Nerds are so annoying." She gave Zack a pointed glare.

"Hey, you didn't have to date me!" he said. "And you didn't have to take this job."

"I took it for you," Kayla said. "I convinced Zoe to help me get signed on because I thought you'd like it. It's the reason I was traveling so much. I was going to surprise you."

"Oh." Zack couldn't manage to say any more than that. That was actually really cool, and it made him feel like a complete jerk for the way things had worked out.

Kayla gave him a cynical smile. "Oh, don't feel too guilty. It's a good gig. Pays well and has definitely expanded my fan base."

She nodded at Greg and Faz, who were practically drooling while they stared at her. Faz brightened when he realized Kayla was looking at him. Zack couldn't help but groan, since he was sure his teammates could hear every single word she said but didn't seem to care. Then again, creators and models treating nerds like crap and them coming back for more was a thing.

"You know, not all gamers are cheaters," Faz interjected. "Some of us know how to get what we want without using cheat codes."

"Ugh." Kayla grabbed the garment bag David Davidson had set on the counter and hurried out of the tent.

With confusion in his eyes, Faz watched her go. "Huh. I thought that was a pretty good line."

"Yeah, it wasn't," Greg said.

"At least I actually said something. She knows I exist now. It's a start."

"You're both ridiculous," Jenny said huffily. She was still eyeing the black dress. "Let's go."

"I could buy that for you to wear to the ball tomorrow night," Zack said.

"I'm not letting you buy me a twenty-thousand-dollar dress."

"Why not?"

Jenny rolled her eyes and stormed out of the tent.

DaEvo chimed.

Your lady is upset. Try the following to make her feel better:

- *Flowers*
- *Chocolate*
- *Apology*

Zack looked back at the dress, not sure what to do. Jenny wasn't his lady, and she had told him not to buy the dress. Should he get it for her anyway? He looked at Faz and Greg, who shrugged.

"I might be back later," Zack told David.

The designer nodded and waved as they left the booth. Jenny stood outside with her arms crossed. Zack studied her from the corner of his eye, trying to decide if he had made the right decision or not.

"Dude, look!" Greg whispered, grabbing Zack's arm. "Is that Zoe Cross?"

"No way," Faz said, studying the woman across the aisle from them. "That's not how Zoe would dress."

"Maybe she's trying to stay under the radar," Jenny said, also staring.

The woman in question wore jeans and a baggy T-shirt, as well as a Star Fury cap pulled low to hide her face, her hair bundled up beneath the cap. Zack turned to look, and DaEvo chimed.

Zoe Cross (Social Level 80.75)
Physique: 94
Style: 43
Reputation: 95
Occupation: 91

Before Zack could decide what to tell his teammates, Zoe turned and waved. "Hi, Zack."

She smiled and walked toward them as Faz and Greg sputtered.

"No way, you actually know her?"

"I thought you were kidding about that."

When she reached them, Zoe asked, "Is this your team? It's nice to meet you all. I look forward to talking to you more at the interview."

Zack nodded and made the introductions.

"It's nice to meet you," said Jenny, who seemed to be the only member of the team capable of speaking. "I'm looking forward to the interview."

Faz and Greg kept staring.

Unlike Kayla, Zoe was apparently used to that. She ignored them and turned to Zack. "I'm sure you're busy with the tournament, but I'm meeting with a few members of my board tonight to discuss foundation details over dinner. My team has been communicating with Mr. MacComack and Doctor Jones, and I'd like your input on a few things if you have time."

"That's great," Zack said, "but we have orientation—"

His words ended in a grunt as Greg elbowed him in the ribs. Zack turned to glare at his teammate. Greg raised an eyebrow and nodded at Zoe. Faz did the same and mouthed, "Go for it," behind his hand. Zack rolled his eyes. They weren't being subtle at all.

"We don't have anything planned tonight," Jenny said. "I'm sure Zack would love to join you for dinner."

Zoe laughed. "Great. Let me add you to the reservation." She turned away from them and tapped on her phone.

Zack turned on his teammates and whispered, "What the hell, guys?"

"It's Zoe Cross!" Faz and Greg said in unison.

"She's high level, right?" Jenny said. "A date with her will give you a lot of game time. I want to make sure you don't run out and abandon us in the middle of the tournament."

"This isn't a date, and I told you I have plenty of game time left."

"You could make it a date, and I've heard that before. We'll all sleep easier if you have extra game time."

As Zoe returned, they all clamped their mouths shut. "All set. My assistant will send the details to you. See you at six?"

Jenny elbowed Zack, and he nodded.

"Yeah, sure," Zack said, trying to ignore the excitement radiating from his teammates. He wasn't excited about a board meeting, Zoe or not.

Zoe also seemed oblivious to it. She continued on, all business as usual. "Doctor Jones and I reached out to the potential hire you suggested. We agree that building the right team is essential for this to work, and she seems like a great fit."

New hire.

Wait.

"You talked to Ashley?" Zack tried to stay calm, but the words came out as kind of a panicked yelp.

Everyone stared at him.

"You and Cassie talked to Ashley?" he tried again, his voice not quite as frantic, but still far from normal.

"Who's Ashley?" Jenny asked, her voice a bit too casual as she looked from Zack to Zoe, trying to gauge the situation.

Zoe simply smiled. "We spoke with her, and she seems lovely. She had a few job commitments she needed to finish first, but then she's going to work part time for us while she finishes her degree."

"That's great," Zack said.

And he meant it, but that didn't keep the depression out of his voice. If Ashley worked part time at the foundation, she would probably quit Gord's. He would have no way to casually bump into her.

Then again, running into her at the foundation would be easy enough if he started being more hands-on there. He could take over a division and ask to have her put on his team.

He swallowed. Ashley didn't want anything to do with him. She wanted space. And unless he wanted to turn into the massive jerk stalker she thought he was, he had to respect that space and give it to her.

He might never see her again.

Zoe stayed silent as she watched him. Then she turned to Greg and Faz. "Have you all been to the Gord's booth yet?"

They shook their heads, still too starstruck to speak.

"You should go." Zoe looked between the two of them then at Jenny, before repeating, "You should definitely visit the Gord's booth while you're here."

Zack blinked as he realized that for some reason, Jenny was smiling now. He shook his head, waving goodbye to Zoe as she left, and tried to dismiss his thoughts of Ashley.

Chapter Fifty-Five

"So what do you think is so awesome at the Gord's booth?" Greg said.

"Who cares? Zoe Cross personally recommended it to us." Faz said. "Let's go!"

He sped away from the group while Jenny gave Zack a little shove to get his head out of the clouds. Zack sighed and quickened his steps to match his friends' pace. His OptiGlasses chimed with a notification from the conference app, and he read it quickly.

"Whatever it is, we need to see it fast," Zack said. "They're opening the arena for orientation in ten minutes."

"It's open all day, isn't it?" Jenny said.

"Yeah, but somebody told Zoe that I didn't have anything this evening and committed me to meet her for dinner, so we need to get an early slot for orientation."

"Oh, right," Jenny said. "You're welcome."

Zack rolled his eyes.

"Maybe they have a cool giveaway at Gord's," Greg said.

"We'll have to come back if there's a line," Zack said, looking at the clock on his OptiGlasses.

"Sure," Greg said. "Maybe they're giving away Zoe Cross

posters."

"I should have had her sign something," Faz said, smacking his forehead. "I met two models today, and I didn't even have them sign anything."

"Yes, because that's how you win over a woman," Jenny said. "Stare at her and ask her to sign a picture of her own face."

"It could work. Lots of models date and marry fans."

"Name one."

"There are so many. It's hard to pick just one."

"That's because you can't think of any."

They rounded the corner and came to the Gord's booth. Zack searched it for whatever special thing Zoe wanted him to see, but it looked about as he had expected. It was definitely one of the larger booths at the con. They were serving food and drinks and had set up mobile gaming stations for those who wanted to play between sessions at the con and tournament rounds. At each of the four corners of the booth, they'd set up ordering stations. The central area was manned by harried and overworked staff prepping orders.

"Weird," Faz said. "It looks normal."

"Maybe they have some good food or something," Greg said. "We need lunch anyway."

"Two minutes," Zack said. "Whatever you're getting, you have two minutes to get it. At this rate, we'll have to sprint to make it back to the arena."

Then again, maybe sprinting wasn't a bad idea. If DaEvo counted that as his exercise for the day, he wouldn't have to hit the gym later. Of course, he'd have to find enough space to sprint for long enough to satisfy the app. In the press of bodies, that might be a little difficult.

"I'll just get a drink then," Greg said. They'd slipped into line while they were talking, and it didn't take them long at all to get to the front of the line "Hey, can I have some coffee?"

The cashier behind the counter was frantically tapping on his tablet, but he nodded at Greg. "Yeah, just a second."

"We're in a hurry," Zack said.

He looked at the promotional poster of Kayla hanging behind

the register and fought the urge to scowl at it. Whatever Zoe thought he would like here, she was wrong. He just wanted to get to the arena and focus on the reason he was there—competing in Star Fury.

"Hey, Ashley, can you help me out?" the cashier called. "System's down again, and we've got customers."

Zack's heart beat faster. It was a coincidence. It had to be. Surely Ashley wasn't—

But a familiar face topped with auburn curls emerged from behind a display, smoothly depositing the cups of coffee she'd been holding, along with the order slip, for another cashier to hand out. Zack's throat tightened as she walked toward them. He had the sudden urge to turn and run, but his feet wouldn't move.

Ashley looked up with a bright smile, ready to serve her customers. The smile slipped when she saw Zack, but she didn't seem nearly as surprised as he was. "Hey."

"Hey," Zack said back.

She didn't look mad. She wasn't yelling. That was a good sign, wasn't it? She might even look a little happy to see him, but maybe that was wishful thinking. Then again, Ashley was pretty outspoken. If she wanted him to get lost, she would tell him to get lost.

"Hey," Greg said. "I'll take some coffee, and we're in a hurry."

His words broke the invisible tension in the air.

"Right. Just a moment." Ashley took over fiddling with the tablet while she sent the other cashier off to grab more coffees, all the while noting Greg's order on a notepad.

Jenny elbowed Greg in the ribs.

"Ouch! What was that for?"

Jenny cast a significant look from Zack to Ashley, but Greg looked as confused as ever.

DaEvo chimed.

Relationship Quest Update!

Due to previous incidents, you must select your conversation partners at the same time. Setting up such conversation and relationship targets will then carry forth for all interactions.

Further confirmation once your first Relationship Milestone (that is, access to the Lovemeter after the first date) on your relationship goals and status will be required for the proper functioning of DaEvo.

Please choose if you are intending to pursue a relationship with:

- *Jenny Romero*
- *Ashley Barnes*
- *~~Both~~ (Please enter Relationship Settings and answer Ethical Polyamory Questionnaire to unlock this option)*

Note: Ashley Barnes Lovemeter is currently at zero, and as such, a new relationship must be completed to begin acquiring relationship milestones and for you to proceed with the relationship once more.

"Here's your coffee," Ashley said, handing the cup to Greg. "Did you want anything else?"

She looked at Zack as she said it. He swallowed, trying to think of something clever to say. By some miracle, Ashley was in Las Vegas and willing to speak with him. He didn't want to mess this up.

"No thanks, we're good," Faz answered. "Pay for your coffee, Greg. We're going to be late for training."

"Right!" Greg fumbled for his wallet, then remembered he could pay with his VIP card and held it up.

Ashley scowled at her tablet, then shook her head. "Our system is still down, so don't worry about it. This one's on the house."

"Yeah?" Zack said. Then he mentally kicked himself. Why was he being so lame? She hadn't even been talking to him.

"Yeah," Ashley said. "I wouldn't want you to be late for training."

"Thanks so much!" Greg said. "Come on, guys!"

He grabbed Zack's arm and pulled him away. Zack shook loose from Greg's grip and tried to pull himself together. Focus. They needed to hurry to the arena and go through orientation so that he could go on his date with Zoe and get points.

Ashley was there. She hadn't yelled at him.

"Hey, do you think that cashier at Gord's liked me?" Greg said.

"What?" Zack's voice came out as a squeak. Greg didn't seem to notice.

"She was acting kind of strange. Do you think she liked me?"

"Hmm, maybe," Faz said. "She did give you the coffee for free."

"The system was down," Zack said.

"Yeah, sure. 'The system was down,'" Faz said, making air quotes as he spoke. "When have you ever gotten free coffee because some corporation's system didn't work?"

"You all are morons," Jenny said.

"We need to focus," Zack said as they arrived at the arena. "We only get one chance to look this place over."

"Right, sorry," Greg said. "I won't let girls distract me from the goal anymore."

"Who knew there would be so many hot girls at a gaming tournament?" Faz said.

"What am I? A pirate wreck?"

When Faz opened his mouth to answer Jenny, Zack elbowed him in the side. Even he had learnt not to walk into that kind of trap.

Jenny grinned at Zack as Faz snapped his mouth shut, realization coming a little late. "Focus, children. This place will be packed with people tomorrow, and they'll be loud. We need to know where we're going."

"Jenny's right," Zack said. "This isn't the time to be thinking about girls."

They signed in for orientation and followed their guide around the arena as he explained the tournament procedures. Where they would wait, how to enter and exit the stage, and how to log in to the official computers. Jenny took notes of important details, and Faz peppered the guide with questions. Zack studied the spaces, looking for anything that might give their team an advantage.

At least, that's what he tried to do. He wished he could follow his own advice and focus on the tournament, but no matter how hard he tried, he couldn't stop thinking about Ashley.

Chapter Fifty-Six

"THESE WILL HAVE A HIGHER COMBO VALUE," Jenny said.

She held up a pair of dress shoes that looked nearly identical to the ones Zack was wearing. She had convinced him to go shopping for a new outfit for his dinner meeting with Zoe so that he could get as many points as possible, and Zack had reluctantly agreed. He hadn't exactly packed DaEvo-approved date wear for the gaming conference.

"Aren't those the same shoes?" Greg asked.

He and Faz had tagged along and now looked as though they were regretting it.

"Just put them on," Jenny said.

Zack put the shoes on and blinked in surprise as DaEvo chimed and awarded him higher Style points for the combination. "How did you know?"

Jenny shrugged and offered a tie. Zack put it on without questioning her, and DaEvo chimed with even more points. He blinked as he hit the highest he'd gotten without climbing into WesterNeon wear, and he didn't look like a psychedelic cowboy either.

"Nice! I'm Stylish again!"

Jenny smirked as if she could hear the capital letter in his statement. "Have a good time. We're going back to the room to swim."

Zack sighed and paid for his new clothes as his teammates left. He had been looking forward to hanging out with them. They didn't often get to see each other in person. Of course, if they made the pro circuit, they'd get to hang out all the time.

As his ride drove to the address that Zoe's assistant had forwarded, Zack watched the bright lights of Las Vegas from the car window. They ended up at a swanky restaurant, and Zack's palms sweat. It reminded him of his first dinner with Kayla.

At least he wasn't wearing WesterNeon this time, and the hostess let him in without a question. Zack followed a waiter to a private room. He was a little early, but Zoe was already there. She smiled when she saw him and offered the chair next to hers. DaEvo chimed, showing him a list of ways to take their relationship to the next level.

Zack swiped them away. He would take conversation points, but that was it. Even the offer of unlimited game time wasn't going to fool him into entering another relationship, and he didn't think Zoe was interested in dating him. He wasn't sure he was interested in dating her either. Yes, she was amazing, but after everything with Kayla, he wasn't sure that models were his type.

"I'm glad you're early," Zoe said. "I just got an email from the chairman of Star Forward. They're interested in joining our hospital initiative, but we have to present a proposal to them. Their meeting is on the last day of the con, so we'll need to pull that together quickly if we want to get on their agenda."

"Star Forward?"

"You know, Star Fury's charity outreach program."

Zack nodded, although he hadn't known until that moment that Star Fury had a charity outreach program.

Zoe grinned. "Dr. Jones told me about your idea to put gaming consoles in pediatric hospital rooms. I passed that idea on to the chairman, and he's intrigued. I've already assigned a staff member to work on the proposal, but I thought you might like to be involved since this project was your idea."

"Yeah," Zack said. "Yeah, that sounds great!"

The door opened, and Zack turned around to greet the newcomer. He was expecting some stuffy board member in an equally stuffy suit. Instead, he saw Ashley. She had pulled her auburn hair back into a ponytail and wore the same green dress she had worn on their first date. The suit jacket over it made it look more professional, but memories of that night flooded back. Zack knew he was staring, but he couldn't help it.

Ashley stared back, although her expression was more of a glare. Unlike Zack, she managed to keep her mouth shut. She recovered from her surprise first and turned to Zoe.

"I put together the reports you wanted." Ashley paused. "Ma'am."

Zoe's lips quirked at the last, but she said blandly, "Great. You've met Zack, right?"

Ashley nodded and took a seat on the other side of Zoe. Zack looked from one woman to the other. What was happening? Was this some kind of weird setup?

DaEvo chimed.

Relationship Quest Update!

Due to previous incidents, you must select your conversation partners at the same time. Setting up such conversation and relationship targets will then carry forth for all interactions.

Further confirmation once your first Relationship Milestone (that is, access to the Lovemeter after the first date) on your relationship goals and status will be required for the proper functioning of DaEvo.

Please choose if you are intending to pursue a relationship with:

- *Zoe Cross*
- *Ashley Barnes*
- *Both (Please enter Relationship Settings and answer Ethical Polyamory Questionnaire to unlock this option)*

Note: Ashley Barnes Lovemeter is currently at zero, and as such, a new relationship must be completed to begin acquiring relationship milestones and for you to proceed with the relationship once more.

Zack refused to let himself be distracted, choosing to keep the conversation with Zoe. He was there for the conversation points. Nothing more. Ashley had made her views clear, and he wouldn't even take points for the conversation with her. Not again.

Relationship Hint: Pay Attention to Your Date
No one wants to play second fiddle on a date. Make sure to keep your attention on the individual you are on the date with to increase intimacy levels.

Zack blinked. He hadn't realized he was staring at Ashley. To be fair, Ashley was staring back at him. Zoe was either oblivious to the tension or an excellent actress. She typed something on her tablet, and Zack's OptiGlasses chimed with an incoming email.

"I just sent you notes for a proposal Ashley created," Zoe said. "As soon as the rest of the board gets here, I'll have her explain."

Zack pretended to read through the report. He was trying to absorb the information, but his brain wouldn't process it. Not with Ashley sitting right there. He looked past the words on his Opti-Glasses to sneak glances at her.

She seemed focused on her tablet, skimming through the information about Star Forward that Zoe had sent to both of them.

He should say something to her. Break the ice somehow.

Zack gathered his courage and took a deep breath, but the arrival of the rest of the board interrupted him. As he watched the well-dressed strangers file into the room, he was glad that Jenny had convinced him to get professional clothes. He looked like he fit in here.

"Let's get started," Zoe said. "Ashley, why don't you outline your plan?"

Zack turned, glad for an excuse to look at Ashley. She explained the stats spreadsheet, how they would implement it in hospitals supported by the foundation, and a plan to expand the program's reach once they perfected the system.

"Expand?" a board member said.

"Once we've proved the effectiveness of the system, we could give it to other organizations," Ashley said. "Disaster relief charities, for example, could use our system to quickly decide what equipment they need to send to affected areas."

Zack blinked in surprise. He hadn't considered expanding his parents' legacy that far, but it made perfect sense. Ashley's eyes glittered with an excitement he found contagious. Why not expand?

Of course, he could already see the problems. They'd need to adjust the inputs for different kinds of disasters and levels, figure out a way to deal with things like shipping costs and reweigh the spreadsheet for basic needs.

Across the table, one of the board members sniffed. "You really think a spreadsheet can make such complicated analysis?"

"Yes, if we have all the data," Ashley said. "I'm working on a survey to send to each hospital to help us gather information on their stats."

"Stats? These are complex medical institutions, not baseball players."

Ashley's expression was calm, but her cheeks flushed as the board members questioned her. "But we can still assign values to various pieces of equipment, track what kinds of illnesses they treat most often, and use those numbers to determine which equipment will have the greatest impact."

"You're still a student," one of them said, "so it's understandable that you would be a bit naive about how things really work. The real world is far more complicated than a table of numbers."

Ashley's face burned red.

Zoe started to say something, but Zack beat her to it. "Of course it is. But we use accounting tables to work out other financial decisions. So why not assign numbers to key stats and weigh them based off expected patient outcomes and usage rates? It's just another financial decision on what to purchase, when, but based off the space and financial constraints in the hospital." Zack leaned forward. "It's just like optimizing the most efficient build matrix for a Star Fury vessel. You just need to designate your required outcome and the software does everything else. The statistic models will work and be way more efficient than individuals analyzing the data, especially as new models will force you to run the analysis again."

"We'll test everything before we roll it out on a wider scale," Zoe said, "but I think this idea has promise. I wouldn't invest in it if I didn't."

"I've already found a small hospital eager to beta test the program," Ashley said. "I just need to set up the survey and input their answers into the spreadsheet."

"I'll help," Zack said. "I know how to automate that."

Ashley blinked at him, and he realized what he had volunteered to do. He would be working closely with Ashley to prepare the test.

So much for his plan to stay hands-off and keep a professional distance.

"I-I won't be able to start for a few days," he stammered. "I'm competing in the tournament and—"

"I'm working for Gord's the rest of the convention," Ashley said. "And I'm sure I could figure it out if you're busy."

"It will go faster if you two work together," Zoe said.

Ashley stammered a little but couldn't come up with an excuse to get out of it. Zack couldn't think of one either. Of course, he wasn't trying hard. Awkward as it might be, he liked the idea of spending time with Ashley again.

"Yeah," he said. "We can collaborate on it."

Ashley glared at him, then nodded as her expression relaxed a bit.

Zoe moved the meeting on to other business, but Zack ignored the drone of conversation. He was too busy looking at Ashley. She was pretending to be focused on the people speaking, but she kept sneaking glances at him as well.

DaEvo flashed a notification.

Warning! Please Pay Attention to Your Date

No one wants to play second fiddle on a date. Make sure to keep your attention on the individual you are on the date with to increase intimacy levels.

Relationship Warning!

You are currently not interacting with your date Zoe Cross and conversation levels are lagging.
Would you like to continue your relationship with Zoe Cross?

Zack read the notification a few times before agreeing to continue his current conversation quest. It made the most sense. Zoe was higher level and he'd promised Ashley he wouldn't force the issue with her. This was entirely business.

So why couldn't he take his eyes off Ashley?

Chapter Fifty-Seven

Zack wiped away beads of sweat and checked the timer on his OptiGlasses. Five more minutes on the treadmill and he would be done with the fitness quest and able to go back to his room and get ready for the day.

The fitness center door opened, and his already fast heartbeat skyrocketed when Kayla walked in.

Detected increased heart rate to a dangerous level.

Scanning status.

Accelerated stress...

Please assume a reclined position and breathe deeply to ease stress levels.

Kayla gave Zack a terse nod before jogging on an elliptical across the room. She put in headphones and kept her eyes straight ahead, ignoring him as he stumbled off the treadmill and completed the round of stretches DaEvo recommended as a cooldown.

He forced himself to stay calm and walk slowly as he left the fitness center, but he broke into a sprint as soon as the door closed. He rounded a corner and collided with Jenny.

"Watch where you're—oh, hey, Zack. Gross, you're sweaty." She wiped at the damp patch of sweat that had transferred onto her T-shirt when they collided.

DaEvo chimed.

Warning! Low Hygiene Levels
Consider taking a shower and changing into a clean pair of clothes before pursuing relationship quests.

"Sorry. I have to work out to keep game time."

DaEvo chimed points for the apology and once again encouraged Zack to ask Jenny on a date. He really wished it would stop doing that. He was almost tempted to set up a bug report.

Almost.

"I'll have to go change now." She turned and walked back with him toward their suite.

"Where are you going anyway?" Zack asked. "I didn't expect anyone else to be up so early."

Jenny shrugged. "I thought I'd beat the crowds and check out the booths first thing in the morning."

"Aren't the booths closed?" Zack frowned. He was certain they weren't open this early.

"VIP access, remember?"

Zack nodded. "Oh, right. Sorry. Still, we saw the vendor hall yesterday."

"And I want to see them again."

She quickened her pace to walk ahead of him, and DaEvo chimed.

Your lady is upset. Try the following to make her feel better:

- *Flowers*
- *Chocolate*
- *A Gift*

- *Apology*

Why was she upset? DaEvo even made friendship confusing. Zack looked at the list of suggested ways to make her feel better.

Buy her a gift.

"You sure you don't want that dress for the dance tonight?"

"I have a dress."

They reached their suite, and Jenny unlocked the door with her ID card. She ducked into her room and emerged in a fresh T-shirt before Zack had time to process a reply.

"I could come with you," he said. "Just in case you change your mind."

Jenny wrinkled her nose. "I'm in a hurry, and you need a shower. See you at breakfast!"

She waved and hurried out of the room. The door slammed behind her, and Greg peeked out from his room, looking confused.

"Is it time to get up already? What's going on?"

"Jenny—" Zack started.

"Forget it. I'm going back to bed."

Zack took a shower and put on a T-shirt and jeans. He frowned at the low Style stats they gave him and swapped the T-shirt out for the button-up shirt he had worn the previous evening. That earned him more points and might help if—

If what, exactly? He was gaming today. That was all. He would not let that app get into his head.

Rather, it already had, and he needed to kick it out!

He pulled off the button-up shirt and put the T-shirt back on. Then he went to the living room and played Star Fury until Faz and Greg got up for breakfast.

Zack: *Jenny, we're heading to breakfast. You coming?*

Jenny: *Meet you there.*

"Where did she go?" Greg asked.

He was still rubbing sleep from his eyes, as was Faz. Apparently, neither of them were morning people. Zack shrugged and punched in the floor number on the elevator. Thank goodness for coffee and energy drinks. They'd need to be on their game throughout the day.

Jenny had already secured a table at the café and looked very pleased with herself.

"Why are you in such a good mood so early?" Greg mumbled.

"Shut up and drink your coffee," she said. "We need to focus on the tournament."

Zack was also curious, but he resisted the urge to ask. Whatever Jenny was so happy about, it could wait.

"Right," Zack said. "Let's go over our strategy."

———

The actual tournament arena consisted of a giant convention hall. Rather than split the teams via Armada or Corsair, the teams had been randomly located at their own tables, where each team sat in a row next to one another. Tall, movable sound barriers blocked the sight and sound of other competing teams, while each table was provided the same CPU and monitor set up. That helped equalize the playing field and, of course, allowed the sponsors to showcase their branding.

The only things the teams were allowed to bring were their own keyboards, joysticks, and mouses. Of course, the majority of players also carried a bag they intended to slip the sponsored gear into, since that was one of the side benefits of making it to the tournament.

"Damn, is this the X-315 Razr mouse?" Greg said, poking the angular mouse with its multiple buttons. "They haven't even released it yet."

"Don't you dare think about using it," Jenny warned Greg. "We don't need you slipping up because you forgot what your hotkeys are."

"He's using it!" Greg pointed at Zack who was setting up two seats over.

"Actually, that one's mine," Zack admitted guiltily. "I got a production copy about six months ago."

"Rich boy," Faz said, elbowing Zack in the side as he finished setting up on the end opposite Greg. "Couldn't have bought one for us?"

"Uhhh..." Zack didn't know what to say. It had been a promotional offer they'd made to him since he was in their VIP program, having automatically upgraded every time they released a new version.

"Whatever. Stop teasing him. Focus!" Jenny said.

"Right. Sorry!" the boys said in unison.

Zack finished plugging in his gear, setting the sponsored gifts aside, and began the process of ensuring all his hotkeys were set up. While he did so, he spoke to his team. "Now, remember, this is a double elimination tournament. With twenty-four teams to play against, there's a maximum of forty-seven games we'll be playing, a minimum of forty-six over the next four days."

"Only if we manage to not lose!" Faz said brightly.

"Stop raising flags, or I'll kill you," Greg said.

"Forty-six if we want to win. They've scheduled a minimum of fourteen rounds each day except the final day. Each round goes for a maximum of forty-five minutes. Each round will consist of two portions—the individual match portion and the team match. Any combat not finished in the allocated time will be resolved based by survivors then damage. Points are given for each surviving member, so the more who survive, the better." Zack looked around, seeing his friends nod.

They offered Zack tight smiles, even though they knew all this.

Catching sight of an incoming official, Zack rushed on. "This is a marathon, not a sprint. Play sharp, play smart, and make sure to hydrate well."

"We got this."

Chapter Fifty-Eight

THEY'D STARTED OUT WELL, winning their first round and being put in the upper—winner's—bracket. Their second battle, after the fifteen-minute break, had become a pure slugfest, broken up only by the last-minute suicidal use of a hyperbomb by one of the enemies. Unfortunately, they hadn't expected Jenny to web their entire team with momentum arresters, resulting in the destruction of everyone but her ship. After that, in the individual matches, Zack's team had managed to eke out a two-for-four win, leaving them the bare winner of that encounter.

Now it was their third battle, and the team was facing another all-Corsair team. The individual fights had gone their way, with only Zack losing in a bad matchup to a heavy missile boat that'd ripped his ship apart before he could close.

Now, in the team match, Zack twisted his head from side-to-side as he scanned the three-monitor set-up they'd been given, searching for their enemies.

"Anyone have eyes?" Zack said.

"Nothing," Faz said.

"Nada," Greg chimed in.

"Working on it." Jenny's tongue half-stuck out of her mouth as she furiously tapped at her keyboard, adjusting the placement of her sensor drones and their settings.

"Damn stealth players," Faz growled.

Unlike the usual set up, the opposing team had decided to heavily invest in stealth systems, opting to use hit-and-run techniques rather than a stand-up fight.

"We sure these are Corsairs and not Veridians?" Greg said, then thumbed the local space voice chat. "Oy! Are you guys Veridians?"

Silence greeted Greg's pronouncement before a rather disturbing chuckle erupted from their headphones. Zack shivered. Even he let off the occasional laser blast, hoping to get lucky. Of course, he was getting nothing.

"Contact! Mines in sector three down!" Faz said. He was already spinning his ship around, opening fire at the ghost ships that had briefly been highlighted by the explosions. His main laser targeted and fired once, burning through the shielding of the lead ship, making its stealth systems lose coherence.

"Gotcha! Nice one with the mines, Jenny," Greg crowed.

"Fire plan S-4 everyone!" Zack barked. He adjusted his ship's trajectory as he spoke, opening fire.

"You sure?" Jenny called as her fingers flashed over the keyboard, repositioning drones.

"Our fearless leader has spoken!" Faz said.

Lasers, missiles, and artillery shells fired on the revealed ship and all around it. Rather than focus fire on the single revealed ship, the group spread their attacks across the region. With well-practiced ease, they covered the entire sector as each team member took their own quadrant. The attacks splashed against stealthed hulls, revealing their prey.

"That's right, that's how pros do eeeet!" Greg crowed.

Zack's eyes flicked, taking in the craft details. His mind spun and his fingers flickered as he highlighted the opposing ships. "Focus fire on beta and delta."

This time around, no one complained as Zack's team focused their attacks on the pair of revealed ships. Unfortunately for their opponents, with most of their ships focused on stealth, their defenses were of a lower order and crumpled under the team's attacks.

In the meantime, the remaining, mostly undamaged ship designated Charlie slipped away while Alpha charged Zack's team, intent on finishing them off.

"All right, we got this, just keep focused," Zack said. "Jenny, you're on Charlie-watch."

Grinning into his headset, Zack and the boys focused fire on the remaining pair, intent on taking down their shields and stealth system. Already, he saw one of the ships listing and he took a gamble, switching fire to Alpha even as his missiles and artillery shells winged their way over.

They had this.

———

"Time!" the referee called.

Groans erupted from all around the convention hall, reminding Zack of where he was. He leaned back, wiping his sticky hands on his jeans.

"I need a drink," Greg groaned.

"No alcohol!" Jenny said.

"I meant an energy drink!" Greg protested.

"Damn Veridian. She should just have let us shoot her down," Faz said.

The group couldn't help but nod. Once they'd managed to kill the first three ships, they had spent the last fifteen minutes of the match searching for the final ship of the team. Rather than just giving up, the last ship had harassed the team at a distance, resulting in a lot of wasted time.

"At least she didn't have a hyperbomb or anti-matter missile," Zack pointed out. That had been what was unnerving, forcing the team to not only split up a little—giving the enemy a chance to damage them—but also stay on their toes the entire time. A single mistake could still have ended with a team wipe.

"Damn straight," Faz said. "Now come on. We only have an

hour for lunch."

The tall Sikh stood, only to be waved down by Zack.

"I got it. The hotel should be delivering food in a few minutes," he said.

"Really? Sweet!" Faz said, sitting back down.

"You didn't have to," Jenny said, but even she sounded less than convinced.

"I did. This is for the team. Less time standing in line means more rest time."

"You got me a Gamer Juice, right?" Greg said, almost bouncing on his toes.

"I did."

A chime in his OptiGlasses shut Zack up.

Physique Alert: Movement is Good!
You have been seated for the last three hours and four minutes. You should get up and move around for your health!

Physique Quest Offered: Take a Thousand Steps!
Reward: +0.1 Physique

Zack let out a groan as he spotted the notification. He automatically swiped accept as he stood. The sudden movement and pop in his knee reminded him how nice it was to actually stand.

"What's up? I thought we were waiting for food?" Greg said.

"Physique quest. I got to walk around," Zack explained.

"Sure, sure…" Faz nodded. "You just want to catch a glimpse of Zoe Cross, don't you?"

Zack rolled his eyes, but at Jenny's urging, he walked off. Maybe he could swing by Gord's and talk—see—stalk Ashley?

Or maybe not.

———

Zack stared at the flashing notification on his screen as he kept running. Taking a page out of the Veridians they'd fought earlier in the day's handbook, Zack had spent the last five minutes running. It was the only way they'd win, and the last few minutes had been a painful game of hide-and-seek in the convenient asteroid field.

"We did it," Zack whispered. Then he turned to his teammates, who were already giving each other high fives. "We did it!"

The team burst into exclamations of excitement as the reality of their latest win set in. They had spent the entirety of the day winning, leaving them as one of the few uneliminated and original winner's bracket teams.

A tournament worker coughed to get their attention as they continued to celebrate their victory, and they looked up.

"Congratulations! You have been chosen as one of the teams to highlight in the tournament. As such, you have an interview with Zoe Cross in one hour." He paused, as if expecting some kind of excited reaction.

Zack and the team simply shrugged. Unlike the other competitors, they had met Zoe before.

The worker gave them a confused look then continued. "We have a green room where you can get ready. Our makeup artists will need to at least powder your faces so you don't shine under the lights, and they can do more if you want."

"Makeup?" Greg said. "Nobody said anything about wearing makeup."

"Oh, that reminds me," Jenny said. "You'll need to change clothes as well."

"What?" the rest of her team said in unison.

Jenny beamed. "You heard me. While you guys were sleeping in, I was negotiating terms for our first sponsorship. It was contingent on us being one of the top teams at the end of the day, which we clearly are."

Zack remembered the determined look in Jenny's eyes that morning. Her gleeful smile at breakfast. For some reason, it all made him nervous.

"Just what kind of sponsorship did you arrange?" he asked.

Rapid footsteps, familiar rapid footsteps approached. Zack twisted his head around to spot David Davidson and a team of assistants carrying clothes.

Chapter Fifty-Nine

"DOES this jacket make me look fat?"

Greg studied his reflection in the backstage mirror, frowning as he checked himself from every angle. The sleek black material of the jacket with the light shimmer in the material mixed with the high collar certainly gave off that impression, Zack had to admit.

"Not fat," Faz said. "Stupid maybe, but not fat."

"You look great," Jenny said.

She was sitting in a corner while a makeup artist worked on her face. David Davidson's team had given all of them the quickest makeover in history, and they still had fifteen minutes before their interview with Zoe. Jenny was the only team member who looked comfortable in their new arrangement.

"When I said I wanted to be a pro gamer, dressing like a weird space vampire was not what I had in mind," Greg grumbled.

Faz mumbled something in agreement, although he looked slightly pleased as he adjusted the steel sword pin David Davidson had included with his outfit. The three men wore variations of the Corsair administrative and civilian flight clothing variations while Jenny was in a long, knee-length dress that hugged her curves. The dress was made of the same breathable and stretchy mesh that made up the men's clothing.

Jenny scowled at Greg and Faz, and the makeup artist sighed as she asked Jenny to relax. DaEvo chimed to let Zack know that his lady was upset. Zack looked at Jenny's glare and knew DaEvo was right. He needed to do something to salvage the situation and cheer Jenny up.

"Forget what you look like," Zack said. "These clothes are lightweight and breathable and designed specifically for gaming. They'll help your performance."

Plus, they were doing wonders for his Style stats. StarFashion was almost as good as WesterNeon, but without the cowboy clown vibe. He could see where Greg was coming from with the space vampire comparison, but no one was likely to laugh so hard they cried because of the outfits. Apparently, that was Zack's standard for acceptable clothing now.

"T-shirts are just as breathable," Greg said. "Besides, we're not competing right now. This is just the interview."

"It's part of the mental game," Jenny said. "We'll intimidate the other players because we look good and have already secured a sponsorship."

The current interview finished, and the players walked backstage. They snickered and whispered to each other as they walked past Zack.

So much for people not laughing at the new outfit.

"Yeah, we're striking fear into their hearts," Faz said. "They're trembling in their comfortable sweats."

"Shut up," Jenny snapped.

"You're on in ten minutes," a production assistant said. "We just need to reset the stage."

Zack's OptiGlasses chimed. Phil was calling.

Zack sighed. It wasn't the ideal time for this, but the interview would provide the perfect excuse to end the conversation quickly. He stepped away from his teammates and swiped his eyes to answer the call. "Hey, I just have a few minutes. What's up?"

Phil chuckled. "Enjoying Vegas?"

"Um, yes?" Zack answered cautiously and braced himself for Phil to explode about something, but the guardian laughed.

"Does your team know they've become Kayla substitutes? You don't have to lavish gifts on everyone you meet. We may need to have a serious conversation about budgeting once this tournament is over."

"I've been doing the fitness quests, so I can spend as much as I want. That was our deal."

"I might have let you off too easy with that."

"Easy? You think working out and eating healthy every day is easy?"

Everyone in the room turned to look at him, and Zack took a deep breath to calm himself. Maybe talking to Phil right before the interview was a mistake.

"Zoe told me about your meeting last night," Phil said. "That you're planning to expand the trust even further and take on more partners."

"It's a possibility."

"You know, if this foundation keeps growing, it's going to need more oversight. You'll need to take a more active role."

Damn, now Zack really regretted taking this call. He did not need Phil pressuring him to take more responsibility right now. "Hey, I have an interview in two minutes. Can we talk about this later?"

"I don't know, can we? Or are you going to block my calls, send my emails to spam, and force me to fly across the country to see if you're still alive?"

"Um, no?" Zack wasn't willing to make any promises. If Phil got annoying enough, he would be tempted. "We have Doctor Jones now. I thought she was going to run things."

"Yes, she'll be a great help, as will Zoe's team. I'm not saying you should take over the whole thing. In fact, I think that would be a disaster. But you can't assemble a team then expect them to run everything the way you want it without any oversight. This is your parents' legacy. You need to be involved."

"One minute!" the production assistant said.

"Hey, I've got to go," Zack said.

He ended the call before Phil could protest and hurried to follow his team to the stage's wings. It was a low blow for Phil to bring up Zack's parents right now, made even lower by the fact that Zack suspected Phil was right. Leaving others in charge had resulted in that nightmarish remodel of the children's wing, and there were probably similar disasters he hadn't discovered yet.

But was he really ready to commit to so much responsibility? In a way, he already had, agreeing to help Ashley with her project. But that was for Ashley. That was different.

"Small crowd," Jenny said, pulling Zack's thoughts from Ashley and back to the thing he was actually supposed to be doing.

The interview.

"Yeah, KayTay is doing a signing at the Gord's booth right now, so most people are there," the production assistant said. "These interviews are mostly to get sound bites for promotional materials, so we don't advertise them as heavily as the later ones."

"We're missing the signing?" Faz said.

He and Greg looked at each other in dismay, and Zack laughed.

Jenny was still studying the audience. "At least this streams worldwide, so we'll pick up more people there."

"Why do you care how many people see us?" Zack asked.

"Sponsorship, remember?" Jenny said, flicking the lapel of his jacket. "We're supposed to talk about how much we like the clothes."

"But I hate the clothes," Greg said.

"Then either pretend you like them or stay quiet and let me do the talking."

The production assistant rolled his eyes and pushed them onto the stage. Bright lights temporarily blinded them as they walked to their places. Most of the audience chairs around the room were empty, but a few people had showed up. Zack wasn't delusional enough to think they were there for his team or the interview. They were obviously there to see Zoe.

She sat on the far side of the small stage, legs crossed, wearing an elegant blue and green blouse-and-pants combo that accentuated her looks and still screamed professionalism. Four chairs sat on the other end, angled to face hers. Zack took the nearest one and looked out at the crowd to calm his nerves.

Mistake.

Ashley sat in the front row. She smiled at him. A cautious sort of smile, as if she hadn't quite decided what to think of him yet.

DaEvo chimed.

Reminder: Lovemeter for Ashley Barnes is currently empty

As such, a new relationship must be started to begin acquiring relationship milestones and for you to proceed with the relationship once more.

Zack stared at the notification. A new relationship? Restarting the relationship. Was that even a possibility? He would have thought not, before last night.

David Davidson had promised that their new clothes were light and breathable, but Zack's skin went clammy as he sweat. He wiped his palms against the tailored trousers to dry them.

"I know how you feel," Greg said. He had gone pale and seemed to be suffering from stage fright, having taken a seat next to Zack.

Faz, on the other hand, waved at the crowd, seeming to enjoy the attention. He'd even found a young lady to wink at. As he scanned the crowd, he grinned and elbowed Greg before pointing at Ashley.

"Look! Coffee girl came!" Faz said in an exaggerated whisper that Zack really hoped Ashley couldn't hear.

"Really?" Greg squinted into the lights and sat a little straighter when he found Ashley in the crowd.

"You should ask her out after the interview," Faz whispered. "Ask her to come to the ball with you."

"You think so?"

"Definitely."

"No," Zack said. "Don't ask her out."

His voice amplified and echoed through the room, and his face went red. Why did the production team have to turn on their microphones at that moment?

Every person in the room stared at him, including Ashley. Zack remembered that this interview was also streaming online and flushed even harder.

Damn. This was bad.

Zoe cleared her throat and seemed to be fighting a smile. She leaned forward a little, the movement refocusing attention on her. "Well, I had planned to ask about your team's bold new look to start the interview, but maybe this is more interesting."

"Nothing is more interesting than StarFashion," Jenny said quickly. "It's innovative clothing for the fashion-conscious gamer!"

She sounded as if she was reading a commercial script, but Zack was grateful for the distraction.

"Yeah, these clothes are really comfortable!" he added with a little too much enthusiasm.

Zoe looked at Zack. Then she winked at him. DaEvo chimed and gave him points, but the gesture seemed more friendly than flirtatious.

"I am intrigued by your team's bold new look," Zoe said. "Tell me what prompted the change."

"We're interested in high performance," Jenny said. "These clothes have a lot of features that will help us in the tournament. It's about the game as well as fashion."

"And what do the gentlemen think about their new outfits?" Zoe said.

Zack looked into the crowd again, avoiding Zoe's gaze like a student who hadn't studied and didn't want to be called on. David Davidson sat in the back row and waved enthusiastically. Zack opened his mouth to speak, then he noticed Ashley again and found he couldn't say anything. He would end up sounding stupid if he said anything about the clothes, and he didn't want to sound stupid in front of her.

Jenny gave her teammates a forced smile that said they would regret it later if they didn't say something.

"I guess it's comfortable," Greg muttered.

"Yeah, the features are cool," Faz said, fluttering his hands over the jacket while shooting a wide-eyed look of helplessness at Jenny.

"The jacket has shock-absorbent wireless charging pockets for all my gear!" Jenny said, taking control of the situation again. She stood, stuck her hands in the pockets, and twirled for the cameras.

The crowd murmured in appreciation, some for the fashion and some for the pockets. David Davidson applauded wildly from the back of the room.

"That does sound useful," Zoe agreed. "I'm sure everyone will be interested to see how your game improves now that you have this extra edge. Now let's talk about your training. Everyone knows how hard Star Fury players train their reflexes and work on their ship builds, but some of you take it a step further. Zack, would you like to tell us about your new fitness routine?"

"What?" Zack said, completely unprepared for the question. "Oh, yeah. I started working out and eating better."

"And what prompted that change?"

Zoe knew it was DaEvo. She was teasing him. She smiled at Zack with a hint of mischief in her expression, and he glared at her.

DaEvo chimed.

Relationship Quest Update!

Due to previous incidents, you must select your conversation partners at the same time. Setting up such conversation and relationship targets will then carry forth for all interactions.

Further confirmation once your first Relationship Milestone (that is, access to the Lovemeter after the first date) on your relationship goals and status will be required for the proper functioning of DaEvo.

Please choose if you are intending to pursue a relationship with:

- *Zoe Cross*
- *Ashley Barnes*
- *Jenny Romero*

- *All (Please enter Relationship Settings and answer Ethical Polyamory Questionnaire)*

Zack stared at the notification. He was getting really annoyed by it prompting him for confirmation each time he talked to more than one woman at a time. Or stared at one too hard. He tried to swipe the notification away, but it refused to disappear. Damn, it really was going to make him choose.

Zack looked at the options, staring at Jenny—his default for the last little while. It made the most sense, and he could do it again. Something made him hesitate to pick her though. Somehow it seemed more important right now.

If he kept choosing Jenny, at some point DaEvo would mistake them for being in a real relationship and force him to buy her gifts, go on dates, and take their relationship to the next level with Relationship Milestones. That felt like a disaster waiting to happen. Jenny might go along with it to help him earn game time, but Zack doubted she would tolerate it for long.

That left Zoe or Ashley.

He was spending a lot of time with Zoe because of their foundation work. He would continue to do so in the future, especially if he took the more active role Phil wanted him to take. But did he want to date her?

Zack exhaled slowly, trying to clear his head. A relationship with Zoe Cross. It was every guy's dream, and he was already living that dream in a way since they had spent so much time together lately. It had been fun. He liked her. But he didn't get the sense that she was into him or wanted to date him.

More important. He didn't want to date her.

The realization went off in his head like an antimatter bomb, wiping away erroneous thoughts. Zack realized he was staring at Zoe, who was waiting for him to answer the question, and turned away. Why didn't he want to date Zoe? She was perfect. With DaEvo and his newfound life skills, he might even stand a chance. He could at least get a lot of conversation points for trying.

He raised his gaze to select Zoe's name from the quest menu, but instead found himself looking at Ashley. His eyes were drawn to her auburn curls, then to her own warm gaze. Ashley offered a small smile as they made eye contact.

The smile made up Zack's mind, and he selected Ashley's name from the list before he had time to think about it more or change his mind. It was probably a mistake, especially since he wasn't even talking to her right now. It was irrational. But sometimes, you had to fly with your gut.

He broke out in another cold sweat as DaEvo chimed and displayed the next notification.

Relationship Notification: Resume Relationship with Ashley Barnes

You are electing to resume a relationship with Ashley Barnes. This option has been generated after your Lovemeter with Ashley Barnes emptied. The process of resuming a relationship with Ashley Barnes will be fraught with difficulty and is automatically set at a higher difficulty level, but you will gain access to Relationship Milestones immediately.

{!----Dev Note: We are defaulting to using the Relationship Milestones algorithm during alpha build-out of the app for ex-relationships. We have input some additional options in such cases, but additional consultation with our relationship therapists, legal, and marketing is required for a proper buildout. This notification is a reminder that, as always, DaEvo is not legally liable for any actions the user takes while following DaEvo prompts.----!}

Was he actually doing this? Risking his game time and stats and personal dignity to try to win Ashley back?

Zack looked down again and smiled. Yeah, he was. Even if it ended in flames and disaster, he had to try.

He was going to win Ashley back.

"What prompted your new fitness routine, Zack?" Zoe prompted again. "How has it helped your Star Fury game?"

"What? Yeah, it helped," Zack said as he tried to pull his mind back to the interview. What were they talking about again?

Fitness. Zoe had asked about fitness.

"Fitness is great. It gives you energy."

Zack realized he was still looking at Ashley and turned away, his face burning bright red.

Chapter Sixty

THE REST of the interview passed in a blur. Zack was vaguely aware of Zoe asking questions. Of his teammates answering. He answered a few and hoped he didn't say anything too ridiculous. He couldn't remember what he said.

Ashley was distracting. DaEvo's constant notifications that he shouldn't ogle other women didn't help matters either. He wasn't ogling Zoe, but he did have to look at her as part of the interview. He didn't really have a choice there.

Stupid DaEvo. He sighed with relief when the interview was finally over. It was the last one of the day, so the production crew turned off the lights and packed up their equipment. The crowd either dispersed or crowded around Zoe, asking her to sign things.

"What time is it?" Faz asked. "You think we can catch the end of the KayTay signing if we hurry?"

"Yeah," Greg said. Then he looked at Ashley, who was still sitting in her place in the front chair as though she was waiting for something.

Zack hoped she was waiting for him.

"Oh, coffee girl!" Greg said. "I was going to ask her out. Why don't you think I should, Zack?"

"Because you'll miss the KayTay signing," Zack said. "You can talk to her later."

Greg gave him a suspicious look, then shrugged and seemed to accept the explanation.

"You want to come?" Faz asked.

Zack snorted. The last thing he wanted was to see Kayla. Faz and Greg laughed and hurried away.

"So, you going to talk to her?" Jenny asked, nodding toward Ashley.

"Um, yeah," Zack said. "I have to. The app."

"I thought you had plenty of game time."

"More never hurts," Zack offered lamely.

"Just don't mess this up. See you back at the suite."

"Wait, where are you going? Don't tell me you want to see Kayla?"

Jenny laughed. "Hardly. David Davidson is giving me a gown to wear to the ball, and he needs to shorten the hem."

She hurried away and met David Davidson at the back of the room. Zack watched them go, then turned back to Ashley. The production crew was putting away the chairs, so she had moved to stand in a corner of the room.

DaEvo chimed.

Relationship Milestones!
You have unlocked Relationship Milestones. Gain bonus points and progress your relationship by completing any of the following:

- *first significant physical contact*
- *in-depth exchange of history*
- *your first kiss*
- *schedule a second date*
- *take her out to an exciting and memorable event*
- *your first [Dev Note—are we even allowed to suggest this? Ask Legal]*
- *become an [#select_variable: relationship type: exclusive;primary;secondary; pair-bonded; metamour]*

- *get engaged*

Note: Due to previous relationship with Ashley Barnes, relationship milestone increases to your Lovemeter will be at a lower level.

You can repair your relationship and remove the ex-relationship penalty to relationship goals for your Lovemeter by trying the following.

- *Showcase your value (i.e. physical, material, or social value)*
- *Acknowledge what went wrong and apologize*
- *Remind her of the good times by repeating a familiar date*
- *Show your affection with a grand gesture*

Zack stared at the notification. Apparently, DaEvo had meant it when it said he'd have to start from scratch. The Lovemeter dropping to zero had erased everything. Even their kiss.

"Stupid buggy app."

Your alpha test bug report has been logged.
Thank you for your help in making DaEvo a success!

Zack swiped away the notification and hurried over before Ashley could leave. "Hey, what are you doing here?"

He mentally slapped himself in the forehead. Very smooth. At this rate, he'd never get a second first-kiss or any of the other Relationship Milestones he was supposed to complete. He felt his face going red.

Ashley laughed a little. "Once I explained to my manager why I didn't want to work the Kayla signing, he told me to stay as far away from the Gord's booth as possible until it was over. Talk about an awkward conversation."

"Oh gosh. Sorry."

Relationship Milestone Hint: Be Specific
When apologizing, be specific about your apology to gain the most from the act.

Zack's heart raced as he thought back to the night of the gala. Of the very spectacular way both those relationships had ended. And yet, Ashley was here. Was he a complete idiot for thinking he could smooth things over with her? She could have gone anywhere in Vegas to get away from the booth, and she was here.

"Thanks for coming to watch my interview."

"I didn't come for you. Amber's watching the live streams from home. I thought they might show the crowd in one of their shots, so I came. She'll get really excited if she sees me."

"Oh. Right." Zack's face flushed even hotter. Of course she wasn't there for him. He was stupid for thinking otherwise. He fumbled to say something else and grabbed the first thing that came to mind. "How is Amber?"

"She's doing well, thanks."

"That's good."

An awkward silence fell between the pair, thankfully interrupted when the production crew herded everyone out of the room so they could finish tearing down the set.

Zack felt a small jolt of panic when they ended up in the hallway and Ashley turned to go. He couldn't let her go yet! He might not get another chance to talk to her, and he hadn't completed any of DaEvo's quests except for spending time with her. "Hey, do you want to go for a walk?"

"A walk?" She looked confused but not angry. That was a good sign, right?

"Yeah, a walk. You know, to look around. I haven't seen much outside the hotel yet. We could walk around and look at things and talk. To each other." Zack shut his mouth to cut off his incoherent rambling.

Ashley waited so long to answer that he thought she wasn't going to, but eventually she nodded. "Yeah, okay. Let's walk."

They walked down the hallway together, getting a little lost before they eventually found their way out of the hotel. The sun had almost set. The lights of the Vegas Strip were on but not showing much since it wasn't completely dark yet. It was a weird kind of transition state. Not blazing daylight or brilliant nighttime light shows, but something awkwardly between. Even the temperature was in that in-between stage, having cooled down a little from the blazing heat of the day.

DaEvo chimed again, reminding him that he still hadn't offered a specific enough apology. Zack gathered all his resolve. He was still playing by DaEvo's rules. He would have to do this and do it right.

"Hey, I'm sorry for how things worked out," he said. "I'm sorry I went out with Kayla while I was dating you. I'm sorry I cost you your job."

Ashley narrowed her eyes. "Did your digital wingman tell you to say that?"

She gestured to the OptiGlasses just as DaEvo chimed and offered points for the apology. Zack pulled the OptiGlasses off his face and stuffed them into one of the many insulated, self-charging pockets on his Star Fashion jacket.

The world looked strange without the OptiGlasses. It was like trying to fly his starship without his navigation computer. Not only was he cut off from DaEvo, he lost all his other apps as well. He didn't know what time it was, or if someone was calling, or how to get to wherever he was trying to go.

Only he wasn't trying to go anywhere. He and Ashley had ended up in front of a fountain. Not one of the ones that did an elaborate show on the hour, just a pool of bubbling water a little off the beaten path. She sat on a nearby bench, and Zack sat with her.

"There, no Dating Evolution," he said. "Now will you believe me when I say I'm sorry?"

She laughed. "I believed you the first time, but shouldn't you be talking to Zoe or Kayla to get points for the tournament? They're way higher level than me."

"I have enough points to get through the weekend."

Even without the OptiGlasses, Zack knew that was the wrong thing to say as soon as the words left his mouth.

"And I'd rather talk to you!" he added quickly.

"What is this, some kind of bonus level? Win back the girl you cheated on?"

"I don't think that bonus exists, and I wanted to talk to you.

Kayla hates my guts, and I feel about the same about her. Zoe is just a friend. We're working together for the foundation. I swear that's all."

Zack wondered if Ashley would believe him if he showed her the quest log where he had chosen her over Zoe when given the option, but he decided against it. She didn't seem to be a fan of DaEvo. Neither was he, but he found he missed the app's prompts. The silence was getting a little awkward.

"I suppose I should say thanks for the new job," Ashley said. "And I suppose I'll be seeing a lot of you at work, so we should at least be civil to each other."

"No, it's not like that! We don't have to work together at all if you don't want to. You can have space. I'll give you space."

"But it's your company." Ashley looked a little confused.

Zack sighed. "Yeah, I know, but I didn't recommend you for the job so you'd feel obligated to spend time with me."

"I can get another job, you know. I don't want to push you out of your own foundation."

"You're not. I barely worked there anyway. I'm not really qualified."

"That's a shame," Ashley said. "I was looking forward to having some help with the spreadsheet."

Were her eyes twinkling, or was it just the setting sun?

"I mean, I can help if you want me to!" Zack said.

He was starting to feel confused. Where was DaEvo when you needed it? Right or wrong, the app would at least offer a suggestion for what to do. They were sometimes helpful.

Then again, Ashley was smiling at him, so maybe he was doing all right on his own.

"Let's try working together," she said. "I miss our lunch meetings."

"I can still bring you lunch!"

Ashley raised an eyebrow, and Zack mentally kicked himself. He could practically hear DaEvo chiming and telling him not to be desperate. He was the textbook definition of desperate, and apparently, he had no game at all without the app's help.

He tried to remember the Relationship Milestones, but all that came to mind was the first kiss. He didn't think they were quite there yet, and he didn't want to blow this a second time.

He added, "Or not. I don't have to bring you lunch."

"I'd like lunch sometime."

Even without DaEvo's cheerful chime, it felt like a win. He had practically asked her out on a date, and she had practically said yes.

"Hey, don't you have another long day tomorrow?" Ashley said. "You should probably get to bed early and rest."

Zack swiped his gaze up to check the schedule and stared at that point a few moments before realizing he wasn't wearing his Opti-Glasses. It seemed he had almost forgotten how to function without them. "Can't. We're supposed to be reviewing the battle footage for the opposing teams later tonight."

"Oh, right. You mentioned that on the interview," Ashley said. "You should still get some rest. It's a lot of gaming, even for you."

Zack smiled at her words of concern. She still seemed to care if he won. That seemed like a good sign.

"Yeah, yeah, I guess you're right." Zack flashed her a tight smile. Maybe there was more than one thing he could win.

Chapter Sixty-One

BRIGHT LIGHTS FILLED THE SCREEN, shrapnel spun off into the void, and Zack listened to the final rumble of their loss. He made a face, pulling off the headset rather than listening to the announcement, only to hear Greg speak.

"Sorry, guys. I tried," Greg said.

His ship had been the last to fall, leaving them one point behind their opposition. At the start of the second day of the tournament, six teams had already been disqualified. Halfway through the day, another two had been kicked out, leaving sixteen teams in the tournament, many of them—like their team now—down a loss.

"Don't worry about it," Zack said, shaking his head. "Sometimes you just mess up, like putting the wrong protein mix and fruit cocktail together."

"What?" the rest of the team cried.

"Oh, right. Umm, never mind." Zack flushed. Damn DaEvo.

Greg said. "Wait, wait. You've been drinking protein shakes?"

"Well, yeah, it's filling, healthy, and you get all the calories you need. Why'd you think I lost so much weight?" Zack said.

"I thought it was all the exercise," Faz said.

"That too."

"You sound like you actually enjoyed those drinks," Greg accused Zack.

"Nah... well, sort of," Zack said as he stood after receiving another notification from DaEvo. He paced in the space behind their table, getting in his steps while he spoke. "It really isn't bad. If you want, I'll order you one for lunch."

"And miss out on the pizza you've been getting for us?" Greg said. "No thanks."

"Yeah. Then again, we could just quaff the drinks and see if we can sneak in to KayTay's second signing session today before it closes when we're done," Faz added.

"I thought you guys went to see it last night?"

"Nah, it was all booked out. You have to pay fifty dollars for a single photo." Faz rolled his eyes. "No way was I paying that."

"Well, she does put her hand around your shoulder..." Greg said.

"There's a—" Faz said.

Jenny warned him, "If you finish that sentence, I'll kick you."

Chuckling, Zack watched the by-play between the group. While they talked, he called up the division rankings, eyeing the loser bracket they were in. The good news, the loser bracket would be easier than the winner's. Of course, at this point, the difference was marginal.

The winner's bracket was filled with a small but elite number of teams that had yet to lose a single round. If Zack's team wanted to win, they couldn't afford to lose another fight.

The stakes were higher than ever.

But for all that, Zack couldn't help but think about later tonight. When he and Ashley were scheduled to work on the spreadsheet further to show it off to Star Forward at the end of the convention.

Maybe there were two events he couldn't afford to fail today.

"Stop moving, you're making me seasick," Faz complained to Zack, breaking him out of his thoughts.

"You guys should try standing and moving too. Get your blood flowing," Zack retorted.

"And mess with this beautiful body?" Greg ran a hand over his plush body, the jacket he wore doing wonders to hide it until he pushed the material together.

Jenny snorted, but surprisingly stood and joined Zack in pacing. "You got to admit, these are actually quite comfortable."

"Except the vampire collars." Faz tugged on his.

"I kind of like it now," Greg said, preening a little at the pair who kept walking. "You still have all that energy, eh? Maybe I should look at all this fitness stuff."

"Maybe you should," Zack agreed.

"Just hook me up with DaEvo." Greg said, grinning. "And KayTay."

A low buzz sounded, reminding everyone they had five minutes. The team sobered, and Zack and Jenny hurried back to their seats. They turned to Zack in unison, staring at him as he debated what to do. Since they never knew till the last minute who they'd be fighting, they couldn't pre-plan builds or order of the individual matches beyond the most basic configurations.

"All right, let's go with configuration six," Zack said.

———

Zack tapped the logout button, watching as Star Fury played its exit screen. He leaned back, exhaling loudly and finally letting himself relax.

"Nice one, Zack," Jenny said.

"Thanks." He looked up, almost expecting the conversation points to start again, but ever since his decision to continue the relationship with Ashley, he was no longer getting conversation points from talking to Jenny. Luckily, anything he'd banked was still available to him, so he was coasting on his remainder minutes till he started the relationship anew with Ashley.

Or whatever DaEvo considered a relationship.

"Yeah, great flying at the end there. I thought he had you for sure, till you dropped those heat-seekers," Greg said.

Zack looked at his friend—who'd taken off Davison's jacket

sometime in the afternoon—and found his lips thinning a little. Greg looked tired, his usual exorbitant cheer dialed way down.

Faz poked Greg in the side. "Come on, we got to get in line for KayTay."

"Just give me a moment." Greg levered himself out of the chair. Almost automatically, he swiped his jacket off the back of his chair.

"You okay?" Zack said with a frown.

"A little tired. Nothing a Gamer Juice can't fix." Greg flashed a grin. "Or maybe a cup of coffee. You think coffee girl's still there?"

Jenny rolled her eyes. "Don't you guys dare take too long. We still need to review the battle footage tonight. We can't afford to get caught out again."

There were serious nods all around. Anything they could glean about their future opponents' tactics would be important.

"Wait, you're not coming with us?" Greg said.

Jenny arched a single eyebrow. "Pay money to take a photograph with that woman?"

Greg flushed. "Yeah, maybe not."

"So, what are you going to do?" Zack asked as he stood and stretched, having shut down his computer. Luckily, the tournament would be locking everyone out of the venue, so they didn't need to carry their gear everywhere.

"There are a few seminars I want to visit," Jenny said.

"Like what?" Faz asked.

"The female gaze and male sexuality in games," Jenny deadpanned.

"Eewwww, nope! KayTay it is," Greg said, bouncing on his feet and grabbing Faz's arm. He pulled the amused man away, the tall Sikh's turban quickly lost in the crowd.

"And you?" Jenny said, still smirking.

"Got a meeting with As—the foundation," Zack said.

Jenny's eyes narrowed a bit before she nodded. "Don't mess it up. And don't be late!"

With those words, she strode out. Leaving him wondering whether she meant late to their meeting tonight or to his not-date with Ashley.

Zack drummed his fingers on the table, trying to focus on the battle videos he was watching in his OptiGlasses of his opponents' matches. But he couldn't focus, not when Ashley still hadn't appeared. He looked up, once again scanning the plushly appointed business center in the convention's connected hotel.

A variety of tables—some just big enough for a laptop and a pair of drinks and others fit to hold a board meeting upon—lay scattered through the business center. Comfortable, adjustable seats surrounded the tables, faux leather a cool covering for the seats. Soft light filled the business center, though the lack of individuals within the room spoke of the current convention's clientele's predilections.

He drew a deep breath, grateful he'd had time to take a quick shower—after DaEvo's usual prompting—and change into something a little less ostentatious. The buttoned-down shirt and pants gave him decent style points while not being too out of place in the business center.

Though, was he trying too hard? After all, Ashley was used to seeing him in his gamer shirts. He pulled up DaEvo's "helpful" notifications again.

You can repair your relationship and remove the ex-relationship penalty to relationship goals for your Lovemeter by trying the following.

- *Showcase your value (i.e. physical, material, or social value)*
- *Acknowledge what went wrong and apologize*
- *Remind her of the good times by repeating a familiar date*
- *Show your affection with a grand gesture*

He was showcasing his value, wasn't he?

"This way, miss," the voice of the business center's attendant broke Zack's thoughts.

He blinked as he realized it was Ashley, still dressed in her Gord's uniform but holding onto her laptop, who had arrived.

Zack hastily stood, smiling at her. "Hi."

Stupid. He should have said something else.

"Hi. This place is… nice," Ashley said, looking around the business center. When the waitress asked if she wanted something to drink, Ashley hesitated.

"Go ahead. It's all being expensed. They also do food," Zack said.

Ashley's eyes narrowed.

"Not a date. Just—I'm hungry, you know? We don't get many breaks."

"Oh, right. Ummm… orange juice, if you have it?" Ashley said to the hostess.

She nodded, then Zack ordered some healthy options for finger food. Hopefully, the curried cauliflower fries were edible.

In the ensuing silence, the pair looked at one another before looking away.

"You should eat. I did notice they didn't give you much time to eat," Ashley said.

Zack blinked, then his eyes narrowed. She knew his schedule? Was that a good sign? Yes, it was a good sign. It had to be.

"Yeah." Zack fell silent and then, casting around for a change of topic, spotted the laptop. "So should we…?"

"Yeah." Ashley booted up the computer before spinning the screen so they both could see it. "So the big problem I'm having is the KPIs. We need to work out the balance between getting the best patient outcomes, most frequent use, and space within the hospital."

"Don't forget skill use," Zack said. "Training. No use having gear if you don't have training."

Ashley nodded. "Right, good point. I have that, but I'm not sure where to get that information. HR, right?"

Zack nodded, tapping on the spreadsheet she'd pulled up. He bit his lip, thinking, before he flicked his fingers. "We could create a secondary database that it would pull data from, with a preset value for now, while…"

He barely even noticed when the waitress arrived with her drink and their food. So engrossed were the pair in their discussion that when his OptiGlasses chimed, letting him know it was time to go, he almost dismissed it.

Spotting the way Zack stopped talking and glanced upward, Ashley's voice cooled. "Your app again? Got a lot of points for this conversation?"

"No, nothing like that." Zack made a face. "I have to go. I've got to do the battle review with my team."

Ashley blushed, looking down. "Oh, right. I guess… I guess you should go."

"Yeah," Zack said. He didn't move.

You can repair your relationship and remove the ex-relationship penalty to relationship goals for your Lovemeter by trying the following.

- *Showcase your value (i.e. physical, material, or social value)*
- *Acknowledge what went wrong and apologize*
- *Remind her of the good times by repeating a familiar date*
- *Show your affection with a grand gesture*

Acknowledge and apologize. He took a deep breath. "About Kayla—"

Ashley's face froze, growing blank.

"I'm sorry," he finished as best he could.

"You should go."

Zack stood. "The spreadsheet…"

"I can finish it," Ashley said. "Thank you for your help, Mr. Moore."

Eyes wide, Zack bobbed another bow before he scurried off.

Stupid, stupid, stupid.

DaEvo sucked.

Chapter Sixty-Two

ZACK GROANED as he pulled on the joystick, trying to get his ship to reorient. In his other monitor, the tracking carats still had his opponent highlighted, so Zack kept his thumb depressed on the fire button, cycling through the artillery rounds.

"A tank and artillery loadout?"

Zack grinned as his opponent's voice went shrill as he vented his frustration with an impressive string of swearing. Last night's decision to mix up their normal loadouts to deal with their new opponents had gone well. Knowing the majority of their opponents were running short-range lasers, both Zack and Greg had switched out the individual fight loadouts to counter their attackers.

Faz, with his faster ship, still ran his original build. It made little sense to adjust to heavier, laser-resistant armor when his ship was so light. He would do better dogfighting, as he always did.

Even Jenny had switched tactics a little, multiplying her mine carrier drones and webbers, focusing on keeping her enemies webbed and at a distance while she picked away at them with her on-board weapons.

"Stand and fight, you cowardly Corsair!"

Unfortunately, it wasn't possible to mute opponents during tournament rounds.

"I am standing still. I'm so slow, even your grandmother could catch me. Not my fault you hit like a Tier V droid."

The frustrated snarl over the headset made Zack grin as he shrugged. The breathable weave in the StarFashion outfit really was nice, and even better, they were given a new set for each day of the tournament. He kind of liked this one, even if it was more Mercantile Captain space vampire than Rakish Corsair space vampire.

"And one more…"

An explosion rang through his headsets as the programmed series of artillery shells went off, blasting his opponent to so much space dust. Smirking, Zack leaned back and cracked his knuckles.

Perfect.

Last night's planning was perfect. He'd even taken the idea of using personnel skills from the medical spreadsheets and plugged it into his own.

Now, if only everything else last night had gone as well.

"Nice one, man."

A clap on his shoulder made Zack smile at Faz. "You're up next."

"Yeah."

"Loadout for the team match? We going to, ummm… D-4?" Jenny said, scrabbling to remember the loadout number.

Zack checked his glasses and nodded. "Yup. D-4."

Luckily, they'd designated each build in Star Fury so it was super simple to swap out, rather than requiring them to individually adjust each component.

As Faz ported in, Zack grinned. They could do this. Already, nearly two-thirds of the teams had been knocked out. If they kept this winning streak going, they could become one of the four teams remaining for tomorrow.

"So how was your foundation meeting?" Jenny asked while they rested between rounds. Even Zack was sprawled in his chair, the entire group exhausted after hours of competitive gaming.

"Great."

"Foundation meeting? Isn't that Zoe Cross?" Greg said, perking up.

"You met with Zoe again? Nice. You taking her to the ball tonight?"

Zack made a face. "No way."

"No way? You're not interested in Zoe Cross?" Greg's jaw dropped. "Are you sure you're fine?"

"Nah, I bet he asked and got shot down," Faz said.

"Oh, yeah. That makes more sense," Greg said.

Jenny was silent, instead watching Zack.

"I didn't ask. Or get shot down. I just… Zoe's nice. But not for the ball," Zack said. "We're not… we're business partners."

"So take out the business." Greg waggled his eyebrows.

Faz groaned.

"It's not like that," Zack said, shaking his head. "I'm here for the tournament, remember? We all are."

"Eh, if KayTay had said yes, I'd take her," Greg said.

"You asked?" Jenny said.

"Of course!" Greg pulled himself up. "What do you think I paid so much for the photo for?"

"Because you're desperate?" Jenny smirked.

He threw up his hands and clutched his chest. "Ouch!"

"Just remember, we're wearing Davison's clothes to the promotional shoot after this and to the ball," Jenny said.

The group groaned in unison, though it was more to tease her than with any real heat. The clothes were actually comfortable. And having the charging ports and hidden pockets had been quite useful for all the swag they had been getting.

"Five minutes!" a voice called.

Another buzzer, and the group spun around to begin the warmup process.

Another fight, another battle, another dance. Then, a different kind of dance this evening.

Zack sighed, wishing he did have someone to bring. But Ashley had looked so angry last night, he hadn't had a chance to ask her to come with him. And now, he didn't have the time.

Maybe she'd be there?

Smiling at the thought, Zack waited till the notification of their new opponent appeared.

Then he focused. Because he wouldn't be doing any promo shoots or going to the ball if he lost.

Chapter Sixty-Three

"One minute to grand entrance," the production assistant said. The harried-looking, floppy-haired brunette production assistant looked stressed, his head cocked as he listened to his earpiece for directions.

"You said that five minutes ago," Faz said.

"Sorry, we're running behind."

The team stood in a small room near the grand ballroom, where apparently, they were going to make a grand entrance as VIPs. As one of the last four teams and the only Corsair team, they were the defacto choice to represent the best-of-the-best for their side.

Thanks to Jenny, they all wore StarFashion formal wear with the high-tech pockets filled with various devices, many of which had been gifts. Everything from smart watches to tiny tablets, cameras, and even a tiny drone had been handed to them as part of their sponsorship.

"Don't forget to pull the toys out from time to time and use them. Comment on how nice it is that they stay charged," Jenny said. She pulled a handheld gaming console from a pocket hidden somewhere in the depths of her black ball gown's enormous skirt and waved it at them.

Faz, Greg, and Zack groaned.

"I did not sign up to be a walking advertisement," Greg said. "I hate this."

"Hey, sorry I'm late!" Kayla said as she burst into the room. She stopped and stared at the team with surprise. "What are you all wearing?"

"StarFashion," Greg said eagerly, forgetting his earlier complaint.

"Hey, we match you!" Faz said, sidling toward Kayla. "I guess that means we should spend some time together this evening."

She sidestepped and moved toward Zack. "Why in the world are you all wearing StarFashion?"

Faz was right in saying they matched. Kayla's StarFashion dress was a form-fitting gown that Zack doubted had room for the pockets that everyone was so obsessed with, but the color and cut had the same space-vampire vibe as the rest of them. Of course, she pulled hers off with grace and beauty.

"Our team is being sponsored by David Davidson," Jenny said.

She and Kayla gave each other appraising looks and wrinkled their noses in disapproval.

"All right, Corsair VIPs," the production assistant said. "Time to make your grand entrance!"

"Is that why you're here?" Zack asked as they followed the production assistant through a hallway. "Because you're the face of the Corsairs?"

"Why else would I be here?" Kayla said. "I'm the face of the Corsairs, and you're the top Corsair players right now. I guess the publicity team decided to group us together."

"Great." Zack briefly wondered how much trouble it would be to switch to the Armada side. It might be worth putting up with their ridiculous notions of honor and crappy ship designs if he could get away from Kayla.

"I'll be conducting your interview tomorrow as well," Kayla said. "Apparently, someone realized we have a history and thought it would be fun for us to be seen together."

"Oh." Zack had other choicier words in mind, but there were too many cameras to let those out.

"Great," Faz said with a wide smile. "We're looking forward to it."

"Please welcome the Corsairs," the Star Fury AI voice announced over loudspeakers.

Kayla's disgusted frown morphed seamlessly into her modeling smile. She strutted into the room as if it were her personal runway, and the crowd went wild. They cheered again as Zack and his team walked in, but with significantly less enthusiasm.

Zack looked around the ballroom, admiring the decor. It was like walking into a space station. Twinkling stars hung from the ceiling and showed through fake windows, giving the impression that the crowd was floating in space somewhere. The ballroom had been divided into several sections where various dungeons or online hangouts had been recreated. Kayla walked toward a corner decorated as Corsair's Cross, and the team followed her. A bouncer dressed as a combat android removed the red velvet rope marked "VIP" to let them in.

"This is cool," Jenny said.

"Yeah," Greg agreed. "Hey, look! It's us!"

The publicity photos they had taken during a break in the tournament had been edited into Armada bounty posters, printed, and hung around Corsair's Cross. Zack grinned. That really was cool. Maybe they had a wallpaper version for his monitor?

The bouncer replaced the rope and another door across the room opened.

"Please welcome the Armada," the AI voice announced.

Zoe Cross led the top Armada team toward a sleek, military-inspired corner of the room marked "Armada Officer's Lounge." The crowd went wild as she waved. She wore the sexy version of the Armada uniform that she wore in her posters and seemed completely at home as she settled into a sleek armchair in the lounge.

"Why don't you play to the crowd too?" Jenny asked.

"I'm here to model the clothing," Kayla said. "Interacting like Zoe is optional."

That seemed to be the case. About half of the attendees sprinkled around the room were cosplaying either their own avatars or famous Star Fury characters. The rest wore varying levels of formal wear or Star Fury T-shirts.

"Okay, Star Fury players," the AI voice said. "Let's party."

The Star Fury theme music blasted through the ballroom, morphing from the standard version into a peppy dance remix.

"Hey, do you want to dance?" Faz asked Kayla.

She narrowed her eyes at him.

He shrugged. "Worth a try. Let me know if you change your mind."

He turned and asked a girl dressed in an elaborate Corsair cosplay instead. She grinned and took his hand. The bouncer lifted the rope for them, and they disappeared into the crowd of people already dancing.

"Hey—" Greg began.

"No," Kayla said.

Greg shrugged and offered a hand to Jenny.

She glared at him. "So I'm your second choice?"

"I didn't technically ask her, so you can still be my first choice if it makes you feel better."

Jenny rolled her eyes but took Greg's hand and pulled him out to the dance floor. The other VIPs also hurried to the dance floor. That left Zack and Kayla standing alone together in Corsair's Cross.

"Don't even think about it," she warned.

"Think about what?"

"Asking me to dance. You're the reason I'm in this mess right now." She gestured to the lively party as if it were an annoying flash mob that had popped up out of nowhere with the sole purpose of destroying her peace and invading her personal space.

Zack looked around, not sure what Kayla objected to.

"You like to dance," he said finally.

"Yeah, but not like this. This is the lamest thing I've ever seen."

Zack could almost swear that DaEvo's annoying "your lady is

upset" notification had appeared, though of course it didn't. Not now that he was with Ashley. Still, he spoke without thinking. "Sorry."

"You should be. This is your fault. I need something to drink." She raised her hand and waved at the nearest waitress.

The serving staff were all dressed in sleek white uniforms that made them look like the androids that served as Star Fury's NPC assistants in various outposts. The servers wore tight hoods pulled over their heads and white face makeup to complete the robotic look. The production team really had gone all-out for this event.

The waitress moved toward them, carrying a tray of drinks. She looked almost unrecognizable with her auburn curls covered by the hood and her face covered in makeup. Almost. Her eyes widened when she saw Kayla, and that familiar gesture was enough for Zack.

"Hey," he said. He should have known Ashley would be working the ball too. She was always hustling, looking for a way to make money. Once more, Zack felt a flash of guilt at his own circumstances but pushed it aside.

Ashley glared at him as the word made Kayla look a little closer as she took her drink. "You look familiar. Do I know you?"

Ashley shook her head and offered the drink tray to Zack. He waited for DaEvo to populate a menu letting him know what he could have. It rejected everything on the tray as too unhealthy, and he sighed. He could have used a drink as well.

"Nothing for me, thanks," he said.

"Stick around," Kayla said as Ashley turned to go. "I have a feeling I'm going to need more of those."

"I can leave the tray."

"No, I want you to stay. I might need you to get something for me."

Ashley frowned, then offered the small bow that the androids always did in Star Fury. She moved a few steps away and stayed there, holding the drink tray as she stared straight ahead.

DaEvo chimed, belatedly recognizing Ashley with its facial recognition software.

Warning! Please Pay Attention to Your Date

No one wants to play second fiddle on a date. Make sure to keep your attention on the individual you are on the date with to increase intimacy levels.

Zack briefly considered strangling the developers. Or at least writing a strongly worded letter asking them to write new algorithms that recognized the nuance of social situations.

He stepped away from Kayla, moving closer to Ashley. "Nice disguise, Veridian, but you can't fool me."

Ashley's gaze remained focused straight ahead, but the corner of her mouth twitched up slightly. It was too subtle for DaEvo to acknowledge it, but it was enough encouragement for Zack.

"It takes some nerve to infiltrate Corsair's Cross. I wonder who your target could be?"

He looked around the VIP lounge before settling his gaze on Kayla. He gave a small nod in her direction and raised an eyebrow, and Ashley's lips twitched again. She was trying hard not to smile. The waitresses had probably been instructed to keep straight faces so they appeared more android-like.

Zack was determined to make Ashley smile.

"Or maybe you're here for me. There's quite a bounty on my head, although I didn't take you for the bounty hunting type." He nodded toward the bounty poster hanging on the wall, then forced his face to go serious. "I should warn you; the bounty is well-earned. I won't go down without a fight."

Ashley snickered. "Please, I could totally take you."

"Ah, so you are here for me."

"A Veridian never reveals her mission. I'm just here to serve drinks."

She winked at Zack and moved toward Kayla, who had emptied her glass and set it aside. Kayla took another drink from Ashley's tray without acknowledging the woman who held it.

For some reason, that made Zack mad. It was as if Ashley didn't exist. As if Kayla thought she really was an android there to serve her. He was still scowling when Ashley returned.

"There's no need to look so upset about your eventual capture," Ashley said. "I'll give you a head start."

"Dance with me," Zack said.

DaEvo chimed points for his asking, and Ashley stared at him. "What?"

"Dance with me. It's my fault you have to work right now. You should be having fun."

"Yeah, it's called a job," Ashley said. "That's the thing about jobs. You work."

"Another drink," Kayla said.

Ashley offered the tray and stepped back into the shadows.

"You have a job with the foundation," Zack said.

"And a job at Gord's," Ashley said. "They're sponsoring this event, so I have to work."

She had that stubborn set to her jaw that she sometimes got, and Zack sighed. He wasn't going to win this one.

"I can't just neglect my responsibilities because I want to spend time with you," Ashley said.

"Wait, you want to spend time with me?" Zack said.

She glared at him, but the damage was already done. Zack didn't try to hide the grin that spread across his face, which only made Ashley glare harder.

Kayla noticed them talking and turned around. "Wait, I do know you. You threw drinks at me at Zoe's gala."

Ashley shrugged and didn't deny it. Zack held his breath, waiting for the inevitable blow up.

Only it didn't come. Kayla looked Ashley up and down, then sniffed derisively and turned away. She pulled a phone from a hidden pocket in her dress and handed it to Zack. "Take pictures of me so I can post something. You know my good side."

Zack was too busy noting that the dress did indeed have pockets somewhere to protest. He fell into the familiar rhythm of taking pictures while Kayla modeled, striking a variety of poses in quick succession.

After Zack handed the phone back, Kayla flipped through the photos and smiled at him. "You've gotten better."

Then she tapped furiously on her phone as she posted to her various social media accounts. Zack turned back to Ashley, but Ashley was gone. He looked around Corsair's Cross and searched the dance floor, but she had disappeared.

Damn.

"Take some pictures with me," Kayla said. "The fans will love it. And so will the Star Fury executives."

She held an arm out to Zack, inviting him to sit beside her on the barstool that was clearly meant for one. He took a step toward her, falling into the familiar rhythm of doing whatever Kayla wanted, then shook his head. What was he doing? This was exactly the kind of thing that had gotten him into trouble before.

"I've got to go," he said.

Zack nodded to the bouncer and hurried out of Corsair's Cross, leaving Kayla staring after him with her lips pursed.

It was loud and crowded outside of the VIP area. Zack found himself swept up in the mass of bodies swaying to the rhythm, and soon he was dancing alone at the center of the dance floor. He caught a glimpse of Faz in the distance—he was the only one of Zack's teammates tall enough to see over the crowd. He seemed to be having a good time.

Zack briefly considered joining his team, then shook his head and worked his way to the opposite end of the dance floor. A plan was forming, and he needed to act on it before he lost his courage.

He found a waiter dressed in the same android costume as Ashley and hurried after him. The man offered a tray of drinks, which DaEvo once again rejected, and Zack shook his head.

"I'm looking for a manager." He flashed his VIP badge in case that was necessary.

The waiter shrugged and pointed across the room toward the Armada Officer's Lounge. "See that door? There's a kitchen and staff room through there."

"Thanks."

Zack smiled at the waiter and hurried toward the door. He pushed through it and found himself in a sea of white-clad waiters. They deposited empty drink trays on the counter, picked up fresh ones, and hurried out again. The only person in the room not in white was a stout man wearing a black T-shirt. Zack hurried toward him, hoping he was the manager.

"Hey, I have a question about a waitress." Zack flashed his VIP badge, not above using his status to get what he wanted.

The man groaned. "Not another one. For the last time, I am now very aware that VI534 model androids are incapable of showing emotion, but I am not going to buy masks and force the waitstaff to wear them all night. This is not up for debate!"

His eyes bulged as he said it, and Zack couldn't help chuckling. The man reminded him of Phil.

"No, that's not why I'm here. One of my friends is working tonight, but I was hoping I could ask her to dance. Is that all right?"

"You want to dance with one of the waitresses?"

Zack nodded.

"And you're not here to complain about masks?"

Zack shook his head. He nudged his jacket open so the VIP badge showed and smiled. "I think you're doing a great job with this event. I'll tell the executives that it was very authentic, and I had a great time."

The manager sighed. "Fine, you can dance with your friend, but she needs to change first. The last thing I need is a swarm of nerds yelling at me about androids dancing."

"Great," Zack said. "Could you write a note giving her permission? I'm not sure she'll believe me without it. Her name is Ashley Barnes."

The man rolled his eyes and muttered something about more drama than a high school prom as he scribbled on a sticky note. "There. But if I get even one complaint about dancing androids, I will hold you personally responsible."

"No complaints," Zack promised.

He scurried out of the room before the manager could change his mind and stared at the crowded ballroom. Now he just needed to find Ashley.

It took longer than he expected. If Ashley had actually been an undercover Veridian, the android disguise would have been an excellent choice. Zack wandered around the ballroom, searching for the bright white uniforms and chasing down waitresses to check their faces. He circled the ballroom twice without any luck. He checked both VIP areas, just in case.

He was about to give up when he noticed a flash of white in the center of a crowd of cosplayers. He hurried toward them, catching snatches of their conversation when the music went quiet.

"One of the better ones. She has a good poker face."

"Still think they should have worn masks."

"Hey, take a picture of us together. I've always had a thing for these androids."

Zack pushed through the crowd and found Ashley standing against a wall and staring straight ahead. Her eyes sparked with rage, but the rest of her face remained stoic as a guy in an Armada uniform leaned close to her for a picture. Zack's anger grew as he recognized Steve from the Gord's in Oklahoma City as the ring-leader of the group.

"I wouldn't do that if I were you," Zack said.

Steve looked up, and his eyes narrowed in recognition. "Oh, it's you. You've got some nerve coming into Armada territory, Corsair. Don't you know there's a bounty on your head?"

He pulled a crumpled poster from the pocket of his uniform and handed it to one of his buddies. They passed it around and glared at Zack. The group tightened into a circle around him.

"There's a ceasefire tonight," Zack said.

"Yeah, we don't trust Corsairs to honor that," one of Steve's buddies said. He pointed at his left eye, which was slightly bruised and swelling.

Zack swallowed. Had they actually gotten into a fistfight with someone? He didn't think security would let things get out of hand at the ball, but the group might land a few punches first. They had obviously been drinking and looked as if they would love to start something.

"You guys remember the hyperbomb that caused a black hole in my quadrant?" Steve said. "This is the guy who dropped it."

The other gamers swore and closed in even tighter around Zack.

He backed up until he was standing beside Ashley, pressed against the wall. He looked at her and met her gaze.

Her lips turned up in just a hint of a smile before she spoke. "If you get thrown out, you'll miss Zoe's big announcement."

"Announcement?" one of the drunk Armada players said. "There's no announcement tonight."

"There is. It's on the agenda they gave us wait—androids," Ashley quickly corrected herself.

"What's it about?" Steve said, frowning with disbelief.

Ashley gave a nonchalant shrug. "As if they'd tell the help. I think it has something to do with a new ship release or something."

"You're lying," Steve muttered.

"Maybe," Ashley admitted. She kept her poker face, made all the harder to read with the white paint.

Zack grinned slightly, though he made it disappear the moment they looked his way, as Ashley bluffed her way through.

"Hey, you know, I heard that new Corsair model muttering something about getting out of the Corsairs as soon as possible. Maybe they're adding a new faction?" another of Steve's groupies said.

Now that the initial anger had dispersed, the group looked a little more uncertain about starting stuff. It helped that the imposing security guards—decked out in Station Security Outfits—had drifted closer.

"Fine, let's just go. Maybe we can get the scoop from her," Steve said, gesturing back to the dance floor.

The group grinned and dispersed, searching for Zoe or Kayla, taking Steve's non-specific language as befitted themselves.

Zack breathed a sigh of relief as the Armada scum dispersed, leaving him alone with Ashley. Together, they slumped against the wall then looked at each other. Then they laughed.

"Thanks for that," Zack said. "I think they really were going to attack."

"Well, that's what you get for crossing into Armada space. There have been a few fights already." Ashley rolled her eyes. "Gamers and drinks don't mix well."

"Right." Zack stared at her, trying to see her expression beneath the thick layer of white makeup. He suspected Ashley might be blushing, but it was impossible to tell.

"I should get back to work," she said, turning to go.

"No, wait!" Zack pulled the sticky note from his pocket and handed it to her. "I talked to your boss. You have permission to dance."

Ashley read the note and shook her head. "He says I have to change first. I don't have any other clothes here."

"Wait." Zack's mind raced. No way was he going to miss the chance to dance with Ashley because of something so stupid. He pulled off his jacket and handed it to her. "Wear this. It will cover most of the uniform."

Ashley considered it for a moment, then grabbed the jacket and put it on. She twirled. "How do I look?"

"Like an android wearing an oversized suit jacket," Zack admitted. "Oh, I know! Pull down your hood and uncover your hair. Androids don't have hair."

He thought it was a good idea, but Ashley scowled. "My hair will be a mess underneath."

"So?"

She kept frowning, and for a moment Zack was afraid she was going to turn him down. Maybe the hair was just an excuse and she really didn't want to dance with him.

Then she shrugged and pulled down the hood. Zack tried not to stare, but he felt his eyes bulging as Ashley's auburn curls escaped. Her hair stuck out on all sides in a frizzy mess. It was like multiple squirrels had been electrocuted and stuck onto her head.

"Is it that bad?" Ashley said.

"No, you look great!"

Ashley raised an eyebrow, and DaEvo remained silent other than to update her Style stats and drop it to the low 20s. It seemed even the buggy app had recognized the compliment as a lie. With her riot of red hair and white face makeup, Zack couldn't help thinking she looked a bit like a clown. But he knew better than to say that, even without DaEvo prompting him.

"You don't look like an android," Zack said quickly. "No one will mistake you for an android. That's what matters."

He offered his arm and smiled as she took it. They pushed through the crowd to the Corsair side of the ballroom just in case any other Armada scum were also watching for an opportunity to collect bounties.

They finally reached an open spot on the dance floor. Zack listened to the music, trying to catch the beat. It was a pulsing "oom-pah" techno rhythm that seemed vaguely familiar somehow.

"Hey, do you want to polka?" he asked.

Ashley listened to the music for a moment, then grinned and placed her hand on Zack's shoulder. It was too crowded for them to polka properly, but they still managed to work their way through the crowd. Other dancers watched them and cheered as Zack and Ashley showed off the moves they had learned in dance class. The crowd clapped when the song ended, and they stopped dancing.

To Zack's surprise, he found a new notification awaiting him in DaEvo, one that he'd missed entirely.

Relationship Milestone Achieved! Significant Physical Contact

Elongated and significant physical contact is an important part of a relationship, creating endorphin and emotional triggers in your date.
+2.5 to Ashley Barnes Lovemeter Level

Sweat ran down Ashley's face, taking some of the white makeup with it. It dripped onto Zack's jacket, leaving a splattering of white on the lapel. His arms were still around her waist, and the moment was achingly familiar. He leaned in closer, staring into her eyes, wondering if he should kiss her.

Ashley blinked and pulled away before he could decide. She smiled at him and pulled him toward the edge of the room. "Is it weird that I kind of miss the tubas?"

Zack laughed, then stopped abruptly as she took off his jacket and handed it back to him.

"Thanks for the dance, Zack."

"Don't you want to dance again?"

"Yeah, but I have work to do. And so do you. They'll be gathering the VIPs soon for a photo shoot."

VIP status was nothing but trouble. Zack watched in dismay as Ashley shoved her hair back into the hood and patted her face to remove the sweat. It was like she was slipping away again. Becoming invisible.

"I'll see you around," Ashley said.

She winked at him and disappeared into the crowd. Zack stared after her, then at DaEvo's notification.

Congratulations! You have reminded Ashley Barnes of the good times.
Relationship Milestone penalties reduced.

You can further repair your relationship and remove the ex-relationship penalty to relationship goals for your Lovemeter by trying the following.

- *Showcase your value (i.e. physical, material, or social value)*
- *Acknowledge what went wrong and apologize*
- *Show your affection with a grand gesture*

Zack was barely aware when Faz dragged him over for a team photo. The rest of the night passed in a blur. Zack tried to keep up with his teammates' excited chatter when they headed back to the suite, but their stories blended together.

"And then Zack danced with clown girl," Jenny said.

"What?"

That snapped his attention back to them. Jenny waved her phone at him, showing pictures that someone had snapped while he and Ashley danced.

"She's really cute. Someone linked her and Kayla's and Zoe's blog and there's now an entire meme about clowns and vampire chic going around the fashion circles. Everyone is saying that clown chic is the next bold step in fashion. David Davidson is thrilled. He's thinking about doing a clown-inspired line once he wraps up Star-Fashion."

"I will quit," Greg said. "Sponsorship or not, I will quit if you make me dress up like a clown."

"So, who is she?" Faz asked as he scrolled through pictures and read the comments. "Nobody seems to know. They're saying she appeared and disappeared like Cinderella."

"A clown Cinderella," Greg muttered. "You guys are so weird."

"She's a friend," Zack said.

When the boys pushed him, Zack kept his mouth shut. He wasn't willing to say more than that. He still didn't know how Ashley felt about him, and he couldn't claim her as his girlfriend until he did. Also, he had to admit, it was kind of fun having a secret, especially since Greg seemed to have stopped focusing on Ashley.

Well, not any more than any other cute girl who wasn't Jenny anyway.

Chapter Sixty-Four

"ALL RIGHT, YOU'RE ON!"

The production assistant shuffled them onto a stage that was much bigger than the last one. In spite of their morning call time for the interview, Zack's team looked moderately alert thanks to a ridiculous amount of coffee and energy drinks.

Whoever had decided to run the interviews in the morning before the final four rounds and after the ball that had ended way too late in the night was a sadist. If Zack ever found him, he would strangle him.

Struggling through the morning's physique quest while mildly hungover and sleep-deprived had been a nightmare, but at least he'd finished it.

"Oh good, a crowd," Jenny said. She strutted over to her seat, sticking her hands in the high-tech pockets of her StarFashion outfit.

"I swear, if she says anything more about those pockets, I'm going to throw up in them," Greg said.

He did look a little green as he looked nervously at the crowd. Zack slid as far over in his chair as he could, nearly colliding with Faz, who was waving enthusiastically. Zack slid back to the center of his seat and squinted into the lights. This stage was surrounded by stadium-style seats, and each seat was full. Was Ashley out there somewhere? The bright studio lights made it impossible for him to see faces in the crowd.

DaEvo chimed. Zack took that to mean Ashley was out there somewhere. The app could see her, even if he couldn't.

Relationship Target Ashley Barnes is present!
Current Lovemeter Level: 2.1/100

Your Relationship with Ashley Barnes is being penalized due to past experience. You can repair your relationship and remove the ex-relation-ship penalty to relationship goals for your Lovemeter by trying the following:

- *Showcase your value (i.e. physical, material, or social value)*
- *Acknowledge what went wrong and apologize*
- *Remind her of the good times by repeating a familiar date*
- *Show your affection with a grand gesture*

Zack had tried the apology multiple times, and that hadn't gone well. Ashley didn't seem impressed by his wealth. That left him with one way to level up the Lovemeter.

"What counts as a grand gesture?" Zack muttered.

DaEvo responded with a more helpful than normal tutorial showing movie clips of over-the-top romantic gestures, as well as a list of suggestions. Some of the options almost made Zack choke before it displayed them all in a checklist format. Some of the ones that jumped out to Zack were:

- *sing to her*
- *use a boombox to declare your love in public*
- *give up something she doesn't like so you can spend more time with her*
- *fight your rival for her hand-in-marriage*
- *tell her you love her in front of a crowd*

Well, crap. None of those looked like good options. Zack stared at the list. Singing was out. Way out. And he definitely wasn't ready to tell Ashley he loved her. And there wasn't a rival. Not that he intended to fight anyone anyway.

That left giving up something she didn't like.

Maybe he should ignore the quest. He and Ashley had parted on good terms last night. The relationship seemed to be heading in a good direction. He didn't need to keep pushing things.

Then again, maybe he did. She had hurried away last night and hadn't responded to any of his texts.

"Damn," he said.

The word echoed through the auditorium, and Zack gritted his teeth. It was like the audio engineers wanted to ruin his life.

"It sounds like you're excited for the final round," Kayla said.

Her voice sounded friendly, but Zack recognized the nasty gleam in her eyes all too well. Why did they have to switch to her from Zoe? There should be some law against having to do an interview with your ex right before the biggest games of your life.

"Sure," Zack said weakly.

DaEvo chimed again to remind him of the quest. Zack looked at the list. DaEvo was wrong as often as it was right. The grand gesture for Ashley was probably a terrible idea.

And yet, there was a reason it ended up in so many movies. There must be something to it.

Kayla leaned forward. The seemingly casual gesture made her cleavage spill out of her shirt, and DaEvo flashed a warning that Zack shouldn't ogle other women while he was pursuing a committed relationship. Zack glared. That was kind of tough when you were sitting close to a woman sticking her chest in your face. What was he supposed to do? Run away?

Actually, maybe that was a good idea. He could swap seats with Faz and stay on the other side of the stage. That would make both of them happy.

The production team gave the sign for them to start, and Kayla turned to smile for the cameras. Zack sighed and leaned back in his chair. So much for that idea.

"Welcome to the final round of interviews for the Star Fury tournament! I'm Kayla Taylor, the new face of the Corsairs! Today, we've got the only Corsair-only team to make it to the last four rounds with us."

The crowd cheered.

Kayla waited, basking in their praise until it died down enough for them to hear her. "Are you guys excited for the finals?"

The crowd cheered again. She had them eating out of her palm and clearly loved every minute. Zack sighed and rolled his eyes. This was shaping up to be a long interview.

"So your team's new look has been generating a lot of buzz," Kayla said. "Jenny, tell me what prompted the change in outfits."

Jenny launched into what had become her usual spiel promoting StarFashion.

"Wow," Kayla said, cutting Jenny off, "you certainly know your stuff! Stand up and let's see these clothes in action."

Jenny stood and gave her usual twirl. Kayla stood as well and joined her in the center of the stage. She wore an outfit nearly identical to Jenny's, but it was skin-tight and much shorter.

"You know my favorite thing about David Davidson's work?" Kayla said. "He knows how to make clothes for all kinds of different body types. Jenny and I couldn't be more different, but he still makes us look good."

She gave a spin of her own, and the crowd roared in approval. Jenny rolled her eyes and sat down with her arms crossed.

"The clothes have to be cut differently," Jenny said. "Your job is to sit there and host events, so it doesn't matter that everything is tight. Since I'll be playing Star Fury, I need to actually be able to move."

She smiled sweetly at Kayla, who returned the gesture with an overly sweet smile of her own.

The tension in the room was making Zack sweat. Or maybe that was the stage lights. Either way, he was once again putting David Davidson's extra-breathable fabric to work.

"I'm sure everyone here wants to know," Kayla said. "Jenny, are you the clown Cinderella who has been generating so much buzz?"

A blurry picture of Zack and Ashley dancing appeared on the screen behind them.

Jenny shook her head. "No, and I don't know who she is. It's very mysterious and exciting. I haven't seen a fashion trend cause so much excitement in years. She's trending at the top of every chart. The memes that have been generated are so much fun, don't you think?"

Jenny said this innocently, but Kayla ground her teeth as she turned to Zack. "So are you going to tell us the mystery girl's identity?"

"No."

Kayla waited, clearly expecting him to say more, but Zack kept his mouth shut. He wouldn't let Kayla bait him, and he wouldn't expose Ashley as his mysterious dance partner until he knew her thoughts on the matter.

"Well, I guess she'll remain a mystery," Kayla said finally. "You've been very caught up in the fashion world lately, Zack. Much more than the average gamer. Tell me, how do you think Star-Fashion compares to some of these more flamboyant trends?"

"Yeah, it's great," Zack said. "My favorite. I love it."

He heard cheering from the back, which could only be coming from the designer. Zack had no idea if the sponsorship was helping Davidson sell any clothes or not, but the designer seemed to be having a good time.

At least someone was.

"You guys may not know this," Kayla said to the crowd, "but Zack and I go way back. He's actually the reason I became interested in Star Fury."

The crowd cheered again. Why were they cheering for everything Kayla said? She wasn't that great.

Kayla patted Zack's leg. It was a brief gesture, almost an accident, although Zack knew better than to believe that.

DaEvo chimed.

Relationship Warning!
*Initiating contact with members of the opposite sex will impact your
existing relationship. If you would like to pursue multiple relationships,
please complete the necessary survey and paperwork.*
Ashley Barnes Lovemeter Level -0.1

Damn it, he wasn't hitting on Kayla!

Zack squinted into the crowd, trying to see Ashley. Did she think
he was hitting on Kayla? She wouldn't, would she? The lights were
too bright for him to see, but he scanned the part of the crowd that
had triggered DaEvo before, and the app flashed a warning.

Your lady is upset. Try the following to make her feel better:

- *Flowers*
- *Chocolates*
- *An apology*
- *Pay attention to her*

Relationship Warning!
*Your Lovemeter Levels are extremely low. If your Lovemeter Levels
empty, your relationship will automatically terminate.*

Damn it! If this was Kayla's way of getting revenge on him, it
looked as though it was working.

Was Ashley actually upset, or was DaEvo imagining things?
With the level of light glare, Zack couldn't even be sure it was seeing
her properly. If DaEvo was right, what could he do about it? He
couldn't go out and buy her a gift. If he yelled at Kayla or ran away,
he would cause a scene.

Then again, maybe causing a scene was the answer. Zack
opened the quest menu and stared at the relationship repair options.
He could possibly still manage a grand gesture. Or a public
declaration.

He'd tried apologizing to her and that had failed. He hadn't even gotten it ticked off. So maybe he needed to do it in public. Declare his love for Ashley.

"So, you've leveled up your fashion," Kayla said. "Do you think that will help your love life as much as it has helped your gaming?"

She brushed her hand against Zack's leg again, lingering longer this time, and DaEvo once again warned that Ashley was upset. He barely had any points left thanks to all that. Faz started to answer the question, but Zack cut him off. This was his chance, and he wouldn't blow it.

"It helped!" Zack yelled.

His teammates and Kayla stared at him. The entire auditorium went silent, and Zack swallowed. He had their attention now.

"It helped," he said again. "The fashion helped my gaming, but something else helped more. Actually, it was someone."

"Oh?" Kayla said.

"What are you doing?" Greg whispered, looking even more green.

Zack stood, fully conscious that he looked ridiculous in the Star-Fashion outfit. "Our team has had a lot of success, but I owe some of mine to someone else."

"I knew it! He's been cheating," someone who sounded suspiciously like Steve called from the back of the room.

Zack ignored him and turned to Ashley. Well, he turned to the part of the crowd where DaEvo said Ashley was. He really hoped she was there. Otherwise he went from kind of looking like an idiot to absolutely looking like an idiot. "I found someone who helped me put the pieces together. Who helped guide me in finding the perfect ship build. Who helped me think of weapon combinations I never would have. She's beautiful and smart and fun, and I wish I had treated her as well as she deserves."

The production team shone a spotlight into the crowd, and suddenly Zack saw Ashley. She was staring at him with wide eyes. He couldn't tell if she was pleased or horrified. Maybe some of both.

"Hey," Greg said, "isn't that coffee girl! Were you dating coffee girl?"

"Oh, some kind of scandal?" Kayla said. "A love triangle within the team?"

She was trying to regain control of the situation, but for once, the crowd ignored her. They were all staring at Ashley. A few murmurs about the clown Cinderella circulated through the room, but Ashley looked nothing like a clown right now. Most of her red hair was hidden under a hat, and she wore jeans and a slightly wrinkled T-shirt.

"I'm no good at this sort of thing," Zack said. "But I messed up, and I wanted to say I'm sorry. Nobody compares to her. And if there's a chance we can work it out, I want to take it."

Ashley's cheeks burned bright red with embarrassment, and her mouth hung open. It seemed Zack had caught her by surprise. Hopefully, that was a good thing.

DaEvo chimed.

Congratulations! You have made a public declaration of affection to Ashley Barnes.
Relationship Milestone penalties reduced.
+10 to Ashley Barnes Lovemeter Level

Relationship Hint! Keep going!

- _sing to her_
- _use a boombox to declare your love in public_
- _give up something she doesn't like so you can spend more time with her._
- _fight your rival for her hand-in-marriage_
- _~~tell her you love her in front of a crowd~~_

Zack was on a roll, and his instincts took over, refusing to let up on the kill. No way was he letting his target escape him! He selected the third option and spoke without thinking. "Ashley, if you'll take me back, I'll give up Star Fury for you."

A collective gasp spread through the audience. Zack's teammates yelled in protest. Kayla was stunned into silence.

Zack blinked, slowly coming back to his senses. His face drained of blood as he realized what he had said. Damn it! Why had DaEvo told him to say that? He couldn't let his team down like that. Star Fury was his life! What would he be without it?

The production crew pulled Ashley from her seat and hurried her to the stage. She protested, then gave up and hurried toward the stage, moving so quickly that she outpaced the production team. Zack had the distinct impression that she was running toward him.

Maybe it had worked? Had he won her back?

Maybe DaEvo knew what it was doing, and it wasn't such a stupid gesture after all. He had won her back. Wasn't love what mattered in the end?

Zack closed his eyes, and memories of the last few months, the last few days of playing in the tournament came back to him. Spending long hours shooting the breeze with his friends—literally and figuratively—in Star Fury. Working out the spreadsheet, poring over it. The chance for his friends to actually make something for themselves, to fulfill their own dreams. The never-ending landscape of the game. His throat clenched and his stomach fell as Zack tried to reconcile himself to his declaration.

"Are you really abandoning us for a girl?" Faz said.

Zack turned to face his teammates. They were staring at him with equal parts surprise and horror. Jenny looked ready to jump up and pound him into the stage, while Greg didn't seem to have any blood left in his face.

Zack swallowed. He couldn't leave them like this. He couldn't abandon them right before the final round of the tournament.

By the time Ashley reached the stage, Zack's forehead was soaked with sweat. Cameras followed her, capturing more drama than they had planned to. Zack stayed frozen on the stage although every instinct screamed at him to run. DaEvo had created a situation where he couldn't win. If Ashley said no, that meant it really was over. That he had miscalculated and blown his chance to get back together with her.

If she said yes, he would either have to abandon his team or backtrack and say he hadn't really meant the offer to give up Star

Fury. Either scenario left him looking like a massive jerk and losing something he really wanted.

What had he been thinking?

His life had been blissfully simple before the app got involved, and now everything was ruined.

Ashley stood there for a minute, catching her breath and getting her bearings. Then she walked toward Zack, her face set in a scowl. "Did you really just promise to give up Star Fury if I date you?"

Zack nodded, not quite able to speak.

Ashley crossed her arms, and her eyes sparked. "That's the stupidest thing I've ever heard."

The crowd's reaction was mixed. Some cheered. Some laughed. Some, and Zack was pretty sure they were his competition, screamed in unison for Ashley to reconsider Zack's offer and have him quit the game.

"It's manipulative and pointless," Ashley continued. "I won't like you more if you give up the game for me, and you won't be happy either. Something like that would make both of us miserable."

"Wow," someone in the crowd said. "My girlfriend just nags me to get a job."

"So that's a no?" Zack said, trying to sort through her answer and still finding himself confused.

"No," Ashley said. "You came here to play in the tournament. You're playing in the tournament."

Behind them, his teammates breathed a sigh of relief. Zack wanted to feel relieved, but he was too stung by Ashley's rejection. DaEvo chimed to let him know he had failed the grand gesture quest.

Ashley noticed his eyes tracking the notification. She snorted in disgust. "I knew it. This is just a stunt for that stupid app. I really hate those OptiGlasses sometimes."

Zack pulled up the quest and stared at it.

Give up something she doesn't like.

Maybe this could still work. He'd just given up the wrong thing.

Zack pulled off the OptiGlasses and snapped them in half. They broke cleanly with a sharp snap. The crowd gasped, and at least one person screamed. Zack ignored their reactions and tossed the pieces on the floor.

"There," he said. "No more OptiGlasses. No more DaEvo."

It wasn't that simple, of course. DaEvo wouldn't just go away because the OptiGlasses were out of commission. But he had enough game time for the tournament, and he could figure out the rest after that.

Ashley looked from Zack to the broken OptiGlasses and back to Zack. She seemed to be having a hard time processing what he had done.

"So now that you know I'm not doing this for points, I'll try again. I like you, Ashley. Will you go out with me? Can we try again?"

"I-do you have any idea how much those things cost?"

Zack blinked in surprise. He'd made his grand gesture and confessed his feelings, and she was talking about money? He really didn't understand women sometimes.

But there was a spark of something in Ashley's eyes that he liked. Respect, maybe? Cautious optimism? She looked down at the OptiGlasses, then up at him again, and smiled.

Zack took Ashley's hand. She closed her fingers around his, holding tightly, and Zack grinned. "I don't actually remember how much they cost, but it was worth every cent."

Ashley snorted, at which point Jenny, fed up with it all, kicked Zack in the back of his leg. "You're lucky she turned you down the first time!"

Hopping on one foot—the crowd laughing at the antics and Kayla scowling at her interview session being taken over—Zack couldn't help but grin.

Maybe everything would work out with Ashley. If she was still standing with him on the stage after everything that had happened, he had a feeling things would go well.

And they were definitely going to win the tournament.

Epilogue

"NEXT TIME, we get Zack's business manager to go over the contracts." Greg scowled as he tugged on the high collar.

They were waiting backstage, about to do the press room interview as the winners of Star Fury's pro-tournament and a new addition to the pro circuit. The entire team was standing around, clad in Davison's StarFashion clothing.

"Actually, Ms. Romero did a good job with the agreement. There might be a few clauses I would have added, but considering the timeframe she completed the deal within, she did well," Phil said as he eyed Jenny speculatively.

To Zack's chagrin, his trustee had flown all the way to Las Vegas for the press conference. The fact that Jenny and Phil had hit it off —on both giving Zack a hard time and talking business—made Zack wince. He had a feeling avoiding Phil and his responsibilities to the trust was going to become much harder.

Of course, Zack was a lot less motivated to avoid them. Especially since his and Ashley's presentation had done so well with Star Forward. Between Star Forward and Zoe's organization, the trust's already doubled budget had nearly doubled again. Between Zack's and Zoe's commitments, the Star Fury tournament circuit was likely where most of their meetings would be held from now on.

"Told you." Jenny poked Greg in the side. "And I noticed you didn't say no to your share of the sponsorship check."

"Well, yeah, but these things are still kinda stupid," Greg said, offering her a weak grin.

"I'm grateful," Faz said, throwing an arm around Jenny's shorter form. "It made my family shut up. At least for a little while."

"They still going to make you give up gaming and go to med school?" Ashley asked, chiming in from where she'd been leaning on Zack's arm.

Zack sneaked a kiss now that she had reminded him she was there. Or maybe because she was cute.

Maybe a little of both.

"Yes. But we've compromised and I'm taking some classes for now," Faz said. "That way when I'm ready to go, I'll have less to catch up on."

The rest of the team grimaced, making faces as they contemplated the future. But Zack found himself breaking into a grin as he looked at Ashley again. She smiled back, and he marveled at her appearance without DaEvo or the OptiGlasses in play. She was radiant, almost literally glowing. Maybe it had something to do with how well they'd done on the presentation. Or the late night talk they'd had afterward, with neither gaming, presentation, nor DaEvo in the way.

DaEvo was now gone for good. Phil had gotten the developers to uninstall everything and remove Zack from intervention mode. And then refused to let Zack buy another pair of OptiGlasses, instead directing him to be a luddite and use a smartphone.

A smartphone! Zack had cheated and gotten a smartwatch too, which helped.

A little.

They were definitely less intrusive, if more inconvenient. And it made Ashley happy.

Which, Zack had to admit, was kind of important.

"Well, I'm not going anywhere," Jenny said, drawing the conversation back on topic. "In fact, I have another half-dozen sponsorship meetings lined up this week. By the time I'm done, we're going to have a real professional team, with newbies, training camps, and all!"

Greg groaned, and Zack laughed. "You know, you can just go with Jenny to the meetings. That way, you can make sure she doesn't go crazy."

"But that sounds like work!" Greg whined in high falsetto. But he did eye Jenny and the clothing with some consideration, so Zack let the topic drop.

"And you?" Ashley said, thumping the side of her head into Zack's shoulder. "You made it. You're a professional gamer now. What's the next mission?"

Zack considered the question. He found himself smiling at Ashley, then at the others who looked at him speculatively. Phil most of all, the trustee nervously tugging on his suit with his long dark fingers. He let the silence linger a little longer, just to make his trustee suffer.

"Next mission?" Zack shook his head. "I think I'm done with missions. And quests for a bit. I think I'm going to focus on Leveling Up somewhere else."

He kept looking into Ashley's eyes as he said it, quite seriously. Ashley met his gaze resolutely before blushing and ducking her head, even as the group let out boos for the cheese and Greg fake-retched.

"All right, five minutes. Now, remember your places." The public relations assistant for Star Fury scrambled over to them, waving to get their attention. He was wearing a pair of OptiGlasses, the latest version to be released. It had a sleeker frame and even better graphic fidelity.

Zack sighed in jealousy.

The PR assistant turned to Ashley and Phil. "You two, please take a seat in the back of the room if you wish to view the press conference. Please stay silent." After a beat, he fixed Zack and Ashley with a glare. "We will not be having any disruptions, will we? No public declarations of love, no tomfoolery? I know it might be part of your brand"—Zack winced—"but let's keep this professional.

"Yes?"

The pair nodded, then seeing each other mimicking the other, burst out laughing.

The PR assistant rolled his eyes as he checked his watch. "Idiot lovebirds."

Zack leaned in and whispered into Ashley's ear, "I think he's jealous. Maybe we should help him out and get him an invitation to DaEvo too?"

About Tao Wong

Tao Wong is an avid fantasy and sci-fi reader who spends his time working and writing in the North of Canada. He's spent way too many years doing martial arts of many forms and having broken himself too often, now spends his time writing about fantasy worlds.

For updates on the series and other books written by Tao Wong (and special one-shot stories), please visit the author's website: http://www.mylifemytao.com

Subscribers to Tao's mailing list will receive exclusive access to short stories in the Thousand Li and System Apocalypse universes: https://www.subscribepage.com/taowong

About A.G. Marshall

A.G. Marshall loves fairy tales and has been writing stories since she could hold a pencil. She perfected her storytelling by entertaining her cousins at sleepovers and writing college papers about music (which is more similar to magic than you might think).

She fills each book she writes with magic, adventure, romance, humor, and other random things she loves. Her stories are designed to sweep you away to magical places and make you laugh on the journey.

You can find her on her website or social media.

www.AngelaGMarshall.com

About the Publisher

Starlit Publishing is wholly owned and operated by Tao Wong. It is a science fiction and fantasy publisher focused on the LitRPG & cultivation genres. Their focus is on promoting new, upcoming authors in the genre whose writing challenges the existing stereotypes while giving a rip-roaring good read.

For more information on Starlit Publishing, visit their website!

You can also join Starlit Publishing's mailing list to learn of new, exciting authors and book releases.

Preview for Princess of Shadows

Princess of Shadows
by A.G. Marshall

Air rushed into Lina's lungs. Her eyes snapped open, but she saw only darkness. She pried her arms away from her sides and rubbed an itch on her nose. Something gritty covered her face. Dirt? She brushed it away.

"Luca? Luca, are you there?"

Her voice echoed through the darkness. Lina inhaled again and coughed on more dust. The sound echoed through the cavern.

"Hello?"

No one answered. The echo faded into a silence like the grave.

Lina pushed herself up on her elbows. Her body was stiff, but she managed to swing her legs around to a seated position. She rubbed the diamond in her ring.

"Illuminate."

A faint glow filled the room. Lina shut her eyes. After the darkness, even the pale light from the diamond overwhelmed her senses.

"Less illumination."

The light faded to a softer glow, and Lina squinted at her

surroundings. She had been in the dark too long to see much. She needed time to adjust. When her eyes recovered enough to open them fully, Lina raised her hand so the light from the diamond filled the room.

She was in a small, dirty cave. Except for the grime and dust, everything was just as she and Luca had ordered it. The tables covered with charms to support her sleep. The scrolls explaining her situation in case a stranger found her. The enchanted mirror.

Lina ran her hand along her stone bed. She traced the swirling vein of silver that ran down the center, and her fingertips tingled with magic.

The seal held.

She stood and walked to a table across the room. Her stiff legs protested, but Lina was too thirsty to care. She had told Luca to keep a pitcher filled with water for her so she could have a drink when she woke up.

The pitcher was empty.

"Just like the donkey to forget something like that," she muttered.

Lina swallowed a few times, trying to relieve her dry throat. The dust that covered the cave had not spared her. She wiped a layer of grime off the enchanted mirror and stared at her reflection.

Her chestnut hair hung down her back in a thick tangled mess. She remembered braiding it before falling under the enchantment. Her bright green eyes twinkled under prominent eyebrows tangled with cobwebs. Lina rubbed them and left a trail of dirt on her face. She licked a finger and wiped her face clean.

Well, cleaner.

Her skin was clear under the dust. No bruises. No sign of a struggle. She looked gray and ghostly in the ring's light.

Lina smiled sadly to herself. The girl in the mirror smiled back. Lina gathered a bit of shadow magic in her fingertips and touched the glass. She studied her reflection for any sign of change.

Nothing. The enchantment had faded. Lina pushed more shadow magic into the glass, but she couldn't bring it back. She and

Luca had enchanted it together. She would need his light magic to fix it completely.

Lina wiped her hands on her skirt. They came away even grimier thanks to the dirt that saturated the fabric of her gown. Lina remembered picking her favorite dress to wear for the enchantment. A pale purple silk frock. It was ruined now. She'd need a change of clothes before she met with the Council.

And a bath.

Maybe two baths.

There would be guards stationed at the end of the hallway. Lina pushed on the door. It crumbled at her touch, and falling bits of wood filled the air with even more dust. She ripped the end off her sleeve and covered her mouth with it. The fabric tore in her hand like a spider web.

Lina pushed her hand through the doorway. Light from her ring illuminated an empty tunnel.

"Luca?"

Her brother's name echoed through the tunnel until silence swallowed it.

Lina's stomach twisted. Luca had promised he would watch her. He might forget to refill a pitcher of water, but even he wouldn't forget something as important as guarding his twin sister while she slept.

Something must have gone very wrong. Had the goblins attacked after all? Had the enchantment failed?

Lina crept down the hallway. One step at a time. Her feet dragged on the rough stone floor. How much time had she spent asleep in the realm of shadows? Everything was easier there. You could fly as easily as you walked. But transitioning back to the realm of light wasn't usually this slow.

Lina reached the end of the tunnel and ran her hand over the smooth stone door. It was just as she remembered. Made from the same stone as the mountain and carved to fit without a single gap.

She studied the door until she found the keyhole. Lina pushed the diamond on her ring into it and turned her wrist. The cavern plunged into darkness as the door swallowed her diamond. Her heart pounded. What if the door was broken? What if she was buried alive?

The latch clicked. Lina pulled her ring out and pushed the door forward. It didn't slide as smoothly as it should have, but at least it didn't crumble like the wood. Gentle white light filled the tunnel. A crisp breeze rustled Lina's hair. She peered around the door and saw stars overhead.

Thank goodness it was night. She wasn't sure she could handle daylight yet. Lina held her ring to her lips.

"Check for danger."

She held her breath. If the light changed to red, there were creatures of darkness nearby. Goblins or worse.

The light stayed white. Its glow matched the moonlight streaming into the cavern. Lina exhaled in relief.

"Extinguish."

Her ring's light faded until it was a normal diamond glittering in the moonlight.

So there was no danger. Luca might be safe after all.

Perhaps the guards were taking a break. Perhaps the danger had passed enough that they didn't need to watch her every second.

Lina slipped around the rock and into the open air. An evening breeze washed over her. She pushed the rock door closed and locked it with her ring. The enchantments should keep the seal safe even when she was gone.

The air smelled just as it should. She closed her eyes and savored the scents. Fresh grass and pine trees. The tang of the ocean. The pale sweetness of snowbells. Summer in Aeonia.

Lina opened her eyes and examined her surroundings. Her heart tightened.

She stood in untamed mountain wilderness. Above her, pine forests reached for the mountaintops. Fields of snowbells stretched below her. Their purple blossoms waved in the moonlight like ocean waves.

This was all wrong. They had buried her in the wrong place. She had watched them carve the marble structures around her cave.

Helped them weave magic into the stones. There should be a pavilion to her left. And where was the wolf statue?

Maybe they had moved her while she slept. A marble pavilion wasn't exactly subtle. Maybe danger had forced them to hide her. To dig another cavern in the wilderness.

Maybe things had gone badly after all. Had there been a battle? Had the goblins destroyed the statue? Lina studied the landscape. The hillside bore no signs of a skirmish. She sat on a mossy patch among the snowbells and studied the bottom of the mountain.

Lights of a city nestled at the mountain's base. Yes, that was right. Mias, the capital city of Aeonia, had been visible from the mouth of the cavern. She remembered the view. Moonlight glistened on the ocean waves and white plaster buildings. She would know that scene anywhere. This had been Luca's favorite picnic spot.

So she was in the right place. What had happened to the marble carvings? She understood removing the pavilion, but the wolf statue had been an important part of the protection charms around her.

Lina stood and studied the space around the door, looking for anything out of the ordinary. Her heart sank.

She didn't remember the moss.

Lina rested her hand on the ground. A faint magical aura permeated it. She dissolved it, crawled to the nearest clump of moss, and pulled at it. She threw handful after handful away, praying she wouldn't find anything under it. Please, let it be just earth.

She jammed her finger on something hard. Lina brushed the dirt away, revealing a gleaming rock as white as bone.

"No."

Lina clawed the dirt and moss away. Please, no. It couldn't be.

A worn marble paw took shape as Lina removed its mossy covering. Claws stretched toward her. She swallowed a sob.

She remembered the shape. She had helped carve it. A fierce guard wolf with sharp claws and green emerald eyes. The claws were dull now, and the wolf's teeth were rounded at the edges. Worn smooth by rain and moss and time.

Time. How much time would it take to crumble the edges of a marble statue to dust?

Lina wiped the dirt away from what was left of the wolf's face.

Something small and round fell into her hand. The wolf's eye. The round emerald gleamed in the moonlight. Tears filled Lina's eyes and left trails in the dust on her cheeks.

"Luca!"

She screamed into the night. Her voice echoed against the mountains and dissolved in the wind. No one answered.

"Luca."

She clutched the emerald in her fist, and the world dissolved in a flash of memory.

"Careful with the peas, Lina."

"They're emeralds, Luca."

"Yeah? They look like peas to me. Think we could trick the chef into putting them in a stew? I'd love to see the king's face when he swallowed one."

"Luca-"

"Come on, Lina! The King of Gaveron has been giving us trouble for ages. Let's return the favor."

"Luca-"

"One last prank before you go to sleep?"

"Luca, this is serious."

He looked at her with piercing green eyes that matched her own.

"I know. Are you sure you want to do this?"

"Yes."

"You're not afraid?"

"I'm a shadow warrior. I've faced worse. Besides, you'll watch over me."

He grinned at her.

"Of course I will."

Lina looked back at the wolf's face. How long would it take to wear marble smooth like that? Decades? Centuries?

Longer than he could live, a small voice in her head whispered. Much longer than Luca could survive.

Lina clutched the pea emerald to her heart and sobbed. She had known this was a possibility. That was the reality of the enchanted sleep. She would wake sometime, but who could say when? Who could say what would be left for her?

Luca had been so confident though. So sure he could find a way to wake her once they had sealed the danger away. They had been a team. Inseparable.

Lina swallowed her tears. Everyone was gone. Not just Luca. Everyone she had fought to protect. Even if they had survived the war, they were gone now.

The lights of Mias twinkled below her. Lina wiped her eyes. Someone had survived. Goblins would not fill a city with light. She leaned on the wolf statue and stood. Her heart pounded.

Lina tore a hole in her sleeve's hem and tucked the pea inside. She clutched the fabric in her fist as she walked down the mountain. One step at a time in the moonlight. She would do as she always had. Go forward. Fight to protect her country.

Pale purple snowbells, the same color her dress had once been, swayed around her.

Read more on Amazon!

Preview for A Thousand Li: The First Step

A Thousand Li: The First Step
by Tao Wong

"Cultivation, at its core, is a rebellion."

Waiting for their reaction, the thin, mustached older teacher stared at the students seated cross-legged before him. Apparently not seeing the reaction he wanted, the teacher flung the long, trailing sleeves of the robes he wore with a harrumph and continued his lecture. Keeping his expression entirely neutral, Long Wu Ying could not help but smirk within. Such a statement, no matter how contentious, lost its impact after daily repetition over the course of a decade.

"Cultivation demands one to defy the very heavens itself. Each step on the path of cultivation sets you on the road to rebellion to defy the heavens, to defy our king. It is only by his good graces and his belief in the betterment of the kingdom that you are allowed to cultivate."

Wu Ying struggled to keep his face neutral as the refrain continued. Usually, he could tune out the teacher until it came time to cultivate, but today he struggled to do so. Today, he could not help but rebut the teacher in his mind. Teaching the villagers how to cultivate was a purely practical decision on the king's part. Most children would achieve at least the first level of Body Cleansing by their twelfth birthday. That allowed them to grow stronger and healthier, even on the little food they had left after the state, the nobles, and the sects had taken their portion.

"The beneficent auspices of the king allow you to cultivate, study the martial arts, and defend yourself. It is only because of his belief that each village must be a strong member of the kingdom that we have grown to the heights we have!"

It had nothing to do with the desire to begin training the villagers to be useful soldiers in the never-ending wars. Or to ensure that the village was not robbed of the grain they farmed by the bandits that seemed to grow in number every year. Or the fact that less than two hundred li away, the Verdant Green Waters Sect watched over them all, searching for new recruits.

"Now, begin!"

Exhaling a grateful breath that Master Su had finally finished, Wu Ying tried to focus his mind on cultivating. That he respected his teacher was without question, but Master Su was a stickler for the rules, which required him to give the same lecture every single time. Even a saint would find it hard to listen after a while. And Wu Ying was many things, but a Saint he most definitely was not.

It didn't help that the state was obviously of two minds about cultivation itself. The three pillars of a kingdom were the government, the populace, and the cultivating sects. A weakness in any of the three would make a kingdom vulnerable. For a kingdom to be stable, each pillar needed to be as strong, as upright and firm, as the others. If any single pillar grew too high, it would eventually lead to the collapse of the kingdom.

Because of that, a wise ruler would support the development of their populace through cultivation, the surest and best form of developing an individual. But a single cultivator, if they achieved true power, could—and had, historically—overturn governments. And so, the state would always view cultivators and cultivation with some degree of distrust.

"Wu Ying. Focus!" Master Su said.

Wu Ying grimaced slightly before he made his face placid again. Master Su was right. He could think about all these thoughts another time. This was the time for cultivation. The time a villager had to cultivate was limited and precious. Stray thoughts were wasteful.

Drawing a deep breath, Wu Ying exhaled through his nose. The first step in cultivation was to clear the mind. The second was to control his breathing, for breath was the source of all things. At least in the Yellow Emperor's Cultivation Method that had been passed down and used by all peasants in the kingdom of Shen.

The first step on the road to cultivation was that of bodily purification. To ascend, to gain greater strength and develop one's chi, a cultivator needed to purify their body of the wastes that accumulated. Starting the process young helped to reduce the amount of such waste build up and speeded up the progress of cultivation. That was why every villager began cultivating as soon as possible. Those children who achieved the first level of Body Cleansing at a young age were hailed as prodigies.

Wu Ying was not considered a prodigy. Wu Ying had started cultivating at the age of six, like every other child in the village, and through hard work and discipline, he'd managed to achieve not just the first level of Body Cleansing but the second. True prodigies, at Wu Ying's age of seventeen, would already be at the fourth or fifth stage. Each of the twelve stages of Body Cleansing saw the conscious introduction and cleansing of another major chi meridian. When an individual had consciously introduced and could control the flow of chi through all twelve major pathways, all the stages of Body Cleansing were considered complete.

Wu Ying breathed in then out, slowly and rhythmically. He focused on the breath, the flow of air into his lungs, the way it entered his body as his stomach expanded and his chest filled out. Then he exhaled, feeling his stomach contract, the diaphragm moving upward as air circulated away.

In time, Wu Ying moved his focus away from breathing toward his dantian. Located below his belly button, in the space just slightly below his hip line and a few inches beneath the surface of his body, the lower dantian was the core of the Yellow Emperor's Cultivation Method. From there, through the flow and consolidation of one's internal chi, one would progress.

Once again, Wu Ying felt the mass of energy that was his dantian. As always, it was large in size but low in density, uncompacted and diffuse. His job was to gently nudge the flow of energy through his body's meridians, to send it on a major circulation through his body. In the process, his body sweated, as the normally docile chi moved through his body, cleansing and scouring away the impurities of life. In time, Wu Ying's normal sweat mixed with the impurities in his body, flowing from his pores. The rancid, bitter odor from Wu Ying's body mixed with the similar pungence coming from the rest of the class, a stench that even the open windows of the building could do little to disperse.

———

Deep in the process of cultivating, none of the students noticed the rancid smell, leaving only Master Su to suffer as he watched over the teenagers. Master Su had long gotten used to the offensive odor that he would be forced to endure for the next few hours as each of the classes progressed. It was a fair trade though, for Master Su received ten tael of silver and, most importantly, a Marrow Cleansing pill each month for his work.

Deep in their cultivation, none of the students moved when a young man shook and convulsed. But Master Su took action, flashing over to the boy with a tap of his foot. Paired fingers raised as Master Su studied the thrashing boy before they darted forward, striking in rapid succession a series of acupressure points along the body. After the third strike, the convulsing slowed then stopped before the boy tipped over, coughing out blood.

"Foolish. Pushing to open the second meridian channel when you have not finished cleansing the first!" Master Su berated the boy, shaking his head. "Get up. Begin cultivating properly. You will stay here an extra hour."

"But..." the boy protested weakly but quieted at Master Su's glare.

"Foolish child!" Master Su growled as he stomped back to his station in front of the class. If he had not been there, the boy would likely have damaged himself permanently. Master Su watched as the boy wiped his mouth clear of blood before he snorted. Luckily, Master Su had been able to quell the rampaging chi flow, but the boy would likely have to spend the next few weeks on light duty at his farm. A bad time for that, considering the planting season they were in. "Stupid."

As the hour set aside for the teenagers to cultivate came to an end and the morning sun cast long shadows on the small village, the village bell rang. Master Su frowned slightly then smoothed his face as the students broke free from their cultivation trances one by one. It would never do for the students to see his concern.

"The session is over. Line up when you are done," Master Su commanded before he walked out of the small, single-room building that made up his school.

Outside, the teacher walked forward slightly, turning his head from side to side before he spotted the growing dust cloud.

"Master Su." Tan Cheng, the tall village head, came up to Master Su.

As the two individuals in the sixth level of the Body Cleansing stage, the pair shared the burden of guarding the village from external threats. It helped that Chief Tan was a lover of tea like Master Su.

"Chief Tan," Master Su greeted. "What is it?"

"The army recruiters," Chief Tan said, his eyes grave.

Master Su could not help but wince. This was the third time in as many years that the army had recruited from their village. The conscripts from the first year had yet to return, though news of deaths had trickled back. The war between their state of Shen and the state of Wei had dragged on, bringing misery to everyone.

"They're going to raise the taxes again then," Master Su said, trying to keep his tone light. Each year that the war dragged on, the taxes grew higher. He wondered how many the army would take this time and did not envy his friend. The first time the army arrived, they had filled the requirements with volunteers. The second time they came, each household that had more than one son and had yet to send a volunteer had sent their sons. This time, there would be no easy choices.

"Most likely." Chief Tan chewed on his lip slightly. As the rest of the villagers slowly streamed in from the surrounding fields, he looked around then looked down, avoiding the expectant gazes of the parents. Whatever came next, few would be happy.

———

"What is it?" Qiu Ru asked. The raven-haired beauty of the class prodded Wu Ying in the back as she tried to peer past the crowd of students who had gathered around the windows. Giving up, she prodded Wu Ying once more in the back to get him to answer.

"The army," Wu Ying finally answered.

As her eyes widened, he admired the way it made them shine— before he squashed his burgeoning feelings again. Qiu Ru had made it quite clear last summer festival that she had no interest in him. Now, Wu Ying had his sights set on Gao Yan. Even if Gao Yan was shorter, plumper, and had a bad tendency to forget to brush her teeth. That was life in the village—your choices were somewhat limited.

"Are they bringing back the volunteers?" Qiu Ru said.

"No. They're too early for that," Cheng Fa Hui said.

Wu Ying glanced at his friend, who had hung back with the rest of them. Not that Fa Hui needed to be up front to see what was happening. He towered over the entire group by a head. All except Wu Ying, who only lost to him by a handbreadth.

"If the army was returning our people, it would be before the winter," Fa Hui said. "That way the lord would not need to feed them."

Wu Ying grimaced and shot a look around the room, relaxing slightly when he saw that Yin Xue had not come to class today. As the nearest village to Lord Wen's summer abode, all the villagers dealt with Lord Wen and his son regularly. Truth be told, Yin Xue did not need to come to their village class, but the boy seemed to take pleasure in showcasing his ability over the peasants. As the son of the local lord, Yin Xue had access to a private cultivation tutor, spiritual herbs, and good food—all of which had allowed him to progress to Body Cleansing four already. In common parlance, he was what was known as a false dragon—a "forced" genius, rather than one who had achieved the heights of his cultivation by genius alone.

If Yin Xue had heard Fa Hui… Wu Ying mentally shuddered at the thought. Still, it was not as if Fa Hui was wrong. If the war was over, it made sense to make the villagers feed the returned sons rather than pay for hungry mouths over the winter.

"Are they here for us then?" Wu Ying mused. That would make sense.

After saying the words out loud, he noticed how the rest of the class stiffened. Before he could say anything to comfort them, Master Su called them out of the building.

Once the students had lined up outside, Wu Ying could easily see the army personnel, two of which were speaking with Chief Tan, while the others watched over the conscripts. As it was still early in the morning, the army had only managed to visit one other village thus far, and as such, there were only twenty such conscripts standing together. Yin Xue sat astride a horse, beside the conscripts but not part of them.

Wu Ying had to admit, the members of the army looked dashing in their padded undercoats, dark lamellar armor, and open-faced helms. But having watched two other groups leave and not return, with only rumors of the losses trickling back via the same recruiters and the itinerant merchant, much of the prestige and glory of joining the army had faded.

"Men, Lord Wen has sent his men to us once again. We are required to send twenty strong conscripts to join the king's army this year." Before the crowd could grasp the significance of the number, Chief Tan announced, "All sons from families who have not sent a child to the front, step forward."

Wu Ying stepped forward. As the only surviving son of his family, he had been safe from the recruiters beforehand. Along with Wu Ying, another six men stepped forward.

"All sons from families with more than one son in the village, step forward," Chief Tan announced.

This time, there was some confusion, but it was soon sorted out with some students pushed forward and others drawn back. By now, Wu Ying counted seventeen "volunteers."

"Why not daughters?" Qiu Ru called.

Wu Ying could not help but grimace at her impertinent words. As the local beauty, Qiu Ru had managed to get away with more impertinent comments than others. Interrupting the Chief while he was speaking was a new high.

"The army is looking for men!" Chief Tan snapped. "Qiu Jan! See to your daughter!"

"This is foolish!" Qiu Ru said.

When Chief Tan began to speak, he was silenced by a raised hand of the lieutenant, whose gaze raked over Qiu Ru. "You are quite the beauty. But our men do not need wives."

The hiss from the crowd was loud even as Qiu Ru flushed bright red at the insult.

"We are here to find soldiers. And you are, what? Body Cleansing one? Women are no use to us as soldiers until at least Body Cleansing four!"

Still flushed, Qiu Ru moved to speak, but her mother had managed to make her way over to the impertinent girl and gripped her arm. With a yank of her hand, the mother pulled Qiu Ru back. For a time, the lieutenant looked over the group, seeing that no one else was liable to interrupt, before he looked at Chief Tan.

"Tan Fu, Qiu Lee, Long Mao. Join the others," Chief Tan said softly.

Everyone knew why he had chosen the three, of course. Their families had been gifted with more than three surviving sons. Even now, their parents would have a single son left to work the farm, turn the earth. A good thing. Better than the families that were left without any. If you didn't consider the fact that now, three of their sons were fighting a war that none of them ever wanted.

"Good," the lieutenant said as his gaze slid over the new conscripts.

Wu Ying looked to the side as well, offering Fa Hui a tight smile as he saw his big friend look sallow and scared.

"Conscripts, return to your homes and collect your belongings. You will not be back for many months. Bring what you need. We will march in fifteen minutes. Gather at first bell," the lieutenant said.

The students stared at one another, looking at the few members of the class that were left, then at the other children. Wu Ying sighed and clapped Fa Hui on the shoulder, giving the giant a slight shove to send him toward his family. As if the motion was a signal, the group broke apart, the teenager's faces fixed as they moved to say their final goodbyes.

Style Quests
Shop for new clothes
Wash laundry and remove worn and torn clothing
Get a haircut from the 21st century
Manicure
Pedicure
Skin treatment
Manscaping
Take a deportment class and pass (locked)
Learn to dance (Choose dance type) (locked)
(more...)

Zack looked at the time display in the corner of his OptiGlasses. Just past seven. Maybe he could squeeze in some grinding before the shops closed. If he got good enough rewards for the quests, he might even be able to squeeze in more Star Fury training tonight. Plus, the higher level would mean more points and time earned the next time he talked to a woman.

He focused on the top style quest, Shop for new clothes, until it selected. DaEvo chimed the cheerful quest music that Zack was beginning to hate.

Quest!
Impress the ladies and level up by improving your style from (Current-style: Unemployed Hobo). Please journey to one of the highlighted stores to begin your makeover quest.

Zack ground his teeth at the word makeover. And then again at the Unemployed Hobo label. He registered a bug report, although that hadn't accomplished anything so far, and went back to glaring at the word makeover. If any of his friends ever found out he had completed a makeover quest for a dating sim...

He would just have to be careful that no one ever found out. Luckily, all his friends were either online or lived in New York. If

75

You're out of time! Would you like to complete a quest to earn more?

As if he had any choice. Zack opened the quest menu and looked over the fitness quests. They were repeatable. Maybe it was worth—

Nah.

He opened the makeover quest menu again. There was still the opportunity to spend some cash and do a little min/maxing. Leveling up his style had paid off pretty well so far.

Style Quests
· *Shop for new clothes (repeatable)*
· *Wash laundry and remove worn and torn clothing*
· *Get a haircut from the 21st century*
· *Manicure*
· *Pedicure*
· *Skin treatment*
· *Manscaping*
· ~~*Take a deportment class and pass*~~ *(locked—see details)*
· ~~*Learn to dance (Choose dance type)*~~ *(locked)*
· *(more…)*

The haircut might be worth looking into. That was easy enough. Manicures and pedicures would be easy as well, although he would have to make sure no one ever found out about them. Dance and deportment sounded like more work than the fitness quests. Maybe manscaping? What did that even mean?

Zack selected one of the websites DaEvo recommended for manscaping and skimmed through a description of their services. He closed the site just as quickly.

Hell. No.

Why would they…? He opened the website again, looked at it again, and shook his head.

No. Definitely not.

That left doing his laundry and buying more clothes.

DaEvo chimed.

Workout Detected
Your increased heart rate indicates that you're working out. Accept an official quest to level up your physique.

Zack glanced quickly through the list offered.

Physique Quests
· *Have a healthy meal (Repeatable)*
· *Walk 2km (Repeatable)*
· *Run 2km (Locked)*
· *Lose 5lbs (Repeatable with limits)*
· *Take a weightlifting class*
· *Lift weights (Locked)*
· *…*

He rejected them just as quickly. Such dumb software. If it detected him exercising, shouldn't it at least give him points for it? Almost, Zack registered a bug, but decided to skip it. He wasn't going to help them fix their damn buggy software that he'd been conned into testing. Anyway, he had almost finished moving the boxes. There was no need to get carried away.

Zack kicked the last box into his apartment. It gave a satisfying thud, and he sank into his gaming chair to examine his loot. If his apartment had looked cluttered before, it now looked as though it belonged to a hoarder. Luckily, most of the boxes were decorated with the brand logos, which would help him sort through them later. The sleek packaging was a strange contrast to the piles of dirty laundry scattered around the room.

Zack retrieved his pizza from the fridge and ate it while he opened a few boxes. DaEvo rated the clothes as he pulled them out, overlaying each item with a pink heart filled with stats. Zack set aside a striped polo shirt, dark wash jeans, and tennis shoes that DaEvo had given high combo points to the night before. He needed

Style Quests
· *Shop for new clothes*
· *Wash laundry and remove worn and torn clothing*
· *Get a haircut from the 21st century*
· *Manicure*
· *Pedicure*
· *Skin treatment*
· *Manscaping*
· ~~*Take a deportment class and pass*~~ *(locked)*
· ~~*Learn to dance (Choose dance type)*~~ *(locked)*
· *(more...)*

Zack studied the list. His first instinct was to swipe it away and forget it existed, but if he wanted to maximize his Style stats, he would have to face these eventually. "What do I get for a haircut?"
DaEvo chimed.

Proper physical grooming is important to maximize points available from your clothing purchases.
Even if you have physical shortcomings, there's no reason to look like a slob.
Style Combo Maximum Upgraded
Physique +4

"Why didn't you mention that yesterday?"
DaEvo remained silent.
Stupid, buggy app. Zack suddenly felt suspicious. Even his high fashion WesterNeon outfit had only reached eighty-nine or so points. That seemed low, considering how cutting edge those clothes were. And some of the best outfits he had bought online were only worth forty-five points. On top of that, this was the second time he'd seen style and physique cross-pollinate. There was definitely something going on.
"What else affects my style points?"
DaEvo chimed.

"You're sick?" Zoe said.

DaEvo chimed.

Relationship Quest Update!

Due to previous incidents, you must select your conversation partner. Setting up such conversation and relationship targets will then carry forth for all interactions.

Further confirmation once your first Relationship Milestone (that is, access to the Lovemeter after the first date) on your relationship goals and status will be required for the proper functioning of DaEvo.

Please choose if you are intending to pursue a relationship with:

- *Tina Evans*
- *Zoe Cross*
- ~~*Both*~~ *(Please enter Relationship Settings and answer* <u>*Ethical Polyamory Questionnaire*</u>*)*

Zack swiped to select Zoe's name and turned back to the conversation. "Just a minor health scare. I'm fine now."

Zoe studied his face, then nodded. "Are you busy right now? I have a few hours before my first appointment, and I meant what I said at the gala. I think our foundations would collaborate well. I'd love to get coffee and chat about the possibility."

"Really?" Zack's voice squeaked, and DaEvo chimed.

Achievement Unlocked! Get a Date!

+60 minutes for non-essential electronics

Bonus: +180 minutes for non-essential electronics due to Social Level disparity

"Unless you're busy," Zoe said.

"Nope. Not busy at all." He would be late for training, but it

Chapter Fifty-Four

"HELLO, ZACK."

Kayla's voice was icy, and her eyes were even colder. She ignored Greg and Faz, who were gaping at her over a display shelf.

DaEvo chimed.

Relationship Quest Update!

Due to previous incidents, you must select your conversation partners at the same time. Setting up such conversation and relationship targets will then carry forth for all interactions.

Further confirmation once your first Relationship Milestone (that is, access to the Lovemeter after the first date) on your relationship goals and status will be required for the proper functioning of DaEvo.

Please choose if you are intending to pursue a relationship with:

- *Jenny Romero*
- *Kayla Taylor*
- *Both (Please enter Relationship Settings and answer Ethical Polyamory Questionnaire to unlock this option)*

Further confirmation once your first Relationship Milestone (that is, access to the Lovemeter after the first date) on your relationship goals and status will be required for the proper functioning of DaEvo.

Please choose if you are intending to pursue a relationship with:

- *Jenny Romero*
- *Ashley Barnes*
- *Both (Please enter Relationship Settings and answer Ethical Polyamory Questionnaire to unlock this option)*

Note: Ashley Barnes Lovemeter is currently at zero, and as such, a new relationship must be completed to begin acquiring relationship milestones and for you to proceed with the relationship once more.

"Here's your coffee," Ashley said, handing the cup to Greg. "Did you want anything else?"

She looked at Zack as she said it. He swallowed, trying to think of something clever to say. By some miracle, Ashley was in Las Vegas and willing to speak with him. He didn't want to mess this up.

"No thanks, we're good," Faz answered. "Pay for your coffee, Greg. We're going to be late for training."

"Right!" Greg fumbled for his wallet, then remembered he could pay with his VIP card and held it up.

Ashley scowled at her tablet, then shook her head. "Our system is still down, so don't worry about it. This one's on the house."

"Yeah?" Zack said. Then he mentally kicked himself. Why was he being so lame? She hadn't even been talking to him.

"Yeah," Ashley said. "I wouldn't want you to be late for training."

"Thanks so much!" Greg said. "Come on, guys!"

He grabbed Zack's arm and pulled him away. Zack shook loose from Greg's grip and tried to pull himself together. Focus. They needed to hurry to the arena and go through orientation so that he could go on his date with Zoe and get points.

Ashley was there. She hadn't yelled at him.

"Yeah," Zack said. "Yeah, that sounds great!"

The door opened, and Zack turned around to greet the newcomer. He was expecting some stuffy board member in an equally stuffy suit. Instead, he saw Ashley. She had pulled her auburn hair back into a ponytail and wore the same green dress she had worn on their first date. The suit jacket over it made it look more professional, but memories of that night flooded back. Zack knew he was staring, but he couldn't help it.

Ashley stared back, although her expression was more of a glare. Unlike Zack, she managed to keep her mouth shut. She recovered from her surprise first and turned to Zoe.

"I put together the reports you wanted." Ashley paused. "Ma'am."

Zoe's lips quirked at the last, but she said blandly, "Great. You've met Zack, right?"

Ashley nodded and took a seat on the other side of Zoe. Zack looked from one woman to the other. What was happening? Was this some kind of weird setup?

DaEvo chimed.

Relationship Quest Update!

Due to previous incidents, you must select your conversation partners at the same time. Setting up such conversation and relationship targets will then carry forth for all interactions.

Further confirmation once your first Relationship Milestone (that is, access to the Lovemeter after the first date) on your relationship goals and status will be required for the proper functioning of DaEvo.

Please choose if you are intending to pursue a relationship with:

- *Zoe Cross*
- *Ashley Barnes*
- *Both (Please enter Relationship Settings and answer Ethical Polyamory Questionnaire to unlock this option)*

- *All (Please enter Relationship Settings and answer Ethical Polyamory Questionnaire)*

Zack stared at the notification. He was getting really annoyed by it prompting him for confirmation each time he talked to more than one woman at a time. Or stared at one too hard. He tried to swipe the notification away, but it refused to disappear. Damn, it really was going to make him choose.

Zack looked at the options, staring at Jenny—his default for the last little while. It made the most sense, and he could do it again. Something made him hesitate to pick her though. Somehow it seemed more important right now.

If he kept choosing Jenny, at some point DaEvo would mistake them for being in a real relationship and force him to buy her gifts, go on dates, and take their relationship to the next level with Relationship Milestones. That felt like a disaster waiting to happen. Jenny might go along with it to help him earn game time, but Zack doubted she would tolerate it for long.

That left Zoe or Ashley.

He was spending a lot of time with Zoe because of their foundation work. He would continue to do so in the future, especially if he took the more active role Phil wanted him to take. But did he want to date her?

Zack exhaled slowly, trying to clear his head. A relationship with Zoe Cross. It was every guy's dream, and he was already living that dream in a way since they had spent so much time together lately. It had been fun. He liked her. But he didn't get the sense that she was into him or wanted to date him.

More important. He didn't want to date her.

The realization went off in his head like an antimatter bomb, wiping away erroneous thoughts. Zack realized he was staring at Zoe, who was waiting for him to answer the question, and turned away. Why didn't he want to date Zoe? She was perfect. With DaEvo and his newfound life skills, he might even stand a chance. He could at least get a lot of conversation points for trying.

He raised his gaze to select Zoe's name from the quest menu, his seat and squinted into the lights. This stage was surrounded by stadium-style seats, and each seat was full. Was Ashley out there somewhere? The bright studio lights made it impossible for him to see faces in the crowd.

DaEvo chimed. Zack took that to mean Ashley was out there somewhere. The app could see her, even if he couldn't.

Relationship Target Ashley Barnes is present!
Current Lovemeter Level: 2.1/100

Your Relationship with Ashley Barnes is being penalized due to past experience. You can repair your relationship and remove the ex-relationship penalty to relationship goals for your Lovemeter by trying the following:

- *Showcase your value (i.e. physical, material, or social value)*
- *Acknowledge what went wrong and apologize*
- *Remind her of the good times by repeating a familiar date*
- *Show your affection with a grand gesture*

Zack had tried the apology multiple times, and that hadn't gone well. Ashley didn't seem impressed by his wealth. That left him with one way to level up the Lovemeter.

"What counts as a grand gesture?" Zack muttered.

DaEvo responded with a more helpful than normal tutorial showing movie clips of over-the-top romantic gestures, as well as a list of suggestions. Some of the options almost made Zack choke before it displayed them all in a checklist format. Some of the ones that jumped out to Zack were:

- *sing to her*
- *use a boombox to declare your love in public*
- *give up something she doesn't like so you can spend more time with her*
- *fight your rival for her hand-in-marriage*
- *tell her you love her in front of a crowd*

"Oh, some kind of scandal?" Kayla said. "A love triangle within the team?"

She was trying to regain control of the situation, but for once, the crowd ignored her. They were all staring at Ashley. A few murmurs about the clown Cinderella circulated through the room, but Ashley looked nothing like a clown right now. Most of her red hair was hidden under a hat, and she wore jeans and a slightly wrinkled T-shirt.

"I'm no good at this sort of thing," Zack said. "But I messed up, and I wanted to say I'm sorry. Nobody compares to her. And if there's a chance we can work it out, I want to take it."

Ashley's cheeks burned bright red with embarrassment, and her mouth hung open. It seemed Zack had caught her by surprise. Hopefully, that was a good thing.

DaEvo chimed.

Congratulations! You have made a public declaration of affection to Ashley Barnes.
Relationship Milestone penalties reduced.
+10 to Ashley Barnes Lovemeter Level

Relationship Hint! Keep going!

- *sing to her*
- *use a boombox to declare your love in public*
- *give up something she doesn't like so you can spend more time with her.*
- *fight your rival for her hand-in-marriage*
- *tell her you love her in front of a crowd*

Zack was on a roll, and his instincts took over, refusing to let up on the kill. No way was he letting his target escape him! He selected the third option and spoke without thinking. "Ashley, if you'll take me back, I'll give up Star Fury for you."

A collective gasp spread through the audience. Zack's teammates yelled in protest. Kayla was stunned into silence.